Anne McCaffrey is considered one of the world's leading science fiction writers. She has won the Hugo and Nebula awards as well as six Science Fiction Book Club awards for her novels. Brought up in the United States, she is now living in Ireland with her Maine Coon cats and a silver Weimaraner. She is best known for her unique Dragonriders of Pern series.

Elizabeth Ann Scarborough is the author of twenty-three science fiction and fantasy novels, including the 1989 Nebula Award-winning The Healer's War and the Powers series, co-written with Anne McCaffrey, as well as the popular Godmother series and the Gothic fantasy mystery, The Lady in the Loch. She lives in a Victorian seaport town in western Washington with her cats, beads and computer stuff.

D1334744

Anne McCaffrey's books can be read individually or as series. However, for greatest enjoyment the following sequences are recommended:

ACORNA'S CHILDREN: FIRST WARNING

Anne McCaffrey
and
Elizabeth Ann Scarborough

CORGI BOOKS

ACORNA'S CHILDREN: FIRST WARNING
A CORGI BOOK : 0 552 15291 9

9780552152914

First publication in Great Britain

First published in the US as *First Warning* by Harper Collins Publishers.

PRINTING HISTORY
Corgi edition published 2006

1 3 5 7 9 10 8 6 4 2

Set in 11/12.5pt Palatino by
Phoenix Typesetting, Auldgirth, Dumfriesshire.

Corgi Books are published by Transworld Publishers,
61–63 Uxbridge Road, London W5 5SA,
a division of The Random House Group Ltd,
in Australia by Random House Australia (Pty) Ltd,
20 Alfred Street, Milsons Point, Sydney, NSW 2061, Australia,
in New Zealand by Random House New Zealand Ltd,
18 Poland Road, Glenfield, Auckland 10, New Zealand
and in South Africa by Random House (Pty) Ltd,
Isle of Houghton, Corner of Boundary Road & Carse O'Gowrie,
Houghton 2198, South Africa.

Printed and bound in Great Britain by
Cox & Wyman Ltd, Reading, Berkshire.

Papers used by Transworld Publishers are natural, recyclable
products made from wood grown in sustainable forests. The
manufacturing processes conform to the environmental
regulations of the country of origin.

*This book is for Jason and
Cynthia Scarborough, with love*

ACKNOWLEDGEMENTS

We'd like to thank Dr Christine Hale, Elizabeth Ann Scarborough's epidemiologist neighbor, who helped us find a way to destroy much of the universe as we might come to know it. As usual, we also must thank Richard Reaser, our science, salvage, and stealthy stuff consultant, and Andy Logan for sustenance. And, as always, we owe thanks to our editors Denise Little and Diana Gill for all of their patience and hard work.

ACORNA'S CHILDREN:
First Warning

ONE

Until the *Condor* encountered the derelict space-ship drifting through deep space, Khorii couldn't understand why the fact that she was taking her first long space voyage had caused so much fuss back home. She had flown on the *Condor* plenty of times when her family shuttled between her home planet of Vhiliinyar and the Moon of Opportunity (known as MOO to everyone except Uncle Hafiz and Aunt Karina now). This trip was just like those ones, only longer, although she did like seeing all the new solar systems and such that Mother and Father, Captain Becker, and her android friend Elviiz's dad Maak were so eager to point out to her.

When Khorii's parents decided to take her on a trip into Federation space to see her mother's human friends and family, Khorii had been afraid it would be really boring. But Mother had her reasons for taking her along. Mother's adoptive human fathers had come to visit when Khorii was younger, but she barely remembered them, and she had not yet met their mates and children. Mother

13

said it was time and past that Khorii got to know them. Mother also wanted Khorii to see something of the worlds that she herself had known as a girl.

But Khorii was on her way, even though her Linyaari playmates, both of them, thought the prospect of a trip into a whole new sector of space was pretty scary. That was despite the fact that they were starborn themselves, and used to meeting other races.

Khorii was scared, too. But not for the same reasons her friends were. She was scared that it would be absolutely mind-numbingly dull, what with all of the adults talking about the Good Old Days and about people who were dead before she was born, as Linyaari adults seemed to do all the time.

At the same time she was worrying about being bored, she *also* thought that this trip *could* be thrilling.

But now, sitting in her berth and staring out through her viewscreen into space, she was not yet thrilled, and she wondered how it could have *possibly* been night for so long. Days and weeks and months full of nothing but darkness. Stars were everywhere, but not one of them turned the morning sky violet, as it was at home when Our Star rose over the mountains.

She understood, of course, the physics of space and light. She knew that it was Vhiliinyar's atmosphere that produced the beautiful skies she longed to see again, and not Our Star alone. Still, she couldn't help feeling that if she touched the tip of

14

her horn to the screen, it might somehow purify the vastness and depth that had swallowed the ship and with it her family and friends, and turn the airless blackness into the light and sweet-smelling air she craved.

She felt a nudge under her arm and lifted it to see her cat Khiindi staring at her while his sides rose and fell with the passion of his purrs. Khiindi loved it out here. Well, he would. Cats loved nothing better than sleeping. Endless nights were good for sleeping. Of course, cats loved sunlight, too, but Khiindi just curled up under the nearest lamp and pretended it was his own personal sun.

Khorii sighed. How she longed to set the ship down someplace larger than the *Condor*, somewhere outside, where she could graze and run and play. And, right now, except for Khiindi, she was lonely. Her foster brother, Elviiz, usually annoyed her by being underfoot and in her way every chance he got, but now that he was closeted with his android father/creator, Maak, Khorii felt abandoned. Her parents, Acorna and Aari, were in their own berth, sleeping after a long watch. They had proposed this trip as a way to spend more time with their family after a long series of missions that had taken them away from Vhiliinyar, but at the moment it felt to Khorii that they were spending their time exclusively in each other's company. She was feeling decidedly left out.

Khorii stretched, yawned, and decided to go see what was happening on the bridge. Maybe she could get Captain Becker, her beloved Uncle Joh, to play a game with her or teach her more about gonzo physics.

When she got to the deck, it seemed that Uncle Joh also had better things to do. He was bouncing up and down in the command seat, alternately wringing his hands and clapping them together before spreading them over the various controls of his scanner array like a concert pianist about to pound out a sonata in one of the cultural vids Mother insisted she watch.

Drawing nearer to her human friend, she saw a spot of drool beaded at the side of his mouth. Becker looked exactly like RK, the ship's feline first mate, when RK was contemplating a particularly tasty specimen of vermin. Khorii rushed forward, worried that Uncle Joh, who was of course quite aged, being a contemporary of her parents, was having some kind of seizure. But then she saw the reflection of his eyes glittering avariciously in three of the scanner arrays and knew he was fine. What he was wearing was simply a heightened version of his characteristic 'Yahoo, salvage!' expression: a mixture of enthusiasm, delight, and greed.

The *Condor* was a ship dedicated to collecting and 'recycling' or selling salvage, and Uncle Joh loved his business. There was very little else that could thrill him so much as a bit of wreckage or refuse. It appeared that he had a particularly luscious bit of salvage in sight this time.

'What is it?' she asked him, sliding into her usual seat beside the captain. She had lived only six Linyaari years, the equivalent of twelve Standard years for a humanoid child, and was somewhat short for her age, even among her Linyaari friends. Khiindi hopped onto the headrest of her chair, which rose a foot or so above the top of her head.

RK, whose given name was Roadkill, was a huge brindled black and gray, very furry, Makahomian Temple Cat. RK had been sleeping in a similar position on the chair above Uncle Joh's head. The feline first mate had been with Uncle Joh since before Khorii was born. Upon seeing Khiindi, RK opened one eye and growled. Khiindi, a gray-striped cat who was large, though not as large as RK, gave a pathetic mew in return. RK was Khiindi's sire, or at least the Makahomian priesthood suspected that he was, and Khiindi always seemed hurt by the older cat's animosity. Khorii reached up and, with one of her three-fingered, single-knuckled hands, stroked Khiindi's fluffy gray tail as it flipped in an agitated fashion against the small, spiraling opalescent horn nestling among the short pink-and-purple-streaked silver curls of her mane. Normally, as a space-faring Linyaari, she should have had silver curls, but she'd been experimenting with dyes to make her look somewhat different from every other star-clad Linyaari person her age.

Like her, every other Linyaari who'd been into space was white-skinned, silver-maned, opal- or golden-horned, and had feathery silver curls growing from head and neck and halfway down the spine. Another ridge of curls tickled the back of her legs from knee to ankle, where her feet ended

17

in two hard, hooflike toes. The dye Khorii had used was pale and sort of messy-looking now, but it had been pretty when she first did it. Aunt Maati said that Khorii's mother had done something similar when she first came to narhii-Vhiliinyar, the new homeworld of the Linyaari that Khorii's mother had helped create.

After a moment of fiddling with the controls that sent the *Condor* in pursuit of its prey, her Uncle Joh leaned back in the chair and pointed to the scanners. 'Khorii, cutie, I am so glad you are keeping me company on this historic occasion. Lookee there!'

She saw a small blip on the screen quickly blossom into a larger blip.

'What is that?' she asked.

'Ah, my child, listen and I will tell you a poem. You like poems, right?'

She nodded, cautiously. Uncle Joh still recited poems and played practical jokes on her as he had done when she was a very small child. To be fair, though, he did the same thing to her parents, so she supposed it had more to do with who he was than with his perception of her. He began:

' 'Twas night just like always as it is in deep
     space
We were scanning for salvage all over the place
When what to my wondering scanners appeared
But a derelict ship, off our port bow, right here!'

Uncle Joh stabbed at a button, and the blip bloomed until it filled the entire screen, revealing

18

itself to be a large luxury space liner, its name clearly legible on its side.

'La Est-trail-a Blanket?' Khorii asked, unsure of how to say the words.

'*La Estrella Blanca*,' he corrected her pronunciation, turning the sounds at the end of the words into long *a*'s. 'It's Spanish, *chica*. Means "The White Star." Historically not the best choice of words, but probably the guy who named her was a businessman, not a space mariner or a historian.'

'Why not a good choice?' she asked.

'It's *very* ancient history, but once upon a time on Old Terra, back when it was called Earth, some people built a huge ship – not a space vessel; it sailed on the water of the ocean, though maybe sailed isn't the right word, since it didn't have sails. It had motors. Anyway, they built a ship so huge that they said it couldn't be sunk. And it did. End of story.'

'And the ship was called *The White Star* also? Like this one?'

'No, it was called the *Titanic*. But the company that built it was called the White Star Line. In Spanish, that ended up being translated into this ship's name. Naturally the *Titanic*'s sinking didn't do the White Star Line any good. For one thing, it wiped out quite a few of the richest people on the planet, who were on that maiden voyage because it was the fashionable thing to do.'

'What is "fashionable"?' she asked. Her Standard was really pretty good, but every once in a while humans, Uncle Joh especially, came up

19

with an expression that had not been covered in her lessons.

'Means all their friends were doing it and thought it was cool, so they wanted to do it, too.'

'Ah.' She thought about that for a moment, but it did not make a great deal of sense. If all of her friends were grazing on one patch of grass, she had always found it helpful to find another patch for herself, which would give her more food and not overgraze that particular area. But maybe that was just her.

Returning her attention to the screen, now filled with the starboard side of the ship, the portion that said 'Blanca,' she noticed a faint pulsing of the indicator light to the right of the scanner array.

'What does this mean?' she asked, touching it.

'Nuts!' he said, touching a volume control, 'it's a distress beacon. Does look pretty old though.' He studied the pulses for a moment, and said, 'I guess they would have been in distress at some point or the ship wouldn't be wallowing around in space like this. We'll just pull alongside her with the tractor beam, board her, and see what's what. I don't wish those people any ill luck, mind you, but that ship would be some bodacious salvage if nobody's still aboard.'

He fiddled with the com system and began talking to his prospective prize.

'Hey, there, you aboard the *Estrella Blanca*, this is Captain Jonas Becker aboard the *Condor*, flagship of Becker and Son Interplanetary Recycling and Salvage Enterprises, Ltd., of which I am the CEO.

We received your distress signal and ask permission to board. Do you read me?'

After turning up the volume, waiting, and going through a number of other procedures, he flicked off the com signal and said, 'Guess nobody's home.' He looked much happier.

After that, he ignored her while she watched him approach the much larger ship and attach the *Condor* to its docking bay hatch using the tractor beam. The tractor beam had been culled, like most of the *Condor*, from another larger and more powerful vessel. Khorii knew this because Uncle Joh was fond of telling her about the heritage of each and every sheet of metal, panel, nut, bolt, screw, and button he had adapted for his ship. Now he reversed thrusters and, with the pull of the tractor beam to override the electronic controls, the hatch opened the rest of the way of its own accord. Becker disengaged the tractor beam and flew into the outer airlock of the liner's docking bay. It irised smoothly shut behind the *Condor*, and the hatch leading to the bay irised open.

'Normally I might have to cut open the hull or extrude a boarding tube,' Becker told her. 'But this baby is large enough that I'll just drive on in there and find us a parking place.' When the inner hatch irised shut behind them, the bay became dark as night, like space itself, without stars. Except for their landing lights, the deck was black and silent. Their lights slid over the hulls of what looked like many other sleek vessels, some larger than the *Condor*, as the ship settled into an empty berth

21

among them. 'The ship's atmosphere seems to be intact – normal O2 levels and reasonable air pressure, but no gravity out there. But I don't like the looks of it. I'm gonna suit up.'

'Should I call my parents or Uncle Maak and Elviiz?' she asked.

'Nah. Your parents need their rest, and Maak is downloading some new programming to Elviiz, so they'll be all plugged in and disassembled and stuff. I'll take the camera to document the findings, in case the company that owns this bird contests my salvage claim. That way, I'll be transmitting back to our com screen and you can watch that and make sure I don't run into any trouble. If I do, then you can call the cavalry. But don't worry, honey, I do this stuff all the time. So does the cat. C'mon, RK. You wanna stink up a new place, here's your chance.'

He clattered down the metal stairs to the lower deck, where the robolift and the first mate's intricately engineered cat hatch and airlock were located. She heard more clanking and banging and a couple of swear words, then the creaking of the robolift descending through the tail of the ship. Before the sound stopped, RK appeared through the viewport, floating through the zero G with his tail lashing like a rudder until he blended into the darkness. When he looked back, his eyes glowed like stars in the ship's lights. Khiindi mewed and jumped down from Khorii's chair.

'Khiindi, come back. The captain didn't say you could go, too!'

22

But almost before her words were out, the flap of the cat hatch announced his departure and he, too, made his appearance outside the hull of the *Condor*, somersaulting nose over tail three feet above the ground or so into the light illuminating the area in front of the viewport. He looked up, blinking at her before righting himself and pushing off after his sire, just as if he'd been in zero G all his life.

Uncle Joh, clad in full protective gear and helmet, lumbered into view, looked after the retreating cat paws and tail for a moment, then made a thumbs-up gesture in the direction of the viewport. She heard each breath he took.

'Uncle, why are you wearing both your night-vision goggles and carrying that huge antique infrared camera?'

'The goggles are so I can see what's here. The infrared detects heat, so if there are any survivors on this ship, which would mean I couldn't claim it as salvage, I'll be able to tell so you and your folks can help them, even though that would, in some ways, pain me. It's also very hard to tell from the pictures I take with this dinosaur what is valuable and what isn't. It gives me a few more . . . shall we say . . . gray areas, allowing for some flexibility in the salvage regulations.'

Watching the antics of Khiindi and RK, he chortled and said, 'Okay, if everything's okay for the two bouncy cats out here, I should be fine.' He removed his helmet, adjusted the infrared camera, and began recording the contents of the docking bay.

The com unit screen broadcast these pictures. While Khorii watched eerie shots of the various silent space yachts in their next-to-last resting places, Uncle Joh uttered appreciative whistles and remarks about what they would bring as salvage. Looking like a strange being with three heads, one of them tucked under his arm, and a third one-eyed head perched slightly to the left of the one sticking out of the neck of his space suit, the captain made his way to the inner hatch and left the docking bay.

The shimmery dark images jiggled as Becker carried the camera down the corridors, silent but for the *creak-thunk* of his antigrav boots, his breath, and an occasional *'whewee!'* when he found something particularly luxurious to record with the camera. Khorii found the details hard to make out, especially since she didn't know exactly what she was looking at.

That is, until the hand appeared. A human hand, dangling limp in front of the camera. The captain uttered an expletive and panned the camera up, then back down again.

'You shouldn't be watching this, kid,' he said into the microphone, his voice grim. 'It's not a pretty sight. There are bodies floating everywhere. I...' His breathing was quicker and shallower now, she noticed. 'I think I'll come back now. We can do this later. I'm not really feeling all that great.' This sounded so unlike Uncle Joh when he had treasure to salvage, even when there were bodies in the mix, that Khorii got really worried.

She was going to ask if she should go get her

24

folks when suddenly Becker tripped, his boots went out from under him, and the camera skewed sideways, to capture the bright red image of an unconscious RK, trapped beneath a body and floating just beneath it in the zero G.

Becker's gloved hand reached up and grabbed his first mate by the tail, hauling him down. She heard both their hearts thumping through the speaker. There was nothing else to hear except . . . there was a familiar plaintive mew off to the right. Khiindi! Had he injured RK in a catfight? Was that why the *Condor*'s first mate was drifting unconscious down the salvage ship's corridor?

Khorii loved cats, but she did not understand what it was in the natures of these two that made them so angry with each other. Her mother Acorna had told her that once when they were on a mission together on Makahomia, before Khorii was born, RK and Acorna had briefly forged a telepathic link. Her mother told Khorii that RK was a perfectly reasonable and highly intelligent sentient creature who simply chose to communicate in his own way the majority of the time. Khorii could hardly wait until her own telepathic talents manifested themselves, as they did for all Linyaari. Perhaps she would be able to communicate with both cats *all* the time, having been raised with Khiindi and RK. Mother had not met RK until she was really quite old, nearly ten *ghaanyi*.

Uncle Joh would not be able to manage the camera and both cats. She abandoned the bridge and slipped into her own shipsuit and antigrav boots, then punched the button for the robolift, which cranked toward her far too slowly. At the last moment, she remembered to grab a flashlight and stepped aboard the lift as it descended into darkness.

Once out of the halo cast by the *Condor*'s running lights, Khorii felt as if she should be creeping forward through the darkness on tiptoe, but she couldn't very well do that while wearing antigrav boots. She did, however, keep the beam of her flashlight rotating in a circle around the path in front of her. Twice the beam picked out a white, dead face staring blankly through the viewport of one of the docked ships. Once the face was black. But no bodies floated or lay across her path.

Leaving the docking bay for the central corridor where she had seen the captain and RK, she was gradually aware of little motes of something fleeing from the beam of her flashlight. They were so concentrated that when she stepped into the corridor, for a time she could not see even with the flashlight because it was clouded by the presence of these – whatever they were. But they fled quickly, and every movement of her flashlight revealed the scene before her more clearly. She almost wished it hadn't.

The dead floated around her like idle swimmers in a lake on a hot afternoon, though they obviously had not had any fun in a long time. There was no smell because the atmosphere was so depleted, and anyway, her horn would have removed the foul odors had they been there. But the dead eyes, the protruding tongues on some of the corpses, the death grimaces on their faces: all of them so sad. Some ladies were dressed in beautiful gowns, some men in fine uniforms with golden braid. They bore no wounds that she could see, though with the lighting so poor, she might have missed them. Then she saw Uncle Joh. To her surprise, he was crawling, not walking, toward her, dragging his inert first mate behind him by the tail.

'Uncle Joh, what is the matter?' she asked. 'Did you hurt yourself?'

'I don't feel so good, sweetie. Better call your mom and dad. RK's sick, too. He's still alive, but just barely.'

'But you were stricken so suddenly!' she said. 'I am afraid to return to the ship, Uncle Joh. I do not know if you will survive until Mother and Father came. Besides, that isn't necessary. I have a horn, do I not?'

'Yeah, but you're just a little bit of a thing.'

'It does not matter. Some of the elders say that the healing power is more concentrated in us younglings. Oh, poor RK!' Khorii said, lifting the first mate into her arms and extricating his tail from the captain's fist. Lowering her horn to his head and tummy she said, 'Wake up, cat. You must help me help the captain.'

RK did, of course. With a wiggle and a flip he was out of her arms and swimming anxious circles around the two of them. As she lowered her horn to the captain's head, RK paddled off into the

27

darkness. By the time Becker was back on his feet, RK had returned, this time with the nape of Khiindi's neck between his teeth while her own cat's head lolled and his limp paws and tail trailed beneath the floating older cat's belly.

'You're a good first officer, RK,' Becker said, giving the cat a pat as Khorii relieved him of Khiindi. 'Got to look after the passengers, even if you don't especially like them.'

RK yawned and paddled back toward the ship. He had had enough. As Khorii touched her horn to the fur between Khiindi's ears, her cat reached for the horn with his front paws, patted it, yawned, and stretched in her arms, then settled against her shoulder, kneading his claws in her shipsuit and drooling with relief.

'Come on, Uncle Joh,' Khorii said, extending her free hand. 'I will carry your helmet for you. We should return to the ship now. This is a very bad place.'

'Yeah, you're right. We need to get reinforcements in here. This liner is way too big for me to catalog the contents alone. Maak can do it much faster than I can manually, and with Elviiz to help him, I'll know how rich we are much sooner! Fortunately, you Linyaari are here and can clean out all the nasty germs or whatever the hell hit me, so all my cargo is nice and negotiable and we can put these poor devils to rest.'

'Yes,' she said. 'Maak and Elviiz can also identify each of these people and which belongings aboard the ship belong to which person so their things may be returned to their heirs. You know, as it says in the Federation Unified Code of Conduct? The one you told Elviiz to make me memorize?'

'Touché,' he said glumly. 'You should think about going into politics yourself, sweetie. You sure know how to take the fun out of everything.'

They did not need to return to the ship to fetch her parents or Maak and Elviiz. The landing had awakened Mother and Father, who rightly guessed it had something to do with salvage. They did not realize the extraordinary circumstances of the stop until coming out onto the bridge, where they tried and failed to raise the captain on the intercom. They activated Maak and Elviiz and met Khorii and the captain halfway down the corridor.

'Joh! What do you mean bringing Khorii out here among these dead bodies?' Father demanded.

'I didn't, Aari, honest, but you can be proud of her. She handled herself really well and kept me and the cats from joining these poor corpses in that great nebula far, far away.'

'Of course she did, Captain,' Mother said, sounding stern. 'And we are very proud of her.' She linked her arm with Khorii's and patted her hand. 'We are simply wondering how you came to be here in a state that required her assistance so desperately that you did not think of the effect seeing so many lifeless people might have on a sheltered female in her formative years?'

'Oh, Moth-*er*,' Khorii said, disentangling herself from the maternal grip in disgust. 'Really. From what Uncle Hafiz and my human grandsires have told me, you were freeing child slaves and confronting criminals at my age. I think I can handle seeing a few deceased people. It isn't as if they could hurt us. Well, not on purpose. I think they must have died from some kind of poison gas that my horn purified when I walked into the corridor.'

Khorii had a lot to live up to – or down. Her mother, called Khornya among their own people, was known and revered as the Lady Acorna Harakamian-Li to the fierce and warlike Terrans. She was the first Linyaari to go among them, well, not on purpose exactly. The human grandsires, asteroid miners at the time, rescued and raised Mother when they found her escape pod traveling where no Linyaari had gone before.

On top of that, Khorii's father Aari was the only one of their people to have survived being captured and tortured by the horrible Khleevi. Together her parents had, in a most *ka*-Linyaari fashion, fought and vanquished the Khleevi in *two* time zones. Of course, the first time they had had help from Mother's human friends as well as from some other Linyaari who helped in a passive way. And the second time, which was actually *earlier*, they had been aided by her grandsire, or mother-father, as the term literally translated from Linyaari to Standard, the language spoken in the quadrant where Mother was raised. Khorii's grandsire and grandam were no less remarkable than her parents, both having recently returned from the dead.

So, really, with a lineage like that, Khorii did not want anyone to think she could not handle seeing a few dead people. RK and Khiindi were no longer in the corridor with the captain and Khorii's parents, who were standing in a cluster, engrossed in discussing what had probably happened to the people aboard *La Estrella Blanca*. Probably the two cats had gone back to the ship, but Khorii wandered up the corridor, shining her flashlight on the path ahead, just in case they'd decided to explore further. Cats did like to explore and, according to Karina, one of her human aunties, curiosity had been known to kill cats in the past, as it had almost done just now. So she thought she had better make sure.

If she didn't find them on the path, she would look upward again, though the bodies overhead were distressing to look at because of their contorted faces, which were empty of everything that made a person a person. Mostly they seemed very sad. She wondered who they had been. From the way they were dressed, they were at a party when they died. Had they been having fun then? Had they died happy? Most of them were probably the equivalent of her parents' age – very old, of course, but not as old as Uncle Hafiz in human years. You couldn't tell as easily with a Linyaari, of course. Her grandparents on her father's side seemed much older than her grandparents on her mother's side, but apparently they were all about the same age as cranky old Liriili, who was very bossy, having once been administrator of narhii-Vhiliinyar, and whose attitude made her seem ancient.

But however old they were, she was sure these people were rather young to have died as they did. She felt sorry for them. She felt even sorrier for their kids. They probably had some, at home, being watched by their grandparents or aunties, as she so often was when her parents were off on a mission. How long would these people have been gone now? Did their children know they were dead even? Probably not. They must still be wondering what had happened to their moms and dads.

At the end of the corridor there were lifts and a very handsome shiny silver-colored spiral staircase extending the length of the ship, descending far below the corridor where Khorii stood, where the engine rooms and cargo holds and other utilitarian spaces were located, to far above, where the bridge would be. In her experience, cats didn't care for the smell of engine rooms so she would try the upper levels first. She reached down and flipped off the antigrav setting on her boots, held her arms over her head, lowered them sharply to her sides, and gave a jump that sent her up the stairwell without actually needing to use the steps. That was usually the fun way to do it, but now the passage was occasionally blocked by a dead crew member. In adjoining corridors branching off the stairwell she saw more bodies. An unusual number of people seemed to have been heading away from the bridge and cabins. Perhaps they had decided to abandon ship but died before they could reach their own private vessels or the ship's shuttles.

At the top of the stairs she turned on her boots again and walked out onto the corridor leading to the bridge and the crew's quarters. Still no cats and many more dead crew members. All seemed to be humanoid at least, if not as human as Uncle Hafiz and Auntie Karina, but that wasn't surprising. Unlike the quadrant of space containing Vhiliinyar's native star system, which had many different species of people, in this quadrant almost all sentient life was human or humanoid, according to Mother and Captain Becker.

And, of course, according to Elviiz's know-it-all data banks. It was totally unfair, in Khorii's opinion, to put a person's school inside a person's already far too superior foster brother. Anyway, it sounded monotonous to her, to have only one kind of people no matter what world you were on. What was the point of going to other planets if everybody else was just like you? That was, she supposed, the best thing about Elviiz. He was different from anyone else on Vhiliinyar, being an android created specifically to be Khorii's companion, teacher, and protector by his father android, Maak, the *Condor*'s android first mate (as opposed to the feline first mate, RK. Uncle Joh was very demo-cratic in his assignment of titles for crew members). As birthing gifts went, she supposed Maak's gift of the ever-present, ever-in-her-way Elviiz was preferable to pricking her finger on a spindle when she was sixteen (by then she would be quite mature of course, in Linyaari years) and falling into a deep prolonged sleep, rather like hypersleep, as the princess in the fairy tale had done.

She'd read that story, along with many, many others, among the books in the captain's extensive dump-rescued library. The *Condor*, with its junk hard-copy library, computerized references, and seemingly endless supply of vids, recycled ancient knowledge as well as refuse. Much of the data Maak had imparted electronically to his son had come from those sources. The way Elviiz acted sometimes, though, you'd have thought he invented all the stories himself. When Maak gave her the birthing gift of Elviiz, unfortunately he had also given Elviiz the birthing gift of both ego and attitude, something previous androids had been without.

It didn't do any good to complain about him to Mother or Father. Maak had been their friend as long as Uncle Joh, and they said they could never have defeated the Khleevi without him. They were sure Elviiz was really as dear to her as Maak was to them. But Maak did not correct every single thing they said or try to stop them from doing anything really interesting, as Elviiz always did with her. In fact, she was surprised to have gotten away from him this long. She expected to hear the clomp of little android boots catching up with her at any moment, telling her to return to the *Condor* while he, Elviiz, got to explore with the grown-ups. Not that she was exploring. She was looking for cats. Really.

The bridge hatch did not respond to its control, so she tried to pry it open, but something seemed to be blocking it. 'I'm sorry, it's the only way,' she said to the bodies floating below her, then backed up to the hatch and gave it a one-legged kick. Her legs and feet had the strength of her equinesque forebears and the hatch, though damaged, opened enough for her head and shoulders to pass through. Shining the beam of the flashlight around the perimeter of the hatch frame, she saw what was blocking it. Three bodies had apparently been wedged into the workings. Parts of them drifted in zero G, but they were stacked atop each other, and each had a limb or a bit of clothing trapped in the iris. Sticking the flashlight under her arm, she reached down and as gently as possible – which wasn't very, dislodged the blockages, freeing two of the bodies to float ceilingward. She saw as she released the dead that, unlike the bodies in the corridors, these people had laser burns through the centers of their chests.

Khorii pushed through the broader opening, bracing her hands on the bottom of the iris and pulling her legs over her head in a sort of supported somersault. As she explored the bridge, she had the odd sense of millions of tiny motes fleeing before her, then disappearing again. What was that? It had happened in the stairwell, too. For a moment the things were quite thick in the thin atmosphere, then, *poof!*

Two officers sat strapped in chairs close to the

36

command console. For a moment she thought perhaps they had survived, but one look at their heads told her otherwise. The darker-haired officer, a man, had a laser burn through the base of his neck that came out the crown of his head. The other, a gray-haired female wearing a captain's epaulet on her uniform, had no mouth, nor was the rest of her face a pretty sight. A laser pistol floated near her hand, which hovered over the still faintly pulsing signal beacon control. On the console behind her hand was a printout. Scrawled across it in ragged handwriting were the words 'Forgive me! I had to do it. Now I will die, too.'

It appeared to Khorii that the captain had written those words just before turning the laser pistol on herself. Clearly, the last moments on the bridge had not been happy ones for anyone.

Khorii was not sure exactly what she was looking for, or even if it existed other than in the ship's powerless computer. A personnel and passenger list maybe. Surely they had such a list? There were – had been – a lot of people aboard this ship. They'd need to know who was in what cabin and so forth, wouldn't they?

But she saw nothing besides the captain's note that was a printout, or even a scrap of paper, much less a book. She climbed back into the corridor. Some of these bigger ships had special offices for the captain, ready rooms, she thought they were called, where the captain presumably got commands and charts and things ready before taking them onto the bridge. Maybe she should try there?

The first door that she opened led into a space that she thought might be such a room. There were pictures of other space vessels on the walls, and a series of important-looking framed documents. Captain Dolores M. Grimwald's certifications and licenses to fly various sorts of spacecraft, citations, and service awards. These were all arranged in a pyramid, seemingly in chronological order from top to bottom. The top one was up a bit higher than she could read by the beam of her flashlight so she turned the captain's swiveling chair around and stood on the seat, training her light on it.

It was a medical license awarded to Dr Dolores M. Grimwald, M.D. The captain had been a physician before she'd been a captain. A healer, like the Linyaari. Why had she killed everyone else on the ship, then? Khorii did not understand.

Except for the framed documents and pictures, there were no papers in the room.

She left it reluctantly, because this was the first room that did not contain corpses. Although corpses didn't bother Khorii, really, not at all, she was getting rather tired of bumping into them and found she was anxious to return to the *Condor*.

The next two cabins were also empty, but in the fourth cabin, she found not only a body but also all manner of nonelectronic record keeping. This was the purser's office, and – to her immense relief – she found the passenger roster she knew had to exist and what cabins the passengers were assigned and what they had paid for them. The purser was evidently someone who liked to have printouts available at all times instead of having to consult electronic devices. Uncle Hafiz was like that as well. She also found a list of crew members along with their cabin assignments, rank, position, and pay scale.

Just what she needed! Now they could notify the families of the victims and perhaps arrange to have them sent to their loved ones for burial or whatever the local custom was. All that remained was to find a ship's log or maybe a personal diary that would give some clue as to how disaster had overtaken these people and what motive a healer/captain might have for murdering her crew and apparently the passengers, too.

From the staircase came the sound of a heavy tread – the *clunk* of little android feet. They'd sent Elviiz to find her, of course. She was afraid of that, though she'd hoped they would all be too preoccupied to send her back before she was ready. It was okay. She was almost ready anyway. Just one or two more cabins to peek into, then she was sure she would have covered most of the officers.

The next door was another office. There she found more paper lists along with duty rosters held against the walls with magnets. There was also a diagram of the ship and the location of all the cabins, along with notations about each passenger. She couldn't read them because they were written in Spandard, the Spanish version of Standard spoken on the ship's homeworld. She did make out the names of flowers and foods. And one more thing sprang out at her near the end – the letters

'S.O.S.' Perhaps she held the key in her hands to what had happened on this ship – if only she could read it. She took the papers down and started to put them in one of the pockets of her shipsuit. As she folded, more of the mysterious motes sprayed off the papers. She touched the papers with her horn, and when the air between her and them cleared, she stuffed them into her pocket.

'Khorii, where are you? Khorii!' Elviiz was calling. Then she heard him mumble, 'Of the two of them, Khiindi is the more reliable.' Then, 'Khorii! Come along now. We are returning to the *Condor* and resuming our journey.'

'What?' she asked, popping her head out of the office. 'The captain would never abandon *this* ship!'

Elviiz looked back at her from the hatch to the bridge. Now the iris was more or less neatly opened. 'Of course not. He will tow it to one of his private storage asteroids, so that we may continue our journey to Maganos Moonbase. He can report his find and make his claim to the authorities there. Now come on.'

Figures, Khorii thought as she followed the android back to the *Condor*. *Just when things were getting interesting.*

THREE

The storage asteroid was not far by space-faring
standards, basically only a wormhole away. One of
the things Uncle Joh was teaching Khorii was how
to navigate the way his father Theophilus had
taught him, using wormholes and 'pleated' space
and other anomalies of physics as shortcuts. Of
course, Maak knew how to do this, as did her
parents, and Elviiz would probably have it in his
data banks long before she flew solo for the first
time; but at least she sort of understood how it
worked, and everyone *else* didn't know all of the
special Becker byways.

'See, this is really not on a commonly used
corridor,' the captain said. 'So I don't have to worry
about somebody disturbing my stuff. It's also,
ahem, a bit out of the reach of the Federation, so I
don't have to comply with a lot of stupid rules and
regulations. It's all mine. My own little world –
actually, I have several.'

He seemed very relieved when they went
through the wormhole. For one thing, the huge

41

liner put a tremendous strain on the tractor beam and the *Condor*'s engines, which were quite powerful compared to her size. 'Whew,' he said. 'Now we're off the main track, and I don't have to worry about someone investigating this particular tail wagging this particular dog. We'll be able to maneuver the *Blanca* into position pretty shortly though. The company cache is coming right up. You'll know it when you see it. I made it easy to identify in case I ever forget to reinstall the co-ordinates when I change our equipment.'

He was always using a newly salvaged piece to upgrade or replace one of the *Condor*'s parts. You couldn't say original parts. He said he figured the whole ship had been replaced quite a few times by now. In outline, it still roughly resembled the carrion bird for which it was named, but its texture reminded Khorii of the patchwork quilts some of the church ladies of Rushima had sent to MOO in gratitude for Mother's help in defeating the Khleevi.

Readily identifiable did not quite cover her first impression however. The name of his company was spelled out in salvage spread over the asteroid's surface followed by, KEEP OFF. DANGER! TOXIC WASTE! BIOHAZARD! EXPLOSIVES!

He watched her face closely, then beamed with pride at her expression. 'Impressive, huh? I wanted to add that trespassers would be fed to the cat, but I was afraid that most salvage thieves who hadn't met RK wouldn't know what a serious threat that was and think I was kidding about the other ones, too.'

That was the last conversation for a little while as the *Condor* coddled and prodded, tugged, backed, lifted, and very gently deposited the huge liner on the asteroid's surface before disengaging the tractor beam. Then they landed for a comparatively brief time while everyone suited up and anchored the liner firmly to the asteroid's surface, then camouflaged it with huge asteroid-colored protective tarps. Then all of them packed as much portable salvage as they could around the ship. None of this threatened the sign, Khorii noticed. Captain Becker had that well protected with a fence around its perimeter.

She reboarded the *Condor*, took off her suit, and waited for the others. 'What about all of those people?' she asked, when everyone had arrived.

'What people?' Becker asked. 'Oh, you mean the stiffs? They'll keep.'

'They *are* people,' Khorii said, with a fierceness that surprised her. 'They have families and homes, and someone is going to be worried about them.'

'You mean in the same way as we were worried about you when you just took off on that death ship and we didn't know where you were?' her mother asked sternly.

Oh, please, Khorii thought. They were psychic even if she wasn't yet. They could hear her mind and *know* if she was in trouble or not, even if they weren't actually reading her at the time.

'Captain Becker is just trying to protect the evidence, *yaazi*, until the Federation can conduct a proper investigation – back where we found the

43

ship. But he's right, you know. Looters could have found it and spaced the bodies—'

'You mean looters who aren't us?' Khorii demanded. 'He doesn't really care about the people at all. You heard him! Stiffs! He just wants the salvage and as much as—'

'That is enough, Khorii,' her father said. 'Come here, youngling, you are agitated. The sights you have seen today have upset you as they would any sensitive person.' He reached for her, and her mother did, but she backed away from them. She didn't want a horn touch to make her feel better. The people aboard that ship would never ever feel any better. She could not believe her parents were going along with Becker's greedy scheme. She could not believe she had ever liked him or claimed him as kin. He was a horrible man. Horrible. She hated him. Well, maybe not hated. Hate was not a Linyaari thing to feel. But she was very, very disappointed in him. And ashamed, too.

Uncle Joh looked angry himself. 'What's the matter with you, kid? Can't you see what we're doing? Those people are better off here. Someone else would come along and space them maybe, the authorities would have a devil of a time telling who was who or how they died. That ship is just too fraggin' big for us to cover and investigate as thoroughly as we should, and, besides, we might mess stuff up for the pros. It's a very delicate situation telling the cops that you've found some salvage you intend to claim, but meanwhile it's full of a lot of inconvenient corpses that you didn't

44

cause to be in that condition. It's gonna take a little time and some finesse to report the wreckage and have it back where we reported it to be. It's not something we can just call in, you know. There will be questions and inquiries and a lot of other stuff.'

'I have a list of the passengers,' Khorii said. 'All their names and where they are from.'

'Good work,' the captain said. 'We can give it to the Federation when we report it and . . .'

'I'd like to do that myself,' she said.

'Khoriilya.' Her mother held out her hand. 'I have heard enough from you for now, young lady. Give me the passenger lists. We will report this immediately.'

Khorii began to protest, even in spite of her mother's tone, but Mother lifted one eyebrow, and she knew better than to argue.

'Okay, then, fine.' She surrendered the various lists she had retrieved, then stomped to her cabin with Khiindi and secured the hatch. She did not feel like talking to anyone. She did not feel like going to visit relatives she had never met or had only met for a short time. She wanted to go home and be with the people she knew. The ones who were around while her parents were off on some mission or other.

Looking around her cabin, she wished she could see the face of Auntie Karina, Uncle Hafiz's wife, when she saw what Elviiz termed the 'modifications' Khiindi had made in the décor Karina had chosen to embellish Khorii's quarters. Auntie Karina would not like it.

Her aunt was very impressed with the fact that Makahomian Temple Cats like Khiindi were sacred on their own homeworld. Aunt Karina set a lot of store by things that were sacred, holy, or otherworldly, and showed her respect for all of them by burning a great deal of strong-smelling incense that made both Khorii's and Khiindi's noses burn and by talking in deep, wavering tones. It had always seemed a little silly to Khorii before, but at the moment it was downright endearing. *Some* people could use a little more reverence.

However, Karina did not really know much about cats, sacred or otherwise. She would never have filled Khorii's cabin with so many little cat statues made of different materials and in all sorts of colors, patterns, sizes, and poses if she'd known what Khiindi would do to them. The fragile ones were all in pieces, which Khorii had stowed in a locker. The soft plushy ones had been clawed, shed upon, nuzzled, drooled on (and sometimes something else, though Khorii purified the spots immediately so nobody would know how naughty Khiindi had been), and torn. Most of them lacked heads or paws or tails and had stuffing hanging out. The 'four-poster' effect, whatever that meant, that Aunt Karina had tried to achieve over Khorii's sleeping hammock with veils had ended up being fringe instead.

Aunt Karina had funny ideas sometimes, and Khorii knew the captain was not happy that she had tried to modify his ship, though he did it all the time. But Mother had said it was thoughtful of

Karina to try to make the ship more homelike, by Karina's standards, for the youngling, since it would be the child's first major spaceflight.

That all seemed so long ago. After recent events, she definitely did not feel like a child anymore.

FOUR

This is Federation Station Alpha adjunct to Kezdet. Please state your name, ship, corporate or galactic origins, registration number, and the purpose of your voyage.'

'Federation outpost, this is Captain Jonas P. Becker aboard the *Condor*, flagship of Becker Interplanetary Recycling and Salvage Enterprises, Ltd. Registration number 333666444555333. I am transporting two Linyaari ambassadors, one of them the Lady Acorna Harakamian-Li, and their—'

'Holy holos, Captain Becker, are we glad to see you! Well, not you. It's Lady Acorna. Maganos Moonbase notified us that she would be arriving soon, and it's not quite soon enough. Lady Acorna?' the dispatcher asked, trying to look beyond Uncle Joh and onto the bridge. He was a very young man, a boy really, with dark hair, skin the color of some of the roan planet-born children of Khorii's generation, and very light eyes. No horn, of course. Like Uncle Joh, he was a human. Mother waved at the screen. 'Maybe you don't remember me, Lady, but you rescued me from a mine on Kezdet a few years ago. Kmal Madari – well, Midshipman Madari, now. There are stories about you and your lifemate Aari going around all the outposts – and Captain Becker and his cat first mate and the android, too. How you all squashed those Khleevi bug monsters.'

'It wasn't quite like that, Kmal. But thank you for remembering me so fondly. We are on our way to take our daughter to visit relatives at Maganos Moonbase. How can we help you? I take it there's some trouble?'

'You bet there is. The whole Solojo star system has been infested with some kind of a plague, and the Federation Health Authorities are scared stiff it's already spread to other systems and worlds in our quadrant. A healer of your caliber – and your husband's, of course – well, you folks are maybe the only hope the victims in the Solojo settlements have left. The docs are baffled – and most of the medical folk are sick or dead as well. This is a killer plague. Even hazmat teams haven't been able to figure it out. We can't evacuate anyone without exposing ourselves and other people. It's a real mess. So when Mr Nadezda and Mr Baird told us you were coming to Maganos, the brass stepped in. They want you to go straight to Solojo, to the settlement on Paloduro. It's the most recently stricken, so there'll be the most survivors or people you can help. We hope.'

'Naturally we'll be happy to assist,' Mother said, with an apologetic look in Khorii's direction. 'But our daughter is with us. It's her first visit here to see her grandparents on Maganos Moonbase. We were hoping to arrive for the birth of Gill and Judit's baby.'

'I understand. I – er – let me patch you through to Federation Health Headquarters.'

The com screen flashed to a woman who looked so tired that when she tried to smile it was as if gravity kept the corners of her mouth down. 'Commodore Crezhale here, Lady Acorna, Lord Aari. Glad you are willing to help us. We will reroute your ship immediately, as soon as one of our fuel ships can replenish your supply. Your Linyaari expertise in these matters will be a godsend to Solojo. However, I have to warn you that Captain Becker and any other non-Linyaari life-forms traveling with you, I repeat, *any* non-Linyaari life-forms, including androids and animals, are under strict orders to remain aboard the vessel at all times. The most rigid sterilization procedure must be used when you reboard your ship to avoid bringing contaminants aboard. Sterile procedure must also be followed on food-stuffs or other supplies. There is to be no cargo taken on your vessel. From what we've observed, this plague crosses species with the greatest of ease, and until we've figured out its transmission method, we're not taking any chances.'

'Hmm,' the captain said, with a glance at Khorii, who had finished sulking and returned to the bridge to see Kezdet. 'Sounds to me like this is not a good time for the ambassadors to be taking their little girl to visit her human grandparents and great aunts and uncles and cousins, is that right?'

'Affirmative.'

'Well, then, maybe we ought to just head back for MOO. We can't take Khorii onto a plague planet,' Uncle Joh said.

Mother stepped forward and said, 'What is the status of Maganos Moonbase? Has there been any report of infection there?'

'Not as far as we know. I'm sorry to interfere with your family plans, but this is an emergency.'

'Aari and I are perfectly willing to do all we can to help halt the plague, and if we are not enough, we will send for other Linyaari to bring more of our technology to help, too, but Captain Becker is correct in saying that we have our child to think of. Linyaari children are not strong enough to deal with this sort of crisis – the healing devices require adult mind control to operate at their highest efficiency. A child would die trying to cope with such a huge demand on her energy. So we must take her somewhere safe. If we can just deliver her to Maganos Moonbase first . . .'

'And Khiindi, *Avvi*,' Khorii said. 'If I go, Khiindi must come with me.' She wanted familiar company. Badly. She did not like the idea of being abandoned among strangers. She didn't agree with it, but she knew she had no choice in the matter. The being abandoned part was nothing new, but she barely knew most of the people they had been going to see. Other than that they were pretty, as she had seen pictures of them, she had no idea what the grandmothers would be like. They sounded very kind, since Grandsire Calum's and Grandsire Gill's wives, the Kendoro sisters, had helped save Mother from all the troubles she was always getting into as a youngling, to hear Grandsire Rafik tell it.

Khorii knew Grandsire Rafik a bit better than the other two. Since he was the nephew and heir of Great-uncle Hafiz, the founder of House Harakamian and the Moon of Opportunity, Rafik visited MOO about once every Standard year to consult with Hafiz on business and to bring Khorii presents and tell her stories.

Once he had brought her a piece of scarlet cloth embroidered with gold and little mirrors. She had put it around herself and carried it behind her in both hands like a sail when she ran but it caught on the bushes and tore one day, so after that she draped it over her sleeping mat. This delighted Khiindi, who had chased the rainbows cast by the reflections on the mirrors and kneaded the cloth full of holes.

'Yes,' Elviiz said, in that annoying know-it-all way he had. 'The child and her kaat must be kept safe. Although I am a Linyaari child, too, I am a Linyaari android child and thus . . .'

'Thus you will accompany your sister-friend where she goes,' Maak said firmly.

'But, Father, I should stay and help you and Captain Becker and my Linyaari parents.' Khorii stuck her tongue out at Elviiz where only he could see. He couldn't stick his out at her in return because he was trying to be so grown-up and was standing in front of the viewscreen where the Federation dispatcher could see him.

'You will help us all best by fulfilling your primary function and keeping Khorii safe,' Maak told him. 'We will have more father-and-son bonding sessions on future occasions. I will be too busy assisting Captain Becker and the first mate to provide you with proper instruction.'

While they were arguing, the commodore, no doubt assuming that her wishes were their command, had signed off, and Kmal the dispatcher was back again.

'I can see we have a problem,' Kmal said. As serious as his voice had been before, he seemed to be trying not to laugh now. Khorii thought maybe he thought it was funny, too, to see Elviiz put in his place. 'Let me check with my superiors and get back to you. Have you spoken with Maganos Moonbase recently?'

'Not yet,' the captain said. 'We haven't been able to get any of Lady Acorna's dads on their private channels. Busy men, I guess.'

'Yes, sir. In that case I'll make contact for you and explain the situation to them, let them know you've gone through channels and everything,' Kmal said. 'Over and out for now.'

He soon reappeared, and said, 'Okay, Lady Acorna, the *Condor* is cleared to orbit Maganos Moonbase and dispatch your daughter and her pet and her droid to the surface. Following that, please proceed to Paloduro with all possible speed.'

When the transmission ended Khorii asked, 'Where's Paloduro?'

'Here,' the captain said, acting like they were still friends, as if nothing had happened. 'I can show you on the charts.' He punched a few buttons, and a star chart appeared on the console screen. 'We're about here,' he told her.

'Where's Vhiliinyar?'

'Way off the chart over there somewhere near where the cats are fighting,' he told her, flipping a thumb back over his shoulder. Khiindi and RK were rolling over and over in a cat pinwheel, growling and hissing at each other. If Khiindi had ever felt any gratitude to his sire for hauling him out of the death-ridden corridor of the *Blanca*, or if RK had ever felt any tenderness for his offspring that had prompted him to save him in the first place, both cats had apparently forgotten about it. 'Now over here is Kezdet, and here is Maganos Moonbase, where you're going. And over here . . .' His hand described a wide arc until his finger stabbed on a dot far to the right of the moonbase. 'This is Paloduro.'

'That's a long way away,' she said, studying the chart. 'Where a plague is concerned, that's a good thing.'

Mother and Father had been talking quietly to each other, but now they came and stood, each of them with a hand on Khorii's shoulder. 'I wish now we had brought the Linyaari ship instead of riding with you, Captain,' Mother said. 'Had we

54

done so, you could take Khorii back to MOO and recruit some of our people to join us.'

'Too late for that now,' the captain told her. 'Besides, the kid doesn't want to go home after coming all this way, do you, Khorii?'

Well, yes she did, actually. She was going to be left alone again.

'You will not be alone, little one,' Father said, reading her thoughts. 'Remember, your human family will be there to meet you. Your mother's foster fathers love to tell stories of her adventures when she was your age. And there will be other younglings there for you to befriend.'

'Think of it as early training for your own ambassadorship when you're a little older, *yaazi*,' Mother said, giving her a hug.

In another two hours the *Condor* was within hailing distance of Maganos Moonbase.

Mother greeted them herself. 'This is Acorna Harakamian-Li aboard the *Condor*, Maganos Moonbase. Please alert Calum and Gill that we will be entering your orbit in approximately four hours.'

'I'm afraid I can't do that, Lady Acorna,' said the young man whose face appeared on the com screen. 'Judit's baby tried to come early, so Calum, Mercy, and Gill all went to the hospital Kezdet-side to be with her. They didn't expect they would all be off base so long, but I'm sure they'll be returning soon. There's been talk in the last few minutes of quarantining Kezdet though.'

55

'Is Kezdet infected, too, then?'

'Not so far and neither are we, but the Federation has proposed a ban prohibiting inter-stellar travel in this sector until they've been able to identify the source of the infection and any vessels that might have been exposed.'

'It is unfortunate, but it makes sense to quar-antine the healthy until you know where the threat is,' Father said. 'From all that's been said, Kezdet is much larger and has a diverse population. It would be more difficult to control a disease there.'

'I still wish Calum and Gill and the Kendoros were going to be there,' Mother said, as if Khorii could not take care of herself, as she had often done before.

'Khorii will probably be better off with the other children even though your fathers will not be there right away. If we cure the plague elsewhere and help contain it, then the quarantine is unnecessary and your fathers and their mates can return to the moon.'

Mother cast a concerned look down at her daughter. Khorii knew she did not wish to leave her alone among strangers. 'The moon *is* a more controlled environment. It is one big school, really, the way we set it up. Even without Cal and Gill here I will feel easier about sending Khorii to the surface alone on Maganos Moonbase than I would sending her down to Kezdet alone to look for Cal and Gill.'

Elviiz spoke up. 'She will not be alone, Mother. I will be with her.'

Mother smiled at Elviiz. 'Yes, you will. I forgot that for a moment. I know you will look after each other.'

'And Khiindi, of course,' Khorii said. Her cat had chosen that moment to disengage from hostilities with his sire and jump to her shoulder for a bout of purring reassurance.

'And Khiindi,' Mother agreed.

Becker chuckled. 'When you were her age, from what I've heard, you were already saving the universe as we know it from all sorts of stuff and scaring the pee-waddin' out of your dads in the process.'

Mother smiled, though she still looked worried. 'I suppose I simply do not want history to repeat itself. My parents were frightened of that when we told them we were taking this trip.'

It was nice that everyone was worried about her, and Khorii almost felt warmly toward the captain again. She hated to bring up another complication, but if they were all too blind to see it, she felt she had to. 'There is a world in the Solojo system? Dinero Grande? I saw it when you showed me the map, Captain. The *Blanca*'s registration said Dinero Grande. I do not think I should go to the Moonbase. I think the people on the *Blanca* maybe had the plague.'

'Your theory is logical, Khorii, but it is not supported by the evidence,' Elviiz butted in. 'The corridor where Captain Becker and the cats succumbed, as did the organic components of Father and I, still held the remnants of a toxic gas.

57

We analyzed it. The crewmen on the bridge were shot. Judging from the input I saw, the captain for reasons known only to herself, or more likely because she lost her reason altogether, frightened the passengers so badly they tried to flee, whereupon she filled her ship's corridors with poison gas. She murdered her subordinates when they attempted mutiny in order to assist the passengers.'

'Besides, youngling, we are Linyaari,' Acorna said, bending down to look into her daughter's face. 'With three of us aboard the *Condor*, no one here would remain contaminated if ever they had been, which, as Elviiz told you, they were not. Please try to stop worrying about that ship. If this plague spreads, I fear you may see far worse things to come. Your feeling for the deceased passengers and crew does you credit, but' – and Mother bent her horn to touch Khorii's, flooding her with feelings of love and security, warmth and understanding, a cradle to support her when her family was gone – 'try to enjoy the school. We hope to return soon.'

'I hope so, too, *Avvi*,' she said, throwing her arms around her mother, then her father, Maak, and finally, because it was expected, Uncle Joh, who gave her a quick bear hug and let her go.

Finally, she gave RK a farewell pat, jerking Khiindi out of the way of the older cat's paw at the last minute, and climbed aboard the shuttle. Elviiz squeezed in between her and the controls programmed to land them safely on the surface and guide them into their assigned docking bay. To Khorii's disgust, Elviiz was also programmed to fly the shuttle manually in case the autopilot failed. Nobody had taught *her* to fly a shuttle yet. *Androids get to do everything first*, she thought.

FIVE

Elviiz didn't get to fly the shuttle manually because
nothing went wrong with the autopilot. Uncle Joh
had made it of 'the best components culled from
the finest scrap heaps in the multiverse, where
castoffs of the very latest obsolete designs' were
abandoned by their owners or manufacturers in
favor of more cutting-edge but, as uncle never
failed to add, not necessarily superior, equipment.
At any rate, the shuttle landed and docked itself
perfectly, then self-activated its com screen so
Khorii, Khiindi, and Elviiz could assure their
family members on the *Condor* that their arrival
had been safe and uneventful.

'In that case, sweetheart, we'd better head for
Paloduro so your folks can heal the stricken and we
can return and all of us have the vacation this was
supposed to be. You mind' – she was going to
scream if Uncle Joh told her to mind Elviiz but
instead he said – 'that your pussycat doesn't get
into too much trouble. He's a chip off the old cat.'

'I will send messages of our progress through

Elviiz's com screen,' Uncle Maak said. 'You must do the same.'

Father's eyes glistened with tears. He had not wanted to let go of her during the good-bye hug. Mother patted his shoulder, and said, 'Khorii, I have every confidence in your good sense and flexibility. The school on Maganos Moonbase is a great place to brush up on your interplanetary social skills. The young people there are from every human and humanoid species in the sector. By the time we return, you will probably have so many friends you won't want to leave.'

Khorii nodded as if she agreed, but she didn't, and she hoped her parents weren't reading her just then because they had enough on their own minds already, without the burden of what she had on hers. What if these human and humanoid younglings didn't like her?

A new face appeared on the com screen. The boy had a roundish fair-skinned face and hair almost as white as Khorii's mane. 'You're Lady Acorna's kid? Cool! I'm Hap Hellstrom. Come on out and I'll show you around. Is that a real Makahomian Temple Cat you have with you? I've never seen one of those before. I had a dog at home before – well, you know, before the place blew up. His name was Boomer and he was a pretty amazing dog. Everyone said so. People I didn't even know asked me about him after he died. I don't mind too much though. I know it's all the balance of nature – well, funny in a way. Not *ha-ha* funny but strange funny. Boomer died, and our planet went boom! But hey, that's how it goes sometimes, and you just have to roll with it, you know what I mean? How do you say your name again? And who's the other kid?'

'Khorii,' she said. 'My mother, whom you know as Acorna, is called Khornya among our people so my name is between hers and my father's, which is Aari. This is my foster brother, Elviiz.'

'Cool sideburns, little brother,' Hap said. 'And I like the white suit with the studs on it.'

'Thank you. My father made me so I resemble a Linyaari version of my namesake, the king of olden times.'

But Hap was plunging along. Khorii had unsealed the hatch and opened it, and the boy came right inside, although there wasn't much room. He was as tall as an adult Linyaari and with his white hair and fair skin lacked only a horn in the middle of his head to make the resemblance at least superficially complete.

'Can I pet your cat? Would that be all right? I like cats. Boomer liked cats, too. Cats all liked him most of the time. Except when he tried to herd them. He was a Lothland herd dog. Hi, kitty. I brought you something. I heard there was going to be a cat coming down, so I made this just for you. Don't rat on me to Tab, though. She runs the 'ponics garden, and she's very strict, but I figured, hey, cats are entitled to catmint, so I sewed it up in this little packet. Ow! Wow! I guess he likes it. I almost lost a finger.'

'Makahomian Temple Cats are like that,' Khorii said. She leaned over to touch her horn to the welts

62

Khiindi had slashed across Hap's knuckles but Elviiz pulled her back in time. This was going to be hard to get used to. When her cat hurt someone who was just being nice to them, it was only natural to want to heal his wound; but the humans weren't supposed to know exactly how Linyaari did it. Though from what she had been told about her mother's exploits in freeing the slave children who were the alumni of Maganos Moonbase, it didn't sound like she had concealed her powers very well, so surely some of these people knew what she could do already?

Elviiz put himself between her and Hap and extruded his bio-wash attachment to cleanse the wound, afterward sealing it with a cello-patch. 'Removing the fingers of human benefactors is a traditional ritual with Makahomian Temple Cats,' he informed Hap. 'Khiindi's sire, the first mate of the *Condor*, Roadkill, or RK as we call him, removed two fingers from Captain Becker when they first became acquainted. The fingers grew back along with other appendages on both the cat and the captain, and now, of course, they are the best of friends.'

'Hey, you *are* a droid, aren't you? Panko said you were – he was the one on com duty when your ship was in orbit – but you sure didn't look it to me. What's with the screw in the middle of your forehead?'

'I am a Linyaari, like my father, so of course I have a horn,' Elviiz said, with wounded dignity.

'Oh, golly, I'm sorry, fella, I didn't mean to hurt

63

your feelings. I think it's cool. And Khorii introduced you as her brother, too. That's really great that you two are bonded like that. Good pals and all that.'

'We are not merely friends or foster sibs,' Elviiz said. 'I am her tutor and her guardian as well to make sure the child does not blunder into harm's way.'

'That's great. Really. I have seven brothers and three sisters . . . somewhere. We got split up during the rescue operation. I don't know where they were taken, but I'm trying to find out. Come on, and I'll show you where you're bunking.'

Khorii started to protest that she had to get Khiindi, but the cat jumped up onto Hap's shoulders and marched back and forth as he led them forward. He didn't seem to notice. Aside from a friendly tug at Khiindi's tail, he ignored the cat's preference as if it happened to him all the time. Well, at least someone was making friends.

Like MOO, the moonbase was a series of bubbles encompassing an environment that would sustain the lives of the people enclosed within it. Unlike MOO, the environment was not especially luxurious or fancy.

Hap showed them to a small cubicle containing a pair of bunks and a couple of lockers for belongings. She and Elviiz sat on the bed.

'No, sport, your room is over in the boys' section with me.'

'But I must be here to protect her,' Elviiz protested. 'If she comes to harm here, my father will be very unhappy with me, as will my foster parents. I prefer that does not happen. So I will stay with Khorii.'

'Sorry,' Hap said. 'She's already got another bunk mate. If you stayed here, too, it might freak out the other girls.'

'I am not a freak, Hap. In many ways, I am more useful than a human male of my age.'

'I wasn't calling you a freak. I just meant the girls would get silly and maybe be a little inhibited, even when they know you're a droid.'

'The way some fully organic beings behave, I am very happy to be a droid,' Elviiz replied. He didn't sniff disdainfully, but he might as well have. The sniff was implicit in his tone. Still, he followed obediently as Hap led him away, promising to return soon to show them both where the dining room and classrooms were located. As they left, at the last minute Khiindi jumped down from Hap's shoulders. The little cat's claws skittered back down the slick-tiled hallway, and he barely caught himself from sliding by the doorway to Khorii's quarters. She scooped him up and sat on the lower bunk petting him, trying to calm him. 'It will be all right, Khiindi. You'll see. Mother and Father will stop the plague, the grandfathers will come back, and, meanwhile, you and I will make lots of new friends.'

As if on cue, a beautiful young girl entered the room followed by an adult woman.

Before Khorii could introduce herself, the girl spoke. 'Get that beast off my bed! And what are you doing in my room?'

The dark-haired girl advanced into the room. Khorii tried to hold Khiindi back. After all, he was a Makahomian Temple Cat, and fierce protectiveness was bred into his bones.

He wriggled from her hands and leaped toward the girl. Before Khorii could utter a warning, Khiindi twined himself around the girl's feet and ankles, purring loudly, weaving figure eights in and out between her feet until she stumbled over him and fell. 'It attacked me!' she screeched, and started brushing at her ankles, as if trying to divest them of cat fur. 'I am very allergic. If I swell up and die, it will be your fault!'

'Here now, what's the problem? What's wrong with you, Shoshisha?' the woman asked. 'Who said anything about your dying?'

'This *person* is in my room, and she brought a tiger with her. It tried to eat me!'

'You are mistaken,' Khorii told her. 'Khiindi did not attack you. He was expressing how much he liked you and he probably expected you to feed him. He expects everyone to feed him.'

Khiindi sat over to the side, washing his right front paw unconcernedly. He paused only to look up at her, squeezing his eyes shut and opening them again, his mouth hanging open as if he were laughing. The little wretch had known exactly what he was doing when he tripped Shoshisha.

'Oh, my goodness!' the lady said. 'You're Lady Acorna Harakamian-Li's daughter, aren't you? I was on my way to greet you, but I didn't realize you were staying *here*. Naturally I assumed you'd stay at the chancellor's quarters, where Mr Giloglie and Mr Baird and their families live.'

'Yes, ma'am, I'm Khorii, and this is Khiindi. My brother Elviiz was taken to the boys' quarters by that nice boy who met us, Hap.'

'Him!' Shoshisha said, tossing her glossy black hair so it rippled and settled back down around her shoulders. 'That explains it. He put you here so he'd have an excuse to see me. He likes me, and he thinks if he spends enough time around me, I'll get used to him, I suppose.'

'He seemed very friendly and kind to me,' Khorii said. 'And since my grandfathers Calum and Gill are not at home, he probably thought I would rather stay with students closer to my own stage of development. It was a thoughtful gesture, but since we are not welcome here, perhaps it would be better if we did stay in grandfathers' quarters until they or my parents return.'

Shoshisha's brown eyes, which had been squinched in temper, widened suddenly as she smiled. 'Oh, no, that won't be necessary. I didn't realize you were related to our beloved chancellors, and of course I see now that you have the horn and look just like the holo of Lady Acorna gracing our assembly hall. I am sorry I overreacted. You startled me and, well, I am quite allergic to most animals.'

'I'm sorry to hear that. It's kind of you to say that I may stay, but Khiindi is my friend, and he must be with me,' Khorii said. She turned her attention to the woman who had greeted her before. A teacher, surely, the woman was comfortably built, had feathery fair hair and very shrewd blue eyes. 'Actually, it would probably be better at the grandfathers' because Elviiz could come, too. You know my name. May I ask yours?' she asked the lady.

'I'm Calla Kaczmarek. I'm the psychologist and psychology/sociology instructor. I also act as the school's guidance counselor. Dr Al y Cassidro, our headmaster and dean of the mining engineering school, has classes all day long and couldn't make it to greet you himself, so he asked me to do it. Your grandpas are old friends of mine, but I only met your mother after she began working with Mr Li. I'm really pleased to meet you. Things have been a little strange around here since the plague scare began, which was unfortunately right after Gill and Calum and the Kendoro sisters landed on Kezdet. But we'll all be fine, and so will you. Come on, I'll show you where to go.'

As they were leaving over Shoshisha's protestations, they were nearly knocked down by Hap and Elviiz. Most people thought droids didn't get excited or any other strong emotion, but Elviiz was an exception. Maak had programmed him to behave pretty much like a Linyaari boy and now he acted like a very excited one.

'Where are you going, Khorii?' Elviiz asked. 'Are you on your way to our classes? Hap says both he and I are far too advanced for the programming the younglings receive in them, but that we are expected to acquire something called "socialization" by attending them anyway. I wonder why my father did not program socialization into me on our journey, so that I could in turn impart it to you? As a part of this aspect of our programming, we are to compete in contests of physical athletic skill called sports and attend gatherings where some aspects of mating are performed in a vertical position. This is known as dancing.'

Khorii smiled. 'We have dances on Vhiliinyar, too, you know, Elviiz.'

'We do? But I have never seen one. Is that because I cannot mate with totally organic females?'

'No. I think it's because you are with me most of the time, and since we've been old enough to attend them, we have been elsewhere when dances occurred.'

'Who's this?' Shoshisha asked, coming out into the hall and widening her eyes at Elviiz. Elviiz, always ready to assimilate, had removed the horn attachment from his forehead. Khorii wondered if she would wish to do the same as time went on. Without the horn, Elviiz's brow was smooth, and he could have passed for Hap's brother instead of hers. Hap's hair was straight and Elviiz's Linyaari-like mane, although as pale as Hap's, curled over his forehead and down in front of his ears, extending slightly onto his jawline. He was now slightly taller than Khorii, as a Linyaari boy her age would be. Except for his hands and feet, he looked quite human and apparently, from the expression on Shoshisha's face, at least one human female found his appearance appealing.

'I am Elviiz,' he said, extending a three-fingered single-knuckled hand made to resemble Khorii's own.

'Oh?' Shoshisha touched his hand experimentally. 'Are you a mutant of some sort? I thought you were human, but—'

'I would not advise taking his hand, Shoshisha,' Khorii said. 'Uncle Joh and Mother have tried to teach him to shake hands, but he does not realize how strong he is. He would never intentionally crush your fingers but . . .'

'That only happened once, Khorii, and I was able to adjust my pressure gauges immediately to compensate,' Elviiz protested. 'Shoshisha is perfectly safe engaging in ritual greeting gestures with me, as you very well know.'

'Pressure gauges?' Shoshisha asked with a frown.

'Elviiz is an android, Shoshisha,' Hap said. 'You should see all the cool attachments he has.'

'Thanks, but I'll pass this time.' She turned to Khorii and smiled sweetly. 'You know, I really am allergic to most animals, but apparently your space cat is different enough that he doesn't bother me. So I wish you two would stay and room with me. I would be so interested to learn all about your planet and your people and what it's like to have a mother like Acorna.'

Khorii did not need to be psychic to know that Shoshisha's reasons for wishing her to remain as a roommate were not as innocent as the human girl said. However, there seemed to be no diplomatic

70

way to decline, and Khorii had been trained from earliest childhood to be tactful in dealing with other beings. Especially when adults were watching. She looked at Calla Kaczmarek, whose mouth twitched with amusement.

'Because I was thinking,' Shoshisha said, 'that if you want to make friends here, it wouldn't be good to look as though you think you're above staying in the dorms with us just because your relatives run this place.'

Khorii suspected that Shoshisha was also thinking that if Khorii chose to stay in her grand-parents' quarters, Shoshisha would make sure everyone *did* believe that Khorii thought herself superior to them.

Calla Kaczmarek coughed. 'Staying in the dorms *would* help with the socialization programming your friend just mentioned.'

'Very well, then, we accept,' Khorii said. 'Only, could you show us now to the hydroponics gardens. I am hungry, and Khiindi will require soil of some sort for his excretory functions.'

'No litter boxes in the room, puh-leeze!' Shoshisha said. 'Can't he use the lavatory like everybody else?'

'I don't know. Aboard the *Condor* part of the garden was reserved for his use.' She did not mention that Khiindi had not always – or even usually – been scrupulous about sticking to his assigned area.

'I can show her where it is,' Hap volunteered eagerly.

71

'Thank you, Hap. If you'd show Khorii and Elviiz the general layout, where the classrooms are, and the other important stuff, I'd appreciate it,' Calla said, then turned apologetically to Khorii. 'I have a class in a few minutes, but I just wanted to say hi and make sure you two – three – were settling in okay. Hap, if you would also show them the curriculum and help them get registered?'

Khorii started to protest that they wouldn't be there long enough to take courses like the other students, but thought better of it. Saying so might give rise to Shoshisha accusing her of being elitist again and of failing to exhibit the proper attitude for assimilation.

The girl needs a few lessons in assimilation herself, Khorii thought, as she followed Hap down the passageway.

Six

Hap led them to a computer terminal and suggested they fill in the forms. She and Elviiz both did so. The curriculum on Maganos Moonbase was essentially directed toward mining engineering, Mr Delzsaki Li's enterprise on the moon before he and Uncle Hafiz had joined Mother in establishing the school.

Other kinds of classes were offered, of course, and several were offered during each time slot, so students had more choices as to what to take when. The psychology and sociology classes taught by Calla Kaczmarek were no doubt designed to help the students deal with the various traumatic events that had brought them here. Steve Reamer, whose daughter Turi had once babysat Khorii, taught gemology and metal-smithing as well as drawing and, oddly enough, symbology. Khorii signed up for those, which were new to her, as well as advanced studies in conversational and written Standard and Calla's classes.

The others all seemed a bit redundant.

Astrophysics, from the course description, seemed fairly elementary compared to the studies she had done with data provided by Elviiz's memory. Maak had equipped his son with not only the basic and advanced Federation courses required for those employed in intergalactic navigation, but also with the quirky theories and star charts compiled by Uncle Joh and his adopted father, the late Captain Theophilus 'Off' Becker. Great-uncle Off had taught Uncle Joh to use wormholes and pleated space as well as other physical anomalies as aids to navigation and shortcuts. She and Elviiz had already mastered many of the other conventional courses as well, and surpassed the lessons offered in the catalog. But she marked something for all of the required time slots, realizing that for the most part what she would actually be studying was her fellow students.

'Here's the 'ponics garden,' Hap said, opening a glass door to a place as moist and green as Khorii imagined the rain forests of Khiindi's native Makahomia might be, from what Mother and Uncle Joh had told her.

Indeed, as they entered, Khiindi began purring loudly enough to drown out the noise of the generators and irrigation system. He sprinted forward, tail aloft, back paws flashing, till he was engulfed by the plants, where he sniffed and licked experimentally. One of them made him sneeze, and he turned his back on it and tried to bury it with digs of his back paws. Then he found a bed of something to roll in.

'Ah, he's found the herb garden,' Hap said. 'Do you know what all the herbs are for, Khorii? Rosemary is for remembrance and is delicious with fish and chicken, thyme is for . . .'

'Are there other cats here?' she asked. 'Or has catmint a use to humans as well as cats?'

'Oh, yes, it's used in tea and is said to be good for stomach upsets and to calm the nerves,' Hap replied.

'That's surprising,' Khorii said. 'It seems to have the opposite effect on Khiindi.'

Khiindi gave her a look that seemed to indicate that he had heard and understood her words but didn't care one bit what her opinion of his behavior was. The cat went right on burrowing into the hydroponics bed.

But Hap bared his teeth at her! At first Khorii was startled, thinking she had done something wrong to make him react with such hostility, then recalled that with humans, that particular toothy expression was usually friendly.

'Khiindi's a cat,' Hap said. 'Cats have their own way of doing things.'

'I've noticed,' she agreed. 'Often.'

At that, Khiindi gave a flip of his tail, and vanished into the catnip patch. Hap continued talking and explaining every single plant in the beds, its uses and properties, dangers and lore, as well as any personal experiences he had had with each variety, while she and Khiindi used the 'ponics garden for their needs. On a Linyaari ship, she would have used the garden the same way

Khiindi did to relieve herself, since Linyaari excrement was high in nutrients that were good for plants and very clean. But humans, as she had learned on MOO, were repulsed by the practice, and so Linyaari wasted their contributions in lavatories when they inhabited human-occupied spaces.

Khorii said, 'It was good of you to wait for us and delay your own meal. We can accompany you now so you can eat, too.'

'Not hungry!' Hap said. 'This is more fun.'

'But it would be a good opportunity to meet other students, would it not?' Elviiz asked.

'I guess so,' Hap agreed, as if reluctant to share them. 'Come on. It's three stories up.'

She wasn't sure what he meant until they reached what he called the 'hubbub.'

'There's one of these at the center of each of our bubbles,' he told her. 'They were designed to make maximum use of the vertical space we have.' A broad, moving walkway ascended in a wide, spiraling path to a series of what seemed to be suspended platforms, staggered so that each level branched off in a different direction.

Khorii counted six levels, including the one they stood on.

' 'Ponics garden, administration offices, most of the recreation areas, laundry, and dorms are on this level of this bubble,' he told them. 'Next one up is the 'puter labs, holo cells, and communications center. That's where I was when you came in.'

76

'It's not associated with the docking bays?' Elviiz asked.

'No. We found it easier to have it all in one place. The idea behind the moonbase, as I'm sure your mom must have told you, is for us to learn to do everything ourselves. We have some supervision from experts and teachers, like Calla, but we're not just learning schoolkid stuff. This is on-the-job training, apprenticeships, vocational-technical education, and all of the cultural essentials kids who live with their families or go to planetside schools would learn as well. And not all the teachers are adults. We also give classes to each other about our worlds of origin. Some of us are from pretty strange places.'

'Is it true you were all child slaves before Mother and her friend Mr Li and Uncle Hafiz rescued you?'

'Well, that was true when they first established the base, but most of those kids have grown up and gone on – of course, some are still teaching here, some you've probably met on MOO. A few of the kids who were little when the Moonbase was established are in the upper levels now. But most of us are orphans, or displaced from our families as the result of a war or some other catastrophe. Shoshisha's family used to rule one of the provincial kingdoms of Zapore, a country located on the most temperate continent of Zilbek, the second planet from the suns of the Ganesha star system. So she's like a princess or something, except that her family got deposed and everybody was sent into exile while she was on an off-world shopping trip, then the exile was made permanent by some of those political enemies, who had her family assassinated. One of her mother's old friends warned her not to return and arranged for her to be smuggled out of the Ganesha system to Maganos Moonbase.'

Khorii sighed. 'She has been through a lot. She must be very unhappy.'

'Why?' Hap asked. 'She's alive, she has us. Life goes on. Besides, it's not like her parents really had much to do with her, you know. People like her are raised by nannies and servants. And her brothers and sisters were all kids by other women in her father's harem. She says they were always plotting to kill each other anyway. No big loss.'

Khorii disagreed. It surely must have been some sort of loss. How could it not be? Even if Shoshisha hadn't been close to her parents, it must have been quite a blow to lose them and have to leave the only home she'd ever known and a position of power and privilege to come to Maganos Moonbase, where she was just a student, like everyone else.

By the time Hap related Shoshisha's background, they had stepped onto the walkway and climbed beyond the computer sector to the third level, whence came the aromas of cooked food.

'Come on,' Hap said. 'I'll introduce you to some of the others in this bubble. Everybody here is more or less your standard-issue humanoid, like me, with a few variations. But there's a more exotic breed housed in the adjoining bubble.'

'How are they exotic?' Khorii asked. She had no doubt that she was pretty exotic to most of these kids.

'Well, we call them poopuus – short for pool pupils, because they live in a big salt-water pool that takes up most of the bubble. They don't have a hub like we do, and they don't have a kitchen because they only eat what they grow in their pool – not vegetarian like you. They like fish and some kinds of seaweed.'

'How did they come to be here?' Khorii asked. 'And how many live in the pool? Do they study the same subjects as the rest of you?'

'Some of the same ones, but they are also studying what's known about oceans on other worlds. I don't know all the reasons behind it. They don't mix much with the rest of us. I've tried to strike up a conversation and, you know, make friends, but they just dive and won't talk to me. There's sort of a language barrier, too. They study Standard but they don't use it among themselves.'

'How do they study if they can't leave their pool?' Khorii asked.

'By computer – only theirs are behind the walls in their waterways.'

His whiskers and ears both twitching thoughtfully while the end of his tail traced curves on the shining plascrete tile of the floor, Khiindi looked up at Hap. It was as if the cat were thinking, thinking very hard. Suddenly his ears pricked up and he lowered himself to a tail-lashing squat, as if stalking prey, then galloped away from them, back down the spiral walkway, bounding off of it from the second level to land on the central street of the bubble. He ran off straight down the street toward the next bubble. The only time he slowed down was when he looked back once to see if they were following him.

'Khiindi!' Khorii called after him as she ran in full pursuit. 'Come back, silly cat!'

'We'd better catch him,' Hap said. 'They're not used to animals around here, I'm afraid. Things are kidproofed to some degree, but not critterproof. There's all kinds of stuff that could hurt him or that he might damage. Your grandpas would not be pleased.'

Although they had stopped at the entrance to the dining hall, it vanished behind them as they chased Khiindi. Khorii called to Khiindi as she ran down the corridor, while students stopped, goggled at her, and moved off to the side to avoid being trampled, finally staring after her as she passed them.

Hap and Elviiz stampeded after her, and at the end of the street they all stopped, panting, seeing Khiindi waiting by the circular doorway into the next bubble as if he were waiting for some vermin to bolt from the hole. The cat looked highly satisfied, as if he'd done something exceptionally clever.

But it was a man, not a mouse, who emerged from the doorway as it irised open. And Khiindi had no interest in him at all. Instead, the cat leaped through the open doorway and was long gone again by the time Khorii, Elviiz, and Hap passed through it after him.

Hap laughed. 'Does Khiindi speak Standard?'

'I don't know,' Khorii said. 'I think he understands it well enough when he wants to. But when he doesn't . . .'

'He is a sentient being on some level,' Elviiz continued. 'He seems to comprehend a great many simple words or phrases, though only those that are not addressed to him as direct commands. He is developmentally challenged in recognition of the simple negative.'

'That's not unusual in cats,' Hap pointed out. 'But are you sure it isn't more than that?'

'Why do you ask?' Khorii wanted to know.

'Because I could swear he understood exactly what I was telling you about the poopuus and that they had fish in their tanks. He took off the instant I said it.'

'But he has never met a fish,' Elviiz told him. 'He would not know what one was.'

'Maybe not, but it sure looked like he knew where he was headed and what he wanted to me. I bet he could smell the fish from where we were and went to find some. I never met a cat who didn't like fish. I think that there's more to that cat than meets the eye.'

Khorii laughed. 'He is not very good at grazing, it's true. And he seems to form his own ideas about what he likes on his menu. My mother says that his sire, RK, is a completely sentient being. Who knows what a cat thinks? I only know that he can be a rare handful.'

As they entered the bubble, the smell of water freshened the air, and a scent Khorii would come to identify with fish and the poopuus who swam in the pool and through the waterways that occupied most of the interior of the bubble. In place of the hubbub moving walkway, water flowed *upward* to another pool, then, on the other side, back down in a playful waterfall.

'It not only serves as a playground for the pool kids, it also helps aerate and recirculate the water,' Hap told them.

But Khorii could barely hear him for the shrill noises and splashing coming from the pool.

The poopuus were much larger than she had expected, very young but with rounded bodies that floated nicely. Their bare skin was the color of a roan Linyaari youngster not yet star-clad, and glistened in the light of the bubble. All of them had flowing hair of a black that was almost purple in its density, and they had very large, prominent dark eyes.

Oblivious to their latest visitors, they leaped from the surface of the pool and dived back into it again. As she drew nearer, she realized that some of the shrill noises were laughter.

'There he is!' Elviiz said, pointing. 'There's Khiindi!'

And indeed, he was there, soaking wet, a fish in his jaws, and carefully borne aloft on the back of a swimming student. The student deposited the sodden cat on the edge of the pool, where Khiindi tried to shake himself while keeping a grip on his fish. His water taxi lingered at the pool's edge, watching the cat with dark eyes round with fascination. Khiindi stood with his front paws on his flopping fish, shook himself vigorously, and head-butted the nose of his rescuer before ravaging the fish.

The language the poopuus used among themselves reminded Khorii somewhat of that of the *sii*-Linyaari back home, the ancient beings who were forerunners of her own race. Her parents had saved the *sii*-Linyaari from extinction by bringing them forward in time, and now they lived in the newly reborn oceans of Vhiliinyar, a development that did not please many of the traditionalists, which Khorii thought was stupid. The *sii*-Linyaari were not the prettiest people, it was true, having tiny horns all over their heads sometimes instead of just the one in the middle, and they did not have the healing power of her own people, but they were great swimmers and good friends of her parents. They had also taught her to swim when she was just a baby. She pulled off her shipsuit.

'Hey, what are you doing?' Hap asked, sounding shocked.

'I am going to go meet these students,' she said, and dived in. She was happy for a change to be taking the initiative herself instead of being herded here and there, even by someone as friendly and well-meaning as Hap. The water felt wonderful, cool but not too frigid, and though it had been a bit murky when she first jumped in, almost immediately it became as clear as glass. Beneath the surface many students – schools of them, she supposed you might say – swam through the deep waters. The bottom contained a veritable jungle of aquatic plant life, including lacy palaces of some shell-like substance that glowed with rainbows of color.

She could hold her breath underwater for a long time, but when she surfaced, halfway across the pool, she found herself encircled by poopuus.

'Hi, I'm Khorii. I'm new here. Who are you?' she said aloud.

'We are the children of LoiLoiKua. You are not,' was the reply. It came from underwater but unlike the bubbling and popping language of the *sii*-Linyaari, the words came in Standard, accented so that the words seemed to be ebbing and flowing with a tide of their own. It sounded like 'We are the children of LoiLoiKua. You are not.' The last words did not seem to be said any more softly, but somehow from a greater depth or distance.

'You do not belong with us, Khorii,' one of them said, surfacing to playfully flick water at her with the tips of webbed fingers.

'Your legs are separated,' another one said. And she noticed for the first time that their legs were fused together from their waists to their knees. 'If you belonged here, your legs would not come apart like that.'

'She does not swim as if her legs are separate,'

84

another one observed. 'She swims correctly, the way of the ocean people,' and he demonstrated the undulating full-body motion that propelled him through the water.

'I was taught by ocean people,' Khorii told them. 'They have no legs at all. They have tails. They were distant relatives of mine, and they didn't care that I have legs. So I didn't think you'd mind either. If you do, I can get out. I just thought it might be friendlier to greet you on your own – well – territory.'

'Look at the water,' another one said. 'Look at the 'puter screens. See how crisp the images appear, how the murkiness of the water has gone since she came.' Khorii did not comment. In another moment, perhaps the observant student would think she imagined the change in clarity. The horn's powers were a Linyaari secret.

'She looks like Our Founder!' said another, this one with long, flowing hair that caught the webs of her fingers and floated up around her thighs.

'What do you mean?' asked one with pale skin and a thousand little brown spots across her wide nose.

'Look,' said the first one, and swam to the edge of the pool. Now Khorii saw that a deep band around the pool's lining was clear, and behind the covering, computer screens waited for students to activate them.

The poopuu with the unruly hair did just that with a squeal pitched to turn the nearest machine on. A series of pictures flashed by – an elderly human Khorii did not recognize, a younger Uncle Hafiz, and her human grandsires, then – Mother!

'Our Founder,' the student said.

'That is my mother,' Khorii said.

'Does she not swim like you? Where is she? Is she here with you?' the student asked excitedly.

'Oh, yes, she swims really well – and correctly, too. But she and my father had to go to another world to help end a plague.'

'Ahhh, do you speak to them in the far talk while they are gone?'

'You mean do I hail them on the ship's computer?'

'Noooo,' the student said. 'Do your water-kin not use the far talk?'

'I don't think I know what that is if it is not using the com units,' she said. She wondered if they were telepathic.

'Mostly we use it only at night, when the others are sleeping,' said a pretty young girl with a face like a full moon. 'Otherwise, it interrupts studies. The dorms are farther from our lagoon than the classrooms.'

'Is it loud then?'

'No, but it carries. It is the far talk. When we are very quiet, we listen for the far talk from our parents and grandparents on LoiLoiKua. They miss us. So we answer back.'

'Could you do it just a little?' she asked.

'Oh, no, Calla asked us not to,' the girl said. 'She said "You should use your 'puters like the land folk." '

Khorii wanted to stay and ask the poopuus more questions, but footsteps echoed through the hallway leading to their pool. Moments later, several children trooped in, led by Calla Kaczmarek.

Oh, bother, what now? Khorii thought. *Looks like I've put my hooves in it again.*

SEVEN

Calla Kaczmarek ordinarily enjoyed the open plan
of the bubbles on the Moonbase. However, at times
it was a pain in the keister. Times, for instance,
when a much-anticipated visitor finally arrived
and was on the verge, some people hoped, of satisfying their curiosity about her, when she suddenly
turned tail and ran away.

Which wouldn't have been so bad except that she
did it where a whole cafeteria full of kids just as
nosy and curious as Calla could see her do it.

She hoped that Khorii wouldn't have to pay for
her small gaffe.

Her hope died when a snarling voice that Calla
knew all too well emerged from the students.

'What, we aren't good enough for the kid of the
great Lady Acorna?' sneered Marl Fidd. This one,
Calla knew, had never been a slave, as Calla had
been during her early years. At least, nobody else
had enslaved the brat. He'd done a good job of tying
himself up in knots, however. Like many of the
newer kids on Maganos Moonbase, he'd been sent

here because the authorities had no idea what else to do with him. He had been found during a raid on a rave shack, plugged into the machines and oblivious to everything around him. He wouldn't say where he was from or who his parents were; but once he got unhooked, the authorities deemed him salvageable and shipped him off to MM. Calla was not at all sure their judgment about him was correct. He was, in her opinion, a punk. A punk with a mean streak a mile wide, and a bully who liked to push around anyone who didn't have the nerve to stand up to him. He was going to cause trouble someday, Calla figured. Big trouble. She only hoped she wasn't around when it happened.

'Maybe she's just bashful,' suggested six-year-old Sesseli in a voice so shy it was seldom heard unless she was called upon directly. As she said it, however, the little girl rose from her seat and started for the walkway.

'Where are you going, Sesseli?' Calla asked.

'To see if I can help. She's come a long way, and she doesn't know anybody.'

'Hap's with her,' Calla said.

'Yes, but he's a big boy, and he talks so much, maybe he scared her. I'll go see.'

'Me, too,' two more voices said in unison.

'Well, I certainly don't think it's right that the poopuus get to meet her first,' said Fawndra Makatia, a good friend of La Shoshisha. 'I'm going to see what's up as well.'

That was the beginning of a general exodus. Calla, being the lunchroom supervisor, their teacher, and their nominal leader, followed them. Since she couldn't seem to stop them, it was her next best option.

The poopuus, as the pupils inhabiting the pool had been dubbed by the general student population, were not, despite the administration's best efforts, well integrated. They were from one of the oldest human colonies in Federation space, and had been on their watery planet for so many years that no one remembered or could find a record of when their ancestors inhabited Old Earth. The theory was that they had been island people to begin with. When their once-idyllic home became so littered with other people and industry that their own identity had all but vanished, their leaders volunteered to colonize, and that was the end of it. Presumably, at some point in its evolution there had been more land on LoiLoiKua, as they called their new homeworld, but apparently when the LoiLoiKua version of the great flood from Terran myth and folklore occurred, the land did not come back – at least most of it didn't. Well adapted to making a living from the sea, however, the new inhabitants found their new sea even more inviting and over the years spent less and less time on land until they became complete sea creatures.

That was what the scientists had decided about them, at least, and it matched some of what the elders of LoiLoiKua had told the Federation when their world joined. The world was in jeopardy now, apparently, and the elders had asked that their young be sent off-world to study and search for new habitats. Calla had not been able to get very far with the LoiLoiKuans, however. They accepted their pool and their own bubble, which was a good thing since it had been built at great expense to the foundation endowed by the late Mr Li and House Harakamian. The poopuus seemed to enjoy their lessons, but they were not eager to mix with the others. No wonder Khorii was drawn to them. Despite her mother's role in the founding of MM, the lone Linyaari girl must feel as much of an outsider as her waterbound classmates.

Calla was still trying to decide if poopuus was a derogatory term or simply descriptive when she reached the interbubble iris.

She felt a moment of anxiety. One other thing they didn't actually know about the students from LoiLoiKua was how they might react, unsupervised, to unwanted company. Their culture was a simple one, even primitive – well, regressed at least. Their reactions might be rather basic.

The anxiety heightened when she saw the pool roiling with poopuus but no sign of Khorii in the pool or out.

Then suddenly the child she was looking for bobbed to the surface, looked startled to see the audience alongside the pool, then gave a small tight-lipped smile and waved.

Smiling, Calla wedged a path for herself among the staring students. 'Khorii, I see you're making friends already, but now the rest of the students would like to welcome you as well. Please come and join us.'

Hap, who she now saw was sitting on the edge of the pool beside the android child, jumped up and picked up her abandoned clothing lying beside the water. As Khorii swam to the poolside, he handed it to her. Crumpling the garment in one hand, Khorii gave a hop and popped gracefully – and nakedly – onto the side of the pool, then began donning the shipsuit as another student might dry off.

Snickers, embarrassed giggles, a wolf whistle and one call of, 'All *right*, horny girl!' greeted her, and the girl looked puzzled. In truth, she was still flat on top, and her lower half was actually covered with some of the same short curly hair as that which feathered down her spine and calves to feet that were surprisingly like cloven hooves.

Calla had never had the honor of meeting Khorii's illustrious mother, and the descriptions she had of her, while they mentioned her two-knuckled three-fingered hands, her curly silver white mane, and, of course, the horn, hadn't really gone into detail about these aspects.

Khorii stood, fully dressed, and said something to the poopuus that seemed to be in their own language. They didn't surface to say good-bye to her, but Calla noticed that as soon as Khorii joined the other students and their backs were to the pool, a fish flipped up onto the side. The Linyaari girl's cat pounced on it.

It seemed that in at least one of the school's populations, Khorii and Khiindi had made some new friends.

* * *

The banner that popped up on every screen in the computer lab said '70,000 BELIEVED STRICKEN, 40,000 PRESUMED DEAD ON PALODURO.'

'THOUSANDS OF NEW INFECTIONS STRIKE TWI OSIAM.'

'250 CASES DIAGNOSED ON KEZDET BELIEVED IMPORTED BY FEDERATION COMMUNICATIONS CREW.'

'MANY FEDERATION RELAY STATIONS FALL SILENT AS PERSONNEL FALL ILL, STATIONS QUARANTINED.'

'QUARANTINE RESTRICTIONS TIGHTEN. FOOD AND WATER SHORTAGES IN PLANETARY COLONIES GO UNRELIEVED. ALL COMMERCIAL INTERPLANETARY TRAVEL SEVERELY CURTAILED.'

There followed an alarming list of cities, continents, space stations, moons, and planets believed to be infected with the disease, along with numbers of reported cases and deaths.

Khorii felt much as she did when sitting inside their pavilion on Vhiliinyar while a thunderstorm raged outside. Inside the weatherproof fabric of the pavilion they were so safe and dry that the wind hardly buffeted them, and the driving rain was only something that glistened in the darkness outside. It was almost imaginary. The plague seemed that way here among all of these healthy young people. Still, her parents were out there in the middle of whatever those statistics really meant, and it worried her. A lot. A whole lot. She knew her mother had done wonders in her lifetime and had seen other emergencies, many of them far worse, in the galaxy, and had coped with them. Her father, too, had battled monstrous Khleevi invaders and lived – the only one of their kind to be tortured by the buglike aliens and survive. But they were her parents – and they were so OLD! She'd found the problem first, after all – the bodies floating in a derelict spaceship. She felt like she should be out there with her parents, where she could protect them.

It took a great deal of effort for Khorii to ignore the escalating fatality figures and concentrate on the simple lessons at hand. Her mind's eye saw space full of ships like the *Blanca*, telescoping inside the hulls where blank-faced people performed an endless macabre ballet in zero G.

Khiindi did not help. He seemed to be as worried as she was. He sat with ears erect, staring at the screen as if he could read it, mewed once, and collapsed across her thighs with a huff of exhaled breath. His face scrunched up in an expression of feline concern – which lasted only until the cat fell over in her lap and went to sleep. That would have been fine except that he then proceeded to snore, then to twitch, run in place, and rake her shipsuit's legs with his back claws while clutching at it with his front claws.

It was as though he were trying to save the universe in his sleep.

She had never once considered leaving her feline friend behind when she left Vhiliinyar, but she soon began to feel as if that indicated a lack of foresight on her part.

He did give her a reason to attend meals with the

other students, however. Not to be outdone in cat bribes by the poopuus, at suppertime Hap, a little girl called Sesseli, and other students insisted that Khorii join them so they could offer Khiindi choice tidbits from their plates.

Khorii happily agreed and brought a selection of grasses and vegetables from the 'ponics garden so she could nibble along, thus blending in more satisfactorily.

This worked well, with Khorii happily chewing between answers to the questions of others, or nodding and asking her own questions regarding some of what they shared – excessively, in some cases – about themselves. Meanwhile one of the boys was foolish enough to voice a question about an astrophysics lesson earlier in the day and was treated to more than he could have possibly grasped in one sitting about the subject by Elviiz, in his most annoyingly superior tutorial tone.

Khiindi ingratiated himself for the sake of future handouts, sitting on first this lap, then that one, walking from knee to knee around the tables and pausing for a wash and brush-up on the lap of Sesseli. He did not even chide the girl when she interrupted his grooming session by stroking his head. Instead, he rubbed his nose and jaw against her hand, then carefully licked his paws and used them to scrub clean the area her touch had tainted.

One set of knees, however, Khiindi avoided. When Khorii noticed this, she glanced at the student being bypassed and caught glares of hostility following her harmless little friend. What could possibly make anyone react that way to a cat? Everyone on Vhiliinyar was extremely fond of cats. The Makahomian Temple Cats presented to her and to her people by the Makahomians reminded the older Linyaari of *pahaantiyiirs*, a feline species many had kept as companions before the Khleevi invasion. Even the rather grouchy Liriilyi had had a *pahaantiyiir* she doted on and had softened considerably when Mother and Father had insisted she be given one of the Makahomian kittens to raise.

An older boy, quite handsome by human standards, reacted the most negatively to Khiindi's adventures in progressive grazing. His glowering heavy eyebrows knitted together over dark eyes that seemed to be trying to turn into lasers to burn her poor little cat to a cinder if only he had the power.

Khiindi passed by him with seeming unconcern but returned to Khorii's lap rather quickly and resumed washing. Casting a slit-pupiled eye in the boy's direction, Khiindi raised a leg and proceeded to clean himself under his tail.

A moment later Elviiz said, 'I feel a message arriving from Dad on the *Condor*.'

Khorii was afraid he'd unfasten the top of his shipsuit then and there and show everyone the receiver screen attachment with which he and Maak both had augmented their chests. Calla had already taken her aside and told her that it went against the school's custom for students to disrobe in front of students of the opposite sex. Khorii had expressed confusion. She had naturally assumed that since all of the poopuus swam without clothing, it was the custom, when among them, to be similarly unclad. Calla said well, yes, but that was among the LoiLoiKuans and it was not the custom for the rest of the students. Khorii asked if this had something to do with mating. Calla said that yes, for the most part, it did. Khorii could not see the relevance since she was a different species from humans and not ready to mate anyway. Neither were most of the other kids, judging from their stages of development.

However, Elviiz had his own sense of what was correct. Communications took place in the computer lab. Therefore, they would receive the *Condor*'s transmission in the computer lab, which was empty now since the students were all grazing – er – dining, Khorii corrected herself.

Furthermore, Elviiz had another idea about propriety, having overheard Calla's admonition earlier in the day. 'One moment, Khorii, and we will both view the transmission on one of these screens. Anyone passing by watching you staring intently at my upper torso might be puzzled and possibly alarmed. Unlike Captain Becker, or even Uncle Hafiz, these humanoids appear to be somewhat skittish.' Thus saying he apparently took his own pulse, but with the result that one of the larger computer screens suddenly lit with the faces of Mother, Father, Uncles Joh and Maak, and RK. Khiindi hopped up onto the table in front of the screen and sat there, his lithe silvery body obscuring RK's brindled gray furriness. Khorii lifted him off the table and held him, scratching his belly so that he forgot to be jealous and overly curious, abandoning himself to blissful purrs.

They didn't really need him to blur the screen anyway, as the reception was unusually poor. The *Condor* had the very best communications equipment the wreckage of the galaxies had to offer and that Maak and Captain Becker could modify to meet their needs. Even so, its range was largely dependent on the booster relays set up by the Federation within its territories and by Uncle Hafiz to connect House Harakamian and the Moon of Opportunity. Since MOO, Vhiliinyar, and narhii-Vhiliinyar were not yet officially Federation members, and at any rate would not fall within the heavily traveled spaceways regulated by it, Hafiz would have been cut off from his supply lines without his own network. The *Condor* operated on both Federation and House Harakamian frequencies, but judging from the snowiness of the video and the static in the sound, both had been affected by the current crisis. Either the personnel who manned or maintained the relay stations were themselves ill or somehow incapacitated by the side effects of it – such as having staff members quarantined away from their duty stations, or needing to attend to family members, perhaps. Khorii couldn't quite imagine all of the reasons involved. After all, this was her first plague. She hoped it would be her last.

'Greetings, younglings,' Uncle Maak said.

'Greetings, Father,' Elviiz said. 'What is your current position?'

Maak gave the coordinates, which placed them a bit less than halfway to the point Uncle Joh had indicated on the star charts. 'There is not actually much to report, but we missed you and communications are becoming increasingly unsatisfactory, as you must perceive.'

'The plague sounds very deadly and extremely widespread,' Khorii said. 'I do not see how you can cure it, just the two of you.'

'We can't, of course,' Mother said. 'But by healing a few of the cases, we may be able to determine the etiology and make other observations that will help the physicians of this area – those who have not succumbed to the illness – in finding a specific cure that does not involve the use of our horns.'

'We've been hearing most disturbing reports,' Khorii told her. 'It sounds as if it's spreading and spreading.'

'You can't take all of those reports to heart, honey,' Uncle Joh said. 'It's probably just a slow news day for the Com Channels, and they're blowing it out of proportion. One relief ship became infected and before they discovered that they'd contracted the disease, they infected some of the personnel on the relay stations – it made it all a lot more visible than it would be ordinarily. I'm sure it's bad, but I doubt it's anything your mom and dad can't handle. And, hey, if they can't, we'll go for reinforcements.'

'The disease, from the data we have gathered,' Maak told them, 'has an erratic gestation period of between one and seven Standard sleep cycles. It appears to have a long life away from its host and is probably transmitted by droplets, as it appears to be highly communicable.'

'We are much needed, Khorii,' Father said. His face was as gentle and loving as always when he looked at her, but strain showed around his eyes and the edges of his mouth. 'The health-care providers have apparently been affected worse than any other sector of the population, and there is no one to care for the ill, especially where the disease has hit hardest, like Paloduro. We are glad you are safe on Maganos Moonbase, which is naturally isolated and has a lower probability of becoming an infection site.'

'What if they find a cure, and because communications are so poor, you don't hear about it?' she asked. And then, since everyone was being so open about answering their questions, she asked the one that was really bothering her. 'What if *you* get this disease?'

'Now, honey, don't get all panicky,' Uncle Joh said. 'Your folks will be fine. Maak and the cat and I will see to it. I guess you haven't been out and about enough to know this yet, but you Linyaari don't *get* sick.'

Khorii nodded, but her worry must have shown on her face, since Mother leaned closer to the screen and touched it with her horn, as if she could transmit her feelings of safety and comfort across the many light-years separating her from her daughter. 'Dear one, please do not worry about us. We've certainly been in more difficult spots than this, and I'm sure that as we work with the Federation's resources at our disposal, we'll be able to bring this crisis to an end very soon.'

The transmission began breaking up then, and Khorii and Elviiz barely had time to say their good-bye before the friendly faces were lost in a sea of static.

'Don't worry, Khorii,' Elviiz said. 'They'll figure out how to stop this plague soon enough.'

Khorii nodded, but she couldn't help nibbling on her lower lip and wondering, *but what if they can't?*

EIGHT

Hafiz Harakamian had not attained his wealth and high position by being a patient man – not unless he was deliberately plotting or stalking something. He expected to be kept informed. And he also expected to be made godfather to the baby being born to Declan and Judit Giloglie as well as any children born to Calum and Mercy Baird or to his nephew and adopted son and heir, Rafik and his alluring lady. These children were related in spirit if not blood to his beloved adopted daughter Acorna and therefore, by Hafiz's reckoning, they all belonged to him as well. He was far too young and virile to be a grandfather, but a godfather – ah!

He made his fifth visit in as many hours to the Moon of Opportunity's communications terminal. 'We have heard nothing from them – any of them – for two days! Two days! I know that Rafik feels he needs no advice in the administration of House Harakamian, but he could send word that he is well, he could say if he has had word from the Giloglies, he could say if the *Condor* has arrived yet at Maganos Moonbase. Am I so interfering, so difficult to talk to, that I am abandoned by my beloved family when they could most use my wisdom? Is consultation with me desired only when they wish to avail themselves of my wealth? By the three books and the Three Prophets I am sorely distressed and feel greatly wronged.'

'Now, Haffy, my potentate of passion,' his lovely wife Karina said, laying a scrumptiously plump beringed hand upon his chest while regarding him from her large and lovely eyes made deepest purple by art and by proximity to the priceless catseye chrysoberyl jewels she bore in abundance upon her shell-like ears, her delicate wrists, and her delicious decolletage. The parts of her person not covered in jewels were swathed in drifts of gossamer in a sunset of purples, lavenders, violets, and plums. His treasure, his beauty, his bride, and yet even her presence did not soothe him.

'Maybe something's just wrong with the relays,' she said. 'One little glitch in the nearest one, and you know how that *affects* our communications.'

'Yes, my delectable dumpling, but to hear nothing! Now that I ponder upon it, no merchant ships have docked of late, none of the cargoes for which I have already paid good currency, no one from home at all.'

'I understand that you are disturbed, O my lord of love, and it pains me to see you so. Therefore, I shall look into my scrying pool and employ my heightened sensitivity to the harmonies of the cosmos to determine what is causing this deplorable lack of consideration on the part of our beloved friends and relations.'

'Oh, that would be nice, dear, how thoughtful, thank you,' Hafiz said, a trifle flatly. Karina meant well and truly believed she had telepathic and even magical powers; although even to him, her doting husband, it was very obvious that for the most part she had all of the psychic sensitivity of a food replicator. Perhaps less. But it did not take any mind-reading ability whatsoever for Hafiz to realize that any implication on his part that her powers were less astounding than she proclaimed them to be would be hurtful to her and detrimental to the recreational marital activities they so deeply and mutually enjoyed.

So he would graciously support her efforts to seek information in her way while he sought the same information in his.

'Go you to prepare yourself, to meditate and free your mind to receive the images in your waters, my lavishly endowed love, and I will join you in an hour's time.'

'Certainly. I go now and await your pleasure, most spectacular of all spouses.'

When she had gone he turned back to the communications terminal and to the young Linyaari boy, Miikaye, interning with his chief communications specialist, and said, 'Send for the captains of the two ships in my private fleet that are docked here. I have a mission for them.'

'That would be finding out why we've had no

104

word from the relays, sir?' the boy asked. Hafiz smiled paternally. Most Linyaari addressed him as Acorna did, as Uncle Hafiz, but it was good that the child had learned the proper form of address to one's employer early. Of course, 'sir' was not as good as 'my lord' as Hafiz's more experienced vassals called him, but it was a start.

'Yes, my lad. You have interpreted my order most correctly.'

The boy smiled, with his mouth closed so as not to show his teeth, since to do so was considered hostile in his culture. 'Yes, sir. Not too difficult considering the number of inquiries you have made yourself already today.'

'Even so, my son, even so.'

When his captains came his orders were simple, 'Go forth and seek the truth. Also seek to repair the accursed relays if they are down again. You, Captain Ling, will follow the course set by Captain Becker and my beloved daughter to the first relay. You, Captain Gallico, will travel to Makahomia, and confer with the regent Nadhari Kando concerning the presentation of a kitten for my new godchild and will also gather intelligence from Nadhari and other useful informants during your journey.'

Both men nodded and withdrew to prepare their ships for their respective voyages.

Practical matters seen to, Hafiz retired to the private and personal garden of delight he shared with his beloved. She was seated beside the glass and titanium birdbath he had ordered to be installed when she requested a small body of water for her prophetic pursuits. Her arms were crossed on the edge of the small pool, her head upon them, and he thought she was meditating perhaps, or catching a quick nap until, hearing him, she raised her head and turned. Her eyes and nose were both red and rather wet.

'Oh, Hafiz, it is truly truly awful. I don't know what we are to do!'

'What, my anxious angel? What demons dare distress you? Tell me that I may slay them!'

'No demons. No clear images at all. But the waters turned black, then red, and that means only one thing, well, two actually.'

'Yes?'

'Gloom and doom. Disaster and despair. Bad omens indeed. Our loved ones are headed into terrible cataclysmic danger. Whatever will they do? However will we help them?'

He peered across her into the birdbath, which looked clear except perhaps for a bit of pond scum. He'd have to speak to the gardener about that. He sighed and stroked her hair. 'Come, my darling, you are overwrought and will spoil your complexion and your appetite. Your Hafiz has already taken steps to evaluate this doom of which you speak. As for worrying about what they will do, please recall, my ravishing raven of revelations, that we are speaking here of Acorna and Aari, who destroyed the Khleevi menace. They will manage.'

'Yes, but, Haffy, they have Khorii with them, and she is just a child.'

'Ah, but she is *their* child. And in that you must take comfort.'

'But that may just be the problem, Hafiz. Have you considered that?'

You know, Hafiz thought, *she might have a point.*

On the fringes of the industrial district of the city of Corazon on the residential and tourist world of Paloduro, third in prominence in the Solojo star system, inside a rented high school gymnasium, a battle raged in an altogether different dimension.

Jalonzo Allende, as Quetzacoatl, struggled for hegemony over the game world with the other contestants in the weeklong Carnivale Marathon Brujartisano Tournament. As usual, his full attention was on his game. As usual, he was winning. Thus he was unaware of exactly when the plague first struck.

A master strategist, Jalonzo made up his decks and plotted his moves with the high intelligence and grasp of complex patterns that had allowed him to progress far beyond his chronological age in his studies of the sciences.

He knew his *abuelita*, his grandmother, devoutly hoped he would someday apply his talents to more realistic and lucrative pursuits than gaming. Jalonzo had plans, but since the death of his parents when he was nine, he hadn't bothered telling people about them much, not even Abuelita. For the moment, the game was what mattered.

Though he had only been playing it four years, since just after his parents died, Jalonzo was a seasoned veteran, a mighty warrior-mage, with more wins than anyone in the city of Corazon. He was proud of his comparatively vast library of game rules, history, variations, and back stories, his albums full of cards and his collection of unusual dice – enough to fill most of his clothing locker at home. He had had to pay for only a tiny fraction of these treasures – the rest were his loot, winnings from his victories.

The other players were not always glad to see him, but most of them said nothing to his face. They all knew that someday soon he would be invited to participate in the holographic tournament held every year on Bruja Prime, the smallest moon of Rio Boca, a moon leased exclusively to the Brujartisano Corporation, who had invented and controlled the game. Also, at six feet five inches, Jalonzo towered over most of the other players, who saw him as just a little scary. Heavy and powerfully built, with black hair and the faint black shadow of an incipient beard, he looked far older than he was.

He had no idea when the first death occurred in the outside world, as he had been busy for the preceding three days slaying the characters of his opponents. The first real death he was aware of was the nacho guy. Camazotz the Bat God was the one who found him. Camazotz, known outside the game as Jaime Martinez, a nervy, thin, redheaded kid who had been losing often enough to have lost interest in the game in favor of food, came into the gym yelling that there was a dead guy on the sidewalk outside the gym. A dead guy with the thermal case of Mucho Nachos, the only place in this part of the city that delivered.

'Is he really dead? How do you know?' Apocatequil the Thunder Bringer, who was also the Prince of Evil, asked, sounding just like Jalonzo would have expected his character to sound: bloodthirsty and excited.

'Is he all bloody?'

'Why would the nacho place send a dead guy, anyway?'

'Can we still get the nachos, or did he do something gross to them?'

Jalonzo almost suspected this was a trick to get him to quit, go outside to check, then they'd shut him out so he wouldn't win anymore. But that was silly. Somebody had to win, and it was a tournament after all. The fun was in playing the game.

And even if it was a trick, he had to look, didn't he? The guy might still be alive.

Jalonzo rose and quickly walked through the sweat and strong-soap-smelling locker room, through the front hall to the entrance. He didn't have to open the door to see the guy. The door was clear plas, as were the side panels on either side of it. The guy really did look dead. There were flies for one thing, but then, they'd swarm around anyone living or dead. But there were an awfully lot of them all over the guy's face. So, yeah, dead probably.

But if he wasn't and the curanderos could still save him? The other contestants crowded against the panels and the door, gawking at the maybe-dead guy.

Jalonzo, mindful of his size and powerful build and careful not to push or hurt anyone, gently moved them away from the door and opened it. Fanning at the flies, he reached for the guy's wrist to find a pulse, as Abuelita had shown him how to do when he was a boy. As soon as his fingers touched the guy's skin, Jalonzo could tell that he was already gone. The skin was way too cool on such a hot day. Also, he stank of something a little more rotten and less rank than most people smelled when it had been hours since they last washed.

Backing away from the guy, he pulled out his hola to call the curanderos. But he couldn't even get a tone. Funny. He had juice, the power cell was full. The little hola looked as if it was eager to talk to him, eager to find who he wanted, all ready to go, but it couldn't. It just sat there in his hand. He looked down the street, thinking, and he noticed that everything was really very quiet for a holiday in that part of town. Usually there'd be a lot of loud music blaring from flitters and maybe some guys who'd had too much *pulque*, people in costume headed uptown to join in one of the Carnivale parades.

The only flitters on the street were silent and grounded, including the one with the Mucho Nacho logo docked a few feet from the door. Where was everybody? Looking back at the gamers, with their faces and hands pressed against the glass, he shrugged. Some of them were scanning the street as he had. Others turned away and were frowning into their holas.

Mucho Nacho's logo was emblazoned like a heraldic device on the thermal container cushioning the upper half of the dead guy's body. Jalonzo could see the hail number and tried it. This time there was a tone but no answer, which was very weird since Mucho Nacho was a busy place, three or four people at least there in the restaurant part to serve customers as well as the delivery guy. The smell of food made Jalonzo's stomach rumble, but he didn't much want any of the nachos under the corpse. He wandered over to the flitter to see what was there, half-expecting someone to yell at him to get away from there. But nobody did. There was nobody, but nobody, to yell anything actually.

He found another order of nachos, also in a thermal container, and took it. After all, the one they ordered was under the delivery guy, through no fault of theirs, and they were owed an order. Then he saw there were five other thermal containers as well, tamales in cornhusk wrappers, a huge basket of taquitos, more nachos, a couple of complete dinners, and some cinnamon churros. And drinks. Well, it wasn't theft. All that food was just going to get cold and rot out there by the time anybody came to see to this guy, so the gamers could eat the stuff and pay for it later.

The containers were easy to lift, and he lugged all five of them plus the drink cooler back to the gym. At least, burdened as he was with food, there was no question about the others letting him back in.

They stood away from the door when he came

111

in, then three tried to push past him to go outside. He shoved the food into their arms, keeping them inside the building. 'No, man, wait,' he said. 'It's no big deal. Nothing we can do. Nothing the curos can do. I called them.'

'How, man? I couldn't even get a ring!'

'Me, neither. But I tried. We'll try again later. Must be a sunspot or something. Or maybe the Carnivale lights have overloaded the grid.'

'What was wrong with him, man?'

Jalonzo shrugged. 'I don't know. Maybe a heart attack? He wasn't bleeding or anything. Anyway, we got eats. We gonna play or what? We haven't finished the game. And it's dead out there.'

NINE

It wasn't until the end of the first week on the Moonbase that things began to go wrong. Up until then, while Shoshisha's public fawning over Khorii was annoying, and there were a few more mean looks from the one boy, looks that were not only for Khiindi but for Khorii and even Elviiz, classes were, if not challenging academically, at least good opportunities for studying human nature.

And then, before she realized it, Khorii's psychic ability began to manifest itself, and she was studying human nature far too closely for the comfort of most of the humans involved.

Furthermore, without realizing it, the human students in her applied astrophysics class were privy to some of her thoughts. This became apparent after a test, when the teacher, Captain Bates, reviewed the results. Shortly afterward, the captain, a pleasant-faced woman with soft, wavy, brown hair, a smile as quick as her keen intelligence, and a pantherlike prowl when she was unhappy about something, prowled back and forth in front of the class. Her expression said that this panther had found more prey than she knew what to do with and was just considering how to use them up without ruining her digestion.

'If I were going to plagiarize a test paper,' she said, 'I would have sense enough to change some of the words and at least a couple of the answers, especially if I were dumb enough to plagiarize answers from the paper of someone else in this class. I would not pass out the test answers to everyone else in the class ahead of time either.'

Everyone looked baffled. At first Khorii was, too, but when she saw the papers, she understood what had happened. The answers on the paper she turned in were hers – and so were everyone else's. All of her classmates thought the answers they'd turned in were theirs because they had put down the answers that were in their heads. She'd put the answers there. Her answers.

She had been sending. *Ulp.* Aunt Maati had told amusing stories about Mother when she first arrived on narhii-Vhiliinyar, after she first began realizing and developing her psychic abilities. She was a strong sender. Everyone on the planet could know what she was thinking almost before she herself did. Of course, that was on narhii-Vhiliinyar, where everyone else past puberty was also psychic, but a strong sender could influence nonpsychics as well. Oh, dear.

She should tell Captain Bates and she would. She would. Only, maybe not right now in front of everybody.

Unfortunately, Captain Bates had to rush off after class, and Khorii had no opportunity to speak with her. She started to go after the teacher, but suddenly she smelled food and the thought occurred to her, *Why bother? It's not like we're real students here anyway. We're only observing. Our education in these matters already far surpasses what they're learning. If everyone else heard our answers, then they heard the right answers, didn't they? Maybe they learned something. Isn't that the point?*

But then she wondered, *What am I thinking? Our answers? They were mine. Elviiz certainly isn't telepathic. It's not the kind of thing his father could program into him.* But before she could pursue that line of thought, Khiindi looked up at her with a wide-eyed stare, whiskers, ears, and tail tip all atwitch. Hmm. He hadn't had a nice fish since the first day they were there, at least, not that she knew of. And some tasty varieties of reed grew in the poopuus' pool. Really, it would be more interesting to lunch with the waterbound students than sitting in the cafeteria while her own lunch wilted watching that nasty boy, Marl Fidd, make threatening faces at Khiindi and make fun of Hap for talking all the time. She wondered what made him so unpleasant. It was as if he wanted to do her harm but was waiting for just the right moment to take her on. Right now, for instance, she knew very well that he would have been nasty to her, too, but Shoshisha made a point of sitting with her and showing everyone what great chums she and her 'alien' roommate were. And Marl liked Shoshisha.

Most of the boys did, in fact. Shoshisha, Khorii had noticed, depended on this fact and cultivated her male acquaintances carefully. All except Hap. She wasn't very nice to him at all. She laughed at the jokes Marl and Fawndra made at Hap's expense. Like there was something wrong with *him*. Really, he was just smarter and a lot more skilled at so many practical things, he ended up doing much of the maintenance in their bubble. For some reason, according to the ranking among the students, that was supposed to make him inferior.

Khiindi put a paw with claws slightly extended against her knee and narrowed his eyes at her.

'Fish,' she said. 'Very well, Khiindi. We will visit the poopuus.' So she and Khiindi headed for the iris door between the bubbles. Meanwhile Elviiz explained to anyone who would listen how the laws of probability were against all of the students in their class coming up with identical equations in answer to the questions as they all headed to the cafeteria.

Inside the air felt fresh and moist. Light dapples danced on the inner skin of the bubble, diffusing the businesslike illumination into something slightly mysterious.

Khorii did not need to call out. Her friends of a few days ago bobbed in the water at the pool's edge, watching their approach. One of them dived and surfaced with a wriggling fish, which Khiindi pounced upon the moment it hit the deck.

Khorii didn't disrobe this time. There was no practical need to since her shipsuit was waterproof

116

as well as fireproof and windproof. It was made of a lighter version of the same fabric from which the pavilions of Vhiliinyar were constructed. She'd undressed on her previous visit to be polite, only to be told that it was actually considered not merely rude but shocking to the other students. The poopuus did not appear to care. No one greeted her in the conventional way, but once she dived in, she was surrounded by so many swimmers the water lapped in waves around her chin and face.

She noticed that the bobbing in the water and the swimming back and forth was rather nervous. 'What's wrong?' she asked.

'What do you know of the sickness?' one of them asked.

'I know that it's very widespread,' she said. 'But my parents have gone to the place where it's the worst to try to contain it at that source and cure as many as possible with – our Linyaari technology.'

'What place is this?' asked another one.

'A place called Paloduro. Why?'

'Because the disease has come to LoiLoiKua, according to the 'puters,' another said, pulling her underwater and pointing at the screen which, beneath the lessons being transmitted, had a plague status banner scrolling through the current statistics, place names of the newly quarantined areas, and, in some cases, links to find the names of the dead in certain locations.

'What's LoiLoiKua?' she asked.

'It is our homeworld. Our parents and elders are there. They sent us here to learn in fresh new

117

waters, hoping that if we do not find a way to save our own world, we might at least escape the destruction of our seas. But all we learned is that now we are far away from our kinsmen while a sickness comes upon them that strikes elders but not children. And we are not there to care for them. I am Likilekakua. I want to go home.'

'I know what you mean. I want to go home, too. This trip is not working out at all in the way I thought it would. But the Federation won't allow any of us to go home now.'

It came to her that she and the poopuus had in common something the other students lacked: living parents.

Khorii did not sleep well that night. She dreamed she was looking through a telescope and saw her mother drowning, much too far away for Khorii to save her. She scanned the pool – which turned out to be a sea, and saw something circling overhead. It was RK, carrying Khorii's father in his mouth as if he were a mouse. Khorii wanted to tell RK to put her father down, but if he did, then Father would drown, too. But someone had to save Mother. Then the dream turned around and it was Khorii who was drowning, though she was actually her own mother. But then RK knew about it and reached out for her, fishing for her with one paw, claws cruelly extended, digging into her shoulder.

She cried out and RK gave her a disdainful look and turned tail. The underside of the tail brushed her face, which was not so bad, but RK also 'marked' her at the same time with some of the hormonally charged tomcat urine that Uncle Joh claimed could eat through steel.

Khorii was really drowning now, gagging and coughing and wiping at her mane. Of course, the smell was dispersed almost immediately by her horn, but the sound of her mother screaming was not.

However, it did change. It was not her mother. It was Shoshisha screaming. 'I'm going to kill it!' she wailed. 'That cat just sprayed all of my new silk underwear. I waited months for it to arrive!'

Khorii sat up, fully awake. That part of her nightmare, at least, was quite real. Shoshisha was on her feet, brandishing a shoe and dodging back and forth around her cot in an effort to head Khiindi off. Khiindi, of course, thought it was a great game. Khorii rose, lay across Shoshisha's bed, and picked her cat up by the nape of the neck before holding him firmly, though perhaps not tenderly, against her.

'Bold, bad cat,' she scolded, but stroked his head as she did, so he broke into a loud purr.

'He ruined it!' Shoshisha was crying. 'I forgot to close the drawer all the way last night and he got in and soaked it with that horrible smell.'

'Let me see,' Khorii said. 'Maybe it's not as bad as you think.'

She wasn't surprised Khiindi had found her roommate's clothing. Shoshisha was very untidy. No doubt this was the result of having been brought up with servants who picked up after her. She left things lying around, drawers half-open,

119

clothing draped from every possible surface. Anyone could have told her that you just couldn't do that around a cat, especially not with anything you prized. But she probably wasn't used to cats.

'Maybe it's not as bad as you think,' Khorii said, raising a handful of soiled silk to her face and almost gagging on the cat musk. Her horn, as if accidentally, touched the affected garments and the smell went away. 'I think if we put them through the swash right away they'll be good as new,' she said, using the students' term for the sonic wash they all used to bathe and do laundry.

Shoshisha's lips clamped together to show that she didn't believe it.

'May I try or not?' Khorii asked.

Shoshisha shrugged irritably and flipped her hand in a dismissive gesture.

Khorii carried the garments into the lav between their room and the adjoining one. Khiindi's interest in the clothing had not lessened, but he carefully kept Khorii between him and Shoshisha.

Khorii closed the door behind her. The walls automatically glowed with light by which she saw that the horn touch had turned the cat urine as clear and odorless as water. She stuck the underclothes into the sonic wash – seven pairs of silk panties and lacy bras, plus an extra sleep shirt, all of the finest quality, soft and sheer as moth wings. Shoshisha might be an exiled and orphaned princess, but she was evidently not a poor one.

'You are very lucky that I am your friend, Khiindi Kaat, or that girl would have your pelt for her knickers,' Khorii scolded. 'And after what you did to her knickers, she'd need it.' Khiindi wound himself around her ankles. When she pulled the underwear out of the swash he mewed for her to return it to him for further destruction.

She held the silken bundle out to Shoshisha. 'See? Good as new.'

Shoshisha snatched it away from her, unbelieving. Then sniffed it, looked surprised, and stuffed it back in her drawer. 'This is a school, you know, Khorii. I'll bet if your grandfathers were here, they would never allow you to bring that – that – livestock in here.'

'Well, he can't go outdoors. There's no atmosphere,' Khorii said reasonably.

'A very good reason to put him out if you ask me,' Shoshisha said.

Of course, nobody had asked her, but Khorii decided to change the subject. She was, after all, training to be a diplomat.

'I wonder how the grandfathers are doing and if the baby is all right.'

'I'm surprised they haven't contacted you before now,' Shoshisha said, clearly meaning to wound Khorii by reminding her she was being neglected.

'I don't think they're able to right now. Besides, everybody is probably busy with the baby,' Khorii said. 'I sure hope they're all right. Are you going to sleep now?'

'If I'm allowed to, yes,' Shoshisha replied.

'We will, too, but I have something to do first. Don't worry. I'll take Khiindi with me.'

She decided to have a late snack and left the dormitories, taking the hubbub down to the 'ponics gardens. The garden appeared much depleted from when she had first arrived. Khorii knew she hadn't eaten *that* much since she'd arrived. There was always plenty on the *Condor*, where the garden was much smaller and there were two other Linyaari and a human to share the harvest. Of course, the school used the 'ponics garden for fresh nourishment for the other students in addition to the starches and proteins they had from different sources.

Leaving the gardens, she decided to try to contact Kezdet and headed to the computer lab and holo suites.

TEN

At the lab Khorii found Hap and Elviiz building a holo-model of a very futuristic-looking structure she assumed was a space station or vessel of some sort. Or perhaps it was simply a cat toy. Khiindi had great fun jumping through it several times and getting scolded by Elviiz until Hap scooped the cat into his arms and held him, belly and paws up. Khiindi struggled, and Hap tickled the fur of his tummy until the cat relaxed and started to purr.

Khorii sat at the console and input the hospital's code. Elviiz asked her what she was doing, and she told him, whereupon he said, 'You will receive no answer. I have tried many times today on my personal unit.'

'But it doesn't take a relay to contact Kezdet,' she said.

'No, but if one is trying to contact the hospital, it may be that the communications personnel are incapacitated. If they are lucky, they are no longer there. I do not think a hospital would be a very healthy place to be at this time.'

He was speaking in Standard out of courtesy to Hap, and she answered in the same language. 'No. I suppose not. The whole idea seems very odd, doesn't it? Having children born in the same place where plague victims might come to be healed? Especially when the plague and some of the other illnesses aren't something the people at hospitals can cure anyway. If only the baby could have waited until we arrived, we could have seen to its safe delivery . . .'

Hap snorted. 'You? What could you have done? You may be a uni – a Lin – whatchamacallit . . .'

'Linyaari,' Elviiz told him.

'A Linyaari, but you're just a little girl. What do you know about delivering babies?'

'What's there to know?' she asked, puzzled. 'You just encourage the mother, and the baby comes out all by itself.'

'Ha!' Hap said. 'What if it's turned wrong or has the cord wrapped around its neck? Do you know how to fix that?'

'Well, no. But why would that happen?'

'You really don't ask when it does, you just have to get the baby turned or the cord unwrapped. With big animals it's hard enough, but with humans – well, and Linyaari, too, I'd think, since you look a lot like us – it often takes surgery.'

'And I suppose you know how to do that?' she asked, feeling a little outclassed.

'No,' he said, sounding a little miserable. 'Not how to do surgery. But I helped deliver calves and colts a lot back home. It's just part of life on an agro colony. I wanted to be a veterinarian, but they don't have classes for that here. Khiindi here is the only four-footed critter around, actually.'

'Yes, and according to *some* people he shouldn't be here either,' she said. She told them about Khiindi's encounter with Shoshisha's wardrobe, leaving out the part her horn played in salvaging the garments. Elviiz would know what she'd done without her having to say, and Hap ought not to know. She had been warned many times by her parents, grandparents, and others that the healing and purifying power of Linyaari horns was a secret. Of course, the secret was only known to every single Linyaari, Uncle Joh, Maak, the human grandfathers and their wives, Uncle Hafiz and Aunt Karina, and other people Mother had helped before she knew to keep the horn's abilities secret. But it was a secret from everyone *else* in the universe who didn't already know.

The secret was safe from Hap. 'Wow,' he said. 'What was it like? Shoshisha's underwear, I mean?'

'Smelly,' Khorii said, wrinkling her nose, 'once Khiindi got done with it. But fortunately I got it clean in the swash. She was really mad.'

'She's pretty sensitive,' Hap said, dreamily.

'Oh, yes,' Khorii said. 'To anything that seems counter to her own interest, she's very sensitive. But she doesn't care at all that Khiindi is far from home and other cats and was only trying to mark as his territory something he thought would make a nice nest.'

'She's not a cat person,' Hap agreed, reluctantly admitting this small fault in his otherwise perfect dream girl.

Khorii rolled her eyes, and Elviiz, seeing this, rolled his, too.

Khiindi stood on Hap's lap with his paws on the boy's shoulder and rubbed his face against Hap's lovingly. How could anyone not be a cat person, he seemed to be saying, when he was so adorable?

Elviiz said, 'Since we cannot make contact with Kezdet or the *Condor*, there is no need for you to violate your sleep cycle any longer, Khorii. You should return to your room and rest.'

'I did sleep before Shoshisha's shrieking woke me up, but I had bad dreams,' she said. 'The poopuus are worried about their relatives still on their homeworld. The news banners reported that the plague has spread there, but it didn't give details. I think they're the only ones besides us, Elviiz, who were not orphans when they came here. I understand how they feel. Of course, I'm not worried about Mother and Father because' – she tried not to look at Hap – 'well, because of our healing technology, but I wish we had gone with them to help. I wish we could help the poopuus somehow.'

'When the *Condor* has finished ministering to Paloduro, perhaps they can go to LoiLoiKua,' Elviiz said. 'Although the probability of that is low, since there are other sites more heavily infected.'

'If my parents were still alive, I'd do a better job

126

of keeping them that way now,' Hap said fiercely. 'I would have just refused to leave if it had been me.'

Khorii started to say he didn't understand but all of a sudden she *did* understand what he meant, how strongly he felt he had failed his family for having been the only one to survive when somehow he should have been able to save them. So instead she changed the subject again. 'Something's wrong with the 'ponics garden. The beets, turnips, potatoes, corn, and carrots are all gone, and so is much of the lettuce and cabbage. There's still plenty of alfalfa and clover, but everything else is looking pretty spotty.'

Hap said, 'That's because the whole school's been eating out of it since the quarantine started. I guess you wouldn't notice, since you don't eat what the rest of us do, but we've been on short rations since right after you came. The supply ship is late. I overheard Calla talking to Captain Bates, and they're pretty worried about it. There's little to feed the replicators to keep them reproducing food either. We've had beans for the main course three times this week already, and Calla said we're going to have to raid the poopuus' fish hatchery next.'

By the time she left the computer lab, Khorii felt so worried and twitchy she was sure she wouldn't be able to fall asleep no matter how hard she tried.

But the room was dark and Shoshisha was already emitting delicate little snores. She had closed the drawers firmly and picked up all of her

127

other belongings from anywhere a cat could mark them. Khorii gave Khiindi a wry smile and an extra pet and settled down. Khiindi curled between her shoulder and her cheek, washing his back and feet and her face with equal attention until she fell asleep.

She awakened sometime later, while the bubble was still dark, to an eerie echoing that sounded a bit like a whistle, a bit like a long moo, and other noises so peculiar she could not readily identify them. Then she was suddenly overcome with longing for her parents and for her homeworld, where the waters covered the ugliness of the land. No, wait. That wasn't how Vhiliinyar looked. Vhiliinyar had mountains and meadows, rivers and streams, as well as the ocean. Then she heard the singing underneath the eerie sounds and understood. This was the far talk of the LoiLoiKuans, calling home.

While the other gamers stuffed their faces, Jalonzo tried again to contact the curos and also Abuelita. When again he had no luck, he thought perhaps the gymnasium was interfering with the signal, though it had not done so before. Certainly the devices had been working when they called Mucho Nacho for delivery. Sometime between then and now something had happened to their holas, to the building, maybe – and he had no reason to think so, really, except for a very small nagging feeling in the back of his mind – maybe to the world?

There was one other person he could contact – as the sponsor of the tournament – who should still be in his office in an old three-story warehouse building a couple of blocks away. He ought to know about the dead guy on the doorstep of his tournament anyway. The sponsor, Miguel Lopez, owned the local Brujartisano franchise. He came to the gym long enough to get the tournament started and tell everyone to have a good time and what the stakes were, but he only sold merchandise to gamers. He wasn't a gamer himself, so he'd given Jalonzo, because he knew him better than the other players, the building keys and gone back to his office. Jalonzo knew where it was because he'd been over there a bunch of times to pick up prizes for other tournaments he'd won. You could see the warehouse from the top floor of the building containing the gym.

Jalonzo climbed the stairs to the top and went back to the hallway between the gym wing and the school wing of the building. It had a good view of this part of the city.

The sun was low in the sky but it never exactly set this time of year – it simply rotated around the horizon. You could still see everything clearly. Usually at this end of town people didn't decorate a lot for Carnivale – that was more to stimulate business uptown and for the tourists. When Jalonzo was little, he had enjoyed going to the parades with his parents, dressing up in the Diablo costume Abuelita made for him. But now it was either too childish or more adult than he wanted to deal with.

He was surprised at first to see the yellow flags with the designs in the middle and mistook them for Carnivale decorations. But he could not avoid seeing the one on the Brujartisano office's warehouse. The design wasn't decorative; it was a biohazard symbol. Most of the buildings he was looking at had quarantine flags on them.

How could that be? It wasn't that way when they'd come to the tournament just three days ago.

He didn't see any activity in any of the buildings, though admittedly he couldn't see much as the windows were all shaded against the sun.

Everything looked about the same as usual, except that there were some people sleeping on the streets – more than the usual homeless who somehow or other found their way there to be homeless in a good climate, where they would not freeze to death. But maybe those weren't homeless after all, or sleeping. Maybe they were like the nacho man. Maybe they were bodies. Here and there he spotted some animals lying in the street and in yards, too.

He really wanted to go out and see what was going on, check on Abuelita, make sure she was okay, but he knew right away that was probably the dumbest thing he could do. Other than getting food out of the truck where the driver had undoubtedly died of whatever it was the yellow flags were about.

Not everything was quarantined yet, but evidently the disease, whatever it was, had spread as quick as a rumor and that, he decided, must be what brought down the communications. The workers were all sick maybe. One little glitch in the system and with no one to fix it, the holas went silent, and probably computers and vid screens as well.

He unlocked the computer lab and tested his theory. There was still power, but the network was down. The vid screens came on but showed static.

Very well. He tried to think what Abuelita would do. She would not panic, she would be thinking of how to help other people. Not the people in quarantine probably. The curos would be helping them. The best thing he could do there was stay out of the way, keep the rest of the gamers out of the way – and keep them from leaving until somebody said it was okay to do so. Not that anybody had told them to stay. If the sponsor was in that building, behind that flag, and the parents of most of the gamers were also behind flags in their pueblos, then perhaps nobody who knew about the tournament could tell anyone else to check on them.

He returned downstairs. He didn't really want any of the food now, but it wasn't like he was sharing it with the nacho guy. It came inside packages after all. And it smelled good. And he was very hungry, when he thought about it. Who knew what else they'd get to eat for quite a while?

He sat down at the table, stared at his cards and the dice for a moment, then threw the cards faceup onto the table, where everybody could see he was set to win again.

'Amigos, I'm bored. I know it's no fun for you guys with me always winning, and it's getting to be where it's not that much of a thrill for me either. So I'll tell you what. Let's play another game – I've been working on this one for a while, and I want to try it out, but I can't do it by myself. If you guys will play along with me on this, I'll forfeit the tournament to whoever wins the new game – and I will just be the evil overlord this time, not a player.'

'You don't mean you are giving up your chance to go to the hologames on Bruja Prime!' Maria Maldanado said. 'You've been heading for that since you started – we all have.'

'I can do it later. If I still want to. It's not like I can't beat you guys anytime I want to,' he said, grinning in his best evil overlord fashion.

'What about cards?' one asked. 'What do we do with the cards?'

'*Sí*, and what about our prizes for winning the individual games? We get those in the real game, not in something you make up.'

He thought about it. Yes, there would have to be incentive. Getting his glory wasn't going to be tangible enough for some of them – some of them weren't very into abstract concepts like glory. They wanted stuff. He had another idea. One that would definitely keep the other gaming freaks interested and occupied. He sighed. He didn't like it. He really didn't like it. But it was the only sure thing.

From his pack he extracted three heavy notebook folders packed with his collections from the last four years. 'We just use the dice for my game – I'll explain the rules. And at the end, when we total who won the most games, each winner starting with the champion and working down to the one who wins the least gets to pick their choice of my cards. Agreed?'

By their words and nods and the expressions on their faces, he could see he had them. He began explaining the new game, all the while wondering when – or even if – help would find them.

ELEVEN

The entity in feline form who was commonly called, but who did not necessarily answer to the name 'Khiindi' reflected, while cleansing the fur below his rib cage, that this mission had somehow strayed far from his initial concept of it. This was, of course, due to the poor planning and incompetence of his bipedal subordinates. If they weren't so young and cute, he would have seriously considered showing them the rough side of his paw. However, since they were in his care, and he was actually rather fond of them, he exercised the patience and strategy all catkind employed when stalking a goal, a tidbit, or, if things were dull, a leaf or a dust mote. All of his wiliness, feline and otherwise, would be required to turn this trip around, and he knew it. Fortunately, he was more than up for the challenge.

Even if his last few missions had gone a bit out of his control, he had never lost his native resourcefulness or the cocky ability to believe in himself that had once been his hallmark, especially back in the days when he'd been known as Grimalkin.

Thus far he had successfully introduced his companions to useful people (even if to date they had proved their usefulness only by providing him with fish). He had also caused less desirable beings to show their true colors by irritating them, so they would identify themselves as enemies. And naturally he had ingratiated himself with all potential allies.

It was really rather exhausting managing so many personnel. No wonder frequent naps were necessary to stay fresh and alert.

Supervising mealtimes was also essential. Because Khorii grazed in the 'ponics garden and Elviiz did not actually require organic nourishment, the poor kids were socially impaired when it came to breaking loaves and fishes with the others. Khiindi sought to ease this gap in social customs by making himself the Linyaari ambassador, allowing other students to pet him and offer him tidbits from their plates. That should encourage them to engage in conversation with Khorii and Elviiz about what a beautiful cat they had, and how friendly, intelligent, etc., etc.

It had come to Khiindi's attention, however, that not all of the students admired him or spoke to him kindly. On one particular day, Khorii was having to search a bit harder than usual for edibles in the garden, and also was trying to think of a way to stimulate new growth. Khiindi, who had no interest in vegetables, got bored and scampered ahead of her up the hubbub and into the lunch-room where Hap, young Sesseli, and several other friends could be counted on to see that a fellow didn't have to rely on the *Condor*'s crunchies for sustenance.

Nothing particularly tasty was being served, Khiindi found to his dismay. Beans again. And not all that many beans, at that. He thought that perhaps, in the absence of vermin and birds to offer to the communal pot, he should start bringing crunchies to the lunchroom and offer to share. All those beans also made for a very heady atmosphere throughout the school.

Of course, he *did* know one place where a tasty meal could still be had for the asking. With a flirt of his tail, which he allowed Sesseli to stroke as he graciously declined the bean she offered to him, he left the lunchroom and headed for the pool, where his friends swam with his intended meal.

So focused was he on this delicious goal that he was taken totally by surprise when a large hand reached down and grabbed him by the tail and held him aloft. 'Gotcha, you mangy flea bag. You want to go in there, do you?'

Pain shot through Khiindi's whole body. Everything from his tail to his whiskers was in agony. Spots of light swirled before his eyes. He snarled and twisted and did manage to sink claws into flesh a time or two, but the other hand brutally slapped him away. Sick and dizzy, he was carried like a dead rat into the poolroom, whereupon his captor began to swing him by the tail. Through his pain, Khiindi heard a girlish scream, then a wonderfully familiar voice say in an uncustomary tone of command, 'Put the cat down and step away from him, Marl. Do not hurt the cat.'

'If it's not the bionic boy!' Marl said, and instead of putting Khiindi gently down, he swung him out over the water and let go, so that Khiindi flew out to the deepest part. When he hit the water, he should have landed hard and possibly injured the parts Marl had not already broken, but instead something held him up and he drifted rather than smacked down to the surface of the pool.

Whereupon, just as he was getting soaked, Lealikilekua dived under him so that he landed on her round back, the water lapping his injuries. By the time she brought him to the edge and deposited him there, the scene had changed.

Out of eyes blurred with pain, Khiindi saw his assailant lying flat on his back on the deck, blood pouring from his nose and mouth and his arm sticking out at an odd angle. The big bully's friends backed away while Elviiz, fists clad in steel attachments, swiveled 180 degrees on his right ankle, challenging any of them to take him on.

Khiindi felt as if his poor tail had been almost torn off. His back was on fire, and his hind legs would not obey him. He wanted to wash his wounds, but his neck would not move in the regular way, so he could not turn his head even to see if his tail was still attached to his hindquarters. He thought probably his back was broken.

Still, it was some comfort to see that his honor

137

was being properly defended and that he was being avenged. Though he could have done without the screaming.

The little-girl scream that cried his name was loud, but Marl's screaming in anger and pain that he'd been murdered was louder. Loudest of all was Shoshisha, bending over the vicious boy, just screaming because she'd never seen anything like that before.

The noise, so close to him, hurt Khiindi's ears and he spat at them all, though the spit actually came out as drool dribbling from the side of his mouth.

Shoshisha was a twit. As for Marl, Khiindi thought for a moment that perhaps he was a shapeshifter who was really at least partly descended from the Khleevi, the horrible buglike race that had had no purpose except to waste, destroy, and eat the rest of the universe.

Lealikilekua, surface-diving for the less noisy depths of the pool, made sure to splash water high enough to soak Shoshisha.

That made Khiindi brighten up a little, as much as he could, under the circumstances.

Hap approached saying something soothing, and Khiindi hoped his friend would help him, but Hap seemed not to see him, intent instead on the embattled Elviiz. Khiindi could not hear what he was saying because of the screaming.

Khorii and four teachers ran into the bubble.

'Turn it off!' Shoshisha shrieked up at the teachers. 'Make her turn that monster off before it kills someone.'

Time for an injection of perspective here. Khiindi mewed weakly and tried to drag himself forward, giving Shoshisha and Marl as wide a berth as possible. His back legs would not hold his weight and his tail dragged listlessly behind him. He cried and cried, trying to alert people to his presence there at their feet so they would not injure his poor tail again or squash him.

Finally, he saw Khorii's beloved two-toed hooflike feet, impossibly far away. Once more he was lifted by invisible hands and carried to Khorii's feet, his battered body gently deposited upon them. He felt small hands caress his head and heard a childish voice saying, 'Poor Khiindi Kitty!'

He tried to answer with another plaintive mew but it died before it escaped his throat.

He saw no more of what was going on around him.

Instead, his past lives, none of them lived wholly in the form of a small cat, flashed before him. He had been many places, seen many things, traveled through many times, and sired many many offspring. In fact, what with the siring and the time travel, he was doubtlessly literally his own grandsire. His lives had always been so big, so grand, so full of activity and vitality, that it seemed impossible it took only one mean male – not even an adult at that – to do him in. It seemed incredible that when his people had decided he would assume the small cat form that they intended – that they would *allow* – him to be killed while in it, small and relatively defenseless. They hadn't been *that* angry, had they? This was just a punishment, a temporary humiliation which, when he had proved how well he could look after Khorii, they would rescind and he would be allowed to shift shapes, forms, and sizes at will as he always had.

And yet, Khiindi knew that something was broken inside. He felt the breath huff out of himself in one last long sigh as his spirit saw the sun come out and pounced toward it, no longer hurting, ready to bask. He wouldn't have been able to eat that fish anyway.

Khorii had just emerged from the 'ponics garden and was on her way to the cafeteria when she was almost bowled over by stampeding teachers, Calla Kaczmarek, Captain Bates, Steve Reemer, and Headmaster Phador Al y Cassidro himself.

Calla and Captain Bates grabbed her by either arm. 'Come along, Khorii.'

'Why? What?' She couldn't be in trouble, could she? She had just been minding her own business, trying, in fact, to improve the moonbase food supply.

'Your droid has apparently malfunctioned and injured one of the students,' Phador Al y Cassidro told her.

'Elviiz? He didn't! He wouldn't. I don't think he *can*!'

'Nevertheless, he apparently did,' Calla told her. 'I first . . . realized he was an android . . . when I asked . . . who his people had been . . . and he told

140

me his father . . . was a modified KEN unit . . . I remember from when . . . I was a child slave . . . before your mother . . . and Mr Li freed us? . . . that the Piper . . . used KEN units . . . sometimes . . . to enforce his will . . . They were *definitely* able . . . to inflict harm on people . . . I know . . . from personal . . . experience.'

Calla's speech came in short gasps because she was talking as she rushed to keep up with the much faster Captain Bates. As it was, her grasp on Khorii's arm was so far behind Captain Bates's grasp on Khorii's other arm that Khorii felt torn between the two.

On the other side of the iris, the bubble was crowded with students and filled with screams, shrieks, oaths that had to do with excretion and mating, and, from the poopuus, splashing. Khorii was taller than most of the kids, however, and over their heads she saw Elviiz swinging from side to side, brandishing fists reinforced with steel. At his feet someone was moaning, shrieking, and swearing while Shoshisha, who was visible, screeched and ranted. Sesseli was emitting a high-pitched childish scream, and the poopuus were squealing agitatedly to one another in their own language.

Only Hap seemed calm. He spoke to Elviiz in a kind and reasonable voice. Shoshisha squealed suddenly as she was drenched, and something landed on the deck beside her. Khorii edged forward, stopping just behind Sesseli.

She started to speak to Elviiz, but Hap

persuaded him to lower his fists first. The teachers closed in. Something wet plopped onto Khorii's feet in all the confusion, but she couldn't see her feet for Sesseli, who suddenly let out her own shrill squeal. 'Poor Khiindi Kitty!' she cried, and started wailing again.

Khorii bent down and saw Khiindi. He was sopping wet and so limp and thin without his silvery fur bushing out that he seemed almost transparent. His back legs splayed out oddly and when she touched his tail his front end contracted in a spasm.

At least he was alive. She knelt to lift him, touching him with her horn as she did so. She couldn't let the others see her healing him, but she couldn't let him suffer needlessly either.

There was no time to explain or to argue. She lifted him, feeling through her arms that his pain had abated, and turned to leave the bubble, Sesseli, still crying, following, trying to give comforting strokes to the parts of Khiindi that dangled from Khorii's arms.

'Khorii, where are you going?' Calla asked. 'You are a healer like your mother, aren't you? This young man is seriously injured.'

'Be back soon,' she said, her voice tight with anger.

Sesseli followed still, so, crooning to Khiindi with her face – and horn – against his wet fur, Khorii carried him (purring by then, but she didn't mention that to Sesseli yet) to the 'ponics garden. Nodding to the first shoots of one of the plants

142

whose growth she had been accelerating before she left the garden, she instructed Sesseli to pick it.

The little girl did so and brought it to her.

'Now, you put it on Khiindi while I hold him and we'll see if he gets better,' she said, not giving the girl a chance to get a good look at Khiindi, who was wriggling around in her arms, until she put the leaves on him.

Whereupon she raised her face and horn from him and looked down into wide and relieved golden green eyes. 'It took you long enough,' she could almost hear him say.

Now Sesseli's squeals were of delight as she jumped up and down. 'I healed him! I healed him! Is he all better now?'

Khorii nodded. 'All better.'

'Now do we go back and heal that boy?'

'Ye-es,' Khorii said. 'But Khiindi is just a little cat and it doesn't take much to fix him. The boy is very large and it will take a lot more leaves to heal him. So let's keep looking.'

Finally, they found the leaves, which she ground up using the hard soles of her hoofed feet, and mixed with water. Khiindi watched attentively throughout this procedure, fully recovered and ready to hunt and vanquish the bits of leaf that flicked out from under Khorii's hoof.

Grinding the leaves gave her a chance to work off a little of the anger she was feeling toward Marl and Shoshisha. It was totally *ka*-Linyaari to be so angry she didn't want to heal someone. Of course, she *would* heal him, but, she reasoned, when there

143

was more than one person wounded, you had to decide who to do first. Khiindi's injuries had been life-threatening, whereas Marl, from her observation, would mend without her help, though slower and more painfully.

They carried the makings of the poultice in a garden pot back to the pool bubble. Khiindi mewed plaintively before going through the iris, and Sesseli picked him up and held him, stroking his head.

Many of the other students had left, including Marl.

'It's about time you came back, young lady,' Phador Al y Cassidro said. 'Marl has been carried to the infirmary. He is in great pain. Your droid apparently doesn't know his own strength. It makes him dangerous. He just attacked that poor boy for no reason.'

Captain Bates stepped in front of him and gave Khiindi's ears a rub. 'How is the little fellow? All better?'

Khiindi licked her fingers.

'Yes, thank you.'

'The poopuus tried to tell Calla what happened but they were so overwrought they had trouble with their Standard.'

'Didn't Elviiz tell them?' she asked, looking around for her friend.

'He didn't get the chance, I'm afraid. Or rather, he didn't take the chance. When you left with Khiindi, before Hap could get him to tell his side of the story, he deactivated himself. Droids have progressed quite far since I was a girl but – can they feel shame?'

An excellent question, Khorii thought as she looked around the poolroom that still held residual tension from the violence that had just happened there.

TWELVE

I think Maak programmed Elviiz to feel much of what I feel,' Khorii said. 'And I'm still really really angry. Why would that horrible boy do such a thing to a poor defenseless little cat?'

'I don't know,' Captain Bates said, shaking her head. 'Maybe if you fix him up, he'll tell you. Maybe,' she said, lifting her eyebrows, 'if he won't, you can read his mind. Although personally I wouldn't want to go there.'

Khorii looked at her uneasily. Had she found out about the test papers before Khorii could confess to sending her answers to the whole class?

(*Can you read me, Khorii? I'm a good friend of your grandfathers, you know. From things they've let slip, I've gathered that Linyaari are telepathic.*)

(*I read you, Captain. My telepathy has been dormant until recently, but I'm learning. Sorry about the exam papers. I'm like my mother. A really good sender.*)

(*At least you sent the right answers*), Captain Bates replied philosophically.

'Where *is* Elviiz?' Khorii asked aloud.

'Phador was all for locking him in a maintenance closet, but I thought maybe it would be best if he were placed in the shuttle you arrived in until this matter is sorted out,' Calla Kaczmarek said.

'I'll go there now,' Khorii said. 'He can't deactivate just because he defended Khiindi from that bad boy.'

'He didn't just defend Khiindi, Khorii,' Calla said sternly. 'He badly injured another student, however much the kid had it coming. With his strength, Elviiz could have prevented Marl from causing more harm to Khiindi without damaging him so badly. Apparently his emotional range includes anger . . . and that's not something most people like to see in a being that is so much stronger, faster, and smarter than humans. For now, Elviiz is fine. If you want to help him, you should take your special poultice up to Marl and see if you can help. We got the arm and jaw set, but it was pretty painful for him. I know what you're thinking, but my guess is that this isn't the first time that kid has had his bones deliberately broken. The way Marl is carrying on, it seems he knows from hard experience just exactly what a broken bone feels like, and how long it'll take to heal. And he's saying things about revenge – "Just like last time," is how I believe he put it. He's a wreck, and he's furious. I'm not saying you have to forgive him. Just think about cutting into his plans to get even by helping out a little.'

It was all Khorii could do not to snort with derision at Calla's suggestion. She didn't want to

147

go near Marl Fidd and didn't want Khiindi near him either. And in her opinion, Elviiz should be congratulated, not made to feel ashamed for defending his family. It was not a diplomatic, pacifistic, or particularly Linyaari way to look at things, but it was how she felt at that moment. Maybe she was a throwback to the Ancestors. The original unicorn forebears of the Linyaari could be rather fierce, according to the old stories about them.

Khiindi, and by extension she and Elviiz, were the injured parties. Just because they were outsiders, and Khiindi was 'just' a cat, and Elviiz was 'just' a droid, while Marl Fidd was one of the students, the teachers seemed to be implying she should make up to him.

Full of indignation, she stalked toward the infirmary, Sesseli following behind with Khiindi still in her arms. When they neared the infirmary, with its medicinal and antiseptic smells, Khiindi leaped down and sprinted away as if he'd never had his tail so much as tugged. Khorii forgot being mad long enough to say to Sesseli, who looked as if she might start to cry, 'It's okay, honey,' she said to the child. 'You don't need to be here for this. If you could keep Khiindi out of trouble while I'm healing Marl, I'd appreciate it.'

Marl was easy to find, being the only patient in the room. And since he was yelling all kinds of things about what he was going to do to her when he got better, Khorii paid him no attention. The health teacher doubled as the medtech. Hap had told her that students were examined by doctors before they came to the moonbase. They were not sent to Maganos until they had recovered from any illnesses or injuries they had. So, for the most part, the student population was healthy and required only a medtech to see to the usual minor health problems kids had. Ordinarily, if someone came down with something more serious or got badly injured, planetside care was within less than a two-hour trip.

Even if there had been a hospitalful of students, Marl would have been noticeable because he was so loud, what with his cursing and fussing and moaning with pain and yelling at the medtech, Mr Singh, in a most disrespectful manner for refusing to give him more and stronger medication.

Squaring her shoulders, Khorii marched up to his bed. She would heal him, but not before she gave him a piece of her mind along with the touch of her horn. In truth, she felt more like goring him with it than healing him, feelings she knew should shame her, but didn't.

Khorii addressed the sadistic Marl, adopting the same no-nonsense voice often used by her Father-Sister Maati, who was raised by the legendary Grandame Naadiina and often had to bring her handsome but rather flighty mate, Thariinye, back down to earth. She hoped that Marl, like Thariinye, had some good buried in him somewhere. She'd seen no sign of it so far. 'Some of my people tried to tell me that my coming here was dangerous because humans are aggressive, warlike, and barbaric people. I did not believe them, because until today all of the humans I have known have been as kind and caring as the Linyaari. But you are evidently a specimen of the bad kind. What is the matter with you, trying to kill an innocent little cat who never did you any harm?'

'Oh, get over it, you spoiled brat. It's just a stupid cat. You shouldn't have brought it here anyway. Everybody else here was lucky to arrive with their own skins. *You* come parading in like some kind of a celebrity with an entourage, no less. Who the hell do you think you are to judge me? All I did was give your fraggin' cat flying lessons. At home we killed lesser beasts all the time. The ones we didn't kill to eat we killed to keep them from eating our food. It's survival, brat. Something *you* have never had to face what with your famous mama and your important human "family."'

Khorii wasn't sure how much she was reading and how much he was saying, but the unfairness of it struck her anyway. 'I can understand how you might resent me,' she said. 'But Khiindi is not me, and he is not a lower beast. His fellows are worshiped on his homeworld, sacred creatures who guard temples and possess great wisdom. If you want to wound me, try throwing *me* in the pool. But you wouldn't do that because you are afraid, are you not? You know if you attempt to hurt me, you might be hurt instead.'

'Yeah, that robot of yours is vicious. I thought they were under orders in their programming not to hurt real people.'

'That shows how much you know. I understand that at one time, Elviiz's father, whom I have known only as a learned and conscientious person, was evil and hurt people all the time to please his mistress. Perhaps Elviiz retains some model, if not racial, memory of that aspect of his father's past. Furthermore, I would not need Elviiz to hurt you to stop you from hurting me. I have other ways, nonviolent ways practiced by my people, of stopping aggression against my person. Right now I feel like forgoing them in favor of stomping on your broken arm with my hard "alien" feet, but that would lower myself to your level. Instead, I am culturally compelled to minister to your injuries. So shut up and do not make me any angrier at you than I already am unless you wish to remain in your current condition longer than necessary.'

'You're lying! You're going to hurt me! Singh! Stop her. She's going to torture me.'

'Alas,' said Mr Singh, 'I am much too busy to hold you down while she does so, evil punk of a boy. So be still and allow the gracious girl to heal you and get your worthless anatomy out of my infirmary.'

Marl let out a low moan, and his eyes shifted back to her. She felt real fear radiating from him. Calla was right. He'd clearly been abused in the past. 'If you are afraid of me simply because I'm standing and you are injured, how do you think poor little Khiindi, who has known only gentleness and love at the hands of bipeds, felt when you nearly killed him?'

151

'Cats don't have feel—' he began.

Khorii saw her vision flicker and burn with shades of red. It was very odd, but she was too angry to think about the phenomenom at that moment.

As she slammed the poultice container down on the table beside his bed, Marl decided that perhaps his statement was the wrong tack to take with her. 'How was I to know you worshiped the damned things?'

'I did not say *I* worship Khiindi,' she replied. 'I said he comes from a planet where his sort are worshiped. He has been my companion since I was a baby. He is more like a brother or sister to me, as is Elviiz, than the subservient creatures you seem to think all four-legged animals should be.'

'Well, you have a pretty mixed-up family, if you ask me,' Marl said with a grunt. 'Animals are only there for people to eat.'

Khorii felt the hair on the back of her neck stand up in shock and anger. 'I do not believe that I asked you for your opinion.'

As she spoke, she concentrated on holding his gaze with her own as she had seen her elders do, and applied the poultice to his various injuries. In a very *ka*-Linyaari fashion, she hoped it hurt Marl like fury.

'I must remove part of your cast to finish the treatment,' she said as formally as possible.

He flinched when she knelt to inspect his arm. She raised it and looked underneath it, as if looking for flaws in the cast. While doing so, of course, she

152

laid her horn against the underside of his arm and imagined the bones mending straight and knitting whole. Then, as if still inspecting it, she took his hand and examined it. She was surprised to feel how warm and normal this hand felt. How could something that seemed so ordinary be so vicious? It had so recently held her poor cat friend in such a cruel grip and with such murderous intentions.

Feeling that the arm was mended, she began removing the boy's cast, smearing on the poultice as she pulled sections off.

He panted with fear at first, but then said, 'Hey, that stuff works pretty good. Bet you could get plenty for it on the black market.'

Her healing gift was a miracle, and all this stunted monster could think of was the profit there was in the process! She glared at him and turned her back. She had taken two steps away from the bed when he said, 'I guess you did this to your cat, too, didn't you? I mean, I guess he's still alive. You didn't say I killed him.' The words sounded both grudging and disappointed.

'No, he lives. But it was not for lack of trying on your part,' she said. 'Without my medicine, he would have died. And, yes, fortunately for Khiindi, our medicine works for all species.' She turned suddenly and faced Marl. 'For your healing to really be complete, you should attempt to make amends to Khiindi for what you did to him and to Elviiz for forcing him to deal with you so harshly.' Once again, she gave the boy a chance to show any mercy or goodness that he had inside him.

'What? Are you crazy? Apologize to a *cat*? And that robot kid almost killed me!' Marl was almost spitting with his indignation.

'Elviiz is an android, not a robot,' she said. 'Your violence activated the aggression in him. He strives to be as Linyaari as I am, having been raised as my foster brother, and we do not believe in such aggressive behavior. You have done him more wrong than he did you. To feel better, you should attempt to mend the hurts you have caused.'

'Yeah, right.' Marl snarled. 'In a million years, if ever!'

So much for Marl's inner healing. Then she did walk away. Behind her she heard Mr Singh say, 'Now then, Marl, pick up the mess your cast has made and get back to your classes. No malingering, no malingering. Go, go. And it would please me if you did not come back.'

It seemed that she wasn't the only person who didn't think much of Marl.

Hafiz brooded over the lists of supplies he had ordered from company headquarters – orders that were as yet unfilled, though some of them were more than six weeks old.

Miikhaye, the Linyaari communications intern, appeared in the doorway.

'Uncle Hafiz, sir, Comoff Harui sent me to inform you that Captain Ling and the *Dervish* are returning.'

'So soon? Did they fix my relays? Did they see the supply ships en route to us? What in the name

154

of the Prophets and Books is causing all of this delay?'

'No, sir, they did not do any of that. As they were entering Federation space they encountered a drone ordering all vessels to return to their last ports of call.'

'Why in the name of all that is holy and valuable? Ships do not conduct interstellar commerce by remaining in port.'

'No, sir. The drone refers to the need for treatment, decontamination, and observation of a quarantine. What is a quarantine, Uncle Hafiz?'

'A quarantine? Why a quarantine?'

Miikhaye shook his head to indicate he did not know and looked expectantly at Hafiz.

'Ah, yes, my son, a quarantine is a rule passed by health officials and other authorities to prevent those who are sick with a communicable disease from mingling with those who do not have it.'

'Oh, well then, sir, that's a relief. At least we do not have to worry about Acorna, Aari, and Khorii. They are Linyaari and can heal any illness.'

'Ah, yes, true. And yet—'

'Sir?'

Hafiz made a wave of dismissal. 'Never mind, my boy. Ask Captain Ling to report to me upon his return, please. And you did well to keep me informed. Do the same when Captain Gallico returns from Makahomia. And, Miikhaye?'

'Yes, sir?'

'You are the son of Khaari, communications officer of the *Balakiire*, the ship commanded by my adopted daughter's aunt Neeva, are you not?'

'Khaari is my mother, yes, sir. Why?'

'Would you tell her for me please that I am desolate that it has been such a very long time since I have had the honor of her company and that of the rest of the *Balakiire*'s crew. I am a lonely old man except for my beloved Karina, and I seek the solace of the companionship of my dear Linyaari friends, especially in the absence of my daughter and her family. Please convey my desire for their presence. As soon as possible. Sooner, even, if they can manage it.'

THIRTEEN

Hap sat beside Elviiz in the spacecraft, wondering how to comfort the droid, if he could feel comfort while he was turned off, and why a droid should need comforting at all. The droid hadn't done anything Hap wouldn't have done if he'd seen what Marl was up to before Elviiz did. Elviiz probably had done it better, of course. Hap wasn't reinforced with titanium and steel.

'Look, my friend, he had it coming. He's had it coming for a long, long time. I don't know why they even sent him here. Most of the kids here are basically good kids who got bad breaks and had no place to go. Marl has a place to go, if you ask me. Prison. Not political prison or anything like that – just somewhere where they put scary people so nobody else has to deal with them. A nice strong place to keep them inside and the rest of us safe out here.'

Elviiz, of course, said nothing. But Hap liked to think he was listening.

It was nice out in the shuttle bay. Even during

'night' inside the bubbles, the stars did not seem as close as they did out in the bay, through the viewscreen. Hap had only ever taken one ride in a spacecraft. He'd been superexcited about it and talked about nothing else for days before until everyone he knew looked pained when he started telling them about it. He'd thought back then, *Boy, if they think I'm full of it now, wait till I get back!*

The truth was, he probably wouldn't have had a lot of high adventure to relate to them if things had worked out like he planned. He was only going to make the runs with the agro tech rep, Scaradine MacDonald, showing people in colonies on other worlds how to use different tools, fertilizers, feeds, and seeds. Scar was a good friend of his family and he had always had time for Hap. His invitation to take Hap with him on this run was like a dream. Realistically, Hap thought Scar might be recruiting him for the companies who employed him. Hap was good with machinery and could fix or build anything, was enthusiastic, loved to talk, loved to teach, and enjoyed agriculture best in the short term – preferably at harvesttime when it came to eating some of the produce. He loved the animals, taking care of them, helping them give birth, bottle-raising the babies. He hated the butchering part, though, and still refused to eat meat, something the other colonists thought was just plain silly.

When he and Scar left New Fredonia, and he watched it grow smaller and smaller as they shot into the atmosphere, he thought he didn't care if he ever saw it again. For a long time he felt bad about that, because he hadn't meant that he never wanted to see his family again. He wasn't really close to his parents, but he liked his brothers and sisters. But all of them had still been home when the planet blew up, as far as he knew. By then he and Scar were at Rushima. When the news came, he hadn't been able to talk for two weeks, and for a long time after that, he couldn't do anything at all. It was like he'd been paralyzed. Scar was very wise about people and tried to comfort him, but when Hap did something really stupid and tried to space himself, thinking that in some way he'd be going where he belonged, with everybody else he knew, Scar decided he wasn't equipped to look after Hap. He'd needed a helper, not somebody to babysit. So, reluctantly, Scar got ahold of Calum Baird and Declan Giloglie, who were old friends, and they agreed to take Hap at Maganos Moonbase.

That had been two years ago, when he was twelve. He was fourteen now. Before long, Scar would keep the promise he made when he dropped Hap off and come back for him. When he felt up to it, Scar said. When he was sane again, Hap thought he meant.

It wasn't such a bad place, though a lot of the other kids seemed sort of babyish to Hap. Not Shoshisha, of course. She felt like – well, he had never got close enough to know what exactly she felt like, but he wanted to. Or had. Having seen her throw a fit about Marl Fidd, her beautiful face twisted with what had to be an unreasonable fear and loathing of Elviiz – on Marl's behalf, he

159

wondered? He was beginning to think she was even more screwed up than he was, and not in a good way. What was that thug to the princess anyway? Had Marl maybe attacked Khiindi because of the underwear incident, which Shoshisha had confided to a half dozen of her best friends?

If she put someone up to being cruel to a harmless little cat because of a bit of urinary carelessness, well, she for sure wasn't the girl he thought she was, and she wasn't the girl for him. Too bad. She *looked* like the girl of his dreams on the outside, but it was starting to look to Hap like the girl inside was all wrong.

Some people thought Khorii was exotic-looking, but to Hap she looked too much like him, too much like the people he grew up around – that is, if you didn't count the horn and the hooves and mane and that kind of thing. Tall, willowy, blond people of both sexes had been plentiful in New Fredonia, along with large, heavy, blond people of both sexes, and redheads of all shapes as well. His sister Fri had hair almost exactly like Khorii's – well, she had had.

As if thinking about Khorii had summoned her, she walked onto the dock and entered the shuttle.

'It was very good of you to stay with Elviiz,' she told him.

'Is he – you know, aware? When he's turned off, I mean? It was weird leading him along behind me like – well, like a broken toy that just went where I told it to go.'

160

'Elviiz is not a robot, he's an android,' she said. 'His bionic parts and attachments are powered down now, but the organic part of him is as aware as you or I would be when we're asleep. I'm sure he appreciated your company.'

'But you want me to go now, is that it?'

She looked startled. 'No, I just thought you'd want to. That you had other things to do. I – have you seen Sesseli? She went to find Khiindi while I healed his assailant.'

'You *healed* Marl?'

'I had to. It is – um, what you would say is – a Linyaari thing. I think the only time someone was injured that we did not try to heal them – I mean by "we" my parents and other Linyaari – was when Khleevi were killed. Of course, Khleevi were not like people. They were more like armed weapons.'

'That's what everybody says about their enemy *du jour*,' Hap said. 'If you're going to be better than us at being pacifists, you'll have to do better than "not quite like a person." '

'Since I never personally met a Khleevi, I cannot effectively argue your point,' she told him. 'Also, I did not realize that the degree of pacifism was a competitive issue? That seems contradictory to me.'

She wished Elviiz were not deactivated. He could sort these things out more logically than she could, and also confuse everyone else in the process.

'You're right about that,' Hap said. He had been sitting still too long and, without realizing it, had begun pacing the small space inside the shuttle, looking inside storage compartments to see what was there. He was rewarded with a find. A bar of chocolate! 'I didn't know your people ate chocolate,' he said.

'We don't,' she said. 'But Captain Becker, whose shuttle this is, loves chocolate. I don't think he'd mind if you had that, however.'

He unwrapped it, stuffed a third of it into his mouth, and chewed thoughtfully. She might not know how to argue like a pacifist, he decided, but she knew how to make a peace offering when the opportunity presented itself.

She stood behind Elviiz and seemed to be massaging his hair, then scalped him, ignoring Hap's surprised yelp. Placing a finger delicately inside his head, she flicked something, and replaced the scalp patch. 'Come on, stop feeling sorry for yourself,' she told him. 'Marl and Khiindi are both mended, so there is no need for you to be disabled.'

Slowly, the android lifted his head, and said in a surprisingly level voice, considering the misery reflected in his posture, 'But what I did was *ka*-Linyaari.'

'Elviiz, you are my foster brother, and as annoying as any blood relative, from what I have seen of such relationships. You are as Linyaari in spirit as I am. I felt like taking Marl apart myself when I saw poor Khiindi.'

'Thank you, Khorii. That means a lot to me,' the droid said.

'However, and I do not say this to be unkind, you are not organically Linyaari. You are not descended from the Ancestors except perhaps to some degree spiritually, nor were you formed by the Friends. You are the child of your father, and, like him, are stronger and possess far more knowledge than any of our people. Have I mentioned recently how annoying that can be?'

'Yes, Khorii. But you see, my position is an ambiguous one. On the one hand I am your foster brother and playfellow, but on the other hand I am your tutor and mentor in matters of data and learning. And I am to look after you—'

'And protect me, right? And so, to keep me from being hurt, you protect Khiindi, too. Which you did. So now, can we please try to contact the grandfathers or the *Condor* from here again? It is possible that the bubble was not as conducive to your transmission as it could have been. Let us try from here.'

'Very well, Khorii, but first I would like to clarify an error in the corollary to your initial hypothesis. I protected Khiindi because he is my friend, too. And there is a great deal of evidence to support the theory that those who harm the small and helpless four-footed beings will also harm two-legged beings when those beings are at their mercy. Therefore, the behavior of those who torture the weak should be corrected when it is first perceived.'

'By breaking his arm?' she asked. 'Perhaps a nice chokehold and a lecture would have sufficed.'

'Oh, come on!' Hap said. 'He had it coming. I'd

have corrected the daylights out of his behavior myself if Elviiz hadn't done it first.'

'In retrospect my reaction to Marl's treatment of Khiindi was – excessive, I realize,' Elviiz replied. 'I will have to modulate my behavior in the future to ensure that it does not happen again.'

Elviiz seemed restored to full functionality, and sent hails to both the hospital frequency on Kezdet and the *Condor*'s private one. There was no answer from either. Khorii sighed and turned to go when the com receiver abruptly crackled to life.

'Maganos Moonbase, this is Rajan Taj, second officer of the supply vessel *Mana* of the Krishna-Murti Company subcontracting to House Harakamian. Do you read me?' The man on the vid screen had dark skin but still managed to look pale, a green undertone beneath the deep brown complexion. His eyes were red and he looked as though he had been crying.

He repeated the hail several times without success.

'Ooops,' Hap said. 'My fault. I'm supposed to be com officer tonight, but it's been so slow, what with the quarantines and all, I forgot.'

A man's brisk voice replied to the hail. 'We read you, *Mana*. This is Phador Al y Cassidro headmaster of Maganos Moonbase. What is it?'

The officer from the *Mana* spoke slowly and, Khorii thought, reluctantly. 'Mr Al y Cassidro, two things.' The man paused for a breath, then said, 'We came to resupply your base, but I regret that we cannot bring your supplies to the surface. Our crew has been stricken with what is surely the plague. Our captain was the first to die, purser followed him six hours ago, and my wife, who is the ship's first officer, and the chief engineer are gravely ill. I don't feel very well myself. I hope you have some food stored away somewhere because we cannot deliver this without bringing the plague to you.'

'That is most unfortunate. Your parent company has always been reliable in the past. You realize I have many hungry youngsters to feed as well as a staff?'

'Yes. I realize this. And so I tell you the second part of my message. Our young daughter Jaya is on board, the only member of the crew who does not appear ill, though she is nursing her mother as best she can. But that is no longer her place. Please allow us to send her to you in our shuttle. If you will make a decontamination chamber for her, she will go through it, wash herself thoroughly, cut off her hair if you insist, and change her clothing before entering an isolation chamber of your choice until you can see that she is disease-free. But do not leave her up here with us – with our bodies – alone on the ship. Promise me you will do this.'

'It's absolutely out of the question. I'm sorry for your daughter, but we are already on short rations, and since yours are unusable, we will have all we can do to feed the children we have. If you are amply supplied, I see no reason why the girl shouldn't do better than my students will, as she will have enough to eat.'

Rajan Taj looked stricken. 'Please, sir. It is not her fault that we are ill. She is only a girl. You must care for children to have so many there. Take pity on her, I beg you.'

'I'm sorry. There is no use arguing. My decision has been made. When the quarantine is lifted, we will contact the Federation Health Authorities to decontaminate your ship and deliver the cargo we paid you for already. If your daughter survives until then, she is certainly welcome until some suitable arrangement can be made for her. That is the best I can do. We have student communications officers running our unit, and I hope that you will not distress them by repeating your futile entreaties. Maganos Moonbase out.'

'Have I mentioned that we don't like that guy much?' Hap asked.

'What is the matter with some of these people?' Khorii asked. 'Elviiz, get second officer Taj back.'

Elviiz was already hailing the stranded supply ship.

'*Mana*, this is the space shuttle *Crow* currently under Linyaari command. Please come in, Second Officer Taj.'

'I – read you,' Taj said, a cough between the first and second word. His face was streaked with tears, and his cheekbones seemed even more sharply pronounced than a moment before.

Khorii stepped up so that her face would appear in the *Mana*'s viewscreen. 'Mr Taj, do you know of House Harakamian's connection with the Linyaari people?' she asked.

'Lady Acorna! Is it really you? We have all heard of you, of course, but never . . .' He broke off, coughing hard.

Elviiz started to correct the man again. Khorii was surprised that Taj mistook her for her mother, because she didn't think they looked very much alike. She took after her father's side of the family. But maybe outsiders couldn't tell. She said, 'Well, perhaps you've heard that I'm here to help with the plague. We will board you and, using our people's special medical skills, heal your crew members of the plague, after which my friend here and I will decontaminate your ship and the supplies for the Moonbase. Permission to board?'

The man looked incredulous and hopeful at the same time. 'What seemed a disaster now reveals itself as the best of luck. Gracious lady, we could not have picked a better place to come.'

When Taj signed off, Hap asked, 'Can you really do that? You're only a kid, and that guy thinks you're your mom.'

'Yes,' she said. 'Only two people need to be healed and a relatively small ship – not like others I've seen – needs to be purified. My parents are doing a whole planet, maybe a star system! They would expect me to take care of small problems like this by myself. We – our healing technology – is certainly up to *that*. We – it – can heal anybody.'

FOURTEEN

Elviiz began the countdown and instrument check while Khorii took the copilot seat and Hap the 'jump seat,' an anachronistic term left over from inner-atmospheric flights when it was conceivable, with the use of a personal sail, actually to jump out of a craft and survive.

Before Elviiz finished his countdown, the hull came under attack. Pounding at first, then a horrible screech like – exactly like – claws scratching metal.

Khorii unstrapped and opened the hatch. Sesseli and Khiindi looked up at her reproachfully for a moment, then Khiindi, tail fully healed and waving majestically, marched aboard. Before Khorii could say anything to either of them, Sesseli darted after him.

'Wait,' Khorii said, as Elviiz continued his interrupted countdown. 'Sesseli, we are going on a special mission to a supply ship orbiting this moon. There are sick people aboard, and they might make you sick, too.'

168

'What about Hap? Hap could get sick,' the little girl argued.

'Thank you for pointing that out,' Khorii told her. 'Hap will have to stay in the shuttle when we go up, until everyone is healed and the atmosphere and cargo are cleansed. Even Khiindi will have to stay in the shuttle until Elviiz and I decontaminate everything and heal everyone.'

'Then I'll stay in the shuttle and keep them company,' Sesseli said.

'There's no room,' Hap said reasonably. 'We don't have another secure seat.'

'Then I can sit on your lap and you can strap us both in and Khiindi can sit on my lap.'

'No, Sesseli, that is not safe,' Khorii said.

But just then another hail came from the supply ship. 'Please,' Taj gasped. 'Can you give us an ETA?'

Khorii took a deep breath, and said, 'We are on our way. Please conserve your strength and try to hang on.' To the others she said, 'Very well, then. We'll all go. There's no time to argue. Strap yourselves in. Elviiz?'

Elviiz had been counting down and checking himself while the others argued, and now he said, 'Prepare for launch.'

This flight seemed much longer to Khorii than the one from the *Condor* to Maganos. During the trip, another message came, with no video.

'Where *are* you?' This was not Taj, and the voice was young, female, and distraught. 'Hurry. Please hurry.'

'We'll be there as soon as we can,' Khorii

169

promised. 'Please, just be patient a little longer. Do whatever you've been doing to treat each other. When we get there we can cure you. Just please hang on.'

Elviiz transmitted their coordinates and an estimated time of arrival but the *Mana* made no reply.

Khorii wasn't worried about being able to cure the sickness once they arrived, but occupied herself with wondering how to do it and hide what she was doing. Elviiz would help, of course. She just hoped Hap, Sesseli, and especially Khiindi stayed out of the way. There was no way to secure the hatch from the outside that could not be undone from the inside. If harm befell either of the human kids, she would never forgive herself nor, she suspected, would anyone else. On the other hand, she thought, brightening, she could always just cure them, too, so it really wasn't such a *big* risk.

She began to feel a little alarmed when they requested docking instructions and received only the computerized voice directing all procedures. She tried to hail the bridge again but got no reply.

She was out of her seat and through the hatch door while Elviiz was still securing their vessel in its berth. 'Hurry,' she said.

Khorii and Elviiz found their way to the bridge from the diagram on the wall of the landing bay, but when they got there, no one greeted them. As Khorii and Elviiz disembarked from the shuttle, Khorii felt as if she were right back on the *Blanca*, though the ship was not dark, and there was plenty of oxygen.

170

It was, however, very quiet, and Khorii's sensitive nostrils picked up the smell of human excrement and something worse before her horn purified the air. Passing a door with a yellow biohazard sign on it, and looking through the small viewport set into it, she saw a single examining table which bore a sheet-covered bulk with feet sticking out at one end. On the floor beside the table lay another sheet-draped figure.

'We can do nothing for them,' Elviiz told her. 'They have been without life for some time.'

Khorii nodded, and they made their way straight to the bridge. On the bridge were three more people, one of them covered with a blanket. Beside the shrouded body lay the man whose face they had so recently seen on the com screen. Rajan Taj.

Khorii let out an involuntary cry and knelt beside him, lowering her horn to his head. He could not be dead. Not so suddenly. They had just spoken. Hadn't she told him to be patient?

'He is without life,' Elviiz said.

'Maybe,' she muttered, and tried to will him to return. Grandsire Rafik had told her a story once about Mother bringing Grandsire Gill back to life when he was shot in front of them. Grandsire Rafik had been certain that his friend was dead, but Mother would not give up, and she restored his life. It was, as far as Khorii knew, the only time Mother or any other Linyaari had done such a thing, but that single story made it possible. If only she tried hard enough. This was not a 'stiff' as Captain Becker had so dismissively termed the people aboard the

171

Blanca. This man was a person. She knew what his voice sounded like and how his face looked when he was worried. Not all blank and waxy like this. He should not be dead. He had a daughter to take care of. He should be here to look after her.

For a moment she saw her own beloved father lying there and with all her might, all her newfound psychic power, she urged him to return. Spots flew in front of her eyes and vanished, but his closed eyes did not open. His chest did not move. His breath did not cast a breeze onto her skin.

'Are you praying for my father?'

Khorii turned away from the body that had contained Rajan Taj. A dark-haired, dark-skinned girl who seemed to be about Hap's age looked down at her from desolate black eyes.

'Because I've already done that,' the girl said. 'I've prayed for all of them.'

'I was – trying to see if there was anything I could still do to help him,' Khorii said, rising. 'But there was not.'

'No, you're a little late for that, Lady – what did he call you?'

'He called me by my mother's name. He used to know her when she lived here, or had heard of her.'

'She's not with you?'

'No, she and my father are fighting the plague on another world. But I have the same skills, and I came to help. I did not take the time to explain that I was not my mother.'

'Oh. Well, you might as well have done. He died anyway,' the girl said, turning away.

'You are Jaya?'

The girl half fell into the command chair, as if her legs could no longer hold her. Her dusky complexion was underlain with a feverish red. Khorii felt heat rising from her skin. The girl's breathing was ragged, shallow, and irregular. 'What's left of me,' Jaya said.

Kneeling next to the girl, Khorii touched her, first on the pulse point at her jawline, drawn sharply against the long curve of her neck. She squirmed away and coughed. Khorii gently raised Jaya so she could put her head next to the girl's chest, as if listening to her heartbeat, but really to touch her horn to it. Jaya coughed once more and sat up, the fever draining from her like an outgoing tide.

'So if you're not your mother, Lady whoever, then who are you?' Jaya demanded.

'I am Khorii; this is Elviiz.'

'Khorii, Elviiz, what took you so long? I'm sure my parents are sorry they missed you.' The words were bitter and reproachful.

Elviiz said, 'Had our civilization developed teleportation technology, we might have been quicker, but as it has not we were forced to use a space shuttle. That requires some travel time. Your father was no doubt aware of this flaw.'

'We truly are sorry we could not be here in time to save your father and mother and are very sorry for your loss,' Khorii said gently, to soften the edge of Elviiz's correct but unhelpful assessment of the situation.

Jaya looked from one of them to the other, and

her eyes, so dry and hot before that there seemed to be no water for tears, flooded and overflowed with them. Khorii reached out a hand to touch her shoulder and comfort her but the girl shrugged it away, demanding, '*Now* what am I going to do?'

Khorii wished she had an answer.

Commander Ray Alcalde reflected that when it came to keeping the subordinates under your command pacified and happy, the Federation could have taken a lesson from him. He had the best record of any Federation liaison governor of a remote and primitive outpost. That was, for the love of the heavens, why he had been chosen to present his work to the Command Council held this year on Rio Boca. He had been unusually excited because the councils were for the most part dull, dry affairs, administrators instructing and admonishing other administrators. Only the odd recreational tour, generally of the most bland and banal variety, was ever included to break the monotony of the droning lectures and award the attendees for traveling so far to participate.

Definitely not what Ray would have chosen as his only trip away from the endless rolling waters of LoiLoiKua, the mournful chanting and dreary singing of the whale people, the drumming on the waters that woke him at all hours. It was hard on the nerves. Before the young were transported to that school near Kezdet, Ray had always liked the singing. That was the period during which he established his reputation as a good governor. The truth was, though they were a superstitious lot and a bit too given to passively accepting whatever befell them – otherwise, they would have moved on when the water overtook the land, not just adapted and evolved into water dwellers – they were easy to govern. They had been happy, satisfied, content. And then some idiot told them that a solar catastrophe was damaging their environment. They did not adapt this time. They became whirlpools of anxiety. What would happen to their young? Their beloved children would perish as would all LoiLoiKuans if their sun and their water betrayed them.

Well, sure. Ray tried to tell them that sort of thing was years, maybe decades, in the future, and they didn't really need to worry about it, but there was no shutting them up until the Federation took the problem under advisement. With unusual speed and efficiency, the children had been lifted into tanks that were loaded aboard a huge cargo ship and transported to Maganos Moonbase. The locals didn't write, of course, since they lived underwater. Neither did the kids. Ray certainly had not been given communications equipment sophisticated enough to allow the kids to hail the homefolk every week or so.

So the adults had stayed unhappy and just a tinge bitter, though they still considered Ray their friend. Little did they know how happy he would have been to turn the whole moist mess over to some fresh new officer who was, as Ray confided privately to his fellow commanders, *heh heh*, wet behind the ears to, *heh heh heh,* get his feet wet.

But he thought, when he got the invitation to speak at the council on Rio Boca, that at least the Federation recognized his work and was rewarding him by sending him home in time for Carnivale.

That would have been wonderful, to see his brothers and sisters again, to get into a costume that excused all sorts of behavior unbefitting an officer and a gentleman, and to parade through the streets to music a whole lot livelier than a LoiLoiKuan lament.

He simply could not believe it when the council ended early and everyone was dismissed, told to report back to their duty stations at once. Just because a few guys had gotten sick. Probably the hotel food. It didn't keep very well in hot climates, and all of the planets in the Solojo system were pretty tropical. The incomers who had set up some of the new industries should have paid attention to his mama and other locals who knew how to preserve and prepare food in the climate. He hadn't had any trouble himself, well, not at first, but he had been ordered back two days before the start of Carnivale. His ship left four hours before his sisters and brothers were due to arrive from Paloduro to catch him up on the news and take in the first of the parades on Rio Boca.

After that, all of them were going back to Corazon on Paloduro to see the hometown events where Ray could let his hair down without quite so much Federation scrutiny.

He was so disappointed and angry he felt literally sick by the time his shuttle docked on the small island containing the goofy sand castle outpost building the LoiLoiKuans had designed as an acceptable surface structure on their world.

He felt as if he was burning up, had started to cough and yes, finally, the effects of whatever bug had ended the conference early began to tell on his own digestion. He threw up on the beach as he disembarked from the shuttle, and almost didn't make it to the latrine. He sat in there for hours afterward, coughing when he wasn't making use of the bowl from one end or the other. He felt as if his chest were in a vise. Finally, he had to abandon the latrine and the castle because there simply wasn't enough oxygen in there. He couldn't get his breath. He dragged himself out onto the beach. He had no idea what time it was when he reached the water because he kept conking out every time he pulled himself forward a little and collapsed into the coughing fits again. What he coughed up had become bloody. *This was some case of dysentery!*

Finally, in his fever, he reached the water's edge and dipped his face and hands into it. He knew it was only lukewarm, about like swimming in pee he always thought, but he was so hot that it felt deliciously cool.

He didn't know when the LoiLoiKuans found him and dragged him the rest of the way into the water, carefully keeping his head above water, while they called for their healers, cleaned him, and sang to him.

He didn't know when the healers reached him and saw him, no longer coughing, eyes fixed and glazed, limbs dangling limply, doing their own slow dance to the rhythm of the waves.

FIFTEEN

Jalonzo was told by his school counselors that, like a lot of extremely bright youngsters, he was intellectually too far advanced beyond his peers for normal socialization. Which meant basically that he didn't have much in common with a lot of the kids at school. He tended to watch other people a lot and not say much unless he had something to say, and sometimes other people misinterpreted his actions and had trouble understanding where he was coming from. He had the same trouble understanding them at times, too. But he pretty much understood gamers, and that and his knowledge of the structure of the games was the only protection he had for all of them.

He felt bad about the nachos. Really bad. Two of the older guys got sick pretty quickly after the new game began. The others, even the girls, were so absorbed in the new game they barely noticed. When Atl of the Flowing Waters cried out as Avilix the Stone-faced slumped across the dice, Jalonzo walked around the table and patted

Avilix, who was actually Jorge Ramirez, on the back saying, 'Good death, Avilix! Now you have to leave until the others can bring you back to life again! I will take you now to the underworld to await rebirth.'

It was a good thing for Jalonzo he was so much bigger than the other kids, even the older ones like Jorge, who was almost twenty. He half carried Jorge away up the stairs. The smaller boy spewed once and Jalonzo ran with him to the upstairs bathroom and got him in a stall just in time. He went back to clean up the mess, then returned to the bathroom. Jorge had fallen forward with his head against the door. Jalonzo couldn't crawl under the door very far but managed to push Jorge's upper body back enough to get the stall open, flush, and with a grimace, clean Jorge before laying him as gently as possible on the tile floor in front of the stall. It was a good place to be for someone who felt the way Jorge did. The tile was cool but not cold because the air temperature was too warm for that. Jorge was burning up.

Lupe Sanchez, Princess Papan in the new game, threw up on the floor. Jalonzo didn't want to be cleaning up girls, so he figured it was time to let somebody else know what was going on. 'Princess Atl, you and Princess Papan have been kidnapped by the Trickster Twins. You come with us to the underworld now.'

'But Jalonzo, I mean Quetzacoatl, I—'

He shot her a pleading look and nodded to Lupe. Her eyes opened wider, her mouth forming

180

an 'O,' and she got up and took Lupe's other side.

He helped Maria get Lupe onto the stool, then went to clean up the mess downstairs.

The gamers might be focused, but they could still smell. 'What's the matter with Jorge and Lupe, Jalonzo?'

'I think there was something wrong with some of the food,' he said truthfully enough. 'If any of the rest of you start feeling bad, let me know. We still can't call our folks or the curos or even the sponsor, and of course you forfeit your standing in the tournament if you leave the building without permission. So we're just parking people near a bathroom till they feel better.'

Later, he switched the game around so that people played in shifts, some of them sleeping on their pads near the bleachers while three or four kept the action going at the table.

When the power went off in the middle of the night, he found candles in the janitor's pantry and flashlights in the security office and everyone agreed that made the atmosphere a lot more authentic.

Only two other people got sick that night which was a good thing, because Jorge died the next morning.

When Lupe died shortly after noon, Maria went ballistic. 'One of us has to go get help. Who cares about the stupid game! People are dead, Jalonzo. Dead!'

'Shhhh,' he said, blocking the sound of her

voice by standing in front of her, even though everyone else was still downstairs. 'We can't go. It's not because of the game. I need to show you something. Come on.'

He led her upstairs to the window and showed her the bodies in the streets and the quarantine flags. The flies were so thick around the bodies that you could hardly see them for the black cloud. 'Nobody has picked those people up, Maria. Not since yesterday. And those yellow flags mean nobody is supposed to go into those houses or come out of them. Abuelita—' His voice caught as he thought about his grandmother. Was she lying sick alone at home worrying about him? Was she already gone? He couldn't believe it. Not his tough little grandmother. She was a doctor. She knew all about this kind of sickness. '—she told me that in the old days, when they had really bad plagues that killed people, the authorities would shoot people who tried to leave a quarantined building.'

'I don't think we need to worry about that,' Maria said. 'Doesn't look like the authorities are bothering with us one way or the other. If they were worried about well people catching something, they'd have taken away the bodies.'

'Yeah, but the thing is – I mean, it's really bad about Jorge and Lupe, but not that many other people seem to be very sick, so maybe the food wasn't very contaminated. If we go out there, with the bodies and the flies and everything, more will get sick, maybe die. So the way I see it, we're all better staying here as long as we can and keeping it quiet as long as we can so everyone can concentrate on the game instead of worrying about their folks and stuff. Because from what Abuelita's told me and I've read, there's nothing we can do without probably making things worse.'

'If you'll unlock the cafeteria, I'll check the freezers and the pantries and see if there's enough food to keep us from starving in the meantime. I might have to get Carlos to help me. He's a good cook. I hate to tell him, though. He's kind of excitable. But we'll have to tell the others something before long. The tournament is supposed to end the day after tomorrow.'

'Maybe help will come by then.'

One thing about the lack of sleep and the hypnotic concentration on the game. When they did have to tell the others, and Jalonzo took them one by one up to the window and told them what he'd told Maria, nobody said much or even seemed very surprised. Jalonzo wondered if maybe some of them hadn't figured it out on their own. He felt very proud of the gamers then that they kept their heads about them. After all, there was really nowhere for them to go. He kept trying to think of something to do, some way to get in touch with people. Maybe he'd go out himself one more time and try to find someone. After all, he'd even touched the dead guy and hadn't gotten sick, so probably he was immune or at least resistant to the mystery disease. Maybe everyone hadn't gotten sick, so maybe there were people out there who were still okay. It was a comforting thought. He hoped it was true.

Khiindi tried to follow Khorii and Elviiz, but they were too fast with the hatch door. Of course, had it not been for his recent traumatic experience, Khiindi knew he would have been plenty fast enough to thwart them, but in his weakened condition he was stuck inside with the youngsters.

They were nice youngsters, but they were not his responsibility, and he wanted none of their 'Nice kitty, it's okay, Khiindi kitty, they'll be back soon. We can't go out there because the air is bad.'

Nonsense! As soon as Khorii's horn hit the oxygen supply it would be plenty safe for anyone to breathe. He knew the power of Linyaari horns better than the average Linyaari did, and he had every faith in her ability to neutralize any contaminant foolhardy enough to cross her path.

She was a mere child and she needed his help. Elviiz, of whom he thought rather kindly at the moment, was, of course, of remarkable intellect, strength, and versatility, but despite his programming, he was also a child. His father had designed him that way, with regular upgrades for 'growth spurts' so that he would be a suitable companion for Khorii.

Of all of the ship's occupants, Khiindi was the only one who was an adult, and not just in cat years. He was a great deal older than any of them knew, older than anyone they knew, and if he wished to get even older, no harm must come to

Khorii.

However, in the interests of continuing to grow old, he thought it would be best if he looked after her somewhere other than Maganos Moonbase, where youthful thugs waited in ambush to wreak excruciating destruction on his poor little cat shape.

Khiindi, feline though he was, could never be mistaken, even remotely, for a tiger or a lion or another of the large predatory members of his genus. Well, there had been a time of course when he could change his shape to resemble one of them, but temperamentally it was not his thing. He was more of a lover than a fighter, more brain than brawn, more apt to use his quick wits than his claws to extract himself from unhealthy situations.

And it seemed to him that the best course of action for him, and therefore, naturally, for Khorii, would be to take charge of this perfectly good vessel, decontaminated by his young Linyaari charge, of course, and go find her parents. He knew from past experience that Aari and Acorna could and would look after him as well as their daughter. Whereas in times past, in other incarnations, in other shapes, he had delighted in exploring new worlds, meeting new people, siring new races upon the most friendly females among those people, new places were infinitely more threatening when one was stuck with a shape that was no more than two feet long, tail extended, ten inches high, ears erect, and fifteen pounds after a particularly satisfying meal.

They thought his present form was descended from sacred Temple Cats who guarded the holy places of their homeworld, Makahomia. The truth was, the Temple Cats were descended from him. He was smart enough to know that temples were not to defend, they were to hide in, and once they lost their value as shelters, you found another shelter. Preferably a familiar one and preferably nearby. With a steady supply of food and water and, not unimportantly, armed two-leggeds to defend the temple *and* the cat.

The thing they had to do was commandeer the ship, find Aari and Acorna and the *Condor*, and leave this plague-infested place to sort itself out while they went *home.* Acorna's human fathers, should they survive the plague, were always welcome to visit them on MOO, weren't they?

Unfortunately, clever though he was, he could not open the secured hatch by himself. For that, he needed an accomplice. Widening his eyes to their largest and most golden green, knowing that his pupils would be round and black as lava in the subdued light of the cabin, he fixed Sesseli with his best stare. 'Open the hatch,' he thought. 'I need to use the litter box, and there isn't one here. Open the hatch now. I will be fine. The air is fine. Open the hatch now. You must do what I tell you, little girl. You are under my spell, within my power. Open the hatch now.'

Sesseli finally noticed him staring and gave him a quizzical and slightly worried look. 'I think the kitty wants something, Hap,' she said, though she kept her gaze locked with Khiindi's.

'Does he?' Hap barely looked up from the instrument panel, which he was studying and experimenting with. 'Don't stare back at him. Cats don't like that. It's okay if they stare at *you*, but if you stare back, they think you're trying to dominate them.'

'No, I don't think so. I think he's trying to tell me something. What is it, Khiindi cat?'

Never let it be said that he was a cat to miss his cue. Still holding her gaze with his own, he stood, looking back over his shoulder in such a meaningful fashion that even a very stupid child couldn't miss the point, and walked over to the hatch.

'Are you getting this, kid?' he asked mentally, and turned away long enough to rise up on his hind paws and scratch vigorously at the hatch. 'Meyowwwt,' he said, quite clearly, but he might as well have been speaking a foreign language for all the compliance with his wishes he got.

So he lifted his tail and gave a mighty squirt of essence of tomcat.

'Oh, boy, Elviiz is gonna have to decontaminate the shuttle, too, now!' Hap said. 'I thought you were a pussycat, Khiindi, not a civet cat!'

Khiindi looked at them pointedly, gave a lick to his shoulder, and scratched at the hatch again.

'No, Khiindi cat,' Sesseli said in her childish but regrettably quite firm voice. She walked over and picked him up under his front legs, compressing his chest and making it a bit difficult to breathe, which made him squirm, but still he was careful not to bite the child. This was not because he was a good kitty. This was because he was beginning to think there was more to little Sesseli than met the eye *or* the nose. 'You can't go out there. You would get sick, and Khorii and Elviiz would have to heal you, too. I guess you'll just have to go in here if you have to go.'

He considered going on her shoes. But actually, he didn't have to. He was simply trying to communicate his wishes and was extremely frustrated to have them thwarted. His Linyaari people never failed to comply. Well, usually not. And it didn't generally matter anyway. But it did now.

Then he realized he had been frozen in cat form far too long and was thinking like some stupid lowbred dispatcher of vermin. He didn't need a person to open the hatch. It was electronic after all, not mechanical. All he had to do was reach the right buttons on the console, which was easy enough to do.

Hap was still playing with everything, reading diagrams and going through sequences for various procedures without actually touching the buttons. He was pleased when Khiindi, seemingly having forgotten his agenda, hopped up beside him and began playing, too. When he thought about the task rationally, he knew perfectly well which buttons to push. He had seen it done often enough in the past and had seen Khorii do it just a short while ago. Pretending to paw innocently at Hap's fingers as they darted for the buttons, he 'accidentally' hit the ones in question. Then before Hap or Sesseli could register the sound of the opening hatch, he leaped, flashing through the opening like a shooting star. He hit the deck running and was far into the landing bay before the hatch reclosed. No one followed. They wouldn't dare. They might catch the dread disease, or so they thought. Khiindi, knowing the power of Khorii's horn, was sure that the area was cleared of contaminants by then. All he had left to do was to get this ship back into space and away from the likes of Marl Fidd.

He raced out of the docking bay but slowed his pace to an exploratory prowl as he entered the ship's central corridor. Hmmm. This was a supply ship, yes? No good, as it was. No good to anyone without a nice Linyaari girl to purify things, but of incalculable value to someone who had access to such a girl. Now then, what supplies did this ship carry exactly? Spices? Replicator fodder? Tools and building supplies?

The first cabin he came to, he stood on his hind paws and put his front ones against the hatch. It gave easily under the full weight of his body, and he strolled in, then bolted out, wishing he still had the ability to hold his nose. Dead bodies! Oh, dear. Did his throat feel a little scratchy all of a sudden? Was that pain in his middle the beginning of some internal lesion? Were sores erupting under his fur, making his skin twitch? Was it not suddenly most terribly hot? And stuffy. Terribly stuffy. Hadn't these people ever heard of O_2?

How long could he live before needing to seek out Khorii to get healed? He didn't want to find her just yet, or have her find him. He did not wish to be found until it was too late for her to leave the ship.

SIXTEEN

You look surprised, Uncle Hafiz,' Neeva said, as he gaped at the horde of Linyaari crowding like a big white cloud with multiple silver linings into his office in response to his request that the crew of the *Balakiire* visit him. 'Did it slip your mind that we are telepathic?'

'Not that we would eavesdrop, certainly not!' Melireenya protested, grinning without showing her teeth. 'That would not be courteous. But when a friend is distressed over the fate of those beloved by both him and us, we cannot help but overhear.'

'I am overwhelmed at your response,' Hafiz said mildly. Neeva, Melireenya, and Kharii were there, but so were Laarye, Aari's brother, Maati, his sister, her mate Thariinye, Aari's parents, and Acorna's parents, plus assorted friends. Even Liriilyi was present, a poisonous female and undoubtedly the least popular Linyaari alive, she had no doubt come to gloat over the fact that the most popular were missing.

'Since you have all read my mind, apparently'

191

(though he thought it more likely they had heard the news in a more straightforward fashion from young Miikhaye), 'you will be aware that I have been informed that much of Federation space is now under quarantine. Apparently the disease in question has attacked many worlds in many sites and has been particularly hard on the administration and troops of the Federation itself. Their relays are down and so, alas, are those of House Harakamian, though I pray our servants and employees will recover. Now that you have undoubtedly read all of my thoughts and probably my wife's as well on the subject, I would like to hear yours.'

'Obviously Aari, Acorna, and Khorii have been called upon to help cure the stricken,' Neeva said. 'And just as obviously, if the disease is already so widespread, they will be unable to contain it alone.'

'And therefore,' Acorna's father continued, 'we must help.'

'Obviously,' Hafiz said. 'But entrance into Federation territory is forbidden at this time.'

'So we understand,' Laarye said. 'But if the soldiers are all sick, who is going to stop us?'

The midday sun melted across the brilliantly colored spires, cones, and domes of Corazon, the heart of Paloduro and its largest population center. Many of the city's inhabitants were in the streets, but a playful breeze that stirred bright yellow flags at doorways, jewel-toned fluffs of feathers and flimsy gilded masks provided the only movement Aari and Acorna saw. Off to the west, a sluggish river clogged with large chunks of some mysterious material struggled to reach an unseen sea.

Strange contraptions of delicate workmanship and rainbow hues seemed to have been cast adrift amid silent flitters and aircars, and – corpses.

Never in her entire life had Acorna been so thankful for the purifying quality of the Linyaari horn. The putrid stench stewing in the heat of the sun gagged her, and she saw Aari's knees buckle. By the time she held out a steadying hand, though, their horns had filtered the air reaching them, and the stink was more bearable.

Acorna was possessed of a peculiar talent no other Linyaari had ever exhibited. She believed it came from being raised by asteroid miners and learning at an early age which drifting rocks might be profitable to exploit. Over the years, her sense of which minerals an asteroid might contain had developed into a finely honed sense of spatial relationships, so that at times, if she concentrated, she could determine what rooms and spaces – and activity – lay behind otherwise impenetrable walls.

The stillness behind the facade of each and every building they passed was as stifling as the heat, as oppressive as the smell, and as appalling as the vast numbers of bodies strewn through the streets like discarded dolls.

Discarded decaying dolls.

193

'We're too late,' she told Aari. 'There is nobody here to cure.'

'It is a large city, *yaazi*,' he said, using the Linyaarí endearment he applied to both his mate and their daughter. 'Everyone cannot possibly be dead already – can they? We had communication from here only forty-eight hours ago. I had the impression there were many people there, although some were sick. Everyone cannot possibly be dead,' he repeated, trying to convince himself.

'Of course not,' she said. 'We aren't giving up, but we must search farther from the city center. I sense no life in any of these buildings, anywhere.'

He scanned the buildings with a wild and haunted expression on his face. 'What if it is very faint?' he asked. 'What if someone is hanging on to the last thread of life and we are their last hope – when we leave, they will die.'

She laid her horn gently against his, and said, 'I sense no one, *yaazi*. But if such a one exists, we must trust that they will find happiness in their transition. If we search each of these buildings, think how many more may die who are farther away but easier to find.'

He nodded. 'Of course.' Looking at the debris and the bodies, he said, 'A colorful people. What strange dress and customs they had.'

'The plague caught them at the height of their Carnivale season,' she said. 'It is a special celebration during which both people and conveyances are costumed, decorated, and disguised to dance in the streets. It is very crowded and people travel from all over the planet and all over this star system – even some others, to be here for it.'

He looked at her quizzically. A multicolored paper pompom whirled past them like the spores from the puff flower until its tendrils caught in a black pool of something that dragged it down.

The Federation had transmitted an informational vid on the Solojo system for them before they landed. It was an unusual system in that it contained four planets nearly equidistant from their sun, all of them class M, habitable worlds, on which the colonies established many years before had thrived and grown. Whereas Paloduro was the most beautiful of the four planets, the center for tourism and the residential center of the system, another world, Dinero Grande, was the administrative and business center. Rio Boca, the planet most distant of the four from the sun, was the usual entrance and jumping-off point for interstellar traffic. However, no communication had been transmitted from there or Dinero Grande in over a week, whereas Paloduro had sent an urgent mayday only two standard days before the Federation enlisted the *Condor*'s help.

'I researched the archives from the beginning while I was on watch,' she explained. 'From what we know of this disease, some of the younglings and the elders should be left here somewhere. But we cannot possibly search all of this on foot.'

They found an abandoned flitter that activated at once when Aari toggled the switch. Using the point where they had landed as the center, they flew in ever-widening circles over the moribund city. The evidence of the Carnivale disappeared within a few blocks. Several times they saw plumes of smoke from the cinders of buildings or vehicles. Then they came to a broad gash in the green of a park. Inside it were the bodies of hundreds, perhaps thousands, of people, not even covered, simply deposited there for later burial. When the plague was over. Now there would be no one left to haul the dead to this makeshift morgue.

But two streets over they saw what looked like purposeful movement – just the flash of what appeared to be a sleeve that quickly passed into a building.

This area had fewer structures that had the businesslike facade of public buildings.

'This is the residential area,' Acorna said. 'People live here. At least, I hope some of them still do.'

'Ah,' Aari said, nodding. 'Yes. The yellow marks on the doors. Do those mean what I think they do?'

'Yes. A yellow flag was the old sign for quarantine. If you recall, we saw some with intricate symbols flying over several of the buildings. But probably by the time these people started getting sick, whichever agency or individual had been doing the marking couldn't keep up.'

She stood still, closed her eyes, and let her sense of what spaces contained guide her through their surroundings. Opening her eyes suddenly, she said, 'Come, *yaazi*. There is life still inside some of these buildings. We can help.'

Without a second thought, the two tall, white-clad, silvery-maned, and golden-horned beings crossed the thresholds of each entrance marked by yellow paint, flags, plastic ribbon, kerchiefs, or bits of clothing. Such symbols were not for Linyaari healers.

Nanahomea sat on shore long enough to strew sea flowers over the body of Ray Alcalde. 'What were we thinking, letting him off-world on his own like that?' her friend Mokilau asked mournfully.

'He had his duties to do,' Nanahomea said.

'Yes, but we could have had a crisis that kept him here. He wasn't very bright. We might have known he'd get into trouble.'

'He wanted to go home,' Nanahomea said, staring sadly at the flower mound that had been their Federation liaison and so-called governor. They didn't need a governor, of course, since they had been governing themselves quite successfully for more years than the Federation had been federated. In fact, if she wanted to get stuffy about it, Nanahomea was actually the queen, but she was only queen as long as she ruled the way her people wished to be ruled. 'He was from that place, and he missed it. People do miss their homes.'

'Yes,' Mokilau said. 'Our young ones do, too. Leave him to the sky now, Nanahomea.'

A single turn of the tide, and she regretted wasting sorrow on Alcalde, who brought death to her people as nothing had ever done before. Her own beautiful daughter, Haina-kolo, and her daughter's mate Keaunini were among the first to die. They did not lose their food as the man did, but though it took two more tides to finish, they gasped and choked and could not dive. At the last, they could breathe neither air nor water, and drowned. Before their funeral chant was ended, many of the mourners who were their friends sickened as well. In two more tides, three in some cases, they, too, stopped breathing.

'It is a traveling sickness, this,' the ancient healer, Nakulakai, said. 'Raealakaldai brought it with him from the stars and when we brought him into the water, he passed his death to us.'

'Why Haina-kolo, then, and Keaunini who were young and strong?' Nanahomea asked. 'Why not me and Mokilau, who have little time left?'

Nakulakai blew bubbles at her. 'If this death is what I believe, you will be joining them soon. We all will. But we must give Keaunini and Haina-kolo back to the sky along with Raealakaldai and these others, too. When they stay in the water, the death rides the tide from their mouths to the mouths of others.'

Nanahomea knew the sense of this, but insisted that each loved one passing into death should be treated with all of the love the living could send with them. Nanahomea and Mokilau bore the bodies of Keaunini and Haina-kolo to the beach themselves and covered them with flowers plucked from the ocean floor by others. The parents of her children's dead friends bore their own children to the beach and did the same.

But that did not stop the tide of death. The lines of mourners grew sparser and the heaps of the flower-covered dead grew larger until they blanketed the beach near the sand house. The ocean floor was bare of its flowers for as far as the eye could see.

Nakulakai told everyone in Nanahomea's home pod that travel was forbidden, as they would take the death with them to the distant pods. Meanwhile the sickness traveled from them like the ripples on water and for many days they heard reports in the far talk of families sickening and of new bodies on other parts of the crater reef. Nanahomea's old sister Hiilei lived beyond the crater reef with her pod, and Nanahomea sent her a message in the far talk the ocean carried for leagues and leagues, asking after the health of her people and the health of the people near them. At first the news was not so bad, as if the sickness had not reached them or been stopped by the reef, but then the word came, far talked from one pod to the next, that Hiilei's eldest son was sick, and his mate.

Nanahomea was glad that the young ones were not there to see their parents die. How would she get word to her granddaughter, Likilekakua, of the last moments of Keaunini and Haina-kolo? That was when she had the most terrible thought of all, worse than anything that had happened upon LoiLoiKua.

If the Federation officer had brought death to

them, might other Federation officers have spread the same death to other peoples in other places? The Federation men were as many as drops in the ocean and had people everywhere. If others among them had the same sickness as Ray Alcalde, they could take it to Maganos Moonbase, where Likilekakua and the other children lived.

SEVENTEEN

Jaya's grief surprised Khorii a little. People on Vhiliinyar didn't grieve in quite that way, seeing death as a simple transition. It tore at Khorii's heart how hard it was for Jaya to accept her parents' transitions to their next lives. Also, she felt a sneaking suspicion that if something happened to her own parents, even though she knew the acceptable attitude of a Linyaari toward death, she might feel much the same as Jaya did.

And although Jaya seemed to want to grieve by herself, and clearly needed time to adjust to the alterations in her world, to the disappearance of the familiar and the invasion of strangers, it didn't take Khorii's newly developing psychic skills to know that the girl should not be left completely alone.

Standing aside, Khorii returned her attention to the bodies on the deck.

'What are you doing, youngling?' Elviiz asked. 'They are, as you have observed, in a moribund state, beyond your help.'

'I know,' she said, softly, wishing she could adjust his volume control. 'But I need to study them for a moment and try to form an image of what the plague looks like, as opposed to other illnesses, so I may identify it if we encounter it again and take preventive measures. Also, we must purify the bodies so that when they are set to rest they won't spread the disease through the flowers if they're buried, through the smoke if they are cremated, or to some curious passerby if they are spaced.' She pulled the sheet aside from the unknown man on the deck. His eyes were sunken deep in their sockets, the flesh of his cheeks had collapsed inwardly, and his skin was as waxy as the artificial fruit Auntie Karina decorated her private dining quarters with because the real thing rotted or was eaten too quickly.

The smell of the man's illness, and probably his death, was strong upon him as she touched her horn to his face. She was glad now that they had not known about the plague when they'd found the *Blanca*. She had been able to imagine the lives that had inhabited the bodies floating around her without having to look at them, and because of the lack of gravity and low levels of oxygen aboard the *Blanca*, the smell had not been as bad as it was here.

No wonder Captain Becker and the cats had been ill. There had been toxic gas there, as they said, but before the gas, the plague had claimed at least some of those people. Luckily her parents and she had been with the *Condor*'s crew and cats when they were stricken. Otherwise . . .

There were stories among the books and vids on the *Condor* that treated the dead as frightening or malevolent. She could not understand this. The body she touched with her horn was solid to her touch, much more substantial than a hologram of a person, for instance, and yet, also much emptier somehow. There was simply nothing there any longer. No one at home.

Khorii arose feeling a bit dizzy, the spots that swirled and vanished adding to her sense of vertigo. It was almost as if she had been leaning over an unfathomably deep hole and was in danger of falling in herself if she lingered too long on the edge.

She told Elviiz, 'Let's notify Maganos Moonbase of our location and that we're decontaminating the ship and – er – personnel so the *Mana* can dock. I wonder if Mr Al y Cassidro had considered that the ship could crash into one of the school's bubbles, which would also be bad for everyone's health.'

'It would kill everyone,' Elviiz corrected her.

'Yes,' she said. 'Definitely unhealthy.'

Elviiz did as she said. Shoshisha had taken over com off duty and did not look very happy about it.

'What are you doing on the com screen, Elviiz?' she demanded, ignoring the information he had automatically imparted when he hailed the Moonbase.

'Communicating with Maganos Moonbase, obviously,' he said.

'So – you guys are up there on that supply ship, right?'

Khorii interrupted. It was rude, but Shoshisha was being curious and not helpful. 'Shoshisha, Khorii here.'

'Oh, really? I thought it was some other student with a horn in the middle of her head.'

'Is there another one?' Elviiz asked. 'I do not believe there is.'

'No, Elviiz. There is not. Shoshisha is being facetious. Shoshisha, we need to speak to the teacher in charge on this shift.'

'I'll bet you do. That would be Calla. Just a nan.'

It was a bit longer than a nanosecond before Calla Kaczmarek appeared in the com screen, but she was out of breath and red in the face, so she had been hurrying.

'Khorii, Elviiz, where are you? Have you seen Hap or Sesseli? We've been looking all over for you kids.'

'That's why I'm calling, Calla. We are aboard the *Mana* with Jaya.'

'All of you?'

'Yes, we took the shuttle. Elviiz and I were going to come alone, but Sesseli and Hap insisted on accompanying us.'

'Oh, no! That's terrible. Khorii, you know you can't return now, don't you? Not until the quarantine is over.'

'I don't see why not. Elviiz and I are capable of

decontaminating the ship so the Moonbase can use the supplies it brought, and Jaya is fine now, except that she grieves for her parents. Mr Taj died before we arrived. But no one is sick now, and no one will get sick as long as we are here to prevent it.'

'Your self-confidence is admirable, dear, but it isn't enough of a guarantee to risk the entire student body if you're wrong.'

'Found them!' Shoshisha's voice piped up behind Calla, and in the viewscreen Khorii saw Asha Bates and Phador Al y Cassidro. Someone else was back there, too; she sensed him but didn't see him.

'I am not wrong,' Khorii said. 'You know my mother can heal and purify – so does the Federation, which is why my parents went to that other planet. My father has the same skills. So do I. It is not a matter of age with us. I can do what I say I can, Calla. I would not boast in such serious circumstances.'

Jaya suddenly came to life. 'It's true, ma'am! I was sick, too, and she did something to me and I'm not anymore. If your stupid boss had sent her to begin with, my dad might still be alive, too.'

'I'm very sorry for your loss, dear, but casting blame does no good. You simply cannot land here. I know you, Khorii, are certain that your special methods can make the ship safe, but what if you *are* wrong? This is not just any disease. If other students became ill . . .'

'Then we'd heal them. We could heal all of you with no problem,' Khorii said.

205

But Calla was shaking her head. 'You'll just have to sit it out up there, dear. Quite aside from breaking the Federation's rules, despite your assurances we cannot risk infecting the other students with the plague. I'll send messages to the Federation and anyone else I can reach to relay to your parents the facts of your situation, but that's all I can do for now. I'm terribly, terribly sorry.'

'But can we not at least land?' Khorii asked. 'No one would need to come near us until you were convinced that we are not sick or carrying any disease, but even though the ship has plenty of fuel at present and the requirements for maintaining orbit are not high, eventually it will run out. It might even crash into the bubbles, then everyone would be dead.'

'We'll simply have to hope that the Federation finds a cure for this soon and lifts the quarantine,' Calla said, shaking her head. 'When you first docked on Maganos, you came from a clean vessel that had not yet been exposed to the plague. That's no longer the case. You must all remain aboard until the quarantine is lifted or the ship can be tested and we have clearance from the Federation.'

Khorii almost told her how wrong she was – that she had been exposed to the plague before she even got there. But that would be telling a secret that was Uncle Joh's. He had been so right about not trying to do anything about the dead people on the *Blanca*. She'd apologize to him as soon as she saw him again.

* * *

'Stupid fraggin' bureaucrats! Darn suckers are gonna kill us all,' Hap said, overhearing the transmissions between the *Mana* and Moonbase.

Sesseli patted his shoulder, and said, 'It's okay, Hap. But one thing's for sure. We can't just stay in the shuttle all the time. Let's go find Khiindi and Khorii and Elviiz.'

'Okay,' he said. 'But we might get sick, too.'

She said, 'If we do, Khorii will fix us like she said, like she fixed Khiindi.'

He smiled at her certainty. Little kids. Even one who had been through what Sesseli had suffered still believed everything would be fine and someone would save them. He'd thought that, too, at one time. He'd thought Maganos Moonbase was his salvation. Think again.

It was okay for him. He was used to it by now and had learned to take care of himself. But Sesseli was just a child. It wasn't fair to leave her on her own like this.

She was right though. The two of them couldn't stay inside the shuttle indefinitely. He hailed the *Mana*'s bridge. 'Khorii, don't forget Sesseli and me. Let us know when you've cleaned the place up enough that we can come out.'

Elviiz appeared in the screen. 'Decontamination of the landing bay and corridors up to the bridge has been completed, Hap. You and Sesseli may join us if you wish, but it will not be pleasant. There are dead crew members here, and the one survivor is rather upset.'

207

In the background he heard Khorii speaking soothingly while another girl ranted.

Hap turned to Sesseli. 'You better wait here till I come and get you, Squirt. We'll get the bodies moved from the bridge.'

Sesseli put her hands on what would someday be her hips, and said disparagingly, 'Really, Hap, I can handle it. Almost everyone in my colony got killed before the Federation came to help us. Besides, I'm worried about Khiindi.'

EIGHTEEN

Khiindi was getting worried about himself. He didn't feel at all well. It was probably all that talk of illness. He had never actually been ill before, but then, he'd never been slung into a pool – well, almost into the pool – by his tail before either. Much as he liked novelty, all new experiences were not necessarily good just because they were new. The truth was, being frozen in this one shape all the time made him less inclined to accept change in other ways, too. Not that anyone sane would like being flung by their tail, but he found it all too easy to degenerate into a purry, lap-sitting, nip-sniffing, kibble-vacuuming, common pussycat, and that alarmed him. Still, his personal philosophy aside, he couldn't see any upside to being ill.

He found a cargo bay and hopped up onto the topmost container for a contemplative scratch and wash. He needed to scratch far more than usual. His left ear really itched, and something bit him near the base of his tail. Fleas? They had fleas on this tub? He hadn't seen a flea since way back before he became Khiindi, while traveling to the more rustic agro colonies. Back then, for the most part, he'd had no fur to infest and did have opposable thumbs capable of wielding antidotes to the nasty bugs.

But now it seemed that as soon as he got one spot quieted, another two itches flared up on other parts of his body. He scratched and bit himself in first one place, then another, until the blood seeped through his fur, but that didn't help anything. What would help was a horn touch, but those among his kind who felt he was so self-centered that he would consider personal comfort above explorations possibly beneficial to the good of all mistook his inherently noble nature.

Besides, there might be something tasty back here that Linyaari and humans would overlook because it chiefly concerned cats.

Not that he had his usual healthy appetite, of course, as poor as he was feeling. But he would need to keep up his strength, no matter the sacrifice involved or his personal feelings on the matter.

He tried stalking stealthily through the labyrinth of containers but had to keep stopping to scratch. And suddenly, with his foot in midair after a swipe at the patch behind his left ear, he heard his scratch being echoed. An echo of a scratch? That was a new one, surely.

'Someone's out there.'

'Of course someone's out there. Someone has to fly

the bloody ship, don't they? Unless you've grown opposable thumbs recently.'

'I don't mean one of those. I mean someone on four feet. Our sort of feet unless I miss my guess.'

'Are you sure it isn't the quarry?'

'Oh, yes, of course I'm sure it isn't the quarry. I can see through these big opaque containers, can't I? How should I know!'

'Just asking,' the other voice said, making itself small.

'Mmyow?' Khiindi inquired. And since the rest of the dialogue was, as best he could tell, conducted by thought transference, he used that mode to ask, *'Who's there?'*

'Vermin Eradication Specialists,' replied the loudest and most mature of the voices. *'This is our patch, you know. You're intruding. Move along now.'*

'Where are you?' Khiindi asked, looking around. Were his eyes growing dim? There was very little ambient light in the storage hold – only a faint glow tube around the perimeter of the bulkhead. But as he rounded the edge of a container the light was sufficient to glitter off three sets of coin-bright eyes. Between him and the eyes were crude bars. These belonged, it seemed, to the ordinary sort of cats. It did not surprise Khiindi that he understood their language, as he had been, in his time, widely traveled, and although his ability to change forms had vanished, his knowledge of languages and customs had not. Also, quite possibly these cats were not as ordinary as they seemed. Khiindi had sired many offspring throughout time and in

211

many galaxies. Some resembled one form and some another, but the most common shape was felinoid. These could therefore be distant descendants of his own, but they wouldn't realize that, and he did not feel it prudent to treat them as anything but common house cats. Or ship cats, in this case. He had, after all, been rather generous with his – uh – affections – and being related to him did not necessarily recommend them as creatures worth cultivating though they would, of course, be superior to creatures who were not of his line. *'Oh, yes, of course, you're incarcerated for the journey,'* he said, with an approving glance at the bars partially concealing their faces. *'You would be. Mustn't have animals running loose on shipboard, or they make an awful mess like that beast aboard Becker's* Condor *. . .'*

'What is he talking about, mammy? It doesn't make any sense,' said the smallest voice.

'Naturally not, child. He's an unstabilized male. Can't you smell him? You have to watch out for his sort. Nothing on their so-called minds but rape and murder.'

The kitten's voice reflected the natural bloodthirstiness of the young. *'Really, mammy? Why does he do that? What's unstabilized mean?'*

'It means he has not had his hormone balance surgically adjusted, as we all have had.' Khiindi saw her tail lashing in the dark like some kind of a whisk broom sweeping back and forth as she paced the front of the cage. *'His kind can think of nothing but sex and lives only to kill little kittens like yourself to*

force their mothers to go into heat again so he can have his way with them and make more kittens, which he would not scruple to kill any more than he would you.'

'I assure you, madame, that although I am, as you say, unaltered, I have no designs on you or your adorable offspring,' Khiindi said in his smarmiest tone. You had to be gentle with beasts such as these – they were only cats, without his superior knowledge or experience. It wasn't their fault they were mere beasts, but to Khiindi that fact made them far less stable and their reactions more volatile than the female supposed his own to be. *'I am Khiindi, and I have worn many guises before donning this cat form for the duration of this life. You are in very grave danger, though not from me. A plague has overtaken the humans – your humans.'*

'These people are nothing to us,' a male voice said, *'and we are only cargo to them. They have not brought us food for weeeeks.'*

By this he knew he meant weeks in terms of feline feeding schedule, which meant they had probably missed two feeding sessions at most. Inflation of the times between food was an ingrained feline cultural characteristic, a survival mechanism to ensure that if a steady supply of food was not received according to schedule, those responsible would be shamed into correcting their dereliction of duty at once. Khiindi had heard Uncle Hafiz Harakamian and Captain Becker discussing this topic once, with the comment that cats would make excellent bill collectors, if only the language barrier could be overcome.

213

'Perhaps, but they were the ones flying the spacecraft and if they cease to do so, none of us will be in very good shape,' Khiindi told him. 'I will help you as best I can.'

'Very good of you, I'm sure,' the male said jovially, but the female spat and hissed.

The kitten said, 'I'm called Kali. If you aren't going to kill me, would you like to play? I'd very much like to have a go at your tail.'

'That's only because yours isn't long enough to play with yet,' Khiindi told her kindly. 'And some other time, I'd be delighted to accommodate you, little one. But we are all in danger now. And the truth is, I don't feel very well. I could do with a little therapeutic grooming, actually.' He heard himself mewing quite plaintively. He pressed himself against the bars and the kitten stuck her muzzle through and went to work on his right ear.

'Get away from him, Kali, he's probably infested with those itchy things,' the belligerent queen said.

'Yes, madame, I am,' Khiindi admitted reluctantly. 'But surely you all are similarly beleaguered?'

'We are not, and it is my belief that it is my enforcement of good hygienic practices on the family that has kept us safe from them. Oh, they tried nibbling at us, but they were quickly discouraged and disappeared.'

'He's crawling with them,' Kali informed her mother with ghoulish satisfaction. 'I expect if we don't pick them off him and kill them, they'll eat him all up. Maybe not his tail, but everything else.'

'I don't think they eat anything up,' Khiindi said, moving away from the bars to preserve his dignity, then ruining it by having to scratch

214

compulsively at his left ear while biting the base of his tail on the other side. He found it hard to work up the necessary vigor, however. His limbs felt heavy, his breath came with difficulty. Even his nose felt sweaty. Also, the figures of the other cats behind their bars were less distinct than they had been. His third eyelid, the nictitating membrane that covered his eye from the inner corner to the middle, had spread across his vision as it did when there was too much light or he was otherwise indisposed. *'But they make you very sick – they are making me very sick – and I hear many have died already.'*

'Poor hygiene,' the female said smugly. *'You're speaking of the two-legged sort, are you not? You know they never wash, don't you? I've never seen one grooming himself. I don't suppose that bothers an unstable male like you though.'*

'You have no idea to whom you are speaking, my dear – uh – puss. Although I am indeed endowed with rather splendid reproductive equipment, I am, far from being unstable, as you put it, the most stable I have been in far more years than you have seen in all of your lives put together. And I can tell you for a fact, stability is highly overrated.'

'So is your opinion of yourself,' she said, with a flick of her tail.

Hmm, perhaps the lady was protesting too much? That would be it of course. The mere sight of his own magnificent physique was enough to send any female of the appropriate species into heat. He kept forgetting the effect he had on the

215

fair sex, having weightier matters to occupy his intellect. Poor puss. She'll just have to wait. He scratched again. Why didn't the vermin leave him and go to the others, where they could, if the reputation of these cats was truthful, be eradicated?

'You lot don't seem to be bothered by these space fleas. What did you use?'

'Stabilization,' the female said. *'It protects us from a variety of ills, including this one. Unfortunately for you, the crew member in charge of stabilization and other procedures pertaining to the health of the four-legged crew members was among the first to die. She neglected to stabilize herself, it seems. So you, too, will be dying soon.'*

'Nooooo!' he yowled.

'Khiindi!' a voice called from far away, 'Where are you, Khiindi? Here, kitty, kitty.'

He tried to arise from where he'd been sitting and run back the way he'd come, but found he could no longer move. It was as if someone were lying on his face and upper torso now – he couldn't seem to get his breath. He yowled again but could barely hear himself.

'Help me!' he told the others.

'Why should we?' the female said. *'There's not enough food left for us, much less an unwelcome stranger.'*

'Food . . .' he told her, though it was difficult to focus his thoughts enough to make a clever answer. *'My people will bring food. Enough for all of us. Fishes . . .'*

The caterwauling of starved, neglected, and mistreated cats filled the cargo hold, spilling into the corridors beyond.

The last thing Khiindi heard was his own pitiful mew.

NINETEEN

Across the street from the building where Aari and Acorna stood, a curtain twitched in an upstairs window. Acorna caught the movement in her peripheral vision and immediately felt the shifting of the space in that building. 'Wait,' she told Aari. 'Someone is coming.'

The someone was a small, hunched woman, who walked with a slight lurch and regarded them through squinted eyes, her mouth screwed up in concentration.

'What exactly are *you*?' she asked them.

'We are Linyaari – a race of healers,' Acorna explained. 'We've come to help you.'

'We have a lot in common then,' the woman said. 'I am Luz Allende, but everyone calls me Abuelita. I am a curandera. Not a curo, not like these modern ones. I use old things because I *am* an old thing. But this is good. I am alive and the young curos are not, so evidently my medicine works better on this sickness.'

'What is it that you've used successfully?' Aari asked.

She shrugged. 'Symptomatic stuff. Heat for comfort, cold for swelling, blankets, food when they can take it, liquids always, flam-go for fever, sit them up when they cannot breathe. That sort of thing.'

'And it works?'

'More often than anything else. And more often on people my age and the children. The others – well, they were mostly too gone by the time I reached them. The younger curos, too. The Federation health teams and epidemiology people, the hazmat teams, all are gone. It is said that many of them died also, in spite of their precautions. I do not know who would wish such a disaster upon us, but it is better for you if you go.' The old woman's voice was cracked and broken, but matter of fact.

'We have special protection,' Acorna told her. 'We have come from many galaxies away to help, and we will. Can you take us to those who are still alive?'

'Oh yes, I can do that. First we will find my grandson. He is with many other young people, playing a game. I hope they are all still there. Our holas – communicators – no longer work, so I have not been able to reach him. But I know where it is. I will take you there.'

They walked to the gymnasium where the woman knew her grandson to be. It was good that they walked, because as they passed each street, doors opened and youngsters came out to join them, sometimes assisting older people, sometimes carrying infants or toddlers.

They were all very frightened, and it seemed to Acorna that the older the children were, the more likely they were to be sick. She and Aari promptly treated everyone showing any symptoms at all and decontaminated the others so that they would not get sick. All of this was done with the aid, they said, of Linyaari medical nanotechnology. The people they treated were so ill, frightened, shocked, or grief-stricken that they probably could have pierced each person with their horn tips and claimed that cured them without causing a stir or having anyone take notice of it.

'We have no data whatever about the possibility of someone being reinfected once they have been cured of the plague. Nor do we know how well disinfecting will correct their prior exposure,' Acorna told Abuelita, which simply meant 'grandmother.'

The older woman shrugged. 'Time will tell.'

By the time the three of them reached the building where Abuelita's grandson Jalonzo was supposed to be playing in a gaming tournament, the crowd following behind them had swelled to hundreds of people. Each of these had been touched by either Acorna or Aari but no one had seemed inclined to go home.

Abuelita took a last look at them. 'I believe they now look to you to feed them, as well as heal them. These are not, you understand, the vigorous and self-sufficient. All are either too old or too young to care for themselves. Something must be arranged. Have you been in touch with the government? Will they send help? At least someone to carry away the bodies and cleanse the homes so that the people will have shelter?'

'We saw no living person until we met you,' Aari told her. 'And we lost contact with the communications center before we landed – the officers in charge did not sound well at the time.'

Approaching the gymnasium, they saw a delivery flitter moored in front of the building. A black cloud hung between it and the door. As they moved closer, they saw that it consisted of thousands of insects buzzing around the swollen corpse of a man whose shirt proclaimed MUCHO NACHO.

'Aiyee,' Abuelita said, shaking her head and almost surreptitiously making the sign of a cross in the air with her fingers. This was the remnant of an ancient religion, as the profile of Paloduro explained in the section on local customs.

Pushing past them, Aari knelt beside the fallen man and discreetly touched his horn to the man's body, dispelling the flies and the odor of death, though not, of course, reviving the corpse.

'You can no longer help him, my son,' Abuelita told him.

'So I see,' he said. 'But we know so little about this disease, I felt I must just make sure. I've cleansed the body of the infection at least, so that our friends there' – he nodded to the masses in the street – 'may pass without harm.'

221

'Bueno,' she said. She squared her shoulders and stepped around the corpse and up to the door, pulling on the handle. But it did not open.

She rapped sharply on the plasglas and peered inside. 'You, chico, open this door!'

Inside, some distance up the hallway, a boy trembled and shook his head.

Abuelita looked as if she would try to kick in the door, but instead she backed away and yelled, frustrated, 'Jalonzo Allende, you open this door right now!'

With a deep sigh she turned back to Aari and Acorna, who did not look at her, but stared steadily at the door, reinforcing her command by sending a mental message to the boys inside. Before Abuelita looked to the door again, it was being opened by a very tall, very large, dark-haired boy.

'Abuelita! How did you know? You're just in time. Some of the older kids are really sick.'

He saw Aari and Acorna then and stared curiously at the crowd behind them. 'Who are they? Neat costumes! I'm sorry, but the tournament is about over so if you've come to play . . .'

'The time for play has ended, Grandson. These people are healers from another world.'

'Take us to your stricken,' Aari said.

What kind of people are those?' Jaya demanded angrily. 'Because you came to try to help us, they are going to make you stay here, too? That's not fair!'

Khorii was a little relieved that the girl's anger

222

was now aimed at Calla and the Moonbase instead of at her and Elviiz. 'I know. It isn't reasonable. They do *know* we can make the ship safe to land. My mother has done that sort of thing lots of times, and it's her fathers who run the Moonbase.'

'There is the quarantine, however,' Elviiz said. 'There are rules.'

'They should be applied sensibly,' Khorii said. She sighed. 'I think all of these people must be distantly related to Liriilyi. They put rules and caution over good sense and the proof they already have of our skills. This is dangerous and silly, and a waste of time when there are dying people that we could help.'

'Yes, it lacks perceptive analyses given the data; however, it is not as silly as suggesting that the teachers are related to Liriilyi. They are human, and she is Linyaari. Our species cannot mate, and therefore cannot be related by blood. She might be an adopted relative, such as those in our family through Mother. But Liriilyi does not care to meet humans when given a chance, so that is also unlikely.'

Khorii rolled her eyes. 'Yes, Elviiz, and that speech was ample chastisement for my little joke.'

'Oh,' he said, and lifted the corners of his mouth, then let them drop.

The com unit was switched off now, and she felt isolated and frustrated by the stupidity of others. These were the people who were supposed to be taking care of her and were too frightened to realize that in this situation, she was the one who could take care of everyone. Well, most of them anyway, under all of the circumstances she had seen so far. Why would otherwise intelligent people choose blindly to follow dumb regulations that should be suspended in this case?

But before Khorii could discuss it any further with Elviiz or Jaya or hail the Moonbase again to try to convince Calla she was right, she heard Sesseli calling her from far back in the corridor. 'Khorii! Khorii, you have to help poor Khiindi!'

The little girl ran forward and grabbed Khorii's hand, tugging it for a while before running back to Hap, who was cradling a limp and drooling Khiindi in the crook of one arm and holding a cage containing three more cats in his other hand. Sesseli tugged a handful of Hap's tunic, as if that would pull him to Khorii faster.

Khiindi was indeed a sorry-looking little beast. For the second time within a few hours, he seemed at death's door. Gently, Khorii scooped him up and buried her face in the soft hot fur of his panting side, burrowing her horn into the nape of his neck. She could almost see – could see – hundreds of small organisms deserting his body. They fled to Hap, who set down the cage of cats to scratch.

Khiindi looked up and Hap sat down, hard, on the deck. Bending to help him up, Khorii brushed his hair with her horn and the organisms fled again. That was very odd. These microscopic attackers were not large enough for her to see, they did not attack her so that she could feel them, but she nonetheless had a sense of them deserting Hap,

224

then being – well, indecisive, if such tiny things could make decisions. They seemed trapped, unable to invade the other cats, or Sesseli, unable to transfer to Jaya or Elviiz. They shimmered in the air for a moment, then, as Khorii lifted her head, they disappeared. When they were alone, she'd have to talk to Elviiz about it. Maybe there was something in his data banks about similar phenomena.

It was interesting, though, that the organisms did not wish to attack Sesseli, Elviiz, Jaya, or the other cats. If her – well, vision, she supposed it could be called – psychic insight perhaps? – proved reliable, it might help her discover something about who was immune to the plague and how it spread.

Elviiz carried Jaya's parents and the other stricken crew members to the room containing the first two victims. Hap offered to help, but although Khorii thought that probably would be safe enough, Elviiz was less susceptible and much stronger.

Instead, Hap manned the helm while Jaya took her on a tour of the ship, so that she could cleanse it of the taint of disease. And also, as Sesseli reminded her, find cat food for the four feline crew members, two of whom were in Sesseli's lap as she sat on the deck. The kitten stood on her shoulder. Khiindi paced back and forth across the console, 'assisting' Hap.

Although the ship was a good size, it was not very complex. The engine room was quite straightforward and the drives built for reliability and a modicum of speed so that the ship could make its rounds efficiently. The crew quarters were neither spartan nor luxurious, the cabins situated near the various duty stations rather than in a block. The cabins for the engineers were adjacent to the engine room, those for the captain and first mate and their daughter near the bridge, and so forth. The seven people aboard the ship when it hailed the Moonbase were the only ones required to run it. The vast majority of the vessel was taken up by a cavernous, warehouselike cargo hold that also contained three tractorlike machines used, Jaya told her, for loading, lifting, and positioning the cargo containers.

'First we should see how the other animals are doing,' Jaya told her.

'There are others? Besides the cats?'

'Oh yes, we transport livestock, companion animals, service animals, and breeding stock from time to time as well as foodstuffs, building materials, tools, machinery, and whatever else the various worlds cannot or do not manufacture themselves,' Jaya told her with some pride. 'They are always very glad to see us.'

'I can imagine. I don't know how the Moonbase plans to get along without your supplies. That worries me more than our own situation right now. Food supplies there are extremely low, and who knows how long this plague will last? Speaking of which, have you a 'ponics garden or some seeds and soil where I might start one? If we're going to be on your ship for a while, I would like to be able to grow my own food. My people are vegetarian and grazers.'

While Jaya located the supplies Khorii would need, Khorii, under the guise of curiosity, poked her head and horn into everything she could reach as she went about the work of cleaning the hold and its cargo of contamination.

'What are you doing?' Jaya asked, descending from the lifter, at the foot of which was a neat stack of various seed sacks, fertilizers, and other gardening supplies.

'Decontaminating the ship,' she said.

'I heard you say you could do that, and I wondered what you meant exactly,' Jaya said. 'How do you know how to do that?'

'How do you know how to run that equipment?' she asked in return. 'It's what my people do.'

'What? Be like some sort of sentient two-legged Lysol?'

'What's Lysol?'

'It decontaminates things, too,' Jaya replied. 'And stinks to high heaven – not that you do because, you know, you don't. You smell good, actually.'

'Thank you,' Khorii said, sincerely appreciating the compliment from the so far rather thorny girl. 'You do not stink, either.'

Jaya grimaced. 'Thanks. So, do you ever think you might want to do something else? I mean, something your people don't do?'

'I do not understand. My people do many things. Do yours not?'

227

'Well, sure. Hobbies, like. Or at least, things that didn't turn out to be what they did for a living. Mom was a scholar before she met Dad. And Dad had wanted to play nine-dimensional chess professionally but when my grandpa died, he took over the business instead. He still plays though—' Her voice shrank to a whisper as she corrected herself. 'Played.'

Khorii, who had continued prowling the containers as they talked, turned back to Jaya and reached out her hand. 'I am so sorry.'

Jaya blinked hard. 'Me, too. Me, too. It's still not real, you know? And – I'm sorry if I made it sound like it was your fault for not being faster. I mean, I know it takes a certain amount of time to get someplace, I just . . . well, I'm sorry, okay?'

'Of course.' She cast around for something else to talk about. Grief was not an emotion familiar to her, and seeing Jaya's made her feel helpless. It was good to know that her own mother and father were saving other parents so their children would not be left alone like Jaya. Like most of the kids on the Moonbase. 'Do you know what you will do now? I mean, after the plague is over? Will you continue working for the Krishna-Murti Company or is there something else you'd like to do?'

'I'm a musician,' she said, sounding as if she were trying on the term for the first time. 'I would like to work at that. Maybe go to school for it.'

'Do you – play an instrument?'

'Yes, sitar sometimes and drum, but also I sing and dance. I learned the traditional dances from the vids Mom brought for studying cultural history. She says I am very good. Said.' Again, the reluctant correction.

'Maybe you would show us sometime? I know this is not a good time now, but perhaps while we are waiting for the quarantine to lift?'

'No, I would like to do it. I would do it in my mom and dad's honor.'

'I understand that my people also sing when someone leaves this life.'

'If you know the songs, I think my parents would like that too . . .'

'I do not know them, but Elviiz does. I will have him teach me. He sings very badly.'

'Which one is Elviiz? The cute white-haired boy with the cats and the little girl or the one with the funny screw-looking horn?'

'The one with the horn. Elviiz is my foster brother, made by his father to be my companion. His father is a very good friend of my parents.'

'Oh? I thought he was a droid.'

'He is, and so is his father. That is why Elviiz did not need to have a mother. But he considers my mother to be his parent as well. He lives with us instead of with his father Maak, so his own father is more like an uncle to him, whereas my father is like his own.'

'They must have more advanced droid technology where you come from,' Jaya said. 'Nobody I know would ever consider a droid to be a relative, like a real person.'

'Elviiz is a real person. He simply has some

electronic and mechanical components in his physical and intellectual makeup. At times his extensive knowledge is very annoying, but at others I confess it is helpful.'

'How about the white-haired boy?'

'That is Hap Hellstrom. He has befriended us since we arrived at Maganos Moonbase. He is not an android, but he is a highly intelligent boy and seems to have many practical skills as well.'

'Good,' Jaya said simply. 'Because I have a feeling we'll need all the help we can get.'

TWENTY

Ordinarily, mutiny was not an option that Asha Bates would consider, but since the people in command on Maganos weren't using their heads, she had no choice. They might not mind being responsible for the deaths of two students, two guests, and an orphaned supply ship crew member, but she refused to sit back and do nothing.

Not that she said anything to anyone about the situation or her plans. Asha had kept her background quiet during her stay on the moonbase, but unlike the others she had not been a slave all of her childhood. When she was six years old, she and her mother had been captured by slavers following the fall of their home city. On the way out of their system, the transport ship carrying them had been hijacked by renegades, former Federation space corps troops turned free enterprise traders – pirates, to be honest. Her mother, who had worked as an entertainer in various bars and clubs, and who could be very convincing to a certain type of

231

man, made sure that the first mate of the pirate ship took a shine to her. As a result, she and Asha joined the crew, and Asha was brought up in the trade. The members of her new family were very successful in their endeavors, and Asha spent several years learning anything anyone would teach her, from spaceship piloting to circumventing security systems to seduction and the art of the con.

Her stepfather's commander was a prudent and wily character. He kept enough military discipline in effect among his crew to ensure that everyone stayed in line and believed in the doctrine of honor among thieves, so that by the time Asha was in her teens, the crew had accumulated enough wealth that they were all able to retire without having ever been arrested. Asha didn't much care for her stepfather, a man named Yan Gron, but he taught her many useful skills. When she expressed a desire to go to the Federation Academy, wanting to do something more with her life than fall back into the legacy of piracy, he saw to it that she was supplied with doctored files that qualified her to attend. Later, she had become an instructor at the academy, but hated all the suffocating regulations. Maganos Moonbase was much more to her taste, allowing her the freedom to accomplish the training that she thought the students needed for the harsh regimen of living and working in space. And if that training bypassed a few dozen of the Federation's rules, then so be it.

But even here, she found herself thinking less of

the Federation quarantine and the head mistress's edict than of one of her stepfather's favorite sayings, 'It's easier to ask pardon than to ask permission.'

She had her own shuttle under a tarp in the maintenance hangar. It didn't need any repairs but was stowed away for the time being. Two hours after Calla had reluctantly informed the kids on the *Mana* that they were on their own until quarantine had lifted, Asha had her shuttle fueled and ready to launch. Having finished her preflight checklist, she was about to board when she realized she was not alone amid the previously deserted docking bays.

'Going somewhere, Captain?'

She turned to see Marl Fidd leaning against the doorway, his head at a tilt, eyes narrowed, watching her.

'Not really. Just getting her ready since there's no one out here. Shouldn't you be in class?'

'Yeah. But this is my practical navigation period. You're the instructor, remember?'

Asha shook her head in disgust. Damn, she had forgotten about it in her rush to get out to the supply ship. 'With everything that's happened recently, it completely slipped my mind, Marl. Give my apologies to the other students and tell them I'll be there in a few minutes.'

'I don't think so, Captain,' Marl said, with a mocking note in his voice.

'What was that?' she asked, with a hint of warning in her own.

'I don't think you're going to class. I think you're heading out to that ship. You believe them, don't you? That the alien and the android can purify our supplies and make them safe, then return without bringing the plague with them.'

She turned and met his gaze, then slowly lifted an inquiring eyebrow, challenging him.

'Because,' Marl continued, managing not to gulp under her hard-eyed stare. 'Because I do. I've seen it. The alien kid – Khorii – she healed my arm right up. She said it was the poultice she used, but Singh tried it later on some little kid who hurt his knee, and it didn't do a damn thing. I've heard the stories about her old lady, too – that she can also do that healing thing. Besides, I saw that transmission – yeah, I know the kids weren't supposed to, but I hacked in – wouldn't want to miss something important just because somebody decided not to consult me for my "own good." None of those kids is sick, are they? I think as long as we stick with Khorii, we're fine. I also think we don't have enough supplies to get us through more than a week, even with pretty strict rationing which, you know, isn't much fun. So what I think, Captain, is that you think the same thing, and you're going to go up there and bring the ship down. Aren't you?'

Asha didn't know this kid very well at all, but she knew his type even before he opened his mouth. Marl was very much like the crewmen she had grown up around. She had no qualms about lying straight to his face, and she was sure he

234

would have no qualms about doing the same if telling the truth had proved at all inconvenient, which, in this case, it hadn't. Even as she tried to persuade him that she had no intention of doing what he had just said, she had to respect him putting it all together so fast.

'Why, no, Marl. *That* would be disobeying orders, and I would never do something like that. I'm a teacher, after all.'

'Yeah. So when do we leave?' He held up his hand, 'And don't bother telling me again that you're not. You can't kid a kidder, Cap.'

'That's Captain Bates to you. And you're not just a kidder, Marl, you're well on your way to becoming a junior criminal. You assaulted Khorii's cat, fought with Elviiz, and lied about what happened. If I *were* going up there, you certainly wouldn't be welcome.'

'Hey, gimme a break. Haven't you heard? I'm an impressionable youth traumatized by being orphaned and left all on my lonesome. A guy can change, you know. Besides, the fight with the droid was pretty one-sided. I may not make top grades, Cap – Captain Bates, but that doesn't mean I'm stupid. I just want to be on the winning side, that's all. And I figure that's where you're going. You keep feeding me this line of exhaust fumes, and I'll just have to go get my speculation validated by other authority figures, if you know what I mean?'

She sighed, but actually, this was the first real indication Marl had shown that he was not, in fact, anything other than sullen and stupid. And if he was with her, then she could keep an eye on him rather than worrying about what he might be doing unsupervised around the moonbase. Besides, even if he tried to cause trouble up there, she had no doubt that Elviiz and Hap Hellstrom could restrain him if she herself could not.

Asha pinned him with her most forbidding stare. 'Okay, then, get on board. And no funny business; I'll be keeping my eye on you the entire time. Let's cut the chatter, shall we, before we have the entire student body joining us for a field trip.'

Hap's voice boomed through the intercom and echoed through the cargo hold. 'Looks like we've got company, Khorii. How is the decontamination coming?'

'Fine, Hap. I believe we're clean now. Who's coming? A Federation inspection team?'

'No, it looks like a ship from the school. They've kept radio silence so far, but I happened to look at the screen and see them,' Hap said. 'I've opened a channel and hailed them, but so far no – oh, wait, now they're responding.'

'Correction,' Elviiz said. 'They are not merely responding, they are docking.'

'Who is it?' Khorii and Jaya asked together, Jaya sounding territorial. She was the de facto captain of the ship, after all. Even if she was a child, the set of her small jaw told Khorii that Jaya thought someone should have asked her permission to board.

'Dunno,' Hap said. 'They've not turned on the visuals. Just a sec. I'll patch it through.'

'This is Captain Asha Bates aboard the shuttle *Nakomas* en route to the *Mana*. Permission to dock?'

'What is *she* doing here?' Hap wondered.

Khorii told Jaya, 'She's the practical astrophysics teacher.'

Jaya nodded, and said aloud, 'Permission granted.'

'Okay, *Mana*, prepare to be boarded.'

'Prepare to be boarded?' Jaya asked. 'Sounds like freebooters.'

Hap was laughing. 'No, that's just Captain Bates. She talks like that sometimes. Captain, this is Hap. Haven't you heard we're supposed to be space lepers?'

'I heard. But I did think you might find some small use for my skills. And it seemed like more fun than being trapped in a classroom for what might be the rest of my life. Situations like this, a person has to decide which way to jump. What can I say? I've always been a sucker for the out group. So do you open the docking bay, or is there a secret code word? Ah! Thanks.'

Jaya and Khorii returned to the central corridor, where they were joined by Hap and Sesseli, the latter clutching Khiindi to her thin chest.

In the docking bay, a slim figure emerged from the *Nakomas*. 'Captain Bates!' Hap said. 'If anyone at Maganos would listen to reason, I should have known it would be you.' Then, seeing the second person climbing out behind the teacher, Hap scowled, and demanded, 'What's *he* doing here?'

'Nice to see you too, Happy,' Marl Fidd said, grinning in pure self-satisfaction.

Khiindi hissed, and Sesseli screeched as the cat laid bloody tracks across her arms and shoulder and shot off back down the corridor.

Khorii knelt and examined the wound, leaning her head close so that her horn touched the little girl's shoulder. She needed a moment to think about these new developments.

'There now. Better?' she asked Sesseli, who nodded, though tears spilled down her cheeks. 'Khiindi did not mean to harm you, *yaazi*,' she said, using the Linyaari endearment that translated meant 'little one,' though her mother and father used it as an endearment for each other as well as for her, and none of them were particularly small. 'He was frightened.'

'I know. He's kind of a 'fraidy cat. But I would have protected him. Doesn't he know I'm his friend?'

'Yes. I am sure that he does. But he *is* a cat and they scratch and run first and think it over later. You would probably do the same if you were his size surrounded by people our size. Perhaps you should go find him now and tell him that you are not too hurt and that you forgive him and will protect him from Marl.'

Sesseli nodded solemnly and ran back toward the bridge.

'Marl assures me,' Captain Bates said, with a

meaningful glare at the bully, 'that if he harms any crew member, whether on two or four feet, we will not have to space him as he'll gladly jump out without a suit. Since there are no barnacles in space, and we can't keelhaul him like they did in the old days, it will have to do.'

Marl's eyes widened as he looked at his teacher during her speech. She narrowed hers in return, and he nodded once.

'He came along to help load the supplies,' Asha continued. 'If Khorii has decontaminated the cargo, we can safely transport it to the surface as originally planned. Uh – how's everybody feeling?'

'Fine,' Hap said. Jaya remained silent and looked down at the deck.

'We did not arrive in time to save the rest of the crew,' Khorii told her. 'Both of Jaya's parents were unfortunately beyond our help.'

'I'm sorry to hear that, Jaya,' Captain Bates said, laying a hand on the girl's shoulder. 'They used to come into the school after their deliveries and visit with us. They brought you to meet us shortly after you were born. They were fine people and good spacers. They'd want this mission fulfilled, don't you think?'

Jaya's mouth twisted, and she stared at the floor, nodding slightly. Khorii caught two trains of thought – Asha Bates chiding herself for being so trite and teacherly when what this girl obviously needed was comfort, and Jaya feeling that her parents would have liked to see her grow up into

239

her own life even more, but that they weren't going to get the chance now. That, and the sudden, crushing feeling of being all alone, surrounded by strangers, well-meaning ones, perhaps, but strangers nonetheless.

'Okay, then, where's the food?' Marl asked, clapping his hands and rubbing them together. 'I didn't come up here just to haul crates, you know.'

Hap snorted and turned his back on all of them, especially Marl and Asha Bates, for bringing him.

Over the intercom, Elviiz said, 'Maganos Moonbase for Captain Bates.'

'Asha, when did you first become suicidal, and why didn't you come to me for treatment?' Phador Al y Cassidro's strident voice demanded.

With a frown Asha headed toward the bridge, followed by Khorii, Jaya, and Marl. When she arrived, the slim woman confronted the vid screen. 'I'm not going to dignify that remark with an answer, Phador. As you can see, I'm not dead yet, nor is anyone else who's come since Khorii arrived. Great galaxies, man, our school was founded by Khorii's mother, who also saved the original student body by means of her extra-ordinary gifts! If her daughter claims some similar abilities, why should we doubt her? We are going to load the shuttles – mine, Khorii's, and the *Mana*'s delivery shuttle – and all of us will return to the surface with enough supplies to see us through this quarantine. I don't know why I'm the only one who realizes that this is the only sane solution.'

'We are teachers, Asha. We follow the rules, however difficult or painful, and set an example for our students to follow,' Phador replied, speaking slowly, as if to a stubborn child. 'I've sent a request to the Federation inspection teams to come and inspect the *Mana* and exempt us from quarantine restrictions, but until they respond in the affirmative—'

'Have they replied at all?' Hap asked. 'Because I sure wasn't getting anywhere on any Federation channels. Face it, the plague has broken down the system. We are on our own, and we have an advantage – we have Khorii and Elviiz.'

'Dr Al y Cassidro?' Khorii said, meeting the teacher's gaze with her own and trying to hold it by sending to him psychically as well as convincing him with words. 'There is no plague here anymore. It went away. I saw it go.'

Calla Kaczmarek intervened, asking, 'You *saw* it go? Khorii, we don't know what causes this plague, but it's nothing visible to the human eye.'

'I know, but I am not human,' she said. 'I am Linyaari. My mother sometimes sees things that are not visible to the physical eye.'

'Does she?'

Elviiz answered. 'Yes, she does. She can tell about the mineral content of asteroids, for instance, just by looking at them. This is documented in your own files by Grandsires Baird and Giloglie. Khornya could do this from a very young age, even before developing her other Linyaari psychic abilities.'

Calla, Al y Cassidro, Reamer, and Mr Singh conferred, then Mr Singh asked, 'And how long have you been able to see the – er – microorganisms in retreat, dear?'

'I have only just discovered this ability,' Khorii admitted. 'I imagine it will develop more fully as time passes. That is how these things usually go, or so I understand from my elders.'

'I see,' the doctor replied. 'Well, you can hope that it doesn't develop too rapidly. Everything around us teems with such microorganisms. I would think that, after a while, such an ability would become quite a burden. You wouldn't be able to see the forest for the – er – trees.'

'I believe I have to be trying to see the particular organisms to do so,' Khorii said, realizing the truth of this only as she said it.

'Maybe so,' Phador Al y Cassidro continued. 'But unless the health inspectors can determine that the plague has gone away for themselves, we cannot risk the entire school on the basis of what you claim is your newfound talent. We also cannot accept cargo from a contaminated ship any more than we can allow you to return before the health inspectors have cleared you.'

'Phador, Calla, Singh,' Asha Bates said, shaking her head. 'You're all suffering from an overdose of overcautiousness, if you ask me. In case you've forgotten what life outside the ivory tower is like, everything involves some kind of risk. But there's a simple enough test here. I am now exposed. If I don't get sick and die as the other crew members

242

did within whatever the incubation period is supposed to be. A week? Two? Then you'll know Khorii's gift worked, and you can accept the food and let us come back to the base. Okay? I think that should be perfectly clear even to the most hidebound bureaucrat. I also think that continuing to argue the obvious is a waste of energy. So on behalf of Acting Captain Jaya and the entire crew I will sign off now. *Mana* out.'

TWENTY-ONE

Jaya had never loaded the delivery shuttle by herself before, but with Elviiz's strength and Hap's mechanical aptitude, the task went quickly.

Marl Fidd, unsurprisingly, was not a great deal of help. He was supposed to be hauling cargo, but instead felt it necessary to sample the more interesting varieties of food first, flinging the cartons every which way in his search for goodies. The Vermin Eradication Specialists flocked to the empties to see if there were any tasty bits left inside.

From a safe high perch, Khiindi hissed down at them. *'Watch your tails!'*

The team leader pulled her head out of a carton, glared up at him with gold eyes, and twitched her whiskers in disgust. *'You stop watching our tails, you pervert.'*

'You wrong me again, female,' Khiindi replied as he feigned a disinterested yawn. *'Were it not for the tiny and rather charming products of your now-barren loins, which I assure you are of no interest whatsoever to me,*

I would not bother to warn you. But that big thug stuffing his face and tossing around the cartons and boxes from which you feast is a cat killer. He tried to drown me by picking me up by the tail and hurling me into a deep pool of water.'

'I already think more highly of him,' the queen said, with an upward jerk of her tail. But she called to her brood, saying, *'Come along, all of you. We have vermin to catch and we don't want to spoil our appetites.'*

Marl didn't seem to notice the other cats at all, but Khiindi made sure that when he fell asleep it was somewhere high and hidden, but close to Elviiz and Khorii. He also made sure his tail was securely tucked beneath his belly.

When Khorii slept, he tucked himself up tightly against her, ready to defend her against Marl or anyone else.

Once the shuttles were loaded and ready to take to the surface, *Mana's* new crew hailed the moonbase again.

'See, Phador?' Asha said, when the other teachers were on the com screen. 'Your canary in the mine is still alive and kicking. I told you Khorii's technology could overcome this, and it has. So if you're not dying to eat your shoes, could we please come back and bring these supplies?'

'We have conferred on this issue, and I have consulted the Federation directives on this subject. You may send the supplies down to us, but none of you may return until the quarantine has been lifted.'

'Why?' Marl demanded. 'Fewer mouths to feed, is that it?'

Phador glared at him. 'The plan is this. I will expose myself to the questionable cargo. If I experience no ill effects, then we may unload it for the use of the compound at large.'

'If it's not contaminated,' Calla turned to him, looking nonplussed, 'surely it stands to reason, since they've been handling it, that they, too, are safe to return?'

'Not necessarily,' he argued. 'We are still unsure about the incubation period. And some of them may be carriers. We cannot take the risk.'

'Well then, you can starve for all I care,' Marl said. 'I didn't bust my hump so that you could take all the food and leave us up here like space trash.'

'No,' Khorii and Asha said together. 'We'll take the shuttles down, unload them and return.'

'You should leave one for our use – for later,' Phador said.

'Ours belongs with this ship,' Jaya said stubbornly.

'The shuttle we arrived in is the property of Captain Becker and the *Condor*,' Elviiz said.

'And since you're going to be so unreasonable about this,' Asha said. 'The *Nakomas* is my personal property, and I will bring her back into exile with me. I suggest that if you need a shuttle, Phador, you do what you do best – run to the Federation.'

They signed off before while the headmaster of Maganos was still spluttering a reply, with Asha muttering, 'Pettifogging bureaucrat.'

Khorii frowned. She didn't have to be a telepath to understand that Phador was very angry. 'While I appreciate what you're doing for the people down at the base, Captain Bates,' Khorii said, 'aren't you worried about what Phador might do to you when this is all over?'

Asha regarded the girl for a long moment before replying. 'Don't you fret about that, little one. He wouldn't dare fire me over this, or I'd spill the news about him keeping the supplies away from the moonbase, when there was absolutely no danger from it, to everyone who would listen, including the Federation. I'm sure this incident will quickly fade away once the plague has been eliminated.' She pushed back from the com console and stood up with a quick smile. 'Of course, if you and your mother had anything to add regarding my conduct, I would be very appreciative.'

Khorii smiled back. 'I think my mother will certainly have something to say about this when she finds out about it. But right now we should get those supplies moonside as soon as possible.'

Elviiz and Khorii both piloted the little shuttle from the *Condor*, although it was packed so tightly the two of them could barely squeeze inside – accompanied by Khiindi, who insisted on going, too. The docking bays were barren of personnel as well as other spacecraft, and the three shuttles set down in an isolated area, with Kezdet shining huge and bright over them and her other moon floating in the sky nearby. Jaya and Hap, Asha Bates and Marl, and Khorii and Elviiz unloaded by hand

247

everything they had used machinery to load on the *Mana*. Khiindi stayed aboard the shuttle and was the only one to see when the com screen, formerly containing Phador's disapproving face, changed to show the picture of a fish. As Elviiz and Khorii reboarded the shuttle, a song poured through the intercom, a complex harmony of many voices filled with melodic melancholy.

'The poopuus are singing,' Khorii said. After the backbreaking work of moving the cargo, she was glad to be able to slump down in the command chair, wipe the sweat from her skin, and stare into space while the chorus of beautiful voices washed over her like the scented and softened waters of Uncle Hafiz's fountains.

'Nice of them to entertain us,' Jaya remarked, from her own shuttle.

'It's not entertainment,' Hap said. 'It's like a hymn. Can't you hear?'

Khorii shook her head silently, but said nothing as the song on the intercom accompanied them back to the *Mana*. While they flew, she saw images in her head of groups of poopuus floating listlessly in their oceans. Then suddenly there was a picture of Khiindi with his paw extended to take a fish, but the fish was not shining, and it did not try to escape. And then Khorii herself appeared beside Khiindi and the fish, and she bent over the water, her body stretching as she reached out to the floating people who yearned toward her. Then she was in the water and all of the other people in it opened their eyes wide and waved their arms back

248

and forth as the song ended on a celebratory note.

When the shuttles emptied out into the docking bay, she told them, 'The poopuus' song contained a psychic message to me,' Khorii said. 'An entreaty. They want me to go to their planet and save their elders.'

'Oh, well, don't let *us* stop you!' Marl said. 'Why don't you just hop aboard a passing meteor shower and go out and save the poopuus and the whole fraggin' universe while you're at it! They're bound to make you the princess of the poopuus in gratitude, and we can all be your grateful subjects, too.'

'Stop that, you mean boy!' Sesseli said, stalking up to him with her hands on her hips and her small chin angled belligerently upward. 'Khorii was just saying what happened. She wasn't bragging, like *some* people would.'

'Get your petite feet out of my personal space, pet, or I'll take *you* by the tail and throw you into the great beyond,' Marl snarled, indicating the star-spangled black bits that showed between Kezdet, Maganos, and the other moon outside the docking bay.

'What do you think, Elviiz?' Hap asked. 'I think in Marl's case, his tongue is a birth defect. Maybe we should perform a procedure on him to correct it.' Elviiz didn't reply, but glanced at Khorii instead, his face flushed with embarrassment.

Marl's eyes narrowed, and he pointed a slightly shaking warning finger at Hap, 'I'm ready for you, smart-ass. And if that monster comes near me, I'll—'

'Yes, tell us, just what will you do, Marl?' Asha, who had been leaning against her shuttle with her arms folded, asked. 'Bleed a lot and hope Khorii can understand your screams well enough to help you with another of her remedies that you're so scornful of? I seem to remember being near her was the main reason behind your noble sacrifice of joining forces with us outcasts.'

Khorii sighed, and said, finally, reasonably, 'Marl, you do not have to be afraid. We Linyaari are peaceful people, and I will not let Hap hurt you. Elviiz is deeply ashamed he broke your arm and will not do it again. But you must not hurt Khiindi or Sesseli or anyone else either, or you will have to be isolated. I think that under the circumstances, that would be rather frightening for you.'

'Frightening? Do I look like a sissy?'

Sesseli glanced at Hap, who stared back at Marl. They both shrugged and nodded.

'Hey, I don't need this—!'

'That is enough,' Jaya said. 'This is my ship now – at least until the Krishna-Murti Company decides to reclaim it – if – if ever anything goes back to normal. And if Khorii thinks her skills can help some other people who are smart enough to let her, I say it's just about criminal to keep orbiting and wasting fuel and wondering if we'll die before we go dry. I think we should go and see if we can save them.'

'That would be breaking the *rules*, sunshine,' Marl said.

'Since when have you ever had a problem with

that, Marl?' Asha asked. 'If you do, however, I'll be happy to let you keep orbiting in the *Nakomas*. Personally, I think Jaya has a point. Khorii, what do you say?'

Relief blew across Khorii like a cool breeze. 'I hate being idle when there is so much to be done.'

Khiindi hopped onto her shoulders and twined himself around her neck, careful to keep his tail tucked. He stared intently at Marl Fidd, who – fortunately – was not looking at him, and tried willing the bully to accept Captain Bates's offer of the perpetually orbiting shuttle. Then the rest of them could head spaceward, finding Aari and Acorna once more after many exciting but not very dangerous adventures, which would somehow, never mind the details, result in glory and adulation for himself.

'Good,' Asha said. 'Shall we tell Phador we're leaving, then? With any luck he'll forbid it, which will make the trip worthwhile even if we don't manage to save another single soul.'

Spying on people was rude, of course. Liriili would have said it was inexcusable; but then Khorii did not want to think of Liriili for a role model, as she was the least empathetic and flexible Linyaari ever born, at least according to Aunt Maati. Besides, this was an emergency situation and, except for Elviiz, Khorii was about to embark on an illegal trip to a strange world with people she did not know very well.

She had found out a little about each of them by then. Hap, for instance, cared about animals, knew how to do many things usually done only by adults, and talked a lot. He could tell you all sorts of things in the same way Elviiz could. But did he talk about the things that were actually important to him? For instance, he seldom mentioned Shoshisha, but the way he had looked at her back on Maganos said that she was probably on his mind a lot. Khorii hoped she was mistaken. Shoshisha she knew well enough to know that she was a very selfish and somewhat hysterical person. Khorii was *very* thankful that Shoshisha was not on the *Mana*.

Captain Bates was a teacher, and obviously a sympathetic one, since she was here. She meant well, and truly had the base's best interests at heart. But on the other hand, she had brought Marl Fidd with her for some reason that Khorii could not fathom. And Marl was angry, selfish, violent, and a bully. Oh, and also besotted with Shoshisha, and very messy.

Jaya had spent just enough time on the *Mana* to learn to operate the loaders, but though she'd managed to load the cargo back on the trip to Maganos she couldn't really fly the cargo ship without help. She missed her parents terribly and had continued visiting their bodies until decomposition took the comfort out of that.

Sesseli was small, friendly, and loved animals. And also stood up to bullies, even at risk to herself.

Which left Marl Fidd, whom Khorii tried to avoid as much as possible. The last thing she wanted to do was to see what was on his mind.

All in all, it wasn't much to go on.

She tried listening in to the thoughts of everyone in general, but they were so confused that she sometimes seemed to hear more inner conversations than there were people on the ship. No, if she was going to learn anything useful, she would have to do it while talking to each person.

Or, in Hap's case, listening to him talk to her. Since he was the first person she met and full of information, she decided to try him first. Finding him turned out to be difficult, however.

Captain Bates sat at the console with Sesseli on her lap. A kitten was curled up in a small furry ball on Sesseli's lap. 'This is the radar screen,' Captain Bates was explaining. 'And do you remember what this is? We talked about it in class.'

'Navigational computer?' the little girl said, pointing to one of the screens.

'That's right,' Captain Bates said. 'You'll be flying this ship in no time.'

She was thinking, *I need to get these kids ready to be on their own. With things the way they are, any or all of us could die at any time, and whoever is left needs to be able to fly this beast. How could Phador be so pigheaded? I thought he really cared.* And Khorii backed off as she got a picture of the captain and Phador Al y Cassidro, locked in a sweaty embrace that she recognized from books and vids aboard the *Condor* as mating, human-style.

So that's really why she wasn't worried about him doing anything, she thought. 'Captain, do you know where Hap is?' she asked quickly.

'I'm not sure. He's been hanging out in the engine room quite a bit lately, so I decided to hold an impromptu lecture down there. He was explaining to us a little while ago about how the drive on this particular model of ship works, but then Marl came in and made a remark that upset Jaya. Before I could stop them, he and Hap got into it, and Jaya ran out of the room. Hap followed her. I'm not sure where Marl went, but I'm keeping Sesseli and the cats with me.'

Sesseli was smiling as she put a small hand on each control in turn, but her large blue eyes were very serious. Her fine curly blond hair was tied into two pigtails with bright-colored ornamental cords with little gold bells on them. Khorii recognized them as being two of the bracelets Jaya liked to wear in thick bunches on each wrist.

Sesseli's thoughts were transparent at that moment. *Just like with Mama,* she was thinking. *But Mama didn't know how to drive a spaceship, I don't think.* The little girl's recollections of her mother were blurred around the face, but seemed to be starting to resemble Captain Bates.

Khiindi jumped off the top of a vent and landed on Khorii's shoulder.

'Except Khiindi,' Captain Bates continued.

'Yes, he will help me search for Hap. They're friends,' Khorii said. Khiindi purred and for a moment she thought she picked up on his thoughts. *'I am not a dumb beast, but I am a beast, with nothing interesting at all for you to read. Concentrate on the people. I have no thumbs. I cannot fly a ship. And*

254

by the way, feed me.' But of course he wasn't really thought-talking to her. Was he?

From Jaya's cabin came the sound of weeping. Khorii had learned that it was best not to bother her while she was grieving, at least not until she gave some indication she wanted to talk. Jaya's thoughts were broadcast through the door and unsurprisingly were of times she spent with her parents, cooking, eating, learning, fighting over whether or not she could go with them, go to a school, a dance, a friend's house. And there were also blurred thought-forms of a very tiny Jaya hunkered down and looking up with enormous eyes at huge feet and legs of other people, happy, powerful people, going about their business all around her. They could step on her at any moment, and there was no one there to protect her.

Khorii raised her hand to knock on the door, then sensed another feeling beneath those Jaya was projecting. Some part of the other girl was enjoying scaring herself in this way, feeling helpless and alone. That was the part that did not want to and was not ready to start living on her own again. Khorii lowered her hand and continued down the corridor.

The door to the cabin where the bodies had been stowed was open, and the room was empty. Khorii closed it quickly, hoping Jaya wouldn't notice.

Was this some macabre prank of Marl's? Didn't that boy have any feelings for anyone but himself? Khorii strode angrily down the corridor. Hearing a lot of thumping and bumping coming from one of the cargo holds, she shoved open the door.

Marl was lying flat on his back with a box labeled SCRUBBERS on his chest. 'Oh, Khorii,' he said, in an uncharacteristically friendly voice. 'The very person I wanted to help me. I just spotted some peanut butter on that shelf up there, but I can't reach it. Give me a boost up so I can stand on your shoulders and grab it and pass it down to you, okay?'

'Wouldn't it be easier to use the loader?' she asked.

'I don't see it, do you?' he said. 'That Hellstrom geek's probably taken it apart to see how it runs. And I'm really hungry.' He tried to look pathetic, but in the days they'd been en route he looked as if he had put on at least ten pounds. 'Please?' he asked. She had never realized he knew the word.

However, his thoughts were anything but polite. In his mind he was huge, especially his male part, and she was comparatively small, and could be broken in half. After he did that mentally, he put her back together again. She also walked very strangely, slinking around as if she were a cat in heat. He had more violent images about what he wanted to do concerning her, before his lust for peanut butter overcame them. Khiindi, he thought, might taste good roasted and covered with peanut butter. This was followed by other disturbing images of himself with every other female on the ship. *I have to warn Captain Bates about Marl*, she thought.

Khiindi dug his claws into her shoulder and tried to hide in her mane as Khorii began backing away. 'I have to do something right now,' she said.

'I *said* "please," ' he said, scowling. 'What do you want anyway?'

'Just a little time,' she said sweetly, but definitely not seductively. 'I'll come back and help you in a little while, honestly. I just have—' She decided not to tell him that she was looking for Hap. That wouldn't go over very well. 'I have something I really need to do first.' That wasn't a lie exactly, but there was no way she was coming back alone. She'd bring Elviiz with her maybe, or just send him, but she was not going to be alone with Marl again. Not with what she saw in *his* mind. She would also have to make sure that the rest of the girls were never alone with him, either.

'Your loss.' He shrugged and turned his back on her, looking for footholds among the shelves towering overhead. 'I'm willing to share.'

Khorii left in a hurry. If he fell again, she did not want to be there to feel compelled to help.

Thumping and swishing sounds came from the next cargo bay, and she could see dim light through the open door. When she stepped inside, she saw that all of the light was concentrated in one corner. Both loaders were parked between her and that area, and cargo had been rearranged in new stacks that formed another wall in back of the loaders. The thumping and swishing sounds came from behind the new wall, accompanied by conversation.

'You realize that this will not impede the decomposition of the bodies?' Elviiz was saying.

'It's not. Supposed. To.' Hap's voice replied, grunting after every other word or so.

Khorii could not see them and walked over to the cargo wall. But it was more complicated than that. The stacked containers did not just form a wall, they enclosed a newly created raised courtyard, a man-made hillock composed of special soils and manures intended for farming colonies that filled the enclosure to a height of about ten feet. The neatly stacked empty bags and boxes that had contained the soils and fertilizers now formed part of the retaining wall. The smell in the bay reminded Khorii of home: rich, loamy earth, and occasional whiffs of other, not so pleasant smells as well. Atop the mound sat five long wooden boxes. Behind them, Hap labored, digging with a shovel, while Elviiz dug with his entrenching attachment, flipping dirt out of his growing hole twice as fast as his human counterpart. She wrinkled her nose as she watched the two boys work.

'What are you doing?' Khorii asked.

'Oh, Khorii, hi,' Hap called. 'There's a ramp over on this side we used to bring the loaders down. Come on around and take a look.'

'We are creating a burial ground, Khorii,' Elviiz answered her question. He always answered her questions, that was the thing about Elviiz. Even ones she asked someone else. Sometimes even if she never actually asked a question at all. That was one of the most infuriating things about him, his almost Linyaari-like ability to know at times what she was wondering, even if she didn't say it. Now, however, his predilection to answer her was coming in handy.

258

'Why?' she asked.

'In order to bury Jaya's parents and the crew of the *Mana*,' Elviiz replied. 'Hap feels it would be beneficial for Jaya's grieving process to observe certain ceremonial folk customs humans use to dispose of the discarded bodies of their fellows.'

Hap planted his shovel in the dirt and mopped his face with his hand, spreading dirt in a comical mask around his eyes. 'I don't think it's good for her to keep looking at the bodies,' he said. 'Her people aren't there anymore, and the longer she looks, the harder it will be for her to remember them how they were when they were alive. I've been building coffins and hauling dirt all week and today, with Elviiz's help, digging the graves. I made some nice markers, too. We can plant fast-growing flowers and shrubs and stuff and make a nice little memorial garden for her to visit.'

Khiindi hopped down onto the mound and began digging enthusiastically in the loose dirt, then squatting over his hole with a look of feline bliss curving his crescent moon cat lips up into his whiskers.

'Eeewww!' Hap said, shaking his head. 'I was going to start on that area next! Elviiz, you've just landed pooper-scooper duty. Funny, I've never seen a cat actually smile before.'

'Khiindi is not like any cat you have ever known,' Elviiz said, before returning to work on his hole. Khiindi strolled off, his tail held high, the look on his face seeming to indicate that he had just blessed the entire area with his offering.

Khorii nodded as she took it all in, not knowing what to say. Between shovelsful of dirt, Hap continued. 'Anyway, we couldn't just space them. For one thing, it's kind of gross because you can see the body float off into space from the ship. It doesn't seem respectful somehow, especially not with the dead person's daughter watching. And also, I would think that the Federation might worry about bodies in space being time bombs for future epidemics. Say everything gets back to normal and we go about our business. Jaya would be held responsible for the ship and what happened to the bodies by both her company and the Federation. We could cremate them, I guess, if we could land somewhere, but we can't right now. And it costs too much in power to refrigerate the room all the time to a temperature that would stop decomposition. We're definitely not storing them in the galley freezer. We don't know how long we'll have to stay on this bird or try to keep it flying. So this seems like the thing to do, you know?'

Khorii smiled and nodded. Only Hap would think something so odd and work-intensive was the logical alternative, but he meant it with a kindness that was almost selfless. She caught a fleeting thought image of him holding Jaya, comforting her, kissing her hair. Boys! Mating was certainly a big part of their thoughts. At least Hap had settled on a girl close to his own age for his fantasies and was doing something nice for her. But she also knew that one reason he was talking so much was that he was afraid it was *not* the right thing to do.

Maybe Jaya would be offended. Maybe her people didn't bury their dead. Maybe she liked being able to look at the husks of her parents and the other crew members. He tried so hard, and yet he felt like he never quite did the right thing to make other people like him. Under his enthusiasm and outer cheerfulness, Khorii felt a great void edged by intense sadness. His life before Maganos Moonbase lay within it, she thought.

'Can I help?' she asked.

'Yeah, we've got the graves about dug now. You want to go get Jaya and let the captain know what's up?'

Elviiz said, 'I will help inter the remains of the crew members, then take the helm, if Captain Bates likes, so that she may make the gestures considered culturally appropriate in this situation. She did say that she knew Jaya's parents.' Khorii nodded and trotted down the ramp, heading for the crew cabins. She passed the first cargo bay at a run, half-afraid Marl would jump out and remind her of her promise. She exhaled with relief when she came to Jaya's cabin, but the smaller girl was no longer there. Khorii found Marl, Sesseli, Captain Bates, and Jaya on the bridge, staring at the viewscreen. A huge Federation ship drifted past, broadcasting the same kind of mayday pulse as the *Blanca*.

'What shall we do?' Khorii asked.

'We can't do a bloody thing,' Marl said. 'They're done for.'

'I might be able to help, in case anyone is alive,' Khorii said.

261

'No,' Captain Bates told her, the tone of command firm in her voice. 'It's too dangerous, and it would take too much energy. That won't be the last derelict we see before this is over, is my guess. Let's save our energy and your skills for one that shows some sign that somebody has survived.'

To Khorii's surprise, Jaya agreed with them. 'Anybody can use the com unit. If they're not well enough to get to it to answer our hail, they would not live until you could board, Khorii.'

Khorii didn't argue. She closed her eyes and opened her mind and tried to feel if there was any life aboard the ship. Whether there was someone and her psychic skills were unable to perceive them, or whether there was nobody left alive there, she couldn't tell, but she nodded. If she had been able to sense anyone, it would have been different.

Jaya looked away abruptly, and Khorii touched her shoulder. 'Jaya, Hap and Elviiz have prepared a resting place for your parents and friends in cargo bay two. They'd like you to come and see now.'

'Me, too?' Sesseli asked.

'Yes, you, too,' Khorii said, hugging the youngster to her side. 'Captain Bates, Elviiz will relieve you so you can come back, too, as soon as he's finished helping Hap.'

Captain Bates nodded, just glad Khorii hadn't made more objection about the derelict. 'I would be honored to attend.'

'Well, I'm coming too. I wouldn't miss this for the world,' Marl said.

He almost choked on his own laughter when he

saw the man- and droid-made hillock, but Elviiz took one step toward him, and he shut up abruptly. Khorii felt certain Elviiz wouldn't attack anyone just for laughing, but she wasn't sure that *she* could have stopped herself from smacking Marl if he didn't stop ridiculing other people's efforts to be helpful.

Hap offered Jaya a last look at her family and fellow crewmen before putting the lids on the coffins, then he and Elviiz lowered them into the holes. Elviiz filled them in with such speed and energy it detracted a bit from the somber tone of the event, but Hap helped Jaya place the markers he had made at the head of each grave. She knelt between the graves of her parents, looking lost. Khorii had an idea. She ran back to cargo bay one where she had made her 'ponics garden and gathered some of the gold and orange blooms already growing on the flowering edible species she had cultivated. Returning to cargo bay two, she climbed the hill and handed the flowers to Jaya.

Jaya stopped crying and looked up at her in surprise. 'Marigolds! How did you know? These are the traditional flowers for funerals and weddings for my people.'

Khorii smiled. 'And they're delicious, too, so they're the traditional flowers for grazing for *my* people.'

As touching as the makeshift ceremony was, she hoped the memorial garden would have little chance to blossom before the ship reached LoiLoiKua, then Paloduro, and she saw her own

263

parents again. Jaya's grief made her nervous, and she couldn't help wondering where her mother and father were and what they were doing.

The gymnasium had been transformed into a makeshift clinic and emergency shelter for anyone well enough to get there. Most of the people were not actually sick, or not very sick, but did need to be decontaminated before they mixed with the others. Finally, after three days of healing, with only an occasional break for one of them to eat or sleep while the other continued to tend the new arrivals, the flow of patients seemed to be stanched.

Aari and Acorna worked tirelessly until every last person who came for their help had received it. Then they made an announcement.

'We need to let any other survivors in the city know that we're here and this is the place to come for help. We also need more supplies to take care of you all. Could we have some volunteers to come with us to try to reestablish the communications systems so we can broadcast to anyone who might be left and also to acquire enough supplies for the people here until we know it is safe for them to return home?'

'I helped design the emergency broadcast system for the entire city grid,' a thin, older man with a shock of white hair told them. 'I can show you where the station is, and I'm pretty sure I can get the equipment going again.'

'Great. Thank you,' Acorna said.

'I will help you hunt for supplies,' Abuelita said.

'We can go to my son's store,' a woman said. 'He sells – sold – camping supplies, sleeping bags, cots, tents, dehydrated food, that sort of thing. It's quite a large place. He was leading an expedition into the jungle when the plague broke out. I – don't know how he is. But I know he would be glad to help, even if he has to start all over – if he can, I mean, I—' Flustered, she broke off as the impact of her words sank home.

'Excellent,' Aari said, smoothly filling the sudden silence. 'I will come with you. We will need more volunteers to load and carry things.'

'I own a fleet of florries. Some of my drivers – died in them. If you can make them safe enough to drive again, we can pick up stuff all over the city.' This was from a tiny bird-like woman. Despite a huge, sculpted, and lacquered wave of blond hair, now a bit bedraggled, and extremely tight skin on her face with eyebrows that looked as if they'd been drawn on with ink, she looked to Acorna to be about the same age as Uncle Hafiz.

'Yes, that would be wonderful.' Florries, flying lorries with a capacity to haul large loads, would be tremendously helpful.

'You two are very tired,' Abuelita said. 'We have many people with resources here. Let us organize ourselves, determine the priorities, where we need you first and who is to help with what. Both of you need to rest. When we are ready, we will let you know where you should go first.'

'The emergency broadcast is the most critical,' Acorna said. 'We must let people know where to come before they lose hope. While they are making their way to us, we can be readying a place for them and for the people already here.'

It took three additional days to gather other survivors, heal them, and decontaminate the means to support them. Aari and Acorna were constantly on the move except when Abuelita and some of the other elders insisted that they stop and rest. They grazed in parks and in the vegetable departments of empty supermarkets. Much of the produce was beyond saving, but some could be restored enough to be edible. Once they felt they had done all they could for as many as were able to receive their help, they moved on.

Corazon contained the largest population on Paloduro, so with help from Jalonzo, Abuelita's grandson, they flew to more remote portions of the planet. Two of the newest settlements, pioneered by a group consisting mostly of men looking for new frontiers, had been totally wiped out, without a single survivor. Some of the other less recently established had a few middle-aged women and a scattering of children, not so much sick from the plague as starving and suffering from other ailments resulting from living in such a moribund environment. This was where the freeze-dried foods and nutrient bars the parties carried with them were tremendously helpful.

But they also needed healing and a safe haven to stay at until more permanent arrangements could be made. Aari and Acorna rose to the task, until the last patient was cured and sixteen centers had been organized, staffed, supplied, and decontaminated. By the time all of that was finished, both Linyaari were utterly drained.

Jalonzo had expected them to be tired, but he was also baffled by the changes taking place in them. He had begun to consider the benign aliens as creatures much like the characters in his games – a constant set of attributes that could be applied in a certain way to achieve a certain result. In real life, he figured, the attributes should remain stable and reliable.

However, both of his heroes began to falter, despite longer rest periods and more open grazing. 'Have you used up all of your secret powers now?' he asked Aari, when they were back inside the flitter, heading back to the place where they had left the space shuttle.

Near the landing site, two retired heavy equipment operators had dug a mass grave in the city's center. Using their gigantic tools with the same intricacy as a laser surgeon, they lifted the bodies from the street and took them to the site, where Aari and Acorna had decontaminated the bodies and the soil. The dead were buried, side by side in neat rows, identified when possible by their ID cards, which were attached to markers erected above each mound. Prayers were said for them, and a slow and beautiful song, accompanied by the haunting, clear notes of a nine-stringed guitar, served as a farewell.

It was an enormous task, and only one of many that still remained.

Acorna wanted to sleep as soon as she sat down in the shuttle. Jalonzo did not leave them, however, but continued to regard them with studious concern. 'Is that why your horns are transparent now and kind of floppy instead of all golden like they were when you first came? Because you used up all your powers?'

'Who are you calling floppy?' Aari asked in between yawns. 'Our horns are simply in their regenerative state.'

'My lifemate is joking, Jalonzo,' Acorna said, in response to the boy's puzzled look. 'The answer to your question is yes. When we become depleted, it shows in our horns. I feel like I could sleep for weeks, but we cannot afford to do that yet.'

'Are you going back to your spaceship now?' he asked.

'Yes, for a time.'

'Can I just ask you one more question?'

'Of course.'

'What if some of the people get sick again? Will you come back? I mean, you couldn't clean up all the plague from the whole city yet.'

Acorna smiled in spite of her exhaustion. 'Actually, that's three questions. We'll try. But we have to hope that meanwhile the Federation will devise a cure for this illness so people can be protected by means that do not require our presence.'

'Hmm. I think I might have an idea about that, but I'd need to use the lab at the university. You didn't decontaminate that, did you?'

Aari shook his head. 'No, and I do not think we could at this time. When we are rested and have seen to the other worlds in your system, we will return to check on the progress of the people here. At that time, we will clear a laboratory for you and others to work.'

'It should be as soon as possible,' Jalonzo said. 'I should have asked you before, I know, but I only got this idea while you were curing everyone. What I was wondering was – I know I am not a Linyaari, but could you show me or tell me something about how your techniques work? Maybe until we have a lab I could use some of them to help people here.'

Acorna shook her head sadly and laid her hand on his for a moment. 'If only we could. You have been a great help. But it is something only a Linyaari can do.'

'I'm really pretty smart,' the teenager insisted.

'We have seen that. But our – methods – are built in.'

'I kind of thought so, but I wanted to ask,' he said with a weak smile. 'I hope your methods get all solid and gold again soon.'

So do I, Acorna thought but didn't say, feeling more depleted than she ever had in her life. *So do I.*

TWENTY-TWO

LoiLoiKua appeared in space as a shimmering ball of aquamarine with a few tiny dots of green. Only one moon orbited it, and the water planet was close enough to its own sun that the star was much larger than Our Star appeared on Vhiliinyar.

The *Nakomas* was well equipped to make a water landing. Captain Bates had tried to insist that she pilot her shuttle, but Khorii pointed out that the risk to her from the plague was much higher than it was to a Linyaari and an android alone, and she was needed on the *Mana*. They would stay in close contact on the com so the captain could monitor their landing and progress.

As the shuttle set down, bearing only Khorii and Elviiz, the Linyaari girl had the odd sensation that instead of having spent a dozen sleep shifts between Maganos and LoiLoiKua, she had simply closed her eyes and opened them to see the vast ocean below her. The scenery had shifted since the Moonbase, but the melodious chant-song of the LoiLoiKuans almost seemed to flow steadily from

270

the voices in the pool to those on the planet below.

'We who are about to die welcome you,' they sang. The line was followed by a harsh, staccato phrase that meant *'Enter at your own risk.'* Khorii heard their message clearly, although they were still too far out of visual range to see any of the aquatic creatures.

She was glad she had finally started reading thoughts, because the chant was not in the same Standard the poopuus used. They must have learned that or improved it once they got to the school. Elviiz, on the other hand, did not read thoughts but had a very sophisticated processor for interpreting languages.

He also had a built-in sensor suite that analyzed planetary environments. 'The water is perfectly safe,' he told her. 'Except for the plague, of course, and the dead fish and other creatures. I imagine the atmosphere is quite pungent by now.'

The poopuus had described their homeworld as having once had landmasses, large islands scattered across the blue-green waters. They spoke a lot of the crater reef, and Khorii saw what she thought must be it as they swooped in to land. Mountaintops poked out of the water in a long line, seeming almost to bisect the portion of the sea-covered planet visible to her.

Closer in, however, was another island and from it rose a large gold-speckled building, topped with many towers, some capped by square chunks of stone that looked like teeth with gaps between, some tapering to graceful points. Its main door was a huge arch, and its windows consisted of smaller arches. From one of the pointy towers flew a biohazard quarantine flag.

'I know what that is!' Khorii said, excited to recognize something from Captain Becker's books. 'It's a big sand castle! Either the LoiLoiKuans or the Federation command here has a sense of humor, or at least they used to.'

'Sand castle?' Elviiz asked.

'Children on Old Earth used to take pails and create them on seashores, modeling and sculpting them from wet sand,' she told him. 'Adults did it, too. Of course, that one would have to be made of more than just sand and water to do the Federation any good, but the form seems to be some sort of bow to traditional architecture. Are we getting a signal? It sounds weak.'

'Intruder, you have been detected by the ASP, atmospheric surveillance program, and are commanded to return to space. This planet is under strict quarantine. Failure to comply constitutes an intergalactic criminal offense punishable by death.'

'If the plague don't getcha, the Federation will, huh?' Captain Bates said over the com unit. The *Mana* had attempted to contact the Federation outpost before establishing its orbit around LoiLoiKua and dispatching the *Nakomas* to the surface, but had received no response. The only reply Captain Bates's remark drew this time was a somewhat weaker and slower repeat of the previous message.

'I don't think anyone from the Federation is home,' Captain Bates said from the *Mana*.

Khorii tried to detect thoughts other than those within the song of the LoiLoiKuans, but found none. 'Perhaps the plague got them already,' she said.

'Probably,' Captain Bates agreed. 'Which means they're not likely to shoot us down anyway. Still, proceed with caution.'

'What's that on the beach?' Khorii asked, realizing that what she had first thought was heavily flowered foliage was growing in an odd place, right at the high-tide mark on the beach. Insects swarmed around it, and it looked as if they were encased in a low-hanging cloud of some kind, full of tiny particles.

Elviiz was silent for a moment as he scanned the motionless forms, then said, 'The remains of several dozen LoiLoiKuans, the blossoms of some mutant form of bottom-feeding frangipangi, seaweed, mineral deposits – shall I list them?'

'No, that's enough. You got good eyes, young fella,' Asha said.

'Thank you. My father upgraded them for me just before we parted.'

'I don't suppose they're just, you know, sunbathing or something?' Captain Bates asked as the *Nakomas*'s cameras provided the *Mana* with a closer look, close enough that the rest of the makeshift crew also could make out the shapes.

'No, ma'am. They are without life.' Elviiz's voice was calm as he relayed the information. 'Certain

273

aquatic mammals have been known to swim up onto the beach beyond the point where the tide can lift them back into the sea. They do this when they are dying or wish to die, according to my files.'

'But we cannot be too late!' Khorii said. 'I hear them singing. Some are definitely still alive. Quite a large number, judging from the volume.'

As the *Nakomas* extruded the pontoons and outriggers that would stabilize it during the water landing, the ocean beneath them swelled into a series of rolling waves that fanned out around the shuttle.

Once the pontoons hit the water and Elviiz shut down the shuttle's engine, several heads broke the surface. Round benign faces, older than those of the poopuus at the moonbase, regarded the shuttle with a mixture of curiosity and dismay. Most of the creatures bore strands of white ribboned through their long dark hair.

She heard them talking among themselves, what they were thinking as well as what they said.

'Who do you suppose this is, some others fleeing the plague and seeking our help?'

'I hope not. We've little enough to give trying to care for our own. I can still hear the ravings of those young Federation troops as they burned with fever.'

'Yes, and many tried to cool themselves by drowning in our water before we could reach them. A lot of protection that was.'

An older female bobbed up to the surface and gestured with a webbed hand, shooing the shuttle. *'You there, don't you know an intergalactic signal for*

274

*plague when you see one? Go away! If you don't have
the sickness, you could catch it from us. If you do have
it, you may bring a mutant strain to finish off what's left
of us.'*

'No, we won't. Really. I am Khorii, a Linyaari healer.
Your children at Maganos Moonbase are friends of mine
and are worried about you. They were all well when we
left. The plague hasn't reached them. But they wanted
me to come and help you.'

'You cannot help us, KoriKori. We are dying.'

'Yes, I can. I've already cured several people.'

The woman looked at the others, who shrugged
the water off their shoulders and nodded.

'Ah,' Elviiz said. 'They seem to be accepting you,
Khorii. Note how they wave their arms in a
graceful welcoming gesture, combining kinetic
symbolism for diving and beckoning, followed by
arms crossed over their chests to indicate
welcome.'

Khorii was already at the hatch, hearing the
spokeswoman as she thought and spoke, though in
her native tongue, saying, *'In that case, come on in.
The water is fine.'*

She took a deep breath and dived into the ocean.
Just before she hit the surface, all of the onlookers
dived deeper into the water, too. She opened her
eyes to see them beckoning to her to follow.

*'Come away from the island where the dead are laid to
rest. It is very dangerous to be there.'*

'Yes, I know. Please take me to those who are still sick.'

'That is where we are going,' the spokeswoman
told her. *'What do you know of this plague, young*

275

healer? Why does it kill my children and spare me? It is unnatural that children should die before their mother.'

'It doesn't always affect creatures that way. On the ship in which I came here, only the daughter of two of the crew members survived. All of the adults died.'

'It is not a natural illness. It goes against the pattern.'

'That's why it's a plague, I suppose,' Khorii said. *'Do you know when and how it came here?'*

'Yes. Raealakaldai, the Federation kahuna, brought it with him when he returned from his Federation council. He was very pleased to go and told us all about it. He was to read a paper on how he well he governed us, and the big council was to be on his homeworld. Or perhaps it was the next world over.'

'Rio Boca, Nanahomea,' said the old man.

'Yes, Mokilau, that is the name of the place. Rio Boca. Raealakaldai was from Paloduro.'

'He was? That's where my parents are. The plague there is terrible, I guess.'

'He caught it and brought it back to us when we tried to heal his sickness. He died, and so did my daughter and her mate. I hope we will not be too late for you to treat my sister's children. They live across the reef far from the house of sand. Of the great population that lived near here, all but a few of us ancient ones are gone.'

'This is a good girl,' an old male said. Khorii knew that he was old because he thought of himself that way, but she saw few of the usual signs of long life. His long black hair bore only a few threads of white, his skin was almost entirely unlined, but his cheeks were no longer round and his eyes were red, as though he'd been rubbing tears from them. How

276

could you tell you'd been crying when you lived in salt water? *'Look how our ocean clears an ever-widening path before her, as if strewing her way with flowers. All of the living fish, fry or old creatures like us, rush to meet us, anxious to swim here.'*

'I have on my purifier,' Khorii said. *'It's something our people know how to do. The same thing that lets us cure illness.'*

'A wonderful gift, to clean the ocean. Does your purifier make the dead fish and bodies drift to the beaches, too?'

'I don't think so. But if it cleans up the water enough, then you'll be able to see better what needs to be – uh – put to rest, will you not?'

As the water cleared, Khorii once more had the sense of many little things fleeing before her, then disappearing entirely. Were those the organisms causing the plague? Surely they must be, since she only experienced the sensation when she was trying to decontaminate something or someplace. It couldn't be all microorganisms her new awareness allowed her to 'see,' or she would be seeing spots before her eyes so much of the time that she might as well be blind. The universe was full of tiny things. Her new sense must have focused itself on the plague in the way that Mother's had once focused itself on the ore content of asteroids.

Though the water was wonderfully buoyant and had been refreshing at first, now, even though the LoiLoiKuans swam on the surface or just beneath it to accommodate Khorii's greater need for oxygen, she was overcome by a lassitude that increased the longer she swam. So tired. She felt as if the ocean was pulling the life out of her, and wondered if she could be catching the plague herself, but that was impossible. Still, the brighter and cleaner the ocean grew, the more tired she became.

'Don't know if I can go much farther,' she said finally.

'We can pull you so you don't have to swim,' the old woman said. 'You just keep up here on the surface, put your hands on my shoulders, and I'll swim for you. A turtleback ride, like I used to give my little granddaughter, Likilekakua, before she was taken to that school you come from.'

'I know her!' Khorii said.

'Tell her her grandmother, Nanahomea, misses her. How is she?'

'Well, the last time I saw her. The poopuus – I mean, your grandchildren, have their own facility at the Moonbase with underwater computers, and they're doing really well. My cat Khiindi made friends with them first because they gave him fish.'

'If you can help us here, your cat may have all the fish he wants.'

'Are you hungry, with so many fish dying?'

'No, actually, we don't eat fish very often. Seaweed is more nourishing and easier to harvest. Are you still feeling tired?'

'Getting better, I think. Having my head out of the water helps.'

A swell of water heaved toward them from the horizon.

'I'll leave you for a moment, my dear. I think my sister has come to meet us.'

Khorii let go, and the lady dived beneath the glittering waters, which had become so clear that Khorii could see her through it, swimming away toward the swell. Khorii could not tell what, if anything, passed between the wave and Nanahomea.

In a few undulations Nanahomea paused, then flipped over and swam back to Khorii. Her smile was as broad as the horizon.

'My sister and all of her family come to greet you, KoriKori. In the past few hours since you slipped into our waters, the sick ones in her family have suddenly begun to feel better. No longer do they cough or bleed, or lose their food from their orifices. They feel well. They are happy. All wish to have a great celebration in your honor.'

'That is very kind,' Khorii said, 'but actually, I am not feeling very well myself. I think I had better return to the shuttle.'

Before I get any worse, she thought.

279

Twenty-Three

So how bad is it down there?' Becker asked, as Aari and Acorna trudged from the shuttle onto the *Condor*'s lower deck.

'Joh, it is bad enough to make any Khleevi very happy,' Aari told him.

Becker gave a low whistle. 'Whew, that bad, huh? Sorry. You guys were down there for quite a long time. I tell ya, Mac and I have been getting kinda lonesome up here. Hell, we could have been to Vhiliinyar and back by the time you guys made it here.'

'That would have been a good thing, Joh,' Aari said wearily. 'There are far too many sick people for just two Linyaari to take care of.'

'What's worse,' Acorna added, 'is that in order to prevent others from getting sick or relapsing, we really should decontaminate the entire planet – any of the planets where the illness has run unchecked over the population.' She sighed and stumbled as she stepped up onto the grated metal ramp.

280

Becker caught her as she started to fall. 'I don't think I've ever seen you this tired. I wish I could tell you I've been able to get a message through to Hafiz on MOO telling him to send in the cavalry, but the relays are down. Everybody's relays. His, the Federation's, everybody's. I thought they might have sorted it out by now, but apparently not. The good news is we're not getting any more bad news. The bad news is we're not getting any news whatsoever.'

'Um,' Acorna said, and she and Aari sleep-walked back to their quarters.

'They seem to have exhausted their fuel supplies,' Maak observed.

'Yeah, well, if they don't wake up in about a day, we'd better wake them and make sure they refuel. Meanwhile we'll twirl around this planet a few more times.'

When Aari and Acorna had not stirred exactly twenty-four hours later, Maak said, 'I will go pick their favorite vegetable matter and grasses from the hydroponics garden now. Would you care for any, Captain?'

'No, but I want to talk to them if they're up to it, so let me take the salad in, okay?'

Maak returned with a Linyaari-woven basket stuffed with grasses, flowers, and vegetables. Becker knocked on the cabin door and when a sleep-muffled voice called for him to come in, he did, and was almost bowled over by a large furry body streaking to the berth of his Linyaari ship-mates.

RK hopped onto Aari's lap and sniffed, then sniffed at Acorna, hopped down, and streaked off as fast as he could.

'I hope Riidkiiyi was not offended because I did not pet him,' Aari said. 'My mind is not working very efficiently, and my hands and legs still feel as if we are on a heavy-gravity world.'

Acorna yawned and stretched, then slumped back against her mate. 'Yes. My thoughts exactly.'

'We just thought you kids ought to eat something,' Becker said, holding out the basket. 'Your horns are looking a little perkier, and I can't see the wall through them anymore, but you've got a ways to go before you're one hundred percent.'

'Very kind,' Acorna murmured.

'Thanks, Joh,' Aari said, before stuffing succulent purple bean sprouts into his mouth.

'Look, guys, this mission really took it out of you. From what you said and the way you look, I think this is a bigger problem than the two of you can deal with. I say we head back to MOO and get reinforcements. It's going to take a whole bunch of Linyaari to stop this bug that's going around.'

'Yes, Joh, but we would need to go back and get Khorii and Elviiz,' Acorna said.

'And Khiindi,' Aari reminded her, in their daughter's tone.

'Of course. Khiindi. That trip alone requires several days, during which more people may sicken and die when we could save them. Not to mention that even with your shortcuts, it is a long trip back to MOO. By the time we returned with other Linyaari, the entire Federation could be infected and much of it depopulated.'

'Yeah, but maybe not. There were a lot of folks down there on Paloduro still alive.'

'And many many dead,' Aari pointed out. 'It is a very strange disease. Some seem to die almost immediately, others appear to have a very high resistance, while still others take a longer period to sicken with the same exposure as those who have already died. Most of those who are left on Paloduro are elders and children.'

'Hmm, and they're gonna be pretty helpless trying to run a planet without sturdy young adults to manage things,' Becker said. He started to scratch his chin and felt a wave of nausea wash over him.

'Not entirely,' Acorna said. 'The elders have much accumulated knowledge of how their city works, and from what we saw the youngsters are very bright and resourceful. We met one very impressive boy who wants us to make the university's laboratory safe for him to work in so he can begin finding a cure. As soon as we have rested enough that our horns are back to normal, I think we should do that.'

Becker, one hand covering his mouth, held up his other hand for her to wait and ran from the room with his thighs locked together. Without the benefit of their horns' air-purifying powers, the Linyaari caught a disagreeable odor from the wind in his wake.

This dissuaded both Aari and Acorna from

283

finishing the rest of their meal and both flopped back against their berth and fell deeply asleep before their heads hit their respective pillows.

Khiindi stalked back and forth in front of the viewscreen yowling his head off. He was very upset indeed and didn't care who knew about it. The screen was filled with the huge blue-green wet planet veined with red-and-black craters and chock-full of fish. How could both Khorii *and* Elviiz have gone off and left him aboard the *Mana*? They *did* know he *liked* fish, didn't they? And they knew that they were leaving him with Marl Fidd, who was just biding his time until he could get ahold of Khiindi again when there was no Linyaari girl around to heal him.

Sesseli was sweet, but she was not big enough to protect him from Marl. She could not pilot a shuttle down to the fishy planet. And worst of all, she had been seduced away from him by the feline wiles of the VES, those sexless and superior-acting animals with whom he could converse, but who had no more sentience in the lot of them than the average turnip.

Forced to find other suitable company, he had tried Jaya next. She had petted him initially, but was a little thick when it came to his signals for treats. Now she was upset with him, holding her ears and squinting her eyes tightly shut as if his quite legitimate protests made her head hurt. If Khorii had stayed here where she belonged, she could have fixed that.

Jaya hailed the shuttle. 'Elviiz, any sign of Khorii yet? Will you be returning soon?'

'Is that Khiindi's voice I hear?' Elviiz asked. 'My auditory sensors can barely read your voice patterns, Jaya, but Khiindi's are transmitting quite clearly.'

'I'll bet! He's driving me completely nuts. If he doesn't stop, I'm going to lock him in one of the cabins or in the cargo hold.'

'Here, Jaya,' Marl Fidd said smoothly. 'Pop him into this bag, and I'll get rid of him for you.'

Sesseli heard that and jumped up, dumping kittens from her lap. 'No!'

Marl fell back onto the deck as if he'd been shoved, and Khiindi found himself suddenly sailing through the air, though not in his normal jumping posture at all. He landed behind Sesseli in the middle of the senior VES, who smacked his face and hissed at him, so his position, though improved, was still not ideal.

Marl gaped at Sesseli in surprise, then grinned, baring lots of teeth in a way that would horrify most well-brought-up Linyaari. 'Whattaya know? The infant is telekinetic.'

'Only when I get really mad,' Sesseli said, jutting out her lower jaw. If she were a cat, her ears would have been flat and her back up.

'I guess I'll have to be careful not to let you know if I do anything I think might make you mad then,' Marl said.

Khiindi decided to stay near Sesseli. Not that he disliked Hap. Hap was large. Hap would protect him. But Hap had discovered the engine room, which was full of smells that offended Khiindi's sensitive nostrils. So Sesseli had suddenly become his best bet for protection until Khorii returned.

'This is the *Nakomas* calling the *Mana*. Do you read me, *Mana*?'

'Jaya here, Elviiz. Yes, we read you. When are you coming back?'

'We're preparing to leave now. The LoiLoiKuans swam back with Khorii a few minutes ago, and I just strapped her in.'

'How was the mission?'

'Oh, it was successful. The LoiLoiKuans are as pleased as a race that has lost a third of their population can be. But Khorii isn't well. I think we should try to contact her parents again, since we're somewhat closer now.'

'I'll get right on it, if you'll give me the data. What's wrong with Khorii?'

'The problem is that she ended up not only healing the sick LoiLoiKuans, but also purifying the ocean here when she dived in. There aren't many boundaries, and it's a lot of water.'

'She can *do* that?' Jaya said.

'Something like that,' Elviiz said. 'This is the *Nakomas* en route.'

'So that's how she does it,' Marl said. 'Duh. It took a while to sink in, but I knew that damn poultice didn't do any good. It's the horn, right? Her handy little all-purpose tool for making everything all better. Well, well, well.'

Khiindi did not like the way he said that.

'And the android's horn is just because he's a silly ass, right? He wants to look like her. I notice he never does any of the actual healing even though she always says "we" are going to decontaminate something or other.'

The scaredy-cat part of Khiindi afraid for his own tail and pelt faded into the background, and the older, more intelligent, if not wiser part took over. This fellow could be a threat to more than him. Something should be done about him, and soon. Khiindi sat and considered, his tail lashing back and forth. Marl had caught him by surprise once, but the truth was that a bully like him was no match even for merely a smart cat, much less a cat who was only apparently a cat and had Khiindi's background. The thing about bullies was, you had to stand up to them, even if you only came to the middle of their shins. Cats could leap, claw, bite, tear, ride, jump, and do many other things to protect themselves if necessary. But very few possessed the wits that Khiindi did, at least when he remembered to use them. It was alarming, really, how being frozen in cat form was causing him to sink into the bestiality of his nature, rather than remembering who he really was and using the skills that had always stood him in good stead. The mental ones anyway. He was an empath by nature and he had not even attempted to figure out why Marl hated him so much. All he could sense was that the fellow loathed felines, or maybe just didn't like *HIM*. He did not seem particularly bent on destroying the VES at all, did not send them the sneers and narrow-eyed threatening looks he cast at Khiindi.

That was not the point now, however. The point was that this – what was the word? Punk? Young thug? – showed signs of being a threat to Khorii. Most of the time, Khiindi let Khorii protect him, even though he was actually with her to protect her. Ordinarily if she needed protecting, Elviiz did it, and often irritated her when he did.

But while Marl had been lazy, annoying, and insensitive, he had not done anything dangerous to anyone since the incident with Khiindi at the pool room. Meanwhile, Elviiz had been shamed by his violent reaction to Marl back on Maganos. He might process twice before acting against Marl again, and that would not be good for Khorii.

Khiindi rose and stretched, putting a paw on Sesseli's leg just to remind her he was there. He would be as vigilant as the VES were at a mousehole. More vigilant, since Khorii and the secret of the Linyaari people were at risk.

Khorii drifted in her sleep, strange, deeply resonant sounds reverberating through her mind, echoing off something far away, or perhaps they were answered? This was the far talk, she realized, the LoiLoiKuan adaptation of the ancient speech of whales from millenniums ago on a world long dead. Like the whales, LoiLoiKua's people spoke to each other across the miles of water separating one community, or pod, from another. But now she thought it might be going even farther.

Then she saw that it was her parents sending a message to her through space. They were swimming through a sea of the little motes that Khorii had come to associate with the plague as they called out to her. But though their faces were straining with the effort and their mouths moving, no sounds came out. She studied their faces to try to read their lips and listened as hard as she could with her mind, but all she heard was 'purrrr purrr purr.' She was no longer swimming, she knew, because most cats disliked water and soft, heavy, furry weight seemed to be piled all over and around her.

'She's waking up,' Elviiz said. 'And she's feeling better, too. Young Linyaari recover from overexertion much faster than their elders, I've been told. See? Her horn is already translucent, and you can detect the golden color now.'

'Elviiz!' Khorii said, sitting up and dumping cats everywhere. 'You aren't supposed to emphasize that kind of thing to – you know?'

'Oh? You have not been very subtle about it at all,' he replied. 'It is not as if they can fail to see the changes in your horn, Khorii. It was right there for everyone to see.'

'Of course it was but . . .'

'And these are all our friends,' he said, waving to Asha, Jaya, Hap, Sesseli, and the cats. It was a sweeping gesture that even included Marl. 'They will not ask questions.'

'I have a few,' Marl said, holding up his hand. Elviiz gave the arm, the one he had broken, a meaningful look, and Marl quickly tucked it behind him.

Khorii observed this with amusement. She was still quite tired, but also felt light and rather cheerful. 'I just saved a whole planet full of people, didn't I?' she told, rather than asked, her crew mates. 'Really, I did very well. Mother and Father should have taken us with them, Elviiz. We could have helped.'

'Yes, we could have,' he agreed. 'But you must remember to heal people *out* of the water next time. Healing an ocean that covers an entire planet is rather ambitious.'

She yawned and stretched and leaned over to pet Khiindi. 'It wasn't all that big a planet really. I'm fine. And I didn't have to swim all the way out to touch the people near the reef because, when I purified the water, it carried the healing with it even to the sick poopuus far away. I must have killed all of the organisms that were in the water, and therefore in the people breathing the water.'

'Too bad you can't do it with people who don't breathe water,' Asha said. 'That could come in handy. As it is, I don't know if anything can really be done to check the spread of this plague now.'

TWENTY-FOUR

Aari and Acorna were awakened by a strange sound. A slow, rhythmic pounding shook the door of their cabin. Calling for the pounder to come in evoked no response, so Aari rose and opened the door.

Maak stood there, something limp and furry draped over one arm. 'We are broken,' he said in a slow, slurred voice much like a recording played on a damaged machine. Aari hurriedly took the raglike form of RK from the android. Maak was emitting sparks from his oral cavity, and the arm that had been holding RK stayed upright, as if carrying something invisible.

'Where is Joh?'

'Broken,' Maak said.

Acorna was now fully awake. Neither of their horns had returned to full opacity yet, but she felt a little better. 'Who is on the bridge, Maak?'

'Brokennn,' he repeated, his already slowed voice deteriorating further into unintelligible noises.

'I'll go, Aari. Here, give me RK.'

291

'He's very—' Aari started to say, but when Acorna felt the cat's body she gasped in alarm.

'His life is nearly gone!' she said, and immediately lowered her horn into the cat's fur while she carried him to the bridge.

To her chagrin, RK didn't immediately rally as she had expected, though he did give a miserable mew and coughed. His eyes were crusted shut with discharge, and the fur of his tail and hindquarters was matted and filthy.

How long had she and Aari slept anyway? The last time they'd seen RK he was his usual boisterous, bouncing, and bossy self. His sickness looked like a feline version of the plague, but how could that be? She and Aari had thoroughly decontaminated the ship before they left. All of the *Condor*'s crew had been in good health then.

Her horn was not functioning fully yet. She could smell the foulness of RK's illness, and it was growing stronger rather than weaker. She saw the side of Captain Becker's head and his arm in the command chair.

'Captain, RK is very ill and Maak appears to be malfunctioning. He said the *Condor* was also malfunctioning. I came to help. We are so sorry we've rested for so long when you needed us. You should have awakened us.'

But there was no reply from Becker. She laid RK in the copilot's seat and knelt beside the captain. His head lolled, and the hand she had thought was merely relaxed actually flopped back and forth when she raised it.

The smell had been coming from him, not RK.

'Oh, Captain Becker, Joh, why did you not call us?' she asked, still reeling from her weariness.

Laying her horn alongside Becker's face did no good. It did not even take away the smell of illness. Unzipping the neck of his soiled shipsuit, she laid her ear against his chest and felt it rise a little and fall back as if taking in oxygen was too much effort, each slight breath he took wheezing through his clogged passages as he exhaled. His heartbeat was loud but quite irregular, as if it was beating any way it could to try to pump his blood, but had to make an extremely difficult effort to do so.

She looked away from him long enough to see that he had set the *Condor* on autopilot, but that their fuel was low.

Aari came out. 'I shut Maak down,' he said. 'I am giving him a fresh energy charge until we can solve what is wrong with his organic components. Where is RK?'

She nodded to the very quiet cat in the copilot's seat.

'Joh, too? Yes,' he said, wrinkling his nose. Automatically, he lowered his horn to his friend's head, but shook his own head when he received no response. 'You tried your horn already, also?'

'Yes, but we are not yet recovered enough to be able to cure even RK. We must take them to the captain's cabin and clean them and try to make them comfortable as we saw Jalonzo and Abuelita do with the victims who were waiting for us to treat n.'

'Fine. I will clean the captain while you clean RK and monitor the *Condor*'s instruments.'

'When you have finished cleaning him, try to sleep again so that your horn will regain its strength, my love. Otherwise I fear . . .' She did not finish saying it, because she could not bear to, and although she tried to hold it back, a single tear welled in her eye.

'Yes,' he said briskly. She knew he ached for their friends, but his eyes held the same steely glint and his jaw the same stubborn set as they might have shown when the Khleevi had tortured him so long ago. In some ways, this had to be worse, for there was no enemy here to be spotted and fought against, only an insidious invader that seemed to threaten them time after time.

'I cannot sleep. Right now I feel about as helpless as I have ever felt in my life. We cannot even pilot the ship back to Vhiliinyar so that other Linyaari could heal them. I do not know what humans do to help each other in these situations. Without horns, they have to rely on other methods, and I have never learned what those are. If I can make Joh somewhat comfortable, I will ransack his library and try to find a way to help him and Riidkiiyi.'

'That is a very useful idea, but we still must continue to rest, *yaazi*, so our horns will recover their power. Nothing humans have done for the plague so far seems to work very well. I don't know if they've ever had to deal with such a disease before. There have been other plagues, but

294

never one so widespread. I fear what those books can tell you may be of limited use. Rest . . .'

'We must keep them alive until we recover enough to heal them though, mustn't we?' he said. 'I do not know how to do that. Joh saved me from a slow death by starvation after I escaped the Khleevi. Because of him, we were able to defeat the Khleevi and rebuild our world. We must do everything possible to save him now.'

'Yes, of course we must. Find the books and when you can rest, give them to me, and I will research, too. Human medicine is imprecise, but surely there is something that will help.'

The com unit beeped for Acorna's attention. It had been so long since anyone had been on the other end, it startled her. 'Acorna and Aari, are you okay? Oh, this is Jalonzo.' He waved from the vid screen. 'Hola. I was just wondering because you're still up there, aren't you, and I thought you were going to go to the other planets.'

'We've had a problem, Jalonzo,' Acorna said. 'We can't go anywhere just now.'

'Well, if you're not, would it be possible for you to come back down here and fix the lab so I can start my research? I have some good ideas about this, and one of the elders is a biologist who is going to help me with some experiments, but I need somewhere to work.'

'No, I'm sorry. We haven't recovered our strength yet.' She thought about mentioning Becker's and RK's illness, but decided against it. It might alarm Jalonzo and everyone else to know that the Linyaaris' own human crew was sick.

'Too bad. As soon as you're better, would you do this before you go, please? I really think I can help.'

'Let's see how things progress, Jalonzo. We have some complications here.'

'Oh. Well, okay. Good-bye then. Uh. Jalonzo out.'

RK coughed and coughed, but produced no hairballs. She wished that *was* his problem. He was so weak afterward, and his breathing was very fast and shallow. She laid her face and horn in his fur again. It felt hot, spiky, and damp. Feeling helpless, she stroked him until he stopped writhing and lay motionless in her lap.

The intercom from Becker's cabin made a scratchy noise. She jumped at the sound, then flipped the toggle, almost afraid of what Aari might want to tell her. 'Acorna, *yaazi*, I have bad news,' he said.

'Worse than it is already?'

'I am afraid so. I have been reading about plagues in these books. I believe that we have both become what was once called a Typhoid Mary.'

'What?' She wondered if Aari was succumbing to the fever himself.

'Typhoid Mary,' he said, and began to read, 'In the early part of the twentieth century on the part of the Earth known as New York City, an Irish cook named Mary Mallon was identified as a healthy carrier of typhoid fever. Although she claimed never to have had typhoid herself, outbreaks of the fever followed Mary from job to job. The health department found typhoid bacilli in her blood and stool. Many people became very ill from her contagion and three died. Eventually she was isolated on a tiny island for the rest of her life.'

'You think we brought the plague back onto the ship to Joh and RK, even to Mac's organic parts?' she asked.

'Yes. I think in our weakened condition, our resistance to disease was down and the plague attacked us. It could not make us sick because we are Linyaari, and we don't get sick, even if our horns are not functioning normally. But we brought it with us to Joh and the others, and even worse, I don't know how we are going to save them.'

Khorii waited her turn for the sonic showers. Hap, who had been in the engine room, went first. Elviiz, whose nonorganic components could be adversely affected by the shower's sonics, sought privacy to initiate his self-cleansing routine and change his clothing.

When Hap emerged, Khorii stripped off her shipsuit and shook it. Linyaari shipsuits were extremely resistant to dirt and body soil and could be worn continually for months if necessary with nothing more than an occasional good shaking. A piece of paper fluttered from one of the deep pockets down onto the deck. Khorii picked it up.

It was a page from the passenger manifest to the *Blanca*. She must have missed it when she gave the rest of the list to her mother. Tucking it inside her shipsuit, she showered, came back out, and dressed. The list could go back in her pocket until later.

Then Elviiz, his toilette completed, returned to the bathing area.

'Look what I found,' she said.

'Ah,' he said. 'The hard copy of the passenger manifest. You do not really need it though, you know. I downloaded all of that information from the ship's computer while searching the *Blanca*'s bridge.'

'You've been holding out on me,' she accused.

'Not really. I have never taken the time to collate the data other than by general categories.'

'We have time now. What general categories did you download?'

'Passenger manifest, crew roster and schedules, personnel files, captain's log . . .'

'You found the captain's log? Why didn't you say so? That's one of the things I was looking for.'

'Why did you not say so?'

'I'm saying so now. Please upload it to the *Mana*'s system so I can read it.'

'I could recite it for you,' he said.

'Actually, I hate it when you do that,' she told him.

'Have it your way then.'

That was one of the good things about Elviiz's being an android. Unless she wanted to do something that would cause her immediate injury or death, he usually agreed to almost any scheme she came up with, and was more than ready to provide any information she wanted. The only thing he wasn't very good at was taking the blame if something went wrong. Her parents always looked straight at her. Being a Linyaari child definitely had its drawbacks. Adults could read your mind, and you couldn't read theirs. But she was working on that . . .

Once Elviiz has finished uploading the information, Khorii settled down at a screen and started from the beginning.

'Captain's log Day 1:

Shipped out of Dinero Grande with a passenger roster of dignitaries, ambassadors, corporate heads, royalty, and Federation and local government officials. Most arrived in their own shuttles now docked in our bay. We carry a cargo of the best the Solojo system has to offer, including the finest new vintages of Rio Boca Rojo, the distinctive wine of that world that is much better fresh than aged.

Day 2: The ship's surgeon reports four cases of fever and respiratory distress among the cargo handlers. The supply officer is also ill. Fortunately, they have time to recover before we need to off-load the cargo to the *Stella Nuevo* at Santa Catrina Station.

Day 3, Hour 14: Two of the handlers, the supply officer, and the ship's surgeon have died of the fever. Two stewards and sixteen of the passengers are now displaying symptoms as well. Infirmary packed to capacity, with only medical aids to provide care. Have contacted the Federation regarding our condition and am awaiting further instructions.

Day 4: I went to see about the welfare of the stricken passengers. All but one had died, and that one died an hour ago. This is a very virulent and aggressive disease, whatever it is. Federation reply advocates staying away from populated areas for fear of spreading infection. They have promised help, but were strangely vague about when to expect their arrival.

Day 5: We are trying to maintain calm and a sense of business as usual among the passengers and crew but forty-six people are now dead or dying. We bypassed Santa Catrina, angering some of the passengers, who threatened to take their private vessels and jump ship. I cannot allow this to happen. Have imposed strict quarantine on the sick, but as soon as one group is isolated, others outside the group come down with the symptoms. The service crew, what remains of it, refuses to interact with passengers. The ship's navigator does not look well either.

Day 8: Peculiar how people refuse to believe evidence they don't like. With crew and passengers dropping like flies around them, the Premier Class passengers, so far mostly unaffected by the disease, have demanded that they be put ashore at Luna

Sangre for the event they plan to attend there two days hence. I have been informed that if the *Blanca* does not dock, these people will be leaving in their private vessels. This I cannot allow. The crew is also turning mutinous. Have contacted nearby Federation outposts, but they seem to be having their own problems with this illness, and no stations near us are equipped to handle more patients. Everyone is frightened, but this illness must be confined to the ship. We have seventy-five dead and fifty near death at this point. There seems to be no treatment. I will do anything necessary to prevent anyone from leaving.

Day 9, Hour 23: I have confined all crew members except essential bridge personnel to their quarters and ordered the passengers to stay in their cabins. The first officer is attempting to wrest command from me. I made the mistake of confiding my contingency plan for the passengers should any of them carry out their threat to escape quarantine. To prevent any from carrying the plague with them, I have changed the course of the *Blanca* to an uninhabited section of space outside of their shuttles' ranges.

Day 10: I am not a monster. It was a medical necessity for the entire universe that I did what I did.

I was forced to execute the first officer and navigator for mutiny. They attempted to stop me from detaining the passengers who panicked and ran for their personal vessels. I could not permit that, of course, and at first I thought I succeeded in hiding it from my senior officers. I did, long enough to achieve my goal. I tried to make it as quick and painless as possible. I simply turned off the scrubbers in the ventilation system on the passenger decks and docking bay and backflushed the vents, reversing the air flow. Though two of the passengers reached their private vessels, as I see on the surveillance cam, none succeeded in leaving the ship. Everyone suffocated. It was not pretty, but it was relatively fast. Once the first officer, Francisco Martinez, looked at the screen and saw the bodies in the corridor, he ordered the second mate and the communications officer to assist the passengers. Of course, I could not allow them to open the door and pollute our air – not that it would have ultimately mattered, but I still had to try to save some of us. I ordered them to stop and when they didn't, I shot them. Martinez looked at me as I resheathed my sidearm. His expression could not have been more amazed if I'd suddenly turned into an alien right before his eyes. He asked, 'What have you done?' So I tried to explain. He directly countermanded my orders, immediately resetting the controls. He succeeded in turning the scrubbers back on and reestablishing normal ventilation, but by then it was too late.

Realizing that anyone still alive would not long survive and if they did, would be in no condition to oppose my orders, I allowed him to do so. When he saw that his counter-measures were of no use, he became deranged and attacked me. While he attempted to restrain me in a bear hug, I was able to free my arm and my weapon. I shot him through the chest, then, once I was free again, I shot him at the base of the skull. It was a relatively painless death, though not, as I had hoped, instantaneous. I made him as comfortable as possible at his duty station, and it won't be long until he's gone. It is my turn now. I cannot operate this ship alone, I cannot allow others to enter it in an attempt to detain me, and I cannot leave the ship for fear of carrying the disease to the outside world. God forgive me and have mercy on us all. Captain Dolores Maria Grimwold, M.D.

'So I was right,' Khorii said, looking up as she finished reading. 'It was the plague.'

'No. It was the captain, as you can see, who was responsible for the total annihilation of the crew and passengers, as I mentioned before,' Elviiz, who had been standing beside her reading over her shoulder, said. 'The plague did kill many of the passengers, but the captain killed the rest.'

'Only to stop the plague from spreading,' Khorii said. 'But this makes me wonder. Why didn't all of the passengers get it? From reading this, it sounds as if isolation really was impossible to enforce. And why didn't the captain herself get sick?'

'She sounds as if she may have been insane at the end,' Elviiz said.

'She knew what she had to do. But she does not mention being sick with the plague. She was a medical doctor herself. What a terrible decision to make!'

'Yes, terrible. It was *ka*-Linyaari,' Elviiz said, in a severe tone.

'Had she been Linyaari or had anyone aboard been Linyaari, no one would have died and none of that would have been necessary,' Khorii replied.

'Danger! Warning! Quarantine alert! This entire sector is under quarantine by order of Federation directive number 000472985-2-FDR. All ships are ordered back to their homeports. Any vessel not complying will be destroyed. Reverse course at once. In precisely fifteen minutes this ship will target your vessel with a diterium warhead.'

The announcement continued over the loudspeakers of the Linyaari ship. 'Firing will begin in fourteen minutes and fifty-eight seconds. Fourteen minutes and fifty-seven seconds. Fourteen minutes and fifty-six seconds . . .'

'What a lovely voice she has!' Maarni said to her husband.

'Yes, isn't it? Especially considering the message,' he replied.

'Federation vessel, this is the Linyaari vessel *Mahiiri*. We are plague-free from another quadrant and are here to help. Do not fire. Have you any plague victims aboard who need our assistance? We have the means to cure them.'

'Firing will begin in thirteen minutes and forty seconds.'

'Well, dear, extrude the boarding apparatus. They are not responding, but it does not look like a drone to me.'

'Nor me. Boarding apparatus extruded. Fasten your helmet, Yiitir.'

'Already done, my love. Shall we?'

'Firing will begin in thirteen minutes and fifteen seconds.'

Once aboard the Federation vessel, they disarmed the warhead as they had been taught and examined each crew member to see if, contrary to appearances, any of them still lived.

'Oh, how sad. All gone. And so very young, too. This makes how many of these ships we've encountered, dear?'

'Six.'

'And how many survivors we have been able to assist.'

'None.'

'I do hope the *Balakiire* will have better luck at Maganos Moonbase, while the rest of us tidy up space out here and maintain communication lines while patching up the Federation's. Surely the youngsters on the Moonbase will be fine. Aari and Acorna are well able to protect a small moon and still prevent the plague from spreading else-where.'

305

'One would think. It does seem to be a very wide-spread plague, judging from all of the threats and warnings we've been receiving. But then, I have no idea what is usual in this sort of situation. There's certainly nothing in our history to inform one, is there?'

'No, dear. Certainly not.'

After conducting a thorough decontamination of the ship so it could be retrieved later by the Federation without risk of infection, they returned to their own craft. Like all Linyaari vessels, the *Mahiiri* was egg-shaped. It distinguished itself from others in the Linyaari fleet by the appearance of its hull, which was decorated with swags of gilt and tasteful patterns in lavender, mint green, and purple.

'Oh, good, the com signal is on. Perhaps there's word from the vanguard even now!'

'*Mahiiri*, this is Naarye aboard the *Haamiiri*. Transmission from the *Balakiire* says that Aari and Acorna did not land on Maganos Moonbase. Acorna's fathers and their wives are all safe at a health facility on Kezdet. The baby boy was born at two o'clock in the morning Kezdet Standard time. He was fifteen inches long and weighed seven and one-half pounds. He is being named Harry, in honor of Uncle Hafiz Harakamian, according to the father. That is the good news.'

'It is indeed,' Yiitir said. 'Hafiz will be so proud. Well, actually, he always is, but this will please him very much.'

'There is also bad news,' Naarye continued.

'Acorna and Aari left without seeing the baby or her fathers. The Federation asked them to help contain the plague.'

'That was to be expected, I suppose,' Yiitir said.

'That is not all. They left young Khorii and Maak's son Elviiz at Maganos Moonbase, but the younglings took a shuttle to an infected cargo ship and left the system. Since communications are down, nobody knows where they are except, of course, for the guess that they are probably going to try to intercept Aari and Acorna, whose mission is in a star system called the – it is not something we can pronounce. I will write it for you in Standard. S. O. L. O. J. O.'

'My stars, that is rather alarming! The younglings out in space all alone on an infected ship.'

'Not entirely alone. Three of the other students went with them and one of the teachers as well.'

'Ah, well, a teacher,' Maarni said, somewhat relieved.

'The *Balakiire* stated its intention of joining Aari and Acorna and probably Khorii's ship as well, but the Federation has requested that we continue to help plague victims and decontaminate critical areas such as the communication chain and health-care facilities. We have agreed, of course, as long as we may maintain our own relay back to MOO as we do so, and the *Balakiire* is free to seek our friends.'

'That sounds fair enough,' Yiitir said.

'Poor children,' Maarni said. 'I hope they can be

located soon so that Khorii can return to the safety of her own family.'

'I believe we are all in sympathy with that sentiment, Maarni. Your assignment will be to visit Uncle Hafiz's headquarters on the planet of Laboue. House Harakamian's enterprises are crucial to the smooth recovery of this sector, according to the Federation.'

'Delighted, Naarye. You can count on us. Please keep us informed.'

'Yes. Naarye out.'

TWENTY-FIVE

The Solojo system, at last!' Khorii said, giving Captain Bates the thumbs-up signal Uncle Joh used to signify he was pleased with the progress of certain events.

'Yep, there's the sun, and we're approaching Rio Boca,' the captain said. 'Khorii, it's your turn to take the helm. You kids are coming along very well. Elviiz took very little instruction, Jaya was already fairly familiar with this ship, though she's a bit vague on programming in courses, Hap was one of my best students and much to my surprise, Marl has taken to piloting like an extinct water-treading avian to – er – water. Even Sesseli has done pretty well at her lessons. You're going to make me redundant if I don't watch out.'

'Do we have enough fuel to make it straight to Paloduro?' Khorii asked. 'I'd love to see my mother's and father's faces when I fly this ship over to rendezvous with the Condor.'

'Looks like it to me,' Captain Bates said.

'We carry extra fuel,' Jaya said. 'That's what cargo bay three is for – extra fuel, extra parts.'

'No problem then,' Khorii said. 'We're on our way.'

She wished Elviiz was there so she could rub his nose in it, just a little. Or Hap, because he'd be pleased. But only Captain Bates, Jaya, Sesseli, and Khorii were on the bridge when she took the helm. And the cats, of course, were sleeping somewhere close by.

Rio Boca was the outermost planet in the Solojo system, but the others were comparatively close in their distance from the sun. All of them had been inhabited for a long time, according to Captain Bates.

'Rio Boca is the "port planet" of this system, where most of the shipping to and from other worlds takes place. It also has a few tourist attractions,' Captain Bates told her.

'Yes!' Jaya said with more animation than Khorii had seen her show before. 'Once Mom and Dad and I took a great vacation to the falls. You can see *la Catarata de la Llorarona*, the Weeping Woman's Waterfall, from space. I'll show you when we get closer. Also the *Sangre de Frida*, Frieda's Blood in Standard, mountains. The waterfall carries the runoff from them and it's the head of the river that becomes the Rio Boca when it reaches the Sea of the Pilgrims' Tears.'

'They have a lot of sad names for things, don't they?' Khorii asked.

'Well, the earliest colonizers apparently had

310

some difficulties. But it's a very rich planet. They have lots of good farmland for coffee, bananas, pineapple, and sugar as well as a lot of the kinds of things you like to eat, Khorii. Fruits and veggies and stuff. They also supply a lot of pharmaceutical companies with crops that have medicinal uses. We actually pick up – we did pick up – quite a lot of cargo here to export to other planets. And they have beautiful jewelry here, too! Dad said it was because the rivers and streams – the Rio Boca and all of its tributaries, are full of gemstones and mineral deposits.'

'It looks beautiful even from here,' Khorii said. She had to concentrate not to be hypnotized by the greenery ribboned with sparkly silver-and-turquoise waters.

'The city of Rio Boca is kind of ugly, actually. Full of docking facilities for spaceships and boring warehouses full of goods. But once you get up the river, away from the port, it's beautiful. Long stretches with no towns or people, just huge plantations.'

'Where does everybody live then?'

Captain Bates said, 'They've divided this system's planetary assets into the functions the people here need. Most of the government and administration for the entire system, as well as the banking and many of the fancier homes of officials and wealthy industrialists, are on Dinero Grande, Big Money.'

'I've always liked the sound of that one,' Marl said, coming up behind them.

Captain Bates continued, disregarding his comment. 'Your parents were supposed to be on Paloduro, which is the planet where most of the population lives. There is some industry there, too, and Corazon, the main city, is famous for its Carnivale, a monthlong masquerade party and parade that was in progress when the plague struck.'

'That's so sad,' Jaya said. 'We got to go to that once, too. It was a lot of fun. I was only little, but Mom made me a leopard costume so I could dance in the parade.'

'I heard something about that when my folks were asked to come here,' Khorii said. 'The Federation health official who talked to them said that Paloduro was the last of these three planets to report an outbreak, so they thought Mother and Father could save the most people if they went there first. The plague must have started way earlier though, before it got reported even.'

'How's that?'

'You know the captain's log Elviiz uploaded to the ship's computer for me to read? It was from a derelict luxury liner we found with all the people dead either of plague or killed by the captain to keep them from breaking quarantine. The registration was from Dinero Grande.'

'Now I find that fascinating,' Marl said, though nobody was talking to him. 'I did when I read that captain's log, too. What a fix they were in. I recognized a lot of big names from that passenger roster. Not all were from these parts, mind you, but a significant number of them were. Just the trillionaires and local government people, none of the royalty. More's the pity. I'd love to get my hands on some crown jewels. I'm a romantic that way, I guess. But actually, I'm a farm boy at heart. There are some agricultural crops and their by-products that particularly interest me.'

'You're not getting your hands on any of it, Fidd, so just forget it,' Captain Bates told him. 'Those planets are all still crawling with plague. There's probably nobody left alive by now.'

'My point exactly,' he said, reaching between the two of them to the instruments. 'They'll have no use for any of it. Why should it go to waste? As for the plague, we have our own little cleaner-upper here in our Khorii,' he said, laying a heavy hand on her shoulder. 'It's perfect, really.'

'Except it's not gonna happen,' the captain told him.

'Oh, I think it will,' he said. 'It seems to me it was meant to be. Here we are in this nice big cargo ship to carry away lots of loot, what with loaders and cargo shuttles and everything and our Khorii to make it all safe as a Federation outpost. Safer, even. It's fate. Has to be.'

'We are not looters,' Captain Bates said. 'We're helping Khorii with her rescue mission and taking her back to her parents.'

He waved his hand dismissively. 'That's all fine. She can do that, too, especially if we bring up enough stuff to fill the bays. Jaya, sweetie?'

'What?' she demanded, her eyes glittering rebelliously.

313

'You can save us a lot of time, my love. Find your parents' files on the layout of Rio Boca's warehouse district for us, won't you? That way we can be most efficient by heading straight for the ones with the best goodies.'

'No!' Jaya said. 'Why would I do that?'

'Because if you don't, I will start by killing Hellstrom, who had a close encounter with a spanner I just happened to be holding at the time. No, don't shriek, he's fine. Or will be when he comes to, if you all cooperate.'

'And if we don't?'

'Then I will grab little friend here' – he squeezed Khorii's shoulder – 'and take the biggest shuttle to the surface. Once we won't get caught in the fringe of the blast, I'll set off the detonator that will explode this ship and all of you with it. And that would be a shame because, like I said, it has all these half-empty cargo bays just waiting to be filled. But there are no doubt other ships docked down there. Khorii can decontaminate one for us to fill with treasure, then she and I will continue on our merry way to Dinero Grande and who knows after that? You lot could come in handy, but you're not really necessary.'

'You're hijacking us?' Jaya asked. 'You're hijacking *my* ship?'

'Not yours, little girl. It belonged to the Krishna-Murti Company, but probably most of them are dead. So it will be the flagship of my new enterprise, and you are all on the payroll, figuratively speaking. Now then, Captain Bates, you take over

314

the helm again and put this bird into orbit around Rio Boca. You'll stay here with Hellstrom, but don't think you can plot anything. I've got him locked in the engine room, and I changed the pass code.'

'And you think we're going to do what you say just because you claim to have set explosives here?' Jaya said. 'Puh-leeze.'

Frowning, Captain Bates said, 'I think that's what we'd better do, all right, kids.'

Marl smiled, showing lots of teeth. 'Good for you, Captain. Did your research on us students, didn't you? Saw my background with the Cholaran Resistance Movement? They hated to let me go, you know. I'm sure they still miss my talent with fireworks.'

'I still don't believe you, you nasty boy,' Sesseli said. 'If you've really got a detonator, let us see it.'

'You'd like that, wouldn't you, chicklet? Then you could snatch it out of my hands, couldn't you? What you and Khorii, great telepaths that you are, failed to notice is that old Marl has a bit of a gift, too. So I'm on to both of you, so don't try to be cute. Just be useful, and we'll get on fine. Now, then . . . I wonder how much cargo you can lift with that tiny mind of yours? Could be quite useful. Ah, ah, don't even think about trying to pick me up and throw me across the room – you might set the detonator off accidentally, and wouldn't that be too bad for poor Hap.'

Khorii wondered where Elviiz was. As if *he* could read *her* mind, Marl said, 'Oh, don't go

315

looking for help from your pet android, Khorii.'

'What did you do to him?' she demanded.

'Not a thing. Not a thing. He'll be a lot of help when it comes to loading my cargo, I figure, once you tell him to do exactly as I say. I gave him a bit of a brain teaser to figure out, and I think he'll be chewing on that until I require his services.'

'Think again, sucker,' Elviiz said, in a low, menacing voice, not unlike one Marl himself used from time to time.

'Stop him, or I'll make you dismantle him piece by piece yourself,' Marl said to Khorii.

'Elviiz, stop,' she said.

'He asked me some ridiculous riddle about some stupid polygamous man who carried his many feline companions in sacks and expected me to ponder it!' Elviiz said. 'Father warned me about that sort of thing. He was trying to trick me.'

'Yes, I was,' Marl said complacently. 'And it worked long enough to accomplish what I needed it to. Now be a good little android and go stand next to Jaya.'

'We're entering Rio Boca's orbit now,' Captain Bates said.

'Great. Let's all go down to the shuttle bay then.'

'Not until you let me look at Hap's head,' Khorii said, folding her arms across her chest. 'I won't leave without knowing that he's not going to die while we're helping you steal from dead people.'

'You're in no situation to demand anything, missy,' Marl said.

'I think I am,' Khorii replied. 'I am the only one

on board this ship you really need to carry out your plan. What I am asking is reasonable and not difficult to do. You should consider what might happen if you do not have my cooperation for decontaminating your precious treasures before you threaten anyone else or refuse to let me see Hap.'

'I – oh, all right. He's all taped up, and he's going to stay that way though, so don't think you'll get me to change that. Come along then. Just you. Captain Bates, you are a reasonable person. You know what will happen if any of you try to take control. Make sure that doesn't happen.'

She gave him a glacial look but nodded once, sharply.

As Khorii followed Marl to the engine room, she wondered – he was so sure of her that he didn't mind showing her his back – if he really had known she was reading him because he could read her, and had deliberately thought repulsive stuff to make her back off. It had certainly had that effect. She had given up trying to read him, and therefore had seen none of his plan coming. She was disgusted with herself. It wasn't the thoughts you read that could hurt you, it was the ones you failed to read. She was going to remember that from now on. She doubted, despite his boasts, that Marl had a great deal of psychic ability, but he was shrewd enough to use the small talent he had to his greatest advantage. And she'd fallen for it. Her doubts about his talents were confirmed almost immediately.

At the engine room door, he input the new code. Apparently she was giving him too much credit to know how to block her from reading him, because she picked the code out of his mind easily. If she was such a good broadcaster that she could give her whole class test results, she hoped the people on the bridge could pick up this transmission, too – D.R.U.A.7. If nothing else, Khorii could send the code so Captain Bates could free Hap after the rest of them left. Although the teacher did not flaunt her abilities, as Marl had just done, Khorii knew she had them. She'd shared thoughts with her teacher on the day of that disastrous test.

Marl stood aside with mock courtesy and motioned her into the engine room. Hap lay on the floor, his hands taped together with heavy utility tape, his arms taped to his torso, his legs taped together at ankles, shins, knees, and thighs. The side of his head was matted with blood, and a red patch had pooled underneath him.

Khorii rushed forward and bent over him, letting out a sigh of relief when she saw that he was still breathing, though very shallowly.

'Do your thing, horn girl, and let's go.'

She laid her horn against the wound, bloodying its tip. At once the scalp wound stopped bleeding and the skin and bone knitted itself together. Hap's eyes opened, and he started to say something, but Marl shoved Khorii aside and slapped another piece of tape over his mouth. Leaving Hap lying in his own blood, Marl grabbed Khorii's arm and yanked her up and out of the room, the door sealing shut behind them.

Marl dragged her to the docking bay door and flipped the toggle on the intercom. 'Okay, you lot, get down here and let's go get my treasure.'

TWENTY-SIX

The *Mana*'s shuttle was the largest and roomiest of the transports that they had, with chairs for three people and a couple of jump seats, besides having a large empty space and nets for cargo.

'Where are the maps I told you to get?' Marl asked Jaya.

'They're in the ship's computer,' she said.

'I know they're in the ship's computer,' he said, mocking her last three words, then shouted at her. 'Where else would they be? Access them, you sniveling idiot, and let's have a look.'

A schematic appeared on the screen at Jaya's fingertips. 'Magnify the writing by each of those,' Marl ordered.

She did this, and he looked until he came to the warehouses for the coffee cooperative, the precious gems and metalwork guild, and the herb and spice growers' agricultural cooperative. He made a pleased sound and stabbed his finger at the last one. 'There. We'll start there. Our beloved teacher forgot to mention that this region is one of the top producers of medicinal and recreational drugs in the entire Federation. Not that the Federation likes it, but they can only control the importing of this stuff, not the exporting from here. Those people on Dinero Grande didn't get rich from hard work and saving their pesos, urchins.'

'Did you plan this all along, Marl?' Captain Bates asked from the ship. 'Is that why you really insisted on coming with me?'

'I'd like to say I was that farsighted, Teach, but actually I have just been well trained to take advantage of strategic opportunities, and this is a huge one. I've been thinking about these warehouses since I heard about the plague starting in Solojo and taking out so many of those pesky Federation plods. And when sweet little Khorii healed my wound I began to realize what an asset she could be. With the *Mana* handily vacated of anyone who could be a serious deterrent to a rising entrepreneur, I knew that fate was in my favor, the Cholabrian gods of pillage were with me, and here we are.'

'Touching success story,' Captain Bates said.

'Oh, shut up and orbit,' he said. 'And let me remind you not to try anything on the ship while we're gone. I've also rigged my bomb with a timer that will go off if I don't come back in time to deactivate it.'

When they had docked where he told them to, he said, 'Khorii, you first, my dear. Make the atmosphere safe for us all. Android, you get us inside. Then Khorii will do her thing again and decontaminate all my souvenirs.'

Khorii left the shuttle, but she wasn't sure what he wanted her to do out there. She saw none of the specks that had vanished before her horn in contaminated areas of the past. Of course, it might be a good thing if Marl imagined the very atmosphere was deadly without her. So she held her head up and walked a zigzag path to the door of his chosen warehouse, and touched it briefly with her horn. Then looked back to the shuttle and nodded.

Elviiz in the lead, the others emerged from the shuttle and joined her. Marl came last. 'Do it, droid,' he said. 'The rest of you stand back and give it room.' He said the 'it' with enjoyment, speaking of Elviiz as if he were a thing.

Khorii looked at her foster brother's stoic face and rolled her eyes. The sides of Elviiz's mouth turned up slightly, and he waved her back. He put his hand on the lock and, with rapid calculation, computed the code key and opened the lock, then the door.

'You are no fun, monster,' Marl said. 'Khorii, debug it.'

Khorii stepped forward, but Elviiz pushed her back and stepped in front of her, striding through the door.

Something inside exploded, and Elviiz staggered back into the street and fell, a huge hole in the skin of his chest revealing the metal shell underneath.

Khorii rushed to his side, and lowered her horn to the wound. Marl stepped across Elviiz's legs and grabbed Khorii by the arm, jerking her to her feet.

Sesseli screamed, her high, piercing cry echoing in the sudden silence.

A man's voice called out from the warehouse. *'Niña?'*

With one fluid move Marl swept the little girl into his arms, holding her tight to him. She tried to turn and glare at him, but the older boy grabbed her by the chin and forced her to look at the warehouse.

'Hey, you, in there! I'll kill this little girl if you don't throw out your weapons right now!'

From inside, heavy footsteps stumped toward the entrance, then they all heard a string of profanity as two pistols flew over their heads and landed in the street beyond them.

Sesseli's face twisted with rage, and Marl suddenly let go of her, his arms flung away from the small child. She turned back toward the warehouse and ran past all of them, crying.

Seeing her chance, Jaya snatched both pistols up and pointed them at Marl as he rushed after Sesseli through the doorway. The man shouted, then let out a yell that ended with a loud crash against something at the opposite end of the warehouse. Jaya reflexively pulled the triggers of both guns, but the bullets burrowed harmlessly into the side of the building, and Jaya herself flew backward and hit the side of the shuttle, sliding down to the ground unmoving.

'The force of the recoil of the Colt 54 Alhambra model pistol is exceeded by the velocity of the projectile by a mere fifty percent,' Elviiz said to no one in particular.

323

Khorii had pulled away from him as Jaya shot and now ran back to help the other girl. She was stunned but otherwise uninjured. Khorii picked up the pistols with two fingers of each hand on each barrel and flung them across the street. They might have come in handy, she could almost hear Hap saying, but she felt a racial revulsion inherited from generations of pacifist Linyaari forebears. Handling firearms was definitely *ka*-Linyaari.

'You coming, Khorii?' Marl asked from the doorway, apparently unfazed by recent events. 'Didn't anybody ever tell you that little girls shouldn't play with guns?' He sounded amused rather than threatened and when she drew near him, shoved her forward into the warehouse.

'Purify the loaders over there and start on the stacks,' he told her, then stepped back through the doorway.

A figure lay sprawled against a pile of cartons and Khorii ran past the loaders to it. An old man looked up at her, blood trickling from the side of his mouth. Still she saw none of the plague aura, as she had started to think of the tiny specks associated with it, surrounding him.

He had a big white mustache and thinning hair on top and looked very angry. *'This is ours,'* he was thinking, though he did not speak.

'It will do you no good if you're dead,' Khorii told him in thought-talk as she lowered her horn to heal his wounds. *'The boy you shot and all of us girls are innocent and mean you no harm. But the tall boy in the doorway is a looter and possibly a killer. I do not know*

324

*how you survived the plague, but I advise you to run
away or hide quickly, before he uses your own weapons
against you.'*

The man thought about it only a moment, then
flipped himself onto his hands and feet and made
a stooping run behind a row of stacked crates. She
did not know if he was still there or if he fled
through another exit. However, he was not in sight
when Marl dragged Sesseli with him by one arm
and Jaya by the other. Jaya's right eye was black-
ening, and her mouth was bleeding. It had not been
a moment ago. Khorii regretted throwing the guns
away. He was not going to let them go ever, was
he? They were going to be his slaves, his minions
to create his own little empire, stealing things that
belonged to the dead and selling them to anyone
who had the money to meet his price, she
supposed. Since the Federation forces had been hit
very hard by the plague, there was no longer
anyone to oppose Marl and people like him. No
one but she and a power to heal and purify that,
unfortunately, didn't seem to extend to the evil
part of human nature.

If her parents were there, she knew they'd think
of something clever to do, something Marl
wouldn't be expecting. She wished they were there
to take charge. This adventure had ceased being
fun when Marl had hijacked the ship. Better yet,
she wished she were with them and nowhere near
Marl Fidd. If she weren't here, if he hadn't figured
out her secret, he wouldn't have dared to exploit
the plague as he was doing. Maybe she could

convince Marl to go to Paloduro. Then he'd be sorry he tried to use the Linyaari to help him carry out his illegal, immoral, and repulsive scheme.

Meanwhile, she went through the motions of purifying the loaders and the stacks of cartons of drugs he pointed to. Actually, they did not appear to be contaminated, showing none of the plague aura. But she pretended to cleanse them and helped stow them on the shuttle anyway.

'Snap to it, kiddies. This is just the first load. There's a lot of room in the cargo bays for valuable stuff like this. I want as much of this warehouse as you can fit in those cargo bays.'

'It will go faster if you'll let me repair Elviiz,' she said. 'He's very strong.'

'Fine, but try anything, and we're going to have to load up another ship because the *Mana* will go nova.' Marl lorded over them with a superior smile on his face, like a man who held all the cards. Right then Khorii knew that, pacifist nature or not, she would do whatever she could to make sure he didn't get away with his despicable plan.

Khiindi was right where he wanted to be, but now what was he going to do? He sat down and thought about it for a while and caught Hap's thought, *'Come on, kitty, it's you and me, why don't you help me?'* It wasn't that Hap knew what Khiindi really was, or that the cat could understand his thoughts. Hap was simply in the habit of talking to, and thinking at, his friends who were gifted with more than two legs. Khiindi considered the situation.

Stupid boy. He was nice enough, but how had he managed to get himself so thoroughly taped up anyway?

Unseen, Khiindi had managed to slip into the engine room behind Marl and Khorii. His original impulse was simply to go where Khorii went since he did not want her anywhere alone with Marl. Unfortunately, there had been no opportunity to slip out of his hiding place before Marl sealed the door again. Not able to reach the control panel set into the wall, Khiindi could not open the door himself. He thought about leaping at the control panel in an effort to open the door, but the nearest counter was several feet away, and while he could cover the distance, the chances of his hitting the correct button were very small, while the chances of him bashing his head into the wall were fairly high. Captain Bates was on the bridge and was the only other human aboard except for Hap. She was much too far away to help and even if he went to the intercom, what was he going to do? Mew at her? He doubted she'd get the point. Besides, even if she did come down, she couldn't get through the locked door either.

No, the hapless Hap was his best hope for release. He was not about to gum up his fangs with that vast amount of tape binding the boy, however. Maybe the hands. That was where those handy thumbs were located. He slid in close to Hap's fingers, which automatically moved to scratch his fur. In spite of himself he purred, but then set to work on the tape. It was not that difficult to

327

puncture, but Khiindi found that he could not position himself properly to tear it away. He stood with one hind paw between Hap's hands and the other outside, while using his jaws to try to rip the tape away without ripping Hap. Hap, ungrateful lout that he was, kept complaining that Khiindi's tail tickled his nose and ouch, he felt that. So Khiindi then tried it from the other direction, back paws on the deck, forepaws and teeth working at the tape from between Hap's wrists. It got too slippery from blood to be of any use, and Hap's mental cursing offended Khiindi's pointed ears. He was just trying to help after all. His claws and teeth wouldn't be any good to Hap if they weren't sharp enough to pierce a little flesh. Some humans were entirely too delicate.

Finally, he clawed a strip about a half inch deep in the tape. Then it wouldn't budge any farther. He grabbed the edge in his teeth and pulled with all his might. Maybe it was true he dug his claws into Hap's hands while he pulled, but even a cat needed traction.

And for all of Hap's mental cursing and muffled moaning, Khiindi finally found the way to free the boy's hands of tape. Hap bled into it so much, it came loose, and between him and Khiindi they managed to wiggle it loose.

By that time Hap had managed to rub the tape off his mouth as well. 'Okay, boy, I don't know how I'm going to stand it, but you have to do my arms next.'

Khiindi sat back on his haunches, panting like a

328

dog. The hands were free, and not lacerated seriously enough to be life-threatening. Nothing Khorii couldn't fix when she returned. But he simply didn't have the strength to go through all that again, and it was entirely possible that by the time they were finished Hap wouldn't have a sufficient amount blood left in him to do anything either.

Let the cursed kid free himself the rest of the way, Khiindi thought, washing the blood from his fur and whiskers with a pristine paw. He would get all matted if he let it set.

Meanwhile Hap was making a nuisance of himself, mentally urging, 'Come back here, you wretched cat, and finish this, will you?'

No, really, he needed a nap and some refreshment before continuing. He hopped up on the table Hap had set up to repair or fabricate some of the things these people used in their spaceships. Khiindi had no idea what they were. Much too primitive for his taste. However, among the tools was a pair of cable shears. Picking these up in his teeth, which would probably be falling out after the abuse they'd just taken, he used the chair, then Hap's leg for steps to get down, stepping carefully. If he jumped too fast, the shears would fall out of his mouth and be much harder to pick up from a flat position.

He did drop them before he got them to Hap's hands, as they were just too heavy for a cat's mouth. However, there was more than one way to free a human without skinning him. Khiindi was a powerful batter, and he slapped the scissors between his forepaws until they rested within Hap's reach. Once he saw the boy's fingers touching the handles of the shears, he figured his work was done and jumped back up on the table to curl up for a well-earned nap. Everything was in Hap's hands now.

TWENTY-SEVEN

The cargo shuttle docked aboard the *Mana*. Khorii and the others were forced to unload it. Marl didn't even bother bringing the loaders in to stow the cargo properly. Once they emptied it, he couldn't wait to go down and get some more.

Khorii had never met anyone like Marl before. She thought Captain Becker, whom she had called greedy once, was the soul of generosity and restraint by comparison. He didn't hurt people to get his salvage, or walk over their injured bodies. And he put away what he acquired before acquiring more. Of course, the *Condor* was much smaller, usually. It varied depending on what parts of what ships Becker was using at the time to patch his own vessel, but it did stay more or less the same size. The size made it necessary to use imagination to find places to put everything. Neatness counted, on a ship like that.

But as soon as the boxes were stacked in the next docking bay, Marl herded everyone back into the shuttle, and they returned to the surface for another load.

On the way down he told Jaya, 'Find us a warehouse where they keep weapons. We're going to need some firepower to hang on to this lot.'

'What do you mean "we"?' Jaya asked.

'Okay, maybe not you babies, but I'm sure I can find some like-minded guys to work for me. This is wonderful. I always wanted to be a warlord when I grew up, but never thought I'd actually have the opportunity. It just goes to show that dreams really do come true.'

Khorii asked cautiously, curious but not wanting to set him off, 'Why do you wish that? I just want to know. We don't have them where I come from. Was your father a warlord, or your mother?'

'How the frag would I know?' he asked. 'I never met my dad, and I don't recall having a mother, though I suppose I probably did.'

'How did you survive until you got to Maganos Moonbase then?' she asked.

'At Maganos they like to quote the old saying about how it takes a village to raise a kid. In my case, it took a military encampment. Actually, my – role models, shall we say? – were on the opposite side from Lord Bendizi, but I always had a sneaking admiration for him myself.'

The odd thing was, since that background would have made perfect sense for breeding the sort of criminal Marl wanted to become, it wasn't true. She could see very clear images in his head of his mother, whom he envisioned in her uniform as a Federation magistrate, and his father, a devotee and minister of a human religion that seemed to involve parallelograms as its most potent symbol.

He had parents. He just didn't like them and had run away from them as soon as he was able to *join* the Cholaran Resistance Movement, which was where he learned how much he liked blowing things up and the benefits reaped by Lord Bendizi from being a warlord.

He was a very twisted sort of person. Reading him did not confer understanding. At least his lust for the cargo spared her the images she had glimpsed before. She wondered where the detonator was. If he could be separated from it before having a chance to use it, his warlord days would be over before they started.

She was much too new at the psychic stuff. She tried to probe unobtrusively for the location of the detonator and the devices he claimed to have set but he caught her. Abruptly she encountered more of the repulsive images of what he would like to do to the crew of the *Mana* – this time not only ugly violent mating practices with the females, but quite hideous disassembly for both Elviiz and Hap and even more terrible fates for poor Khiindi and the other cats.

Marl leered at her. 'Gotcha. I told you I know how to deal with your sort. Give you something to think about, eh, little girl? Get used to it because even if I have to kill everybody else, you and me are a team. Maybe after you've been around me for a while you'll change your attitude about some of it.'

Khorii snorted. She didn't mean to. She wouldn't have done it if she'd thought about it because obviously he was a pretty dangerous person. But he sounded so much like Aunt Maati's mate Thariinye boasting, as he always had done, about his way with females that she couldn't help it. The images in Marl's mind blew away with anger and, very strangely, embarrassment, and she saw a momentary flash of him giving Shoshisha something and her laughing at him. He knew about all that dreadful stuff he put in his mind to stop her – he had probably seen it and had memories of it. But she was very glad to see that it wasn't really him. He was bad enough, but there might be something in him to salvage, as Becker would say, if she could just think of a way to stop him.

'What was that, horn girl?'

'Nothing,' she said. 'I got something in my nose is all.'

They picked up the second load, and this time he and Jaya used the loaders to stow it in cargo bay one, while Elviiz, his organic bits repaired by Khorii and the manufactured ones self-repaired, carried the rest. Sesseli couldn't lift anything else with her mind at the moment. She had to sleep. Marl had tried to make her do it, and Khorii put her foot down. 'She's exhausted. *You* try lifting all those heavy things with your mind when you're no bigger than she is. If you want her to do it when speed counts, then let her recuperate now.'

She carried what she could while on board the *Mana*, but kept reaching out with all her senses, trying to find Hap. He was still inside the engine room but he felt freer – in more pain than he had been after she'd healed him, but he was partially free. While the others continued to the cargo bay, and Marl gloated over his booty, she slipped away and used the code she'd read from Marl's mind to unlock and open the engine room door.

Hap looked up, his arms still partly bound to his chest, but his hands and feet and lower legs free. Blood was everywhere, but she saw that it was from minor wounds on his hands. Khiindi lay on the table, sleeping the sleep of the just. Well, the just fed, perhaps. Hap kept cat snacks in the engine room for Khiindi and the other cats. She hadn't realized the cat was in there, but that did explain the wounds on Hap's hands. Khiindi woke, stretched, yawned, jumped down, and leaped through the hold in the slightly irised door without so much as a mew of greeting.

Khorii slipped inside to free Hap, ignoring him shaking his head.

'Khorii, what are you doing? Get out of here,' Hap said. 'Don't give Marl a reason to come looking for you.'

Khorii snatched up the shears and began cutting Hap's bonds. 'Just a few seconds, and I'll head back.' She understood what he was getting at. They would all be safer if Marl didn't know Hap was free, and he could look for the explosives that way. With one more snip the last of the tape binding Hap parted. She nodded and backed out, leaving the door unlocked, then hurried to the cargo bay.

Khorii wanted to send a message to Asha Bates, but she wasn't sure of her mental aim over the length of the ship. She didn't want Marl to be able to intercept anything she had to say to the captain.

Picking up her load again, she toted it to the cargo bay. Marl and Jaya finished stacking their cargo, and all of them returned to the shuttle. Just before she left the bay, Khorii thought she caught the glint of a slitted green-gold eye high up among the stacks.

'We've cleaned out all the entire stock of cackle juice and rhiosapam, which will bring an absolute fortune on the black market,' Marl said, rubbing his palms together with glee. 'We'll get the rest, then go for those weapons.'

But as Jaya lowered the shuttle onto the street, it was suddenly surrounded by a group of old men and young boys, all brandishing weapons of either an explosive or agricultural nature. The warehouse guard who had shot Elviiz pointed angrily at the shuttle.

'Up!' Marl shouted, but Jaya was already lifting off, amid a hail of bullets, pitchforks, shovels, brooms, wrenches, crowbars, and other items that bounced off the hull. Sesseli, who had slept through the whole thing, sat up and rubbed her eyes. 'Huh?' she asked.

Khorii gathered her into her arms, and said, 'Shhh. It's okay. There are more enterprising free

336

marketeers who survived the plague here than Marl counted on, that's all.'

Marl pounded on the viewscreen and screamed at the people below, 'You're all supposed to be *dead*! Lie down and die and give someone else a chance, you selfish zombies!'

Elviiz opened his mouth, no doubt to make some remark about the lack of logic in Marl's command, but Khorii put her finger to her lips and shook her head.

As they returned to the bridge, she lingered by the engine room but sensed at once that it was empty.

'That place sucks,' Marl told Captain Bates. 'Take us to the Big Money, honey! I need to pick out my mansion, then we'll go borrowing from the neighbors.'

He didn't notice her turning on the signal beacon, because she'd done it while he and the others walked from the docking bay to the bridge. He wasn't especially looking for it, of course, since space was full of such beacons now, and most of them went unanswered by other ships with their own mayday beacons pulsing into empty space.

Aari and Acorna held on to the lives of their friends with every shred of will and skill they possessed. The problem was, it took both of them to keep both Becker and RK alive and that meant neither of the Linyaari had a chance to get enough rest, and neither of their horns regained enough power to cure the captain or even the cat.

337

Acorna stroked RK and hung pouches of new fluids to flow into his veins. Abuelita had taught them how to rig up and sterilize makeshift kits for administering intravenous fluids for waiting patients. But everything they administered seemed to leak out of the patients as quickly as it went in.

Furthermore, the water and air supplies were both getting low, and neither Linyaari had enough power left to purify other sources.

In between putting cold cloths on Joh's neck, armpits, and groin to keep his fever down, Aari kept up a steady psychic stream of memories of their adventures together, of all the times Joh had saved his life.

Acorna rubbed RK's head and ears and the places behind his whiskers and reminded him of when they were in close psychic communication on the cat's homeworld of Makahomia. She asked him to recall all of the beautiful jungle temple cats he'd met, including the one who had borne him the litter of kittens from which Khiindi had come. *'Remember, Roadkill, that you are no common feline, but regarded as a superior life-form on Makahomia. Think how sad Nadhari and Miw-Sher would be if you depart this life without saying farewell to them. Also, you should remember that you are a very mature cat, spiritually as well as physically, and have probably already exhausted most of your other lives. You must hang on to this one as long as possible. Continue your long nap, continue your passive feed, but do not leap into your next life yet. It may not be there when you land.'*

If only they could take the two of them to the

surface, where even in isolation they could receive the food and water she and Aari had purified when their horns were potent. But from their research they both feared that the plague they carried may have mutated when filtered through the Linyaari system. They might kill the survivors they had just rescued, and Joh and RK as well.

One at a time, each had taken a break from their psychic interaction with their respective patients to try to send a long-distance message to their own people, praying that somehow it would get through. Then it was back to the grueling efforts of trying to keep their friends alive.

Jonas P. Becker was not a religious man, even though his first mate was of a species worshiped on the planet of Makahomia. Becker had been orphaned, enslaved, then adopted and raised by his scientist foster father, Theophilus Becker, to be a scientist. Of sorts.

The thing was, when you got to a certain level of theoretical physics, it was very difficult to tell if you were talking science or religion. Much of it sounded similar. Religion – maybe – was more like theoretical history with some miracles thrown in here and there. The courtesy and suspension of disbelief Becker accorded alien priesthoods and cat deities did not extend to human holy rollers and missionaries.

He was not sure he had a soul. He knew there was a core of stubborn self, of course, but he felt that it was unlikely to sprout wings, ascend any higher than he already was above the *Condor*, or learn to play a harp.

So he was totally unprepared for what awaited him after he had emptied his guts, coughed up his lungs, and felt as if the Khleevi bug-eyed monsters were taking revenge on him by pulling his brains out his ears and his skin off his muscle, his muscle off the bone. That was the kind of pain that he was feeling.

But then, although he was in no less pain, he suddenly shifted places, as if he'd gone through a wormhole and come out the other side. The pain was there, but it was beside the point. The point was that bright light at the end of the wormhole – yep, he was in a wormhole all right. He became sort of alarmed when he realized that he was passing through the hole toward the light ass over teakettle without the *Condor* surrounding him.

He became aware of a voice in his head, Aari's voice, and he said, just kidding, *'What light through this here wormhole breaks?'* and Aari replied, *'Light? Oh, no, Joh, you see the light when you are dying, it says here in* Ancient Terran Myths of Life and Death. *Do not go to the light, Joh. You do not belong there yet.'*

But Becker tumbled ever closer and closer, though now it seemed he was bodiless. Except, it wasn't true that there was no *Condor* around him. Not exactly. He *was* the *Condor*, all patched and bolted together, and he was roaring through that wormhole focusing more and more intently on that light. If he could just see what it was – just a little closer.

'Joh. No! You are slipping from me. Do not go to the light. Do not look at it.'

And from somewhere Becker formed the thought, *'Then you look at the damn thing. Don't you guys ever check the scanner array?'*

That said, he continued dying.

Twenty-Eight

As spaceflights went, the one from Rio Boca to Dinero Grande was a mere commuter hop.

On the bridge, everything seemed uneventful. Marl remained firmly in charge, though he might have been more suspicious of the unnaturally meek demeanor of the rest of the crew. But flushed with the success of his first venture, he no doubt figured he had them cowed. He had stepped out of sight outside the bridge door to turn off the timer to the bomb, then come back inside.

This time, instead of orbiting, Marl insisted that since there was no one to enforce the Federation quarantine, the *Mana* should land in the private port attached to the mansion of his dreams.

'You're just the most helpful little thing, Khorii,' he said. 'That passenger roster you brought from the derelict is great. I just pick out the ones from Dinero Grande that I recognize – like these. The woman was a major exporter to drug companies, and her husband was in the shadier side of the business. I've heard about their place. It's a

342

bloody palace. Ought to do nicely for my *pied-à-terre* here.'

While the *Mana* was en route, he enthused about the baths of rock crystal and the kitchen large enough for fourteen chefs with an oven so large that it could hold two entire oxen.

Captain Bates suddenly said, 'That's odd.'

'What?'

'Look, the com board just lit up. It looks like the Federation relays have been reestablished.'

Marl looked, and said, 'All at once? Nah, that doesn't mean anything. Those are all remote. Nothing from around here. Don't get your hopes up. Nobody's going to be calling up to rescue you.'

Just then the com unit beeped. Captain Bates toggled up the vid. '*Mana*, this is Acorna Harakamian-Li aboard the *Condor*. Please do not count on us for aid. We are extremely contaminated and have two very sick crewmen on board. We read that you are in trouble but if it is at all possible for you to get word back through other vessels to Maganos Moonbase and the Federation, please ask them to send word to the Linyaari home-world. Our own people are our only . . .'

Khorii ran forward. Her mother's voice had poured over her like a shower of comfort and warmth until she took in the words, then she felt frightened as she never had been before. Marl blocked her way and pulled the toggle back, then reached over and shut down the distress signal.

'What a clever captain you are, Asha,' he said. 'I

may have to kill you once we land. The truth is, I don't need any of you anymore.'

'Marl, that was Khorii's mother we just heard,' Captain Bates said. 'Why don't you get out here on Dinero Grande and go live happily ever after, but let us go try to help them?'

'Okay, fine,' he said, and although Khorii couldn't believe it, she relaxed enough to release some of the tightness that had constricted her chest since hearing her mother's voice.

'Everybody but Khorii can run off and rescue everyone in sight.'

'It's her parents, Fidd. And she's probably the only one who can help them.'

'Tough,' he said. 'Because she's the only one who can help me, too, and in case you've forgotten, I still have the detonator. Land this thing, dammit. You can off-load my cargo, then Khorii and I will leave, and you can take off and go do anything you bloody well choose.'

It came to Khorii suddenly that they needed a distraction, and she flashed a message to Captain Bates, hoping that Marl was too full of his own plots to intercept hers.

On the way down to the surface the ship began bucking and jerking as if it were a lightweight flitter. Everyone not seated fell to the deck.

'I thought you knew how to fly this thing,' Marl said.

'Turbulence,' Captain Bates said, and shrugged. 'Sorry. I don't make the weather.'

'*Again*,' something told Khorii, and she told the captain.

'*The device is strapped to his inner left forearm*,' something or someone told her. The voice was as familiar to Khorii as her own, yet she had no idea whose it was.

But the information did them no good at all. Marl was the only one besides Captain Bates who was strapped into a chair.

They landed, and Marl said, 'I can't really wait around while the menial stuff gets done before I see my new digs. Come on, Khorii. You can clear my path with pure air and uncontaminated luxuries. The rest of these folks, if they wish to leave when I say the word, can unload my cargo.'

Her heart sank. Marl pushed her out the hatch ahead of him. She was alone with him on the ground, while aboard the ship she imagined the others going to the cargo bay for the loaders.

She also imagined, because she sort of heard it from the same familiar and yet totally strange source as before, that it was entirely possible that there was no longer anything for the detonator to detonate.

There was an uncertain comfort if ever she had heard of one. Khorii couldn't take the chance that the mystery voice was wrong, however, so she kept going, waiting for her chance to escape.

She did as Marl told her, clearing the way up through the wilted, unwatered gardens to the great carved doors of the home. She led him through the halls to the bedrooms with the mattresses forty inches thick, hoping he might decide to fall asleep so she could escape, but of course that didn't happen. In two of the beds lay corpses, and she purified the air there. Like the other places where she had seen the plague, the air was filled with the specks that fled before her horn. It wasn't quite so bad here though, since the rooms were so large and airy.

'You'll have to remove those bodies later,' he told her.

He saw the baths made of rock crystal, some of which were golden, some of which were pink. Unfortunately, recent neglect had allowed scum to settle in the perpetual pools flowing over the sides of the bath from waterfalls that fell across gemstone cliffs. The falls were reduced to a trickle now, clogged with dead flowers and leaves from the untended gardens.

And last, she entered the kitchen with him. It stank of rotten food, but the freezers had not fully defrosted, and there were dried stores as well.

'Yes,' he said, 'this suits me fine. Let's see if they've unloaded my cargo yet.'

They walked back through the ruined flowers and weeds just as Jaya and Elviiz drove the loaders back into the docking bay.

'Is that it?' he asked.

'That's it,' Jaya said. 'Now, let Khorii go so she can see her parents.'

'I don't think so. Like I said, I need her. The rest of you can go though. Give my regards to the moonbase!'

They headed back toward the mansion as the ship lifted off and disappeared into the atmosphere. Then, as they walked into the kitchen, before Khorii could stop him, Marl pressed his right hand against his left forearm.

'What did you just do?' she demanded.

'Got rid of witnesses and evidence,' he told her. 'Get over it. You didn't really think I was going to let them go, did you? And the crowd management was getting to be stressful. Now come on and fix us something to eat.'

'Can't make me,' she said. She expected to be overcome with grief and fury, but actually, felt her insides freeze to an icy calm. 'You've just done your worst, you vicious, stupid boy. Why do you think I'd ever do what you say now?'

'How about because I'm bigger, older, smarter, and meaner than you, and I can make you afraid in ways you cannot imagine?' he said, advancing on her as she backed toward the door, not in a hurried or frightened way, but slowly and deliberately.

'You had it the right way around before,' she told him. 'You need me. I don't need you. This entire house, except for the very steps I took and the very places I touched my horn to, is infested with organisms that will make you look exactly like those bloated bodies in the beds. If you set a foot wrong or try to go anywhere I didn't go before you, you will die just like them.' And while he was thinking that over and trying to decide when to pounce, she sent images of herself in three other places in the room. She sent images of the plague germs

347

everywhere, of bodies lying as thick on the marble and carpeted floors of the mansion as they had on the beaches of LoiLoiKua. When he started spinning around the room trying to decide which one of her to attack, she slammed out of the kitchen, running through the house by a different path than they had come and out into another garden.

An inarticulate howl of rage rose from the house, and Khorii looked back to see Marl burst out of the house and race after her, his face a snarling mask. Although Khorii was light on her feet at the best of times, she still hadn't fully recovered from the healing she had performed on the poopuus' planet, and her energy flagged almost immediately. She heard the older boy panting over the slap of his feet on the ground, and knew that he had closed the distance between them. Then fear lent her speed, and she practically flew down the rest of the hill, heading back to the landing dock.

Rounding a corner of a building, Khorii staggered and nearly fell. She didn't see anyone who could help her. The streets were still completely deserted.

'Stop – Khorii – stop right now!' Marl yelled from behind her. She kept going, looking for someone, anyone.

Her legs buckling, her sides aching, Khorii reached the dock just as a large shadow passed over her. She looked up to see the *Nakomas* descending from above, interposing itself between her and Marl, who screamed in frustration. The shuttle hatch opened and she leaped inside, relief making her knees feel like sap. Elviiz was in the pilot's chair, and Khiindi hopped onto her shoulder.

'The others are undamaged,' Elviiz told her. 'Hap escaped his bonds and the engine room. Then he located all of the explosives Marl Fidd set. Hap spaced them, using the airlock from the docking bay, while the *Mana* orbited Rio Boca and the shuttle was on the ground. The detonator Marl wears is out of range of those explosives. As soon as all our friends were out of Marl Fidd's reach, Khiindi and I brought the shuttle to fetch you.'

Even though Elviiz never really liked to be hugged, she hugged him anyway.

Back aboard the *Mana*, Captain Bates coached Jaya in setting a course for the coordinates of the *Condor*, still orbiting Paloduro.

In another relatively short commuter hop they were within boarding distance of the ugly, awkward-looking patchwork ship. Khorii thought it had a certain style and distinction she had failed to notice before, an individuality that made it rather homey.

She could read the distress of her parents even before she left the *Mana*. But until she was safely aboard the *Condor*, she could not read Uncle Joh Becker or RK at all.

She expected her parents to rush up to embrace her, but she did not see them. However, over the ship's intercom, her mother's voice said, 'Khorii, *yaazi*, we cannot come out and meet you, but you

349

have come just in time. Go to Uncle Joh's cabin. There you will find him and RK still alive, we hope. They were a few seconds ago.'

'Where are you?' Khorii asked, bewildered. '*Aavi*? Mother? Mom? Papa? Daddy?' she said, using some of the words she had learned on Maganos Moonbase. 'Why aren't you here?'

'We will explain later, *yaazi*,' her father said. 'Please heal Joh and RK. We cannot for the same reason we are not there to embrace the stuffings out of you.'

Jonas Becker, lately absorbed by the *Condor* which was absorbed by a wormhole, felt himself shrinking back out of the hull and into his skin. It wasn't unbearably hot and dry anymore, his skin. It was moist and cool and his throat and his butt and every other part of him didn't hurt anymore. His chest expanded and contracted without complaint while the air went in and out.

Opening an eye, he looked into Khorii's anxious face. 'Uncle Joh, don't die, okay?'

'Does that mean I'm forgiven for being a greedy old goat who dishonors dead people by calling them stiffs?' he asked, and the words came out as smoothly as ever, though they sounded really loud to his ears.

'Mostly,' she said. 'You were right about most of what you did with the *Blanca*.'

'Me? Right? My child, those are healing words, a balm to my soul and music to my ears. Hiya, Khorii, give your old unk a hug?'

Her horn touch had even done something about the sickly odor that had been clinging to him.

He sat back up, and demanded, 'Now, what do you mean "mostly"?'

RK barely felt the sweet touch of horn, for he was too far sunk in his misery. Even though he felt his skin tingling, his whiskers sensing the softness of someone holding him on one side, the brush of a hand on the other, he did not think he could possibly pull out of the nosedive he had been in for so long.

'Giving up that last life, are you? Good. You are a wretched old creature well past your prime. You should die and bequeath your cushy job as a ship's officer to some deserving young cat who will do the job properly. You're no good to anyone anymore anyway. You have been a fickle mate, an abusive sire, and the fact that your two-legged companion is fond of you owes more to his eccentricity and enjoyment of a good fight than to any virtue of yours.'

Who was this unsympathetic, unperceptive, rude animal saying all of these terrible things to a dying hero?

'Hero?' the upstart continued. *'Why, I saved my girl and all of her friends with nothing but my wits, my claws, and teeth. It's a good thing for all of those children aboard the* Mana *that there is so much more to me than just your sorry DNA. I freed a boy who had been held hostage, then let myself out to follow one who hid things that would have destroyed all of the others, including my charge. I peeked into the destroyer's mind when he*

351

thought nobody was looking and learned his secrets, and led the other boy to them. Together we spaced them so when he took our girl, he had nothing to use against her and, of course, she came back to us like we were her food dishes.'

'Braggart,' RK mumbled, the expression on his face changing from ill to furious. 'Upstart. Ingrate. Heretic. Liar.'

'Am not.'

'Rrrrr, too,' the older cat growled from his deathbed, then flipped to his feet, knocking the healing horn away from his hide, leaped through the air, his no-longer-dank-and-matted fur bristling, and gave chase to the other cat, who wore a mocking smile as he streaked out of the room.

TWENTY-NINE

Khorii was more devastated than she would have believed possible. She had waited so long to be with her mother and father again. How could they lock themselves in their cabin and refuse to come out to see her? She wanted nothing more than to be held by them and reassured that she was not an orphan like so many of the other kids she'd met recently. She had parents and they loved her and during the past few weeks she had come to realize that she loved them so much it made her throat ache from the huge lump that had appeared there as she tried to comprehend why they would not see her.

She felt as if she'd come through the desert, and they were withholding water. She stood touching the door to the cabin in which they had locked themselves and absently stroked the plasteel sheathing of it. She understood now what they had done and why they had done it, but it didn't make her yearn for them any less. But at least she understood. At first she had not when they tried to explain, and Uncle Joh tried to explain. Finally, it was Elviiz who explained it so that she could understand.

'Your mother and father carry the disease, although they are not affected by it,' the android said. 'They think it is possible they can give the disease to Linyaari now,' he told her. 'They do not wish to contaminate you.'

She knew so much how lethal the plague was, but the idea of her parents having it was ridiculous.

'Although they have rested and returned many days ago, their horns are still transparent,' Maak told her, looking none the worse for wear after having his own organic parts healed by Khorii and his nonorganic ones repaired by his son. 'While they were exhausted and their resistance was lowered, the plague somehow attached itself to them, your father said. It was they who infected the captain, the feline first mate, and me.'

Khorii had come to the door then. 'Elviiz and Maak say you carry the plague? How is that possible?'

'We are not sure, *yaazi*, but it certainly seems to be,' her mother said over the intercom. Since Khorii had not had her psychic powers when she left them, they were used to talking to her with their voices instead of sending thought-talk, and that took less of the precious energy they needed to revitalize the power of their horns. She did not attempt thought-talk herself because she liked the solidity of their voices. If she could not actually see and touch them, at least she could actually hear them.

Her mother continued, 'This has never before happened with any Linyaari. This plague is extremely tricky. If you want to help, love, you might go down to Corazon and find Jalonzo Allende. He will show you a laboratory to decontaminate for him to work in. You'll like him. He's a nice young genius about your age. Take Elviiz. They'll be fast friends.'

She wanted to whine that she did not want to leave them, that she wanted to see them both right now, but stopped herself. She was not a baby, after all. She was a six-and-a-half-*ghaanye*-old star-clad Linyaari with full psychic powers. Did Father whine about what had been done to him? Did Mother complain because she had been raised by humans far from Vhiliinyar? No, they had made the best of their situations, and as their daughter, she would do the same.

Khorii stood back from the door and asked through the intercom, 'Can my other friends come, too? I mean, is the area decontaminated enough for them to land safely and leave the ship?'

'Yes, I believe so. Jalonzo and the others can show you where we've been.'

'I think I'll be able to tell,' she said.

Her parents sent mind touches. At last she was ready to receive them and accept reassurance and love. It was almost as good as physical contact, if not as satisfying. She could not smell their scent that was so much a part of her own. She could not feel her father's strong arms close around her like a fort, protecting her against any harm. She could not look into her mother's beautiful silvery eyes or curl her mane into rings for her fingers. But the mind touches relaxed her and made her smile, and she sent one back loaded with all the love she could muster for them, which was a lot indeed.

Straightening her back, Khorii put her hand to the door once more and nodded to Elviiz, who came into the corridor with Khiindi on his shoulder, that she was ready to return to the *Mana*.

By the time Khorii returned from decontaminating the huge college laboratory in downtown Corazon, Jalonzo Allende, the large boy with the long black hair and brown eyes that were shrewd yet innocent at the same time, had thoroughly bonded with Elviiz and Hap Hellstrom.

'You should have seen them! Everybody got really involved in this game, and I just made it up. We didn't even use cards or anything.' He explained to them the magical system he'd invented, and, as Khorii listened, it sounded to her as if Jalonzo had turned the plague into a game with each symptom being a monster or a curse and each person who survived being gifted with some kind of special protective amulet.

Although Jalonzo's first language was Spandard, he spoke excellent Standard as well. When he could not explain something adequately in that language, Elviiz translated for Hap, and did the same for Elviiz when Hap enthusiastically interrupted saying, 'It's cool that you don't need cards, Jalonzo, but wouldn't it be fun to make up your own with some really amazing artwork? I can just see Sangrojo on a card, all oozy and red, and Kuklukan as a wind dragon with an Aztec-looking face, and Santanina would be beautiful, kind of like a fairy.'

'In addition to which, Jalonzo,' Elviiz said, 'cards or some form of tangible artwork present a marketing opportunity not to be overlooked. Perhaps instead of dice you could employ some more distinctive device?'

'*Sí, sí,*' Jalonzo said. 'Such as throwing bones – maybe shaped like vertebrae or small skulls – ahh, I have it, dice but with holograms of skulls inside them that glow in different colors, the colors representing the magical properties . . .'

'Ahem,' Khorii said, clearing her throat and trying not to roll her eyes. 'The laboratory is cleared now, Jalonzo.'

'Oh, *gracias*, Khorii,' he said, suddenly all of the enthusiasm turned to awkwardness as he looked down at the slender, silver-maned girl. 'Uh, how are Aari and Acorna doing? Are their horns back to normal yet?'

She shook her head. 'I do not think so.'

'What do you mean? Haven't you seen them?'

'No. They wouldn't let me near them. They think they gave the plague to Captain Becker and RK, and they're afraid a variety that can attach to them might be fatal to Linyaari even when their horns are fully functional.'

'Extremely unlikely,' Jalonzo said in an authoritative tone surprising for one so young, 'But I can

357

see why they'd want to be careful. I mean, it makes sense, given, the shape that they were in, that they passed it on to their human – I mean, to susceptible beings of other species, since one was a *gatito*. But I don't see why that would change the plague.'

'But Linyaari have always been able to destroy any illness or heal any injury with our horns,' Khorii reminded him. 'If those organisms I kept seeing were able to attach themselves to my parents and mutate into something that is immune to our healing abilities, then everyone is really in trouble.'

'True, but there are still a few things that we don't know about this plague – like how it infects its victims,' Elviiz said. 'I have a theory about that that I have been collecting data on ever since this epidemic began. Jalonzo, besides people, what other kinds of animals died here on Paloduro?'

'We lost a lot of cats and dogs and horses and many other kinds of animals here, too. Not all of them, but quite a few. But we noticed something interesting. Lots of people died, and their pets didn't. A lot more feral cats and dogs died than pets, I guess because the pets got good diets and regular visits to the vet and . . . and a lot of them were neutered,' he finished.

'As we were coming down, I saw fields with steers in them, but no cows,' Elviiz said.

Jalonzo's brow furrowed as he pondered this information. 'Aari, Acorna, naturally,' he said, grinning at Khorii, who didn't quite understand his expression. 'Is RK? Neutered, I mean?'

'No,' she said. 'Neither is Khiindi. He got sick, but I healed him.'

'But all of the mousers we were carrying to Rushima were,' Jaya interjected. She'd been silently watching the boys bat the conversational ball back and forth. Jaya hadn't always been a quiet person. Her mother used to scold her for chattering so much and singing to herself all the time. Losing her parents had made her feel empty of talk or feelings or even sensible thoughts for a while. But listening to the boys was giving her a lot of new ideas, even if she hadn't been able to get a word in edgewise. 'Maybe that's why they didn't get the plague.'

'Oh, what do you know about it?' Jalonzo said without thinking. Anger flared in Jaya's eyes. The older boy thought fast, needing to backtrack. He didn't want to make her angry. He only wanted to impress her with how smart *he* was. This new girl was so pretty, and he knew he wasn't especially handsome or athletic or anything.

Khorii was reading everyone's faces and feelings and thoughts effortlessly now as she had not been able to do on the *Mana*. Maybe her friends were less guarded out in the open, and without Marl to use everything they said against them. 'I'm sure Jalonzo didn't mean what he said,' she interjected, with a meaningful look at him.

'Uh, no, I'm sorry, Jaya,' Jalonzo said, recognizing the opportunity she had handed him. Then his eyes widened, and he nodded and apologized again, this time sincerely. '*Really* sorry because you're actually right.'

'Yes, of course—' Jaya said, then realized he meant more than that she knew which cats were sick and which ones weren't. 'You think the neutering had something to do with it? But how could it? None of the people who survived were neutered that I know of, at least.'

'No,' he said. 'Not that. And of course the usual stuff like how healthy they were to begin with made a difference – some of the kids in our group who died had other stuff wrong with them, too. It was part of the reason they got into the game. I'm not sure exactly what the trouble was, but I remember that one of them had a heart problem from birth and there was something wrong with the girl, too. Before the plague, I mean. But when you consider it, we were all exposed because everybody ate the nachos the dead delivery guy brought. And we are all, you know, kids.'

'Hormones!' Hap said, snapping his fingers as he got the point. 'All of the adults say kids going through puberty are a mess of hormones. Either too active or not active enough – that's probably why I got it, but Sesseli didn't. Jaya's younger than we are, but she's a girl and they – uh – girls are different.'

'None of us had been eating well,' Jaya said. 'There was food, but everyone was too sick to fix it, and the air supply had really become polluted. I'd have had to be made out of plas – sorry, Elviiz, no offense.'

'None taken,' he said.

Khorii said, 'But Elviiz, if it was hormones, why

360

did your father get sick, too? Droids don't . . . do they?'

'Father had been experimenting,' he said. 'Making me instilled in him the joys of fatherhood, and he . . . wished to experience it again. But you know my father, Khorii. He always thinks the organic way is better than the electronic or mechanically engineered, even though I am living proof . . .'

'That's another thing!' Jalonzo said, so excited by his own idea he forgot to ask where Maak intended to find the hormone-enhanced female android necessary to complete his experiment. 'It's engineered. The plague I mean. That's how come it selects certain people – or animals – based on hormones.'

'You mean someone started it on purpose?' Jaya asked. 'Why?'

Before the boys could speak, Sesseli spoke up. 'That's easy-peasy,' she said. 'So that there would only be little kids and grandmas and grandpas, but no moms and dads to take care of them.'

'Or teachers to teach them,' Khorii continued. 'Or police to protect warehouses and valuables . . .'

'Or Federation officials to investigate the plague itself or anything else,' Hap finished. 'Which is why we're the ones to figure all this out. Everybody who got close enough to study it got zapped. We've already seen how the incubation period varies so some people were infected for a long time before they got sick and died and had a chance to infect other people in the meantime. Or maybe it was

361

their general health again that decided when the disease struck, I don't know.'

'It worked really well, too,' Jaya said. 'Except for people who weren't in the area like Captain Bates or people lucky enough to have Khorii there to save them when they got infected, like you, Hap.'

They all looked at each other, then Hap summed it up. 'Well,' he said. 'That sucks.'

Khorii said, 'With the lab now ready for you to use, Jalonzo, perhaps there is something we can do about it after all.'

'I'll help you, buddy,' Hap said. 'I want to kick its viral butt.'

'I should be able to be of assistance, too,' Elviiz said.

'I can help,' Khorii said. 'Definitely. But first I think we should also collect specimens from my mom and dad to see if they are incubating a new Linyaari-specific strain, as they fear.'

She, Sesseli, and Jaya took the shuttle back to the *Mana* while the boys ran off toward the lab. Sesseli slipped one of her hands into Khorii's left hand and Jaya's right as they walked through the ship. Captain Bates half turned in her chair when they entered the bridge.

'There's good news and bad news, ladies,' she said.

Khiindi, who had opted for the *Mana* over the *Condor* where his sire held the ironclad alpha cat position, deserted Captain Bates's lap for Khorii's shoulder.

'The good news is that the communications

362

relays are now open all the way back to the Moonbase and Kezdet. Congratulations, Khorii, you are a great aunt. The bad news is that we've had a number of other distress calls from colonies in the next system. The nearest two are moons, Luna Frida Kahlo and Luna Diego Rivera, colonized by a company based on Dinero Grande.'

'None farther afield than that?' Khorii asked. If the plague was a deliberate attack, as they suspected, it must not have been as thorough as the perpetrators hoped.

'Not that I've heard about so far. The Federation posts were the hardest hit, and the word about quarantine got out elsewhere. But it seems that the moons were infected after every other place. Some of the first victims are still alive.'

'We'd better hurry then,' Khorii said.

THIRTY

As the *Mana* left Paloduro space, Khorii watched the speck that was the *Condor*, then the speck that Paloduro became fade into the distance. Finally, the Solojo sun itself became just a very bright star, but not so bright as the red giant that illuminated the entire Solojo system. The planets themselves were harsh and full of noxious gases, but the twin moons that orbited the third planet, Calaca del Muerto, had been bubble-colonized like Maganos Moonbase. The purpose of the colonies was to cultivate and tend experimental genetically engineered crops, according to the general information the *Mana*'s crew had downloaded from Federation data banks.

The com unit beeped, and Khorii saw her mother and father again. 'Khorii, we heard you're on your way to heal some people on two different moons,' her father said. 'You know we would never want you to withhold compassionate aid to others, but do not let them exhaust you. This is very difficult to say, *yaazi*, but even if a few people die while you rest, you must risk it, or you may have the same problem your mother and I have now – and you could infect your human companions.'

'Don't worry, Dad, Mom,' she said, again using terms she'd learned on the Moonbase. Although she understood why it had to be, she was still hurt and also angry with them for refusing to see her. 'I have it under control. Also, you should know that the boys have a theory, which so far has been borne out by all of our observations. We think that the plague has been deliberately engineered so that it attacks beings with certain hormone levels. We think it has something to do with being able to reproduce. Most of the plague victims aren't kids my age or elders. The farm animals and pets who were altered also mostly survived. So we think I'm immune. But we could be wrong. So I guess if I come back tainted, I'll go in with you, and we'll just have to get Captain Bates to lock herself airtight in the cargo bay or something until we can cure this. Jaya's already had it, and, if we're right, Sesseli is immune. But we need you to send blood and tissue samples down to the planet for analysis, so they can work on understanding how the plague in you has been changed.'

That would show them they should not underestimate her! She had grown up a lot since she saw them last and they needed to realize that. Already she knew more about this plague they were supposed to cure than they did.

'*Yaazi*,' her mother said, holding her gaze through the com unit as if she were right beside her. 'Captain

Becker and RK should have been immune, too. Remember, they were exposed aboard the derelict which, as we all found out from Elviiz's data, *did* carry the plague. They had it and we cured them and that should have made them immune if immunity is conferred by recovery from the disease. So Jaya could still catch it again if you become exhausted enough to expose her. We certainly hope you and the boys are right and that you are all immune because of your age and hormone levels, but we were immune as well until we became very tired. I'm very proud to hear you thinking this through, but the things causing these illnesses can mutate, Khorii. They can change the rules on you before you know what game they are playing. *Promise* us that you will rest when you need to.'

Chastened, Khorii nodded, and again felt like crying because she couldn't see her parents when she needed them the most. But she swallowed her tears and gulped hard, then looked out the viewscreen again. She had too many other things to do to sit here and wallow in her misery.

Captain Bates touched her hand. 'It's time, honey.'

Khorii had never felt so alone in her life as when she finally got her wish and piloted the shuttle down to Luna Diego Rivera. But she had formed a plan even while discussing the risks of this mission with her parents. A figure clothed in what looked like a helmeted shipsuit waited for her at the entrance to the nearest bubble.

'*Señorita*, we are so grateful you have come. Your

people are said to be able to work miracles with this disease. We have many afflicted now, and two have died.'

As politely as she could, she said, 'Then there's no time to waste. Do you have a pool?'

'Pool?'

'Um – water – large body of water. A pond, lake, pool, sea?'

'*Sí!*' he said. 'Oh yes, we have a reservoir for watering our plants and for drinking water for ourselves.'

'Good. Please take me there and bring everyone else, too.'

'But we have quarantined the sick ones, *señorita*, as the Federation ordered.'

'If you don't want them to die, unquarantine them. Have the older children – but no one over thirteen Standard years, and any elders who live with you bring them to the water. I'll treat everyone before I'm done – um, how many of you are there here?'

'Six thousand, *señorita*.'

'And how big is the reservoir? How many people would it hold?'

'We do not put people in it normally, *señorita*, so I do not know,' the man said. He was no doubt a senior scientist, and he was looking at her as if reconsidering the idea of having her help them.

'I suppose we'll find out. Which way is the reservoir?'

'Straight ahead, following this street to the last bubble.'

'Fine. You gather the sick ones and bring them there, and I'll meet you. Please trust me, and bring them as soon as you are able.'

Khorii realized her reassurance might not be enough, so she broadcast a silent psychic message and hoped the colony had enough people who were sufficiently receptive that they would not have to rely on word of mouth alone. *'Hola, people of Luna Diego. I am Khorii, of the Linyaari race from the planet Vhiliinyar. I have the ability to help cure your colony of the illness, but I must treat many of you at once. That is why I want you to bring your sick ones to the reservoir. When you arrive, help them into the water. Assist the ones who cannot support themselves so they don't drown.'*

As she broadcast, people came, at first in pairs or trios, then a steady flow from the rows of small flat-roofed dwellings lining the street. Beyond the buildings, to the edges of the bubble's horizon, were greenhouses and fields, untended and empty.

When Khorii arrived at the reservoir, she could see two or three hundred people already in the water. She stripped off her shipsuit and jumped over the side of the round sunken pool. She clapped her hands to get everyone's attention. 'When I dive, duck the heads of the sick people into the water at the same time,' she told them with both her voice and her mind. She saw nods of under-standing, heard a few spoken or shouted replies of '*Sí*,' and many questions from many minds she could not take the time to answer.

She nodded and dived under the surface. At first

she could not see even the nearest faces and bodies, only the countless plague specks that clouded the water around her as if dirt had been poured into it. But almost at once, the specks flowed away and vanished, and she beheld the faces and bodies of a lot of people who were having trouble holding their breath. By then she knew that once the specks were gone, the people would be cured.

'*Up!*' she ordered, and surfaced herself.

Once the others saw the condition of their friends and loved ones, the main problem was to keep them from drowning each other in their hurry to get into the water with her.

It took about thirty immersions to free everyone of the disease. At the end she felt a bit soggy but nowhere near as exhausted as she had been after purifying the ocean for the LoiLoiKuans.

'Does Luna Frida have a pool like this?' she asked the nearest convalescent.

'*Sí, señorita, gracias*, you are an angel, a saint . . .'

Khorii shook her head, water droplets flying from her silver hair. '*Gracias.* That's very nice of you, but I'm not. I simply have access to powerful alien medicine that works the way you just saw. Would someone please get on the com unit here and tell the people of Luna Frida I'm coming and what to do? But tell them not to dunk anyone until I get there, okay?'

Someone met her on the path in a little cart. '*Señorita*, we do not normally swim in our pool. How can we clean it so we can use it again to drink from?'

369

'I think you'll find it cleaner and more pure now than it was before we went for our swim,' she told him with a smile. 'My medicine also has that effect.'

The healing process on Luna Frida began in much the same way. But it was a larger colony than the one on Luna Diego, with fifteen thousand people, and by her twentieth dunk, Khorii realized that she was too exhausted to continue. More people were ill here because, since she visited Diego first, more had had a chance to become infected or to get sicker. She couldn't bear just to let people die, but her parents were right. Could she really risk the lives of Captain Bates, Jaya, and maybe even Sesseli, not to mention the people who were expecting to be saved and might not be because of her overextending herself? Also, if she became too tired to finish this job properly, the ones she had already cured could become reinfected if her parents were correct about Uncle Joh's and RK's first contact being no protection.

She felt protest from some of the minds of the more receptive Luna Fridans who were aware of her conflict. How could she let them down? She was as good as killing them!

Khorii thought and thought, then came to a decision. If she exhausted herself trying to save as many as possible, she could be with her parents again. That was a better alternative than what these people had to face. She took a deep breath, readying herself to plunge back into the water.

'Hey, Khorii! Are you going to hog the swimming hole or can anybody play?'

370

'Great-aunt Neeva?'

'Right behind you, youngling. Flying around trying to decontaminate all of those smelly old Federation outpost relays is dry work. Can we come swimming with you and your friends?'

'We?'

'Melireenya and Kharii of course, and Maati and Thariinye. We contacted the Condor, then the Mana, to find you. Don't worry, little one. We, as the humans say, have got your back. And we heard what you did on LoiLoiKua, so we have cleverly divined the moistened nature of your master plan.'

The hard footfalls of two-toed Linyaari feet clattered behind her, and what parts of her had begun to dry while she was debating her decision to continue healing were soaked all over again as five Linyaari bodies dived gleefully into the reservoir, leaving a grateful Khorii to sink to her knees, smiling and crying with relief at the same time.

Standing outside her parents' cabin door aboard the Condor once more, Khorii came to believe something she had always thought was mere folklore concerning the origin of the Linyaari people. It was said that the Ancestors who lived in a secret place on Vhiliinyar were part goat. They looked very much like small, bearded, cloven-hooved, horned horses, and Khorii had never wanted to believe they could be related to a lowly animal from old Terra mostly known for providing smelly cheese. But now her parents' stubbornness made her think of the legendary hard heads of the goats, and she was pretty sure that she numbered those humble animals somewhere in her evolutionary chain.

'Okay, I understand. You are trying to protect me and everyone else in the multiverse, as usual. But, look . . . There's something I forgot to tell you, probably because you haven't let me see you yet and it slipped my mind. I can see the plague.'

'Are you sure?' her father asked. 'How?'

'The same way Mother can tell the mineral content of asteroids and that sort of thing. I can see the life-forms that make up the plague. I've been able to ever since we found the derelict. I see all these little specks, and when they see my horn coming, they run for it and just vanish.'

'I'm very proud of you, darling,' Mother said.

'But the thing is, if you are still infected or affected or whatever, if you'd just let me see, I could tell you for sure. Then you'd know.'

'Khorii,' her father said a little sternly, 'we've already explained.'

'*Sí, sí, sí,*' she said in the rather mocking singsong she'd picked up from Jalonzo over the last few days while she'd been trying to decide what to do about her parents and the mission in general. 'But as I've already explained, and the boys assure me that this is true, and furthermore Grandsire Kaarlye and Grandam Miiri think they are using sound scientific logic, kids don't get the plague. At least, not yet. The odds are we don't get any mutations either because we think this was deliberately set to attack active healthy adults during their reproductive years, not kids or elders. So – so you should let me

372

in so I can tell if you are carrying the plague.' Khorii's voice quavered for just a moment, and she sucked in a deep breath, trying to be strong.

What if they still refused? Would she ever see them again? *Don't be silly*, she scolded herself. *Of course you will.*

Very much to her surprise, the door irised open. Although Khorii wanted to rush inside, she stepped in slowly, and the door shut behind her.

'Oh,' she said. Blue specks floated around each of her parents as they moved. None seemed to be trying to drift toward Khorii, but they didn't vanish either, despite the fact that her parents' horns were once again their usual color and shape.

'Blue specks,' she said.

Her mother nodded. 'We told you. It's a mutant strain. It would almost have to be. And it could infect you or other Linyaari.'

'Not me,' Khorii said. 'Not yet. And not elders or other Linyaari kids. So I want a hug. If you infect me, the worst that can happen is I get to stay with you. But I'll know if I'm okay.'

Stiffly at first, then with great enthusiasm, all of them hugged and kissed and cried, and Khorii tried to tell them all of her adventures in one long thought.

When she finally stepped away, none of the blue specks clung to her but neither had any been removed from either of her parents.

Captain Becker's impatient voice boomed over the intercom. 'So, what's the verdict?'

'Guilty as charged,' Father said, with a sad smile.

Uncle Joh took a deep breath. 'Okay, then. Well, as your captain and your social secretary today, I need to tell you that there are some other people here to communicate with you.'

'People? Who?'

'*It's us, Aari dear,*' Grandam Miiri's voice said. '*Your father and I have a plan we need to discuss with you.*'

Two Standard days later, Elviiz, Khiindi and Khorii waved good-bye as the *Condor* headed back to Vhiliinyar, accompanied by Kaarlye and Miiri.

Khorii could hardly breathe for the tightness in her chest that had nothing to do with the plague. Her parents and the *Condor* crew were returning to their homeworld, where Kaarlye and Miiri would guide them to a special private enclave built for the Ancestors, who were the oldest beings on the planet and said to be the wisest as well. Khorii had reassured everyone that the strain of the plague Mother and Father carried could not attack her grandparents any more than it had attacked her. Therefore, they and the elders should be safe. Although she had been able to cure Captain Becker and RK of the mutant strain, her horn had no effect on the strain surrounding her parents, nor had she been able to disinfect the *Condor* totally. So all of them, Mother, Father, Uncle Joh, RK and even Maak, would wait with the Ancestors while she and her friends, human, feline, and Linyaari alike, searched for the malevolent entity who had created the plague and for a permanent cure.

374

It was only a temporary measure, Khorii told herself. She had no doubt that soon they would all be together again for good, but it could never be soon enough to suit her. And woe to the person or persons or beings or whatever who had caused so much suffering throughout the galaxy, for as she stood on the bridge watching the *Condor* fade into space, Khorii vowed to find the entity that had done this and bring that entity to justice.

It was her mission. And it was a mission that she would pursue if it took her to the end of the galaxy or beyond.

GLOSSARY OF TERMS AND PROPER NAMES IN THE
ACORNA UNIVERSE

aagroni – Linyaari name for a vocation that is
a combination of ecologist, agriculturalist,
botanist, and biologist. *Aagroni* are responsible
for terraforming new planets for settlement as
well as maintaining the well-being of populated
planets.

Aari – a Linyaari of the Nyaarya clan, captured by
the Khleevi during the invasion of Vhiliinyar,
tortured, and left for dead on the abandoned
planet. He's Maati's older brother. Aari survived
and was rescued and restored to his people by
Jonas Becker and Roadkill. But Aari's differ-
ences, the physical and psychological scars left
behind by his adventures, make it difficult for
him to fit in among the Linyaari.

Aarlii – a Linyaari survey team member, firstborn
daughter of Captain Yaniriin.

Aarkiiyi – member of the Linyaari survey team on
Vhiliinyar.

abaanye – a Linyaari sleeping potion that can be
fatal in large doses.

Acorna – a unicorn-like humanoid discovered as an infant by three human miners – Calum, Gill, and Rafik. She has the power to heal and purify with her horn. Her uniqueness has already shaken up the human galaxy, especially the planet Kezdet. She's now fully grown and changing the lives of her own people, as well. Among her own people, she is known as Khornya.

Ali Baba – Aziza's ship.

Allende, Jalonzo – a young genius from the planet Paloduro.

Ancestors – unicorn-like sentient species, precursor race to the Linyaari. Also known as *ki-lin*.

Ancestral Friends – an ancient shape-changing and space-faring race responsible for saving the unicorns (or Ancestors) from Old Terra, and using them to create the Linyaari race on Vhiliinyar.

Ancestral Hosts – *see* Ancestral Friends.

Andina – owner of the cleaning concession on MOO, and sometimes lady companion to Captain Becker.

Aridimi Desert – a vast, barren desert on the Makahomian planet, site of a hidden Temple and a sacred lake.

Aridimis – people from the Makahomian Aridimi desert.

Arkansas Traveler – freight-hauling spaceship piloted by Scaradine MacDonald.

Asha Bates – teacher on the Maganos Moonbase.

Attendant – Linyaari who have been selected for the task of caring for the Ancestors.

377

Avvi – Linyaari word for 'daddy.'

Aziza Amunpul – head of a troop of dancers and thieves, who, after being reformed, becomes Hafiz's chief security officer on MOO.

Balakiire – the Linyaari spaceship commanded by Acorna's aunt Neeva.

Basic – shorthand for Standard Galactic, the language used throughout human-settled space.

Becker – *see* Jonas Becker

Bulaybub Felidar sach Pilau ardo Agorah – a Makahomian Temple priest, better known by his real name – Tagoth. A priest who supports modernizing the Makahomian way of life, he was a favorite of Nadhari Kando, before her departure from the planet. He has a close relationship in his young relative, Miw-Sher.

Calla Kaczmarek – the psychologist and psychology/sociology instructor on Maganos Moonbase.

Calum Baird – one of three miners who discovered Acorna and raised her.

chrysoberyl – a precious catseye gemstone available in large supply and great size on the planet of Makahomia, but also, very rarely and in smaller sizes, throughout the known universe. The stones are considered sacred on Makahomia, and are guarded by the priest class and the Temples. Throughout the rest of the universe, they are used in the mining and terraforming industries across the universe.

Commodore Crezhale – an officer in the Federation Health Service.

Condor – Jonas Becker's salvage ship, heavily modified to incorporate various 'found' items Becker has come across in his space voyages.

Crow – Becker's shuttle, used to go between the *Condor* and places in which the *Condor* is unable to land.

Declan 'Gill' Giloglie – one of three human miners who discovered Acorna and raised her.

Delszaki Li – once the richest man on Kezdet, opposed to child exploitation, made many political enemies. He lived his life paralyzed, floating in an antigravity chair. Clever and devious, he both hijacked and rescued Acorna and gave her a cause – saving the children of Kezdet. He became her adopted father. Li's death was a source of tremendous sadness to all but his enemies.

Dinan – Temple priest and doctor in Hissim.

Dinero Grande – a world in the Solojo star system.

Dolores M. Grimwald – Captain of the ship *La Estrella Blanca*, deceased, an early victim of the space plague.

Domestic Goddess – Andina's spaceship.

Dsu Macostut – Federation officer, Lieutenant Commander of the Federation base on Makahomia.

Edacki Ganoosh – corrupt Kezdet count, uncle of Kisla Manjari.

Egstynkeraht – A planet supporting several forms of sulfur-based sentient life.

Elviiz – Maak's son, a Linyaari childlike android, given as a wedding/birth gift to Acorna and Aari. According to Maak, the android is named for an ancient Terran king, and is often called Viiz for short.

enye-ghanyii – Linyaari time unit, small portion of *ghaanye*.

Fagad – Temple priest in the Aridimi desert, who spied for Mulzar Edu Kando.

Felihari – one of the Makavitian Rain Forest tribes on Makahomia.

Feriila – Acorna's mother.

Fiicki – Linyaari communications officer on Vhiliinyar expeditions.

Fiirki Miilkar – a Linyaari animal specialist.

Fiiryi – a Linyaari

fraaki – Linyaari word for fish.

Friends – also known as Ancestral Friends. A shape-changing and space-faring race responsible for saving the unicorns from Old Terra and using them to create the Linyaari race on Vhiliinyar.

Gaali – highest peak on Vhiliinyar, never scaled by the Linyaari people. The official marker for Vhiliinyar's date line, anchoring the meridian line that sets the end of the old day and the beginning of the new day across the planet as it rotates Our Star at the center of the solar system.

With nearby peaks Zaami and Kaahi, the high mountains are a mystical place for most Linyaari.

ghaanye (pl. *ghaanyi*) – a Linyaari year.

gheraalye malivii – Linyaari for navigation officer.

gheraalye ve-khanyii – Linyaari for senior communications officer.

giirange – office of toastmaster in a Linyaari social organization.

Grimalkin – an Ancestral Friend who became entangled with Aari and Acorna in their voyages through time. He even impersonated Aari for a while. He was punished for his impudence by his people, who trapped him in the body of a cat and took away his machinery for time travel and time control. He has become Khorii's boon companion – she calls him Khiindi. He is the key to a number of secrets that none of the humans or Linyaari are privy to, including the fate of Khorii's lost twin.

GSS – Gravitation Stabilization System.

haarha liirni – Linyaari term for advanced education, usually pursued during adulthood while on sabbatical from a previous calling.

Hafiz Harakamian – Rafik's uncle, head of the interstellar financial empire of House Harakamian, a passionate collector of rarities from throughout the galaxy and a devotee of the old-fashioned sport of horseracing. Although basically crooked enough to hide behind a spiral staircase, he is genuinely fond of Rafik and Acorna.

Hap Hellstrom – a student on Maganos Moonbase.
Heloise – Andina's spaceship.
Highmagister HaGurdy – the Ancestral Friend in charge of the Hosts on old Vhiliinyar.
Hissim – the biggest city on Makahomia, home of the largest Temple.
Hraaya – an Ancestor.
Hrronye – Melireenya's lifemate.
Hrunvrun – the first Linyaari Ancestral attendant.
Iiiliira – a Linyaari ship.

Iirtye – chief *aagroni* for narhii-Vhiliinyar.
Ikwaskwan – self-styled leader of the Kilumbembese Red Bracelets. Depending on circumstances and who he is trying to impress, he is known as either 'General Ikwaskwan' or 'Admiral Ikwaskwan,' though both ranks are self-assigned. Entered into devious dealings with Edacki Ganoosh that led to his downfall.

Johnny Greene – an old friend of Calum, Rafik, and Gill; joined the Starfarers when he was fired after Amalgamated Mining's takeover of MME.
Jonas Becker – interplanetary salvage artist; alias space junkman. Captain of the *Condor*. CEO of Becker Interplanetary Recycling and Salvage Enterprises Ltd. – a one-man, one-cat salvage firm Jonas inherited from his adopted father. Jonas spent his early youth on a labor farm on the planet Kezdet before he was adopted.
Judit Kendoro – assistant to psychiatrist Alton Forelle at Amalgamated Mining, saved Acorna

from certain death. Later fell in love with Gill and joined with him to help care for the children employed in Delszaki Li's Maganos mining operation.

Kaahi – a high mountain peak on Vhiliinyar.

Kaalmi Vroniiyi – leader of the Linyaari Council, which made the decision to restore the ruined planet Vhiliinyar, with Hafiz's help and support, to a state that would once again support the Linyaari and all the life-forms native to the planet.

Kaarlye – the father of Aari, Maati, and Laarye. A member of the Nyaarya clan, and life-bonded to Miiri.

ka-**Linyaari** – something against all Linyaari beliefs, something not Linyaari.

Karina – a plumply beautiful wanna-be psychic with a small shred of actual talent and a large fondness for profit. Married to Hafiz Harakamian. This is her first marriage, his second.

Kashirian Steppes – Makahomian region that produces the best fighters.

Kashirians – Makahomians from the Kashirian Steppes.

kava – a coffeelike hot drink produced from roasted ground beans.

KEN – a line of general-purpose male androids, some with customized specializations, differentiated among their owners by number, for example – KEN637.

Kezdet – a backwoods planet with a labor system based on child exploitation. Currently in economic turmoil because that system was broken by Delszaki Li and Acorna.

Khaari – senior Linyaari navigator on the *Balakiire*.

Khiindi – He is supposedly Khorii's cat, one of RK's offspring. He is, however, much more than that. He is actually Grimalkin, an Ancestral Friend who got into more mischief than his shapeshifting people approved of. They trapped him in the body of a cat and gave him to Khorii, as penance for his harm to her family and also to allow Grimalkin time to work out his destiny.

Khleevi – name given by Acorna's people to the space-borne enemies who have attacked them without mercy.

Khoriilya – Acorna and Aari's oldest child, a daughter, known as Khorii for short.

Krishna-Murti Company – The shipping and supply company that subcontracts to House Harakamian and owns the *Mana*, Jaya's ship.

kii – a Linyaari time measurement roughly equivalent to an hour of Standard Time.

ki-lin – Oriental term for unicorn, also a name sometimes associated with Acorna.

Kilumbemba Empire – an entire society that raises and exports mercenaries for hire – the Red Bracelets.

Kisla Manjari – anorexic and snobbish young woman, raised as daughter of Baron Manjari; shattered when through Acorna's efforts to help

384

the children of Kezdet her father is ruined and the truth of her lowly birth is revealed.

Kmal Madari – a child saved from slavery in a mine on Kezdet, he grew up to become a midshipman in the planet's space force.

Kubiilikaan – the legendary first city on Vhiliinyar, founded by the Ancestral Hosts.

Kubiilikhan – capital city of narhii-Vhiliinyar, named after Kubiilikaan, the legendary first city on Vhiliinyar, founded by the Ancestral Hosts.

La Estrella Blanca – A luxury liner from Dinero Grande. It became a plague ship. Captain, crew, and passengers all perished.

LAANYE – sleep learning device invented by the Linyaari that can, from a small sample of any foreign language, teach the wearer the new language overnight.

Laarye – Maati and Aari's brother. He died on Vhiliinyar during the Khleevi invasion. He was trapped in an accident in a cave far distant from the spaceport during the evacuation, and was badly injured. Aari stayed behind to rescue and heal him, but was captured by the Khleevi and tortured before he could accomplish his mission. Laarye died before Aari could escape and return. Time travel has brought him back to life.

Laboue – the planet where Hafiz Harakamian makes his headquarters.

lalli – Linyaari word for 'mother.'

lilaala – a flowering vine native to Vhiliinyar used by early Linyaari to make paper.

Linyaari – Acorna's people.

Liriili – former *viizaar* of narhii-Vhiliinyar, member of the clan Riivye.

LoiLoiKua – a water planet in the human Federation, with human-descended inhabitants that have become fully water-dwelling.

Lukia of the Lights – a protective saint, identified by some children of Kezdet with Acorna.

Ma'aowri 3 – a planet populated by catlike beings.

Maarni – a Linyaari folklorist, mate to Yiitir.

Maati – a young Linyaari girl of the Nyaarya clan who lost most of her family during the Khleevi invasion. Aari's younger sister.

MacKenZ – also known as Mac or Maak, a very useful and adaptable unit of the KEN line of androids, now in the service of Captain Becker. The android was formerly owned by Kisla Manjari, and came into the Captain's service after it tried to kill him on Kisla's orders. Becker's knack for dealing with salvage enabled him to reprogram the android to make the KEN unit both loyal to him and eager to please. The reprogramming had interesting side effects on the android's personality, though, leaving Mac much quirkier than is usually the case for androids.

madigadi – a berrylike fruit whose juice is a popular beverage.

Maganos – one of the three moons of Kezdet, base

for Delszaki Li's mining operation and child rehabilitation project.

Makahomia – war-torn home planet of RK and Nadhari Kendo.

Makahomian Temple Cat – cats on the planet Makahomia, bred from ancient Cat God stock to protect and defend the Cat God's Temples. They are – for cats – large, fiercely loyal, remarkably intelligent, and dangerous when crossed.

Makavitian Rain Forest – a tropical area of the planet Makahomia, populated by various warring jungle tribes.

Manjari – a baron in the Kezdet aristocracy, and a key person in the organization and protection of Kezdet's child-labor racket, in which he was known by the code name 'Piper.' He murdered his wife, then committed suicide when his identity was revealed and his organization destroyed.

Marl Fidd – a student on Maganos Moonbase, and a true cad.

Martin Dehoney – famous astro-architect who designed Maganos Moonbase; the coveted Dehoney Prize was named after him.

Melireenya – Linyaari communications specialist on the *Balakiire*, bonded to Hrronye.

Mercy Kendoro – younger sister of Pal and Judit Kendoro, saved from a life of bonded labor by Judit's efforts, she worked as a spy for the Child Liberation League in offices of Kezdet Guardians of the Peace until the child-labor system was destroyed.

Miiri – mother of Aari, Laarye, and Maati. A member of the Nyaarya clan, life-bonded to Kaarlye.

mitanyaakhi – generic Linyaari term meaning a very large number.

Miw-Sher – a Makahomian Keeper of the sacred Temple Cats. Her name means 'Kitten' in Makahomian.

MME – Gill, Calum, and Rafik's original mining company. Swallowed by the ruthless, conscienceless, and bureaucratic Amalgamated Mining.

Mog-Gim Plateau – an arid area on the planet Makahomia near the Federation spaceport.

MOO, or Moon of Opportunity – Hafiz's artificial planet, and home base for the Vhiliinyar terraforming operation.

Mulzar (feminine form: Mulzarah) – the Mog-Gimin title taken by the high priest who is also the warlord of the Plateau.

Mulzar Edu Kando sach Pilau dom Mog-Gim – High Priest of Hissim and the Aridimi Plateau, on the planet Makahomia.

Naadiina – also known as Grandam, one of the oldest Linyaari, host to both Maati and Acorna on narhii-Vhiliinyar, died to give her people the opportunity to save both of their planets.

Naarye – Linyaari techno-artisan in charge of final fit-out of spaceships.

naazhoni – the Linyaari word for someone who is a bit unstable.

Nadhari Kando – formerly Delszaki Li's personal bodyguard, rumored to have been an officer in

388

the Red Bracelets earlier in her career, then a security officer in charge of MOO, then the guard for the leader on her home planet of Makahomia.

narhii-Vhiliinyar – the planet settled by the Linyaari after Vhiliinyar, their original home-world, was destroyed by the Khleevi.

Neeva – Acorna's aunt and Linyaari envoy on the *Balakiire*, bonded to Virii.

Neo-Hadithian – an ultra-conservative, fanatical religious sect.

Ngaen Xong Hoa – a Kieaanese scientist who invented a planetary weather control system. He sought asylum on the *Haven* because he feared the warring governments on his planet would misuse his research. A mutineer faction on the *Haven* used the system to reduce the planet Rushima to ruins. The mutineers were tossed into space, and Dr Hoa has since restored Rushima and now works for Hafiz.

Niciirye – Grandam Naadiina's husband, dead and buried on Vhiliinyar.

Niikaavri – Acorna's grandmother, a member of the clan Geeyiinah, and a spaceship designer by trade. Also, as *Niikaavre*, the name of the space-ship used by Maati and Thariinye.

Nirii – a planetary trading partner of the Linyaari, populated by bovinelike two-horned sentients, known as Niriians, technologically advanced, able to communicate telepathically, and phleg-matic in temperament.

nyiiri – the Linyaari word for unmitigated gall,

sheer effrontery, or other forms of misplaced bravado.

Our Star – Linyaari name for the star that centers their solar system.

Paazo River – a major geographical feature on the Linyaari homeworld, Vhiliinyar.

pahaantiyir – a large catlike animal once found on Vhiliinyar.

Paloduro – a planet in the Solojo star system, infested by the space plague.

Pandora – Count Edacki Ganoosh's personal spaceship, used to track and pursue Hafiz's ship *Shahrazad* as it speeds after Acorna on her journey to narhii-Vhiliinyar. Later confiscated and used by Hafiz for his own purposes.

Dr Phador Al y Cassidro – headmaster and dean of the mining engineering school at Maganos Moonbase.

piiro – Linyaari word for a rowboatlike water vessel.

piiyi – a Niriian biotechnology-based information storage and retrieval system. The biological component resembles a very rancid cheese.

Poopuus – water-dwelling students on Maganos Moonbase.

Praxos – a swampy planet near Makahomia used by the Federation to train Makahomian recruits.

PU#10 – Human name for the vine planet, with its sentient plant inhabitants, where the Khleevi-killing sap was found.

390

Rafik Nadezda – one of three miners who discovered Acorna and raised her.

Red Bracelets – Kilumbembese mercenaries; arguably the toughest and nastiest fighting force in known space.

Rio Boca – a planet in the Solojo star system.

Roadkill – otherwise known as RK. A Makahomian Temple Cat, the only survivor of a space wreck, rescued and adopted by Jonas Becker, and honorary first mate of the *Condor*.

Roc – Rafik's shuttle ship.

Rushima – a planet invaded by the Khleevi and saved by Acorna.

Scaradine MacDonald – captain of the *Arkansas Traveler* spaceship, and galactic freight hauler.

Sesseli – a student on Maganos Moonbase.

Shahrazad – Hafiz's personal spaceship, a luxury cruiser.

Shoshisha – a student on the Maganos Moonbase.

sii-Linyaari – a legendary race of aquatic Linyaari-like beings developed by the Ancestral Friends.

Siiaaryi Maartri – a Linyaari survey ship.

Sinbad – Rafik's spaceship.

Sita Ram – a protective goddess, identified with Acorna by the mining children on Kezdet.

Solojo – a star system in the human galaxy, one of the first infected with the space plague.

Smythe-Wesson – a former Red Bracelet officer, Win Smythe-Wesson briefly served as Hafiz's head of security on MOO before his larcenous urges overcame him.

Spandard – A variant dialect of Standard Galactic Basic, once known as Spanish.

Standard Galactic Basic – the language used throughout the human settled galaxy, also known simply as 'Basic.'

stiil – Linyaari word for a pencil-like writing implement.

Taankaril – *visedhaanye ferilii* of the Gamma sector of Linyaari space.

Tagoth – *see* Bulaybub.

techno-artisan – Linyaari specialist who designs, engineers, or manufactures goods.

Thariinye – a handsome and conceited young space-faring Linyaari from clan Renyilaaghe.

Theophilus Becker – Jonas Becker's father, a salvage man and astrophysicist with a fondness for exploring uncharted wormholes.

thiilir (pl. *thilirii*) – small arboreal mammals of Linyaari homeworld.

thiilsis – grass species native to Vhiliinyar.

Toruna – a Niriian female, who sought help from Acorna and the Linyaari when her home planet was invaded by the Khleevi.

Twi Osiam – planetary site of a major financial and trade center.

twilit – small, pestiferous insect on Linyaari home planet.

Uhuru – one of the various names of the ship owned jointly by Gill, Calum, and Rafik.

Vaanye – Acorna's father.

Vhiliinyar – original home planet of the Linyaari, destroyed by Khleevi.

viizaar – a high political office in the Linyaari system, roughly equivalent to president or prime minister.

Virii – Neeva's spouse.

visedhaanye ferilii – Linyaari term corresponding roughly to 'Envoy Extraordinary.'

Vriiniia Watiir – sacred healing lake on Vhiliinyar, defiled by the Khleevi.

Wahanamoian Blossom of Sleep – poppylike flowers whose pollens, when ground, are a very powerful sedative.

wii – a Linyaari prefix meaning small.

yaazi – Linyaari term for beloved or 'little one.'

Yaniriin – a Linyaari Survey Ship captain.

Yukata Batsu – Uncle Hafiz's chief competitor on Laboue.

Yiitir – history teacher at the Linyaari academy, and Chief Keeper of the Linyaari Stories. Lifemate to Maarni.

Zaami – a high mountain peak on the Linyaari homeworld.

Zanegar – second-generation Starfarer.

BRIEF NOTES ON THE LINYAARI LANGUAGE
by
Margaret Ball

As Anne McCaffrey's collaborator in transcribing
the first two tales of Acorna, I was delighted to find
that the second of these books provided an opportunity to sharpen my long-unused skills in
linguistic fieldwork. Many years ago, when the
government gave out scholarships with gay
abandon and the cost of living (and attending
graduate school) was virtually nil, I got a Ph.D. in
linguistics for no better reason than that: (a) the
government was willing to pay; (b) it gave me an
excuse to spend a couple of years doing fieldwork
in Africa; and (c) there weren't any real jobs going
for eighteen-year-old girls with a B.A. in math and
a minor in Germanic languages. (This was back
during the Upper Pleistocene era, when the Help
Wanted ads were still divided into Male and
Female.)

So there were all those years spent doing things

like transcribing tonal Oriental languages on staff paper (the Field Methods instructor was Not Amused) and tape-recording Swahili women at weddings, and then I got the degree and wandered off to play with computers and never had any use for the stuff again . . . until Acorna's people appeared on the scene. It required a sharp ear and some facility for linguistic analysis to make sense of the subtle sound changes with which their language signaled syntactic changes; I quite enjoyed the challenge.

The notes appended here represent my first and necessarily tentative analysis of certain patterns in Linyaari phonemics and morphophonemics. If there is any inconsistency between this analysis and the Linyaari speech patterns recorded in the later adventures of Acorna, please remember that I was working from a very limited database and, what is perhaps worse, attempting to analyze a decidedly nonhuman language with the aid of the only paradigms I had, twentieth-century linguistic models developed exclusively from human language. The result is very likely as inaccurate as were the first attempts to describe English syntax by forcing it into the mold of Latin, if not worse. My colleague, Elizabeth Ann Scarborough, has by now added her own notes to the small corpus of Linyaari names and utterances, and it may well be that in the next decade there will be enough data available to publish a truly definitive dictionary and grammar of Linyaari; an undertaking that will surely be of inestimable value, not only to those members of our race who are involved in diplomatic and trade relations with this people, but also to everyone interested in the study of language.

NOTES ON THE LINYAARI LANGUAGE

1. A doubled vowel indicates stress: **aavi, abaanye, khleevi.**

2. Stress is used as an indicator of syntactic funtion: in nouns stress is on the penultimate syllable, in adjectives on the last syllable, in verbs on the first.

3. Intervocalic *n* is always palatalized.

4. Noun plurals are formed by adding a final vowel, usually **-i**: one **Liinyar**, two **Linyaari**. Note that this causes a change in the stressed syllable (from **LI-nyar** to **Li-NYA-ri**) and hence a change in the pattern of doubled vowels.

For nouns whose singular form ends in a vowel, the plural is formed by dropping the original vowel and adding **-i: ghaanye, ghaanyi**. Here the number of syllables remains the same, therefore no stress/spelling change is required.

5. Adjectives can be formed from nouns by adding a final **-ii** (again, dropping the original final vowel if one exists): **maalive, malivii; Liinyar, Linyarii**. Again, the change in stress means that the doubled vowels in the penultimate syllable of the noun disappear.

6. For nouns denoting a class or species, such as Liinyar, the noun itself can be used as an adjective when the meaning is simply to denote a member of the class, rather than the usual adjective meaning of 'having the qualities of this class' – thus, of the characters in *Acorna*, only Acorna herself could be described as 'a **Liinyar** girl' but Judit, although human, would certainly be described as 'a **linyarii** girl,' or 'a just-as-civilized-as-a-real-member-of-the-People' girl.

7. Verbs can be formed from nouns by adding a prefix constructed by [first consonant of noun] + **ii** + **nye**: **faalar** – grief; **fiinyefalar** – to grieve.

8. The participle is formed from the verb by adding a suffix **-an** or **-en**: **thiinyethilel** – to destroy, **thiinyethilelen** – destroyed. No stress change is involved because the participle is perceived as a verb form and therefore stress remains on the first syllable.

enye – ghanyii – time unit, small portion of a year (**ghaanye**)

fiinyefalaran – mourning, mourned

ghaanye – a Linyaari year, equivalent to about one and one-third earth years

gheraalye malivii – Navigation Officer

gheraalye ve-khanyii – Senior Communications Specialist

Khleevi – originally, a small vicious carrion-feeding animal with a poisonous bite; now used by the Linyaari to denote the invaders who destroyed their homeworld.

khleevi – barbarous, uncivilized, vicious without reason

Liinyar – member of the People

linyaari – civilized; like a Liinyar

mitanyaakhi – large number (slang – like our 'zillions')

narhii – new

thiilir, thiliiri – small arboreal mammals of Linyaari homeworld

thiilel – destruction

visedhaanye ferilii – Envoy Extraordinary

DRAGONSBLOOD
Todd McCaffrey

A deadly plague has begun to wipe out the
dragons and fire-lizards, leaving mankind no
defence against the deadly Thread which has just
begun to fall in the Third Pass. Tantalized by a
song that seems to suggest that Lorana can find out
how to heal the dragons, the Harper Kindan and
Lorana race against time to solve the clues that
Wind Blossom left behind.

Can they find the cure in time to save Lorna's
queen, Arith, and the rest of the dragons? If they
don't, there will be no dragons left, and all life on
the planet will be devoured.

And how could Wind Blossom, Pern's last
geneticist, know of a peril 400 Turns
after her death?

With an introduction by Anne McCaffrey:

'*Dragonsblood* is a good yarn, fitting perfectly into
the Pern series, yet something I don't think I would
have thought up myself. Enjoy, as I did, another
point of view about Pern'

'A proper Pern novel . . . bodes well for
future volumes' *SFX*

0 552 15208 0

CORGI BOOKS

A LIST OF OTHER ANNE McCAFFREY TITLES
AVAILABLE FROM CORGI BOOKS